Vanessa studied English and Australian literature at the University of Sydney and dreamed of one day writing fiction. She then went on to immerse herself completely in writing about real people, working as a journalist for eighteen years. Vanessa has been a news, medical, entertainment and arts reporter for *The Daily Telegraph* and her writing has appeared in numerous other publications. She's happy to now, finally, be creating fictional characters. She lives in Sydney with her husband and daughter.

Also by Vanessa McCausland

The Lost Summers of Driftwood

The Valley of Lost Stories

The Beautiful Words

VANESSA McCAUSLAND

HarperCollins*Publishers*

Quoted material on page vi from *Johnny Panic and the Bible of Dreams* by Sylvia Plath, Faber and Faber Ltd, London. Reprinted with permission.

Quoted material on pages 86, 168, 179 and 205 from *The Bell Jar* by Sylvia Plath, Faber and Faber Ltd, London. Reprinted with permission.

Definitions on pages 1, 3, 13, 32, 50, 68, 83, 91, 100, 107, 121, 129, 141, 161, 176, 190, 201, 219, 229, 238, 250, 265, 273, 291, 299, 303, 308, 315, 319, 324, 327, 331, 337, 345, and 352 from *Macquarie Dictionary & Thesaurus, Combined Edition,* Macquarie Dictionary Publishers, an imprint of Pan Macmillan Australia Pty Ltd, Sydney, 2012. Reprinted with permission.

HarperCollins*Publishers*
Australia • Brazil • Canada • France • Germany • Holland • Hungary
India • Italy • Japan • Mexico • New Zealand • Poland • Spain • Sweden
Switzerland • United Kingdom • United States of America

First published in Australia in 2021
by HarperCollins*Publishers* Australia Pty Limited
Level 13, 201 Elizabeth Street, Sydney NSW 2000
ABN 36 009 913 517
harpercollins.com.au

A catalogue record for this book is available from the National Library of Australia.

ISBN 978 1 4607 5958 5 (paperback)
ISBN 978 1 4607 1318 1 (ebook)
ISBN 978 1 4607 8959 9 (audiobook)

Cover design by Hazel Lam, HarperCollins Design Studio
Cover image by shutterstock.com
Author photograph by Sally Flegg Photography
Typeset in Bembo Std by HarperCollins
Printed and bound in Australia by McPherson's Printing Group

FSC www.fsc.org MIX Paper from responsible sources FSC® C001695

To my beautiful first readers – Kirstin, Karina, Danielle, Ali and George

'Whereon those … first years of my life
sealed themselves off like a ship in a bottle –
beautiful, inaccessible, obsolete:
a fine, white flying myth.'

'Ocean 1212-W', by Sylvia Plath

PALM BEACH, SUMMER 1996

lighthouse *(n.)* – a tower or other structure displaying a light or lights for the guidance of vessels at sea.

An early moon had risen, casting a pale silver light over the sand. The world was turning blue, as though the day could no longer hold onto its colours. In the fading light she could see the lighthouse at the far end of the beach, a luminous streak in the sky. Kase had walked the track to it so many times during the day but never at night. She wondered what the cold, dark ocean would look like from high above. The bonfire crackled and the waves washed against the shore. The murmurs of her friends reached her; voices lulled by the heat of the fire and the wine.

'Want to walk up to the lighthouse?'

It was as though Sylvie had read her mind. But Sylvie was always reading her mind. There was a line of communication running between them and they had long ago stopped saying 'jinx'.

'Yes. Want to see if the others are up for it?'

'Nah,' they said in unison and linked arms.

'I'm cold.' Kase huddled into the thin lines of Sylvie's ribs.

'Here.' Sylvie took off her scarf and wound it around Kase's neck.

It smelled like Sylvie. Vanilla musk mixed with smoke from the fire. As she stood, the world tilted slightly. 'Are you as drunk as me?' she asked as Sylvie steadied her.

'A bit. Not too bad. Not as bad as the others.' Sylvie pulled her close against the early summer breeze.

They walked in silence, the soft, cold sand numbing their toes, the salty air on their lips. They reached the bank of bush leading to the lighthouse and Kase looked back. The fire was like a warm beacon. A shiver ran through her. 'Are you sure we shouldn't get the others to come?'

'It looks like they already are.'

Kase could just make out the forms of their friends moving towards them up the beach, sea-salt ghosts hovering in the dusk air. Tristan, Gabe and the others. She yelled to them, but the breeze snatched her voice before she and Sylvie walked into the bush.

CHAPTER 1

friend *(n.)* – someone attached to another by feelings of affection or personal regard.

Sometimes the words were light, like tissue paper. She could feel them brush her skin, a sweet caress. Other times they were dark and heavy – stones, or rotting bones to be carried deep in your gut. Sylvie didn't know if other people experienced words like she did. She assumed everyone held a word in their mind and felt its tiny pulse. Felt them under their skin, in their eyes, pricking to tears. Sylvie had long ago found the word to describe what she was – a logophile. The list of her beloved words sat in her heart like a balm. *Elixir. Lullaby. Eloquent. Pristine. Ethereal.*

But it wasn't just words. Everyone thought her job was boring. *Don't you get depressed going into people's homes after they've died? You're too smart to be a cleaner.* But they didn't understand what she really did – which was find people's stories. Stories were hidden everywhere if you only cared to look, to listen. She collected the stories of the dead like an archaeologist digging up treasures. Everyone had one. They were hidden in the bags of clothing Sylvie emptied from wardrobes, the shoe boxes she found at the back of cupboards, filled with letters, even in the piles of unpaid bills to be cleared from tabletops. She couldn't bear for the stories to be lost. She'd read once that stories only survived three generations and then they were gone, blown away by the winds of time. The proof: What does anyone know of their grandmother's mother?

Sylvie opened the front door to the smell of wilting flowers. Houses decayed so fast without their people in them. She took a deep breath and then stepped inside. Discovering someone's world gone cold always made her heart ache until she got to know them a little better; until she found their warmth, their essence. She stepped into the light-filled room and the bay windows drew her gaze. The ocean. The sky. And lining the walls, books – dozens and dozens of books. This was a special world. And by the looks of the room, filled with flowers now fading on their stems, a special lady.

She took her notebook out of her pocket and wrote:

Sylvia. 91. Lover of books. Gazer over oceans. My namesake.

Sylvie's mother had named her Sylvia at birth, but somewhere along the line Sylvie's name had morphed. It was funny how people always found the names that suited them.

She brought in her bucket of supplies and cardboard boxes and placed them carefully on the thick cream carpet. She was meant to wear covered shoes, but she found herself easing her feet out of her sandshoes to feel the soft pile. Bare feet sometimes felt too familiar, but already it was as though she knew Sylvia. The family had stripped the house of valuables and it was Sylvie's job to clean out the last of the possessions to get it ready for sale. Everything left was to go to charity or the tip.

Sadness moved through her as she looked around the room. So many once-precious things to be discarded.

She could see the ghosts of shapes in the dust – furniture that had been sitting there forever, now gone. Such a beautiful old house was bound to have held some treasures. She gazed around at the shelves. Had no one wanted to take any of these books? A tingle ran through her. She knew she was meant to stack them into a box for the pick-up at the end of the week, but she also knew she would go through them, each one a key to who Sylvia had been, the other worlds she had escaped to in her ninety-one years.

There was a knock on the door behind her and she swung around, heart thumping.

A man wearing an expensive suit stood on the doorstep. 'Are you the cleaner?' he asked.

'Yes,' said Sylvie, hating how small her voice sounded. She felt his eyes on her, no doubt appraising what she was wearing. She knew a flowing dress was not the most practical thing to wear to clean a house but slipping one on made her happy. She liked to think it was her way of showing respect. Like when her mother was in her religious phase and made Sylvie wear her Sunday best to church.

He strode past her into the loungeroom. His shiny black shoes looked like cockroaches on the clean carpet and Sylvie cringed.

'Smells like old people,' he said, his nose crinkling. 'But the house is worth an absolute fortune.'

Sylvie wanted to ask whether he was a real estate agent or perhaps a greedy, rude, distant relative, but she kept her mouth shut and picked up her bucket, slipping her feet back into her shoes, and moved towards the hall that she saw led to a kitchen. She felt his eyes on her, watching her, no doubt noticing her slight limp. The familiar rush of shame flooded her.

'I won't be long. Just need to do an evaluation. The family wants this place empty and ready for sale by the end of the week, so you've got your work cut out for you.'

Sylvie nodded. At least there was no pity in his voice. 'I work quite quickly,' she said, avoiding his darting eyes.

'I presume you've got a dump bin coming for all this stuff? There's a lot of crap still here. Looks like the old biddy was a bit of a hoarder. That's what the son said.'

Sylvie felt anger rise and colour her face. She had cleaned hoarders' houses and this was nothing like them. She wanted to slap his smug face. Instead she bit the inside of her lip and walked away from him down the hall.

'The skip will come tomorrow,' she mumbled.

He followed her and they reached the kitchen. The view was even more spectacular from here – the jutting jaw of the coast falling to the smooth curve of the harbour.

'The new owners will pull all this out and make it sleek as,' he said.

But all Sylvie could see were the tiny, soon-to-be-erased markers of Sylvia's life. Of a life well lived. The tray with a floral teapot. A pile of books, the top one still bearing a bookmark. An empty fruit bowl in the shape of a hen.

The man walked off into an adjoining room and Sylvie breathed out. She had a bad habit of holding her breath when she was nervous.

She got to work cleaning out the kitchen, wrapping the crockery and cutlery and placing it into a box. She imagined all the meals that had been eaten off these pale blue floral plates, the celebrations toasted with the vintage champagne flutes.

The man returned, dusting his hands in front of him. 'Upwards of ten mil, I'd say. Huge old place. Views from all the bedrooms. Apparently the family was just waiting for her to die. They couldn't get her into a nursing home. Imagine, one person living alone in this huge place. Maybe they even slipped her one. Bingo, instant millionaires, all four kids.'

Sylvie's breath quickened and she longed to scream at this man, to push him out of Sylvia's house, but instead she scrunched a piece of newspaper into a hard ball.

The man moved closer and peered into the box. 'Bet there are a few things of worth still here. Wink wink. The family cleaned it out in such a rush. Want their money ASAP. Just saying … a cleaner's salary can't be much. Not for this depressing work.'

Sylvie felt her shoulders bunch to her neck. She bit down the words forming on her tongue. 'I don't find it depressing,' she said, her voice a whisper.

He studied her for a moment then clapped his hands so loudly she started. 'Each to their own, I guess. Okay, I'm done and dusted. Out of here.'

She watched him stride down the hall and slam the front door behind him.

The sudden quiet was like a soft pillow and she relaxed into it. She took a deep breath. *I'm sorry you had to have that man in your house, Sylvia.*

She stood and stretched her legs. Now she could finally explore the rest of the house and find out who Sylvia was. She found the well-tended garden. Sylvia had loved roses. She found the living room where Sylvia had obviously spent most of her life. She had loved crosswords and newspapers. She found the study with a long timber writing desk in front of a window that overlooked the garden. A stack of leather-bound books sat on the desk. Sylvia had been a writer.

The room was bathed in light, refracted through the stained glass at the top of the windows. Sylvie sat down at the desk in a square of blue light and ran her fingers over the cracked leather spines. These were journals. Surely her family had wanted to keep these. Perhaps they hadn't realised their significance; she would keep them aside. She took the top book and pressed its pages open.

Here was Sylvia, the real woman. Sylvie felt a quiver down her spine as she began to read. She allowed herself only twenty minutes. She had always read fast – she swallowed whole books in a day. She closed the journal and took her notebook from her pocket. It was a habit she'd begun after the accident when she hadn't been able to trust her short-term memory. She had to write important things down so she wouldn't forget. She'd continued because the writing of words, the cataloguing of feelings, calmed her. She wrote down four words.

Best friend. Lost. Regret.

The words felt heavy, sodden; they pulled at her heart. She slipped the notebook back into her pocket. Now she understood Sylvia and could properly commence her work. It seemed they shared more than just a name. The connection was uncanny. Sylvia had been lonely too. Her family never visited – her children lived interstate … they were busy. There was too much time to think in this empty house alone and the past haunted her. Her best friend's name had been Rose. Rose and Sylvia.

Sylvia and Rose. Girlhood friends, and her most true person for so long. But they had fallen out. Rose had closed up to her, become a stranger. Sylvia never knew exactly why, but she'd been too proud to reach out, to breach the years of distance. But she had never forgotten, never recovered. *Best friend. Lost. Regret.*

Sylvie thought about the invitation stuck to her own fridge door.

> *Please join us to celebrate Kase's 40th Birthday. As one of her nearest and dearest you're invited to an intimate long weekend of everything 'Kase', from book talk (naturally), to lashings of red wine, to skinny dipping in the sea (not compulsory but we all know it will probably happen). We're holding it on our private island off the Tassie coast, so we can all commune with nature while we celebrate the wild force that is Kase Fowler.*

Those same four words had come flying at her when she'd opened the thick, creamy invitation. *Best friend. Lost. Regret.*

It had been so long. Twenty-three years. Why had she even been invited after everything that had happened? But she felt pulled, like the sea drawn back. And now here was a sign. Did she want to finish her life with the regret and longing that Sylvia had? When you were young you believed life would be full of soul-deep connections. That there would be many who understood you without needing words, who laughed with you without being able to stop, and who felt deeply known to you as soon as you met. Someone who you could never forget. But now she knew they were rare and precious things. Fleeting things. Like memories.

Sylvie thought about her small flat behind the cafe. Her tiny life – words and death. Kase had been her everything at seventeen. They'd had dreams of such a big life. And Kase was living that life – an award-winning, bestselling author, academic husband. A part of Sylvie stirred uncomfortably at the thought. *That could have been me.*

It all led back to that night at Palm Beach, up at the lighthouse. But there was no story for that night. The words were gone. Or maybe they had never been. The doctors said it was normal after a traumatic brain injury – not to remember. There was only thick black silence, like a cloak. She had never wanted to know more, not really. Perhaps it was a small mercy that her brain had forgotten. Blank, like the cassette tapes she and Kase had recorded over so many times.

Sylvie ran her fingers over Sylvia's final words. Sylvia who was no more. Who had nothing left to lose. Who had died with the name of her friend written in her last pages. *Rose.* Sylvie felt the pull of her own past, like a rip that ran cold and deep beneath the safe shallows. She thought she heard a loud whisper in her ear, or it could have been the wind coming off the sea, playing in the sheer curtains through a crack in the window. Three words that made her heart beat fast: *Be brave. Go.*

* * *

She woke to the sound of coffee beans grinding. It was the same sound, the same smell every day. It wasn't such a bad way to greet consciousness, except that she didn't drink coffee. There was the slide of chairs on concrete, the clash of cutlery and the hum of human voices growing louder. Sylvie got up and made herself a tea then sat in her bed with her book as the cafe filled on the other side of her bedroom wall. A high laugh. A baby crying. A thin partition separating her from life. She was happy listening to its muted chaos, safe behind the wall.

She tried to focus on the story, but her eyes kept skipping over words. This morning the sounds seemed louder, the smells stronger. Now bacon frying. She must be hungry. She stood in front of her small refrigerator. Kase's invitation slipped off the front. It was soon. At the other end of the country. She'd have to take leave from work. She'd have to reply to Kase. She didn't have the words. The paper was too thick to scrunch into a ball so she folded it as small at it would go and threw it in the bin. She was not brave.

She looked into her empty fridge. When had she run out of food? Books were her sustenance. She would spend her last pennies on stories rather than meals. And she so often had to clean out other people's refrigerators, it was no wonder she was never hungry. But for some reason she was hungry now, and what she wanted was bacon. She looked over at the lukewarm tea and open book by her bed. She wanted food. She pulled yesterday's dress over her head and stood in front of the tiny bathroom mirror, applying lipstick. Was she really doing this? It was so rare she chose reality over fiction.

She walked through her tiny courtyard filled with succulents and potted plants and out the side gate. The sky was high. The world seemed too boundless. Around the corner the cafe was overflowing with people, inside and onto the pavement. She took a step back. There wasn't anywhere to sit, she should just go back to the quiet world of her book. But she looked at the muffins and the eggs and her stomach growled. She'd just say hello to the owner, her landlord, and order a takeaway.

She had to wait in line inside. It smelled like eggs frying and toast cooking and aftershave. There were kids playing on the floor, groups of friends conversing loudly, couples reading newspapers.

She ordered a bacon and egg roll.

'Love, you're going to have to speak up.'

'Mr Jones, it's me Sylvie, from the flat behind the shop.'

The man wiped his hands on his apron and looked at her properly. 'Oh Sylvie. I haven't seen you for so long. Nice to see you, love. Breakfast is on the house.'

Sylvie felt unaccountably sad as she thanked him. A couple got up from the prime table beneath the window. Sylvie sat down.

'Are you waiting for anyone else?' A woman about her age with a baby on her hip stood with her hand on the chair opposite.

Sylvie shook her head.

'Can we take this?' The woman nodded towards a group of people, towards her family and friends.

Sylvie nodded. She watched the woman drag the chair over to her table. She felt her eyes fill with tears. The words were here now and so was her breakfast. *Alone. Unaccompanied. Lonely.*

CHAPTER 2

wild *(adj.)* – living in a state of nature.

The sails clanged in the wind and a fine salt spray wet her face. Sylvie stood on the jetty at Kettering with her small suitcase and waited. The boats were like ghosts, hovering in their misty moorings. She scanned the horizon for the water taxi. The water was the same flat grey as the sky, and whispers of cloud clung to the shoreline. She pulled her rain jacket closer. Salt was in her hair, on her tongue; it was seeping into her, washing away the stale airport air. She was completely alone, but strangely, she didn't feel as lonely as she had in the cafe only a week ago. She watched two eagles wheeling above, their cries almost lost on the cold wind.

It was summer, but Tasmania operated on a different weather pattern to the rest of the country. There was something raw and wild and shifting about this place. It frightened and energised her in equal measure. She couldn't believe she had come. She had spent so long just finding the words to accept.

Dear Kase, Thank you for the invitation. I'm really looking forward to your party and to seeing you after all these years. Your island looks beautiful. Sylvie x

Kase's reply had been perfunctory, but not without some rapport, as though the two of them were work colleagues who shared a desk – close by proximity, rather than childhood friends, twinned in every sense and cleaved apart a lifetime ago. Sylvie had written back, counselling herself to seem normal. She knew what normal was meant to look like at nearly forty. Mother. Wife. Career woman. Kase wasn't a mother but her eminent career as an author was like a baby, growing fatter every year. Sylvie wasn't normal, but she knew the words to make her appear so.

Really busy with work but have managed to get some much-needed time off. I will arrive Friday. The others had all arrived the day before, apparently. Her whole body convulsed with cold and she felt tears build behind her eyes as she thought about the people she was about to be thrown back together with. People she hadn't seen in half a lifetime. *Strangers.* And yet they had once been woven into her very fabric.

Be brave. She thought of Sylvia who never got closure with Rose. *This is a chapter you need to close.*

She braced herself against the cold. A tiny boat appeared through the mist.

'Heading out to the island? Sylvia Dane, guest of the Fowlers?' a man called.

'Yes, hi,' she called in return, but her voice was lost on the wind.

'This is our warm Tasmanian welcome.'

He tied the rope to the jetty, and she passed him her bag and climbed down a ladder and into the boat, blinking back water from her lashes. She slipped and felt him steady her, his hand on her back.

'Sorry. Are you okay? I'm Holden.' Warm brown eyes hid under a beanie and hood.

'Yes, hi,' she said, breathless. 'Thanks, it's slippery.'

'Take a seat … sorry it's so wet. I'm the local water taxi operator, or party taxi in this case.'

'Or the main character from *Catcher in the Rye*.' She chastised herself and picked at her fingerless gloves. This wild weather was making her more uninhibited than usual. *Stupid*. He didn't look like a literary type.

He revved the motor and the smell of petrol filled the air. 'You can hardly talk, Sylvia, or should I say, Sylvia Plath?'

She smiled, surprised, and felt the hairs on her arms lift. 'How did you know I was named after her?'

'The intuition of someone named after a literary character I guess,' he said, winking.

She felt herself blush. 'Just call me Sylvie.'

'Parents who name their kids after famous literary characters have a lot to answer for.'

She laughed. 'I know. My mother is incorrigible. You've read Plath?'

He nodded. 'Sure have.'

She felt bad for judging him. The boat moved out into the channel and the words swirled around her as she took in the sky, painted black with dabs of yellow where the sun was pulling at the clouds, trying to get through. The water churned and frothed below her, a mirror of her insides. The boat crested a wave, and she was thrown against the side, her hands gripping the seat, knuckles as white as the foaming sea below.

'Is it always this choppy?'

Holden shook his head. 'No, you got the extra special treatment. But it's only a twenty-minute trip across the channel and there's a big fire lit at the house … and I think everyone's already drinking wine.' He checked his watch. 'At 11 am.'

She found herself laughing. That sounded like Kase. It was funny how someone didn't change all that much from fifteen to forty. Maybe it would be exactly the same. Maybe they'd fall into the same easy rhythm, joined at the hip, finishing each other's sentences, laughing at things other people didn't find funny. Maybe the past was far enough away now that they could forget.

But there was a rift, as deep and dark as the place Kase's brother had fallen. They had never spoken again after that night. *Were there words for such a tragedy anyhow?* Sylvie had been there when Tristan fell, but she had no recollection, no memory. Kase had been there too. Sylvie had swallowed the pain of Kase's silence and moved on with her life, altered as it was. She had let the past lie, careful not to unsettle the dust. But now she was roaring towards it, the wind whipping her face, the salt stinging her eyes.

She saw Bruny Island come closer into view ahead. The grass was straw-coloured, like tufts of unruly golden hair. The trees were ancient, tall and gnarled like a giant's limbs, leaning into cliffs that fell away to crashing waves. The wild beauty of it sent a rush up her spine. But that wasn't where they were headed. Kase's island was in the D'Entrecasteaux Channel, between Bruny and the mainland. Kase had bought the private island several years ago, presumably when her books had become bestsellers overseas.

The gulf between their lives now seemed as deep as the channel they were crossing. The water was darker here. Holden's voice was small against the sea. He pointed skyward.

'Our resident eagles. Tail and Claw.'

'Oh, I think I may have seen them before, on the mainland. Are they following us?'

'They know me. They nest over the headland, where my cabin is. I'm sort of the caretaker of the island.'

She wanted to ask more, but the wind was swallowing their words. As they approached the island, she saw the headland with two majestic blue gums rising from it. Holden eased the throttle back and pointed up to the house. Its timber was raw, as though it had been gnawed on by salt air, but it was as beautiful, honed and natural as the trunks of the trees that surrounded it. The building had been architecturally designed to merge into the landscape, camouflage with the brown earth, the black rocks, the grey water. A long timber deck ran its length, and several levels were built into the slope. Big glass windows surveyed the bay like blinking eyes. Below it, a small boatshed rested on the lip of the water, a long jetty jutting out like a tongue.

Kase and her mother, Fran, had lived in Hobart since they'd fled Palm Beach to start again after Tristan's death. Sylvie thought she remembered that Fran had grown up in Hobart. It was funny how the place you were born never left you. She knew that Kase had a home in Hobart as well as the island. Sylvie imagined what that would feel like to have a mother who wanted to be wherever you were.

Holden cut the motor and they drifted, the squall of gulls and the slap of ocean on the hull the only sounds. He handed her a card. It read 'Holden's Water Taxi Service'.

'My mobile number. If you want a tour of the little coves, help building a fire, supplies of any kind, a lift to Bruny or back to the mainland, I'm your man.'

Sylvie's heart swelled at the warmth in his voice. At least she had an escape plan. Almost an ally. 'Thanks, that's very kind,' she said as he helped her out of the boat and handed over her bag and her small leather backpack.

'No problems, Sylvie Plath.'

She laughed. 'Bye, Holden Caulfield.'

She hadn't thought about *The Catcher in the Rye* since she was fourteen and read it in one sitting in bed on a rainy day. And now here she was, about to face the universe her teenage self had once starred in.

Holden smiled under his hoodie and turned the boat around. She watched him speed off into the bay then took her notebook and pencil out of her dress pocket and wrote four words. *Holden Caulfield* ... *Bookish* ... *Intrigued* ... She slipped the notebook away. It had become like a nervous tic. A crutch. She wasn't even aware she was doing it, she didn't even have to do it anymore. Her memory was much better now, but somehow the writing down of words calmed her. Steadied her. As though the recording of feelings exorcised them from her body. She was aware it was not a normal thing to do. She was going to have to resist writing in it while she was here, but how could she hide the other physical reminder of the night that everything changed?

She was acutely aware of her limp as she started down the jetty, her right foot dragging ever so slightly with each step. The rain had eased and her heart was pounding as hard as the waves on the rock shelf. She remembered Sylvia's words. *Be brave*. She clung tightly to them as she climbed the slope and then the wooden stairs to the house. She stood on the deck and looked back out at the view.

The grey water of the bay stretched beyond a gentle slope covered with blue gums, pines and that same straw-coloured grass. The beach was a wild stretch of white sand, framed at either end by dark rocks and oyster flats. Bruny Island crouched in the distance. Sylvie breathed deep, the air cold and fresh. She felt a ripple just under her skin. It was so pristine here, so beautiful, she didn't know where to put the feeling. She took out her notebook but then put it back into her pocket. She needed to appear normal now.

She turned and pulled on the thick, salt-encrusted rope to sound the bell that hung at the front door. A low gong. No movement from inside. She eased the door open and stepped in. It smelled like wood, smoke, candle wax and home-cooking.

'Hello?' She should have come yesterday so that she wasn't the odd one out. *Who am I kidding?* She was always going to be the odd one out.

She moved through an entrance foyer with coats on hooks and gumboots lined up ready for the onslaught of the elements. To the right was a loungeroom with exposed timber beams and rustic floors. It was warmed by Persian rugs in muted colours, white linen sofas, chunky mohair throws and a fireplace that smelled like it was still smouldering. Sheer curtains billowed softly at the windows facing the sea. Sylvie had the urge to run her fingers along the spines of the books in the bookcase and curl up with one in an armchair. She wasn't sure if it was the books and the cosy atmosphere that made it welcoming, or the fact that it felt like Kase.

She followed her nose until she arrived in the kitchen. She dropped her bags next to an island bench. Pots and pans hung over an industrial stove and from the sink there was a view along the coastline. The kitchen was modern, but with nods to the elements of nature that surrounded them. Shells sat on the windowsill, a metal anchor leaned against a wall, and there were hues of navy blue, grey and cream. A perfect mirror of the rawness outside. The Fowlers had always had beautiful homes, and this was another.

She followed the sound of voices until she reached a glass door, which opened to a covered deck. Everyone was sitting around a weathered teak table. Sylvie's body was rigid with nerves and she found herself unable to speak. But Kase saw her and jumped to her feet.

'Oh my God, Sylvie!'

Kase's arms were around her, squeezing her tight, and she might have been a teenager again. Tears pricked her eyes at the warmth of the greeting, at the same sweet scent of Kase's hair. She said a silent prayer to Sylvia.

Kase drew back and shook her head. 'You look the same. How is that possible?'

Sylvie laughed. 'So do you.'

'But just really old, right? Middle-aged.'

'No. The same.' Sylvie squeezed her arm.

'Surely we've improved with age. Remember how short I used to wear my hair? I was trying to be Winona Ryder.'

'We were all trying to be Winona Ryder.'

'Or Drew Barrymore.'

They said it at the same time, their voices chiming in unison. They looked at each other, their eyes wide with shock. Their secret language, the line of silent communication was still intact. It felt like it had never gone away.

Kase's rich, deep laugh pealed out, and with it came the silver edges of so many good memories. *Full. Brimming.*

'No, you were just you, Sylvie Dane,' she said, still holding Sylvie by the shoulders. Kase pressed her lips together, holding back emotion, and gestured around to the table. 'Everyone, this is sweet Sylvie, my long-lost friend who has come all the way from Sydney.'

Sylvie's face grew hot, and her fingers twisted her wet dress into a knot. It felt good but strange to be seen for who she used to be. She had forgotten, but Kase remembered. Or was Kase just focusing on the past to avoid the so obviously changed woman standing before her right now?

'You remember Mum, Fran. And this is my husband, Henry. And you remember Rachel, and you know Gabe, who used to be in our little posse. His wife, Trina, and their kids are around somewhere, too.'

Sylvie's eyes flicked from Rachel to Gabe. She forced a smile onto her face and swallowed. Of course. Why wouldn't Kase still be friends with her brother's best friend? For most people, life moved on after death. Those who knew Tristan no doubt helped to keep his memory alive. And no one knew Tristan better than Gabe.

But Rachel, Gabe's sister, the girl who'd tormented her and Kase from age fourteen to seventeen, how was she here as one of Kase's nearest and dearest?

Sylvie chastised herself. Maybe it was only natural they'd stayed in touch, become closer after Tristan's death. Jealousy twinged inside her, like a discordant string, an old feeling. She opened her mouth to greet them, but two kids rushed at the table like little gusts of wind, energy high, just like their father's had been.

'Steady on. Don't take all the food,' Gabe cautioned them as they grabbed muffins and pastries.

'Dad, can you come and see this sea creature we've found? It might be poisonous,' one of the kids said.

'Can you go with them, babe? I just want to have a coffee in peace,' said Trina – Sylvie assumed – flopping down at the table.

'So much for our long-awaited child-free weekend.' Gabe rolled his eyes. 'The grandparents fell through at the last minute, and now behold the tag team.' He gestured to his wife, drained his coffee and followed the kids down the steps that led towards the beach.

'Oh, we love having the kids,' said Kase.

Fran stood and embraced Sylvie warmly. 'Oh, it's been too long. I still remember how much you loved my carrot cake.'

Sylvie laughed at Fran's greeting. Perhaps all the usual pleasantries were not available to them, given the events of the last time they'd seen each other. Still, a warm seam opened inside her remembering that cake. 'You know, I can still taste that cream cheese icing with the walnuts down the middle.'

'It was from a packet, you know, but I never told you that because I think you had this picture of me as the ideal mother who baked from scratch, which I quite liked.'

Kind. Soft. Present. The ideal mother. Yes. I did think that. So far removed from her own mother, who was absent, indifferent to Sylvie's whereabouts. How many times had Fran picked her up from places? Fed her dinner? Given her a toothbrush and fresh sheets to sleep in. Asked them how school was, what was going on with friends. Unlike Evangeline.

'How is your mother?' asked Fran.

Sylvie nodded. 'She's well. Busy. Living in Istanbul at the moment.'

'Oh, how glamorous.' Fran's voice was laced with a tiny hint of sarcasm.

Sylvie cringed inwardly. *Glamorous, beautiful, free-spirited.* Words frequently bestowed upon her mother.

'Come, sit down. Can I get you a coffee or tea? Or there's morning wine, which is of course permitted for such momentous birthday celebrations.' Fran winked.

'Tea would be great, thank you.'

Kase nudged her. 'Come on, have a mimosa. It'll warm you up. It's my birthday and I'll make people drink breakfast wine if I want to.' She poured a glass from a big jug and handed it to Sylvie.

Fran passed her a cup of tea and a soft mohair blanket. 'And it looks like you could use this too. Sit, sit. Get cosy.'

'Thanks.' Sylvie sat between Fran and Kase and wrapped the blanket around her damp legs. She hadn't realised she was shaking, couldn't tell if it was from the cold, or nerves.

Kase reached out and squeezed her hand. 'I can't believe you came. I mean I was hoping, but I didn't even know where you were living.'

'How did you find me?' Sylvie took a sip of the sweet cocktail, enjoying the sharpness of the alcohol in her throat.

'My agent knows Evangeline and she emailed her and asked for your address.'

'Oh.' Her mother hadn't mentioned this in their recent email exchange.

'She's doing well, isn't she? Shortlisted for two prizes in recent years.' Kase sat back, crossing her legs under her in the exact same way Sylvie remembered, as though she was made of a bendier substance than the rest of them.

'Can you still put your legs behind your head?' Sylvie wondered out loud.

Kase laughed. 'I don't know.' She pulled a leg out from under her and proceeded to stretch it up until her ankle fitted neatly behind her neck.

Fran rolled her eyes. 'Kasey June Fowler! Really? At the table?'

'How the hell did I not know you could do that?' exclaimed Rachel. 'Did you know about this sorcery?' she asked Henry.

Kase's husband shook his head, a bemused look on his face. 'What do you think? She gave me a demonstration on our first date.' They all laughed. 'No. I didn't know.'

Kase attempted the second leg but failed. 'Not as flexible as I used to be then,' she said. She took a swig of her drink. 'And what about you? Are you still writing?'

Sylvie laughed. 'Me?'

Kase widened her eyes. 'Yes, you. Star English student. Famous author mum. You were born to be a writer.'

'No.'

'Really? You don't write at all?'

Sylvie shrugged. 'Work keeps me busy.'

'What is it that you do for work?' Rachel asked from across the table. Sylvie took in her neat honey-blonde hair, dark manicure and chic black turtleneck jumper. Their family had always had money and now it showed.

'I'm a cleaner.' Sylvie felt a mixture of shame and defiance saying this in front of all these people from her past.

She saw Rachel's eyes glaze over; she clearly hadn't changed since high school. *Superficial. Hungry.*

'No, I refused to believe it when I heard,' said Kase. 'You can't possibly be, because how on earth do you clean houses in those beautiful dresses of yours?' Her face was open and free of judgement, and Sylvie laughed. *You still know me.*

She shook her head. 'How do you know I don't wear overalls?'

Kase rolled her eyes. 'I just know. You would never.'

'I clean out furniture and things from houses after people pass away. I like to dress up out of respect for them.'

Kase smiled. 'How interesting. What do you have to do exactly?'

'I go in after the family have taken everything they want, and I pack up the rest for charity or the tip. There's a lot of going through old things. Finding things in the backs of wardrobes, in long-forgotten places.'

'Oh, now that's interesting,' said Rachel, leaning on her elbows and narrowing her eyes. 'That's not a cleaner, that's a death curator.'

'That's a dramatic interpretation. Can you tell she works in the theatre?' added Kase.

Sylvie laughed. Rachel had always had a flair for the dramatic. She felt her shoulders drop and the clench in her gut ease a little. She took another sip of her drink. The fresh salty air and the sweet sharp wine were good. Now she wanted the conversation to steer away from her. She knew what came next.

All the questions: Don't you find it depressing? Do you have to move dead bodies? *Morbid curiosity.*

'So what book are you up to now?' she asked Kase.

'The one about the long-lost friend showing up at the party.'

Kase shot her a cheeky look and everyone laughed, but Sylvie felt the tightness return to her throat. *Abandoned, not long-lost. There is a difference.* Her eyes met Kase's and she saw amusement there, but also something else. There had been a time when she could read her friend's every expression.

Kase waved her hand dismissively. 'No, not really. Though it's not a bad premise for a book. I'm running short of ideas at the moment. Bit of a dry patch creatively, despite the next one being due soon. I really must be getting old.'

'I want to read something about a death curator now,' said Rachel. 'Can you write that? Richard, my director, can turn it into a play.'

'Why don't you get Sylvie to write it? She's always been a far better wordsmith than me,' said Kase.

Sylvie shook her head, feeling a rush of embarrassment at everyone's eyes on her, remembering all the dreams she used to have, how good with words she used to be. *I was better. But I never did anything with it.*

'Don't be silly,' she said.

'You are. We both know it. Our Year 12 English teacher knew it. Your mother knew it. I have no idea how I've published five books and you're working as a cleaner.'

There was a ripple of awkward laughter but the words hung in the air like the mist sweeping towards them across the bay. Sylvie felt the cold stain her cheeks. She didn't know what to say, so she said nothing, and then they all felt the fine mist of rain, slanting sideways, like icy pins.

'Oh, that's cold. I think it might be time to light the fire and think about lunch,' said Fran, rising and collecting the mugs. Sylvie busied herself with helping clear the table and Kase hugged her again as they went inside. But her words sat within Sylvie like the dark stones glistening under the bruised sky on the beach outside.

SPRING 1996

The mall smelled like sweet cinnamon doughnuts and cheap perfume. Kase took a sip of Diet Coke to quell her hankering for fried sugar. It didn't work. She bought two doughnuts, one for Sylvie. Her mouth was salivating as she held the sticky, oily bag and waited at their meeting spot outside Sportsgirl. They totally needed to update their spot to somewhere cooler. God, they were lame sometimes, but she secretly liked that it was her and Sylvie, the misfits, against the world.

Kase checked her Swatch. Sylvie was always late. Annoyance flitted through her, but not because of the tardiness. Sylvie had beaten her in the English exam. Again. It was only by two marks, but it always felt like ten. It was clear Mrs Washington favoured Sylvie. Of course the child of an author was going to get better marks. *Whatever.* Kase looked at her watch again and opened the bag of warm doughnuts. She ate one and licked the sugar granules from her fingers, then eyed Sylvie's.

'Hi,' Sylvie rushed up to her, breathless. Beads of perspiration had oozed through her new pancake foundation that was a shade too dark around her jawline. Kase made a mental note to tell her.

'I nearly ate yours, you're so late.' Kase handed her the bag.

Sylvie made a face. 'Argh. Should I? I already ate a whole brown bread roll from the canteen for lunch. You know, those really heavy ones? It still feels like a brick in my stomach.'

Kase rubbed Sylvie's belly, affecting a baby voice. 'Oh, hello little bread belly. You're so cute.'

Sylvie batted her hand away and frowned. 'You're cruel. Leave my baby alone.' She rubbed her belly affectionately. 'Don't listen to Aunty Kase, she's just jealous because she's never incubating baked goods in her flat-as-hell stomach.' She shot Kase a look of mock rage.

Kase lifted her uniform, sticking out her stomach and revealing a pair of pink undies to the world.

Sylvie clapped a hand over her mouth and squealed, pulling Kase's uniform down to her knees. 'Oh my God! You nutter. You just flashed the entire mall.'

Kase shrugged, her face deadpan. 'I'm pretty sure that guy over there appreciated it.'

Their eyes landed on an ancient man whose back was bent like a hairpin over his walking stick. Laughter erupted from them and they linked arms and ran.

They reached the fountain at the centre of the mall and sat down, breathless, buzzing. The hot afternoon sun illuminated the blue dolphins jumping over each other and the rush of the water filled their ears. They were in their pre-hysterical mood. It was as though both of them were silently egging each other on, daring the other to laugh harder. Kase peeled off her school shoes and socks and stood in the ankle-deep water. She made an elaborate bow to the woman giving her a hard side-eye.

'These adults need to take a chill pill. It's freaking hot.' She splashed Sylvie.

Sylvie shrieked and peeled off her own shoes and socks. They waded in the water, splashing each other, heady with the disapproving glances coming their way.

Sylvie linked her little finger through Kase's. It was something they did sometimes, if they were unsure, or defiant, or just needed the other person to know, *Hey, I've got your back. I'm here.*

'Oh my God, I'm soaked.' Sylvie got out and picked up the doughnut bag. 'I've worked up an appetite now.'

'Go on, eat the doughnut. Give bread baby a twin.'

Sylvie bit into the treat and moaned appreciatively. She offered Kase a bite.

'We'll take turns on my exercise bike later,' Kase said, her mouth full.

'Definitely no Viennetta for dessert,' said Sylvie, rubbing her belly. 'I'm not ready for triplets.'

'You say that now …'

'You always have way too much tempting food at your house. Evangeline only ever has cheese. She thinks cheese and crackers with a piece of apple and red wine constitutes dinner.'

'That's why I love your house. At least she lets us drink. My parents are under the illusion that Trist and I don't touch alcohol.'

'Yeah, that's how loving parents are meant to be.'

'Your mum loves you, she's just way more worldly and realistic. She knows us better than my mum.'

'How's this for a metaphor? My mum is brie on crackers, Fran is melted cheese on toast. I'd prefer your mum any day. So oozy and comforting.'

Kase rolled her eyes. 'Gee, anyone would think you were a nineteen out of twenty English student.'

Sylvie nudged her. 'There's hardly any difference between seventeen and nineteen.'

There is to me, thought Kase. *And I'm pretty sure to you too.*

'So, what are we going to wear to the end-of-year beach party? We need to plan our outfits. And which friend of Tristan's is having it? The hot one who looks like Kurt Cobain?' Sylvie asked, licking the sugar from her fingers while eyeing a green floral dress in a shop window.

'Yeah, Brent. He's dumb but pretty.' Kase pulled her away. 'Come on, let's go to Vinnies. I saw a dress you'd love there. You're going to look exactly like Drew Barrymore.'

'Why thank you, Winona,' Sylvie said, linking her arm through Kase's. 'If we really want to look like Winona and Drew, I think we'd better go to my place tonight. No temptations. All that's in the fridge is vodka. My mother classes vodka as a food group.'

'Have I told you I adore your mum?'

They looked at each other and laughed.

'Are you thinking what I'm thinking?' Sylvie asked.

'More doughnuts,' they said in unison, laughing and steering each other towards the food court.

Kase mock-flirted with the boy at the doughnut shop for Sylvie's benefit until her friend and the boy reddened sufficiently. They ate the sticky carbs, feeding each other as they left the mall and stepped onto the main road barefoot, purposely avoiding the crossing and running across the double lanes just to feel the shot of adrenalin.

CHAPTER 3

swell *(v.)* – to rise in waves, as the sea.

'You're shivering,' said Fran, touching her shoulder as they went inside. 'You're still wet, I'm going to run you a bath.'

Fran dismissed Sylvie's protests and gestured to follow her up a short set of stairs into another wing of the house. There were the same big windows with views over Bruny and the bay, woven rugs covering timber floors, hallways lined with paintings of the local landscape and tables covered with candles and vases of dried flowers.

'This place is incredible,' said Sylvie, running her fingers along a distressed-timber sideboard. She wanted to ask how long they'd owned it, but didn't. Probing into such things felt weighted, difficult.

'Kase and I moved to Hobart after we sold Palm Beach,' Fran said, answering Sylvie's unasked question. 'We wanted a fresh start. And I grew up in Hobart, so it felt like home, I guess. Then after Ted and I separated, I needed a job, so I started running our place in Hobart as a B&B. When Kase's books took off, she bought me this place to run as a guesthouse. I mean, it had been in my family generations ago. My grandfather owned it for a while, so I think the owners liked that there was that connection, felt that we'd keep the spirit of the place. But honestly, I couldn't believe she bought me an island. She doesn't do things by half, our Kase.'

Sylvie laughed, feeling a rush of unexpected affection for Kase's big heart. 'No, no she doesn't.'

'But it's …' Fran shook her head. 'It's been a godsend. It keeps me busy, looking after other people.'

'You don't feel too isolated out here by yourself, when you don't have guests?'

'Well, you met Holden in the taxi – he helps out with handyman stuff and is a fantastic cook. And Kase runs writing retreats here sometimes.' Fran paused at a doorway. 'Here's your bedroom and there's a lovely bath in the ensuite overlooking the bay.'

Sylvie put her bag down on the beautiful eggshell-blue linen bedspread and followed Fran into a bathroom. Fran turned on the taps in a beautiful stone bath sitting under a sloping ceiling of exposed wood.

Sylvie couldn't remember her own mother ever drawing her a bath, though surely she had when she was little. But to be looked after as an adult, that was something foreign to her. That was something special. She felt a fondness unfurl as Fran handed her a fresh towel.

'Take your time. Warm up your bones. Would you like a cup of tea or a glass of wine in here?'

Sylvie smiled and shook her head. 'You are so kind, Fran, but no, I'm fine. This is just perfect.' She had forgotten just how much Fran had been part of her life. How Kase came as part of a package. It had also been Fran. And it had been Tristan.

She peeled her damp clothes from her body and sank into the hot water. A pleasant chill crept through her as she eased in up to her shoulder blades. Through a small window, the sea chopped and changed below, whitewash flecking blue-grey waves. Dark clouds and sunlight warred over the water. She had not expected the rush of warmth she had felt coming back to these people. How they could feel more like home than her own home, even after all this time. The balm of that realisation came with a prickle of discomfort at just how good it felt, how much she'd missed it.

There was a knock on the door and Sylvie sat up, wrapping her arms around her knees to cover herself.

'It's just me,' said Kase, poking her head in. 'Mum made me bring you some herbal tea. I remembered you liked peppermint but hated chamomile. 'May I?'

Sylvie nodded, trying to reassure herself with the thought of all the times they'd seen each other naked as teenagers. Kase came in and placed the steaming mug on a wooden rack at the end of the bath.

'Thank you. You've all been so welcoming. I'd forgotten how amazing Fran was.'

Kase shook her head and sat on the edge of the bath. 'You've forgotten how we worshipped Evangeline because she let us drink and smoke at your place and she was so gorgeous and young-at-heart. I wanted her to be my mum.'

Alluring, creative, bohemian. 'Maybe I have forgotten,' she said. But really, Kase had been the only one who had adored Evangeline's libertine parenting. Sylvie had gone along with the hero worship, but all she'd ever wanted was a normal mum. Not a cool mum. Just a mum like Fran. *Evangeline is not here now running a bath and sending up tea.* Sylvie felt another flash of jealousy, like a mild electric shock. Kase still didn't realise everything she had.

Kase stood. 'God, look at me. Sorry, here am I just sitting here while you're essentially naked. You know me, no boundaries.'

Do I still know you? The words floated in the air like the tail end of Kase's vanilla scent as she left the room.

* * *

A storm brewed over the slate-coloured water and the house felt like it was unmoored in the choppy wash and churn of the bay. They had closed all the doors, but still the smell of rain and salt and fish seeped through the cracks, like the rock pools below, leaking into the sea. Sylvie felt herself cower as lightning cracked in the distance. Her world was usually so contained, as predictable as lines on a page. And now she was here, feeling exposed, at the mercy of the people as much as the elements.

Sylvie found herself sticking close to Fran in the kitchen, helping her rinse the mugs and stack the dishwasher and then chopping vegetables to accompany the two roast chickens stuffed with herbed butter and garlic.

'Thanks for helping,' said Fran, checking on the birds roasting in the oven. 'I don't expect Kase to pitch in – it's her celebration – but I did expect the others might offer to help. We'll rope them in to do dinner. Nurturers like us need to stick up for ourselves or we get walked all over.' She gave Sylvie's arm a squeeze.

Sylvie smiled. Her eyes were drawn to Kase's husband who was sipping red wine in front of the fire, talking with Rachel. He hadn't said a word to Sylvie, but she could tell he was an introvert. He had that thin-skinned quality. She could see it in his watchful eyes, in the silent twitch of his lips as he listened. She knew only that he was in the philosophy department of Hobart University. Sylvie imagined he was the balance to Kase's wide open immunity to life.

Kase was half-reading the paper, half-conversing with Trina, who was tucked in front of the fire with a cup of tea and a book splayed open on her lap.

'It's so nice to have everyone here. It's almost like the old days,' said Fran.

Sylvie smiled to cover her feelings. She could never tell Fran that she was shocked Kase and Rachel were now apparently close friends. She watched Fran toss vegetables in olive oil with her hands. Her face was different. Still suffused with kindness, but there was a sadness, a droop to the corners of her mouth that Sylvie didn't remember her having before. Sylvie's hand found her notebook and she itched to write down the words: *Fran … Loss. Grief. Endurance.*

'It means a lot to Kase that you came after all this time,' said Fran, her eyes suddenly shining. 'It feels like a reunion of sorts. Though we've stayed close to Rachel and Gabe since Tristan died.' Perhaps Fran realised the subtext of her words: *We've stayed close to everyone except you.* It hung in the air as pungent as the sting of onion in Sylvie's eyes, because she added, 'Truth be told, it feels like having Tristan's friends around keeps his memory alive.'

Sylvie pressed her hand to her chest. 'I'm so sorry, Fran. It must be hard … these milestones.'

'Sometimes I wonder what his wife would have looked like. What my grandchildren would have looked like. Would they have his same bright blue eyes? His knowing chuckle? He was such a handsome boy.'

Sylvie's breath was shallow. The onion and garlic on the chopping board were making her eyes water and she swiped under them. How had she thought she could cope with this talk of the past? Of Tristan? It had been twenty-three years since he'd died. But standing here surrounded by his family, she might have been seventeen again and in their kitchen. Tristan opening the fridge door and taking out every condiment to make one of his towering sandwiches. Tristan flicking his hair off his face with his thumb, the lopsided charm of his smile. The hope humming inside her like a song, on that last night he was alive. The only thing she did remember. The way he had finally, after all those years, noticed her on the beach, before they walked up to the lighthouse. And then, just when it felt like the beginning of things, it was the end, and he was gone, and there was only the blackness.

The knife she was holding clattered to the floor.

'Are you okay?' asked Fran, her eyes concerned.

Sylvie bent down to pick it up and the world spun. She needed to get some fresh air, but it was raining now, the water sleeting against the windows. A peal of panic rose through her. *Empty … Blank … Abyss …* She needed to take out her notebook. To write the feelings out of her, but she knew she couldn't. It was another excruciating reminder of how much she'd changed, another reminder of that night on the clifftop.

Another reminder of how far she was from who she used to be around these people. She wished suddenly that she was home in her small, safe bedroom. Her four walls surrounded by all her books, all her known words.

Fran touched her shoulder. 'Oh, Sylvie, I'm sorry. Sorry, I didn't even think. Is it hard to talk about that night? I know you and Kase drifted apart after everything that happened. Kase took it all very hard. Very hard.'

Sylvie steadied herself on the bench. 'It's okay.' *I have no words for that night, no memories,* she thought. *It's not just hard to talk about that night, I can't talk about that night. And I can't talk about how you and Kase abandoned me.*

She was about to excuse herself when Holden stepped into the kitchen, a box in his arms. He was breathless.

'Storm's coming over the channel, so I thought you could do with some more supplies. It's going to get cold tonight.' He slid the box onto the bench. 'Wood, whisky and wine, and some chocolate fudge from Bruny,' he said, peeling a wet raincoat from his body.

Sylvie realised she hadn't really seen him under his hood. His dark hair was cut short but still longish on top and curled under his ears where it was damp. He had deep-set brown eyes below strong brows and a nose that stopped him from being traditionally handsome. His tanned skin had the same warm quality as his voice and eyes.

Kase was up from her spot by the fire. 'Oh, you are just perfect. A man bearing wine and chocolate. Is there anything better for your birthday? Henry, take note.'

Henry looked up and rolled his eyes behind his glasses.

Sylvie's eyes met Holden's as he walked towards her. 'How

are you settling in, Sylvie Plath? You didn't catch your death of cold coming across the channel, did you?'

She laughed shyly, shifting her gaze. She couldn't remember the last time a man had flirted with her, if that's what he was doing. She'd forgotten the feeling of inexplicable energy flowing back and forth with a person. 'No, I'm fine.'

'Holden, you should stay for lunch. Or dinner, or linner, or whatever we're having,' said Rachel, taking a bottle of whisky out of the box and inspecting the label. 'I can see just how this afternoon is going to play out.' There was a twinkle in her eye. She hadn't changed. Still thought she could seduce every man on the planet.

'I really don't mean to intrude on your special celebration,' Holden said evenly, refusing to flirt with Rachel.

Sylvie smiled on the inside. *You really are Holden Caulfield, sniffing out the phonies.*

'No, no, you must stay. Look at that weather. We can't have you going out into that again. Sit by the fire. Put your feet up. Warm up.' Kase took the bottle from Rachel's hands.

Holden rubbed the back of his neck. 'Oh, I've got quite a bit to do this afternoon.'

'I daresay there won't be many water taxi jobs with a storm like that brewing,' said Fran, nodding towards the window. 'Come on, stay. You need to eat lunch.'

Holden's eyes met Sylvie's. 'Oh okay, arm twisted. It smells damn good in here.' He took a bottle of red wine from his box and cracked it open. 'You *have* to taste this.'

Sylvie was acutely aware of his body behind her as he took beautiful stemless glassware down from the cupboard and poured the wine.

He handed a glass to her and Fran. 'The cooks get first drinks.'

Sylvie took a sip and rich berries, earth and smoky wood combined on her tongue. It felt like she was drinking the landscape outside. 'This is really good.'

'I knew you'd love it.'

Intimate. Known. Sylvie's fingers found her notebook, but she withdrew them.

Gabe and the kids came through into the kitchen, shaking rain from their jackets and hooting with the cold. Trina was up and ushering the children in front of the fire. Kase grabbed towels from a bathroom and dried their hair until they laughed.

'We got any beer?' Gabe was standing beside Holden on the other side of the kitchen bar, his hands on his hips, cheeks florid with cold.

Gabe had been a tall boy and now he was a tall man. Sylvie thought he perfectly fit the stereotype of the editor of a major metropolitan newspaper, though she wouldn't have guessed the relaxed surfer boy who'd lived at the end of the Fowlers' street would have amounted to someone who ran a newsroom. She ignored his comment about the beer and busied herself with putting vegetable scraps into the compost bin. He could get his own beer.

'Sure, mate.' Holden grabbed a bottle from the fridge and opened it.

'Got any chips or dips? This Tassie weather sure gets the appetite going.'

Holden opened the pantry with an ease that everyone who'd ever been in Fran's kitchen had. There were jars of preserves, stacks of cans and bulk bags of pulses and rice. Sylvie thought about her own bare cupboards. She wondered what it would be like to live with such abundance. It also reminded Sylvie of how remote this property was. This was clearly a stockpile against disconnection from the outside world. A tiny pulse of panic went through her at the thought of being stranded here.

'Help yourself to anything,' Fran chimed in. 'Holden knows his way around this kitchen because he helps me cook for some of our bigger groups. And he's helping cook for the party tomorrow night.'

'Are you a chef?' asked Sylvie.

Holden nearly choked on his wine. 'God, no. I just like eating.'

Fran raised an eyebrow. 'He's being humble. He's as natural a cook as I've ever seen.'

Gabe grabbed a large packet of crisps and opened it. He was about to put a chip in his mouth when one of the kids ran and took it from his hand.

They all laughed at Gabe's expression. 'Seagulls inside the house,' he said, wrangling a handful of crisps before the kids took off with the packet.

'You have cute kids,' said Sylvie, finally attempting conversation with Gabe. She knew she was only 'the cleaner' to him and Rachel. She'd seen it in both their expressions, but she wanted to be polite, for Fran's sake. It was obvious to Sylvie that Fran had substituted Gabe for Tristan and that Kase had replaced her with Rachel.

Gabe rolled his eyes. 'They're cute ... in small doses.'

'How old are they?'

'Jessie's ten and Rocco's twelve. Lucky for us they seem to like each other's company. You got kids?'

Sylvie arranged her face into a smile. 'No. No kids.'

The way he addressed her she might have been a stranger. She was a stranger now, despite all those years living in each other's pockets, the outliers, the two best friends of Kase and Tristan. If Kase and Sylvie had been twinned, so had those two.

'Smart woman. Lucky you,' said Gabe, amusement in his voice.

She forced the smile to remain, but when he turned at the sound of his kids, she let it slip from her face.

'What about you, Holden? You saddled with the little buggers?' Gabe asked with the same blithe amusement.

Holden stiffened, his glass halfway to his lips. A shadow passed over his face, so fleeting Sylvie may have been imagining it.

'No.' The word felt like a stone being dropped onto the floor. *Leaden. Flat.*

She searched his face. *Forlorn.* Her fingers traced the outline of her notebook. Her mind scrambled for a change of subject; she needed to rescue him.

'You must have seen some incredible storms come over the island,' she said, as the sky uttered another deep growl.

'Ah, yes, I'm a bit of a sucker for a good storm. The weather here has a mind of its own. It's like this now, but you watch, in a few hours the sun will be out. That's what I love about Tassie.'

They exchanged a smile and Sylvie thought there was a tiny hint of gratitude in his.

'Pretty special spot this island,' said Gabe. 'I couldn't think of anything better than getting away here for a few days and throwing a line in. Drinking whisky and kayaking. That's what the website said you could do here.'

Holden nodded. 'Well, there are fishing rods and kayaks in the shed. I can point you in the right direction.'

'So, Fran's got you working pretty hard by the looks of things. You're like the island concierge or something are you?'

Holden shrugged. 'Yeah, I guess you could call it that. I'm the practical guy. I help out with maintenance and the like, and the rest of the time I operate the Bruny water taxi. I do a lot of trips to Kettering.'

Sylvie imagined a life skimming across the water like a smooth flat stone, skirting the wild edges of Bruny Island, the only sound the hum of the motor, the roar of the wind and the high call of birds. Holden's job was as solitary as her own.

'Sounds like a pretty good gig actually,' said Gabe, sipping his beer.

Trina had joined them in the kitchen, searching for more potato chips and pouring them into a bowl. 'Sylvie, didn't you say you were a cleaner? You could work here too. If you're going to clean bathrooms it may as well be some place beautiful.'

Her eyes flicked to Holden's face. She hadn't thought she was ashamed of what she did, but now she felt humiliation crawl through her. Why did these people have to keep bringing up what she did for a living as though it was the only part of her that mattered? They didn't understand the poetry of what she did, the people's stories she found and respectfully lay to rest. All they saw was a badly paid job with no social cachet. But if it didn't matter what they thought, why was she feeling so embarrassed?

Holden shot her a small smile. 'What do you think, Sylvie Plath? Would you clean a room with a view?'

Sylvie's heart lifted, like the sea eagles they'd spotted from the boat. 'I'm pretty sure E.M. Forster would take that job. But I much prefer a room of one's own,' she said with a soft smile. He had rescued her in the same way she had rescued him.

'Ah yes, Virginia Woolf would rather like it here, I think,' he said taking a sip of his wine and winking.

Gabe and Trina exchanged a puzzled look. They took the chips and wandered off into the loungeroom, following the sound of their kids.

'Sorry, the pitfalls of being named after literary heroes,' said Holden, mumbling into his wine.

Complicit. Undercurrent. Connection.

Sylvie smiled and took a large gulp of her own wine, feeling hope fill her out to the edges.

'Did I hear we're discussing literary heroes over here?' asked Rachel, picking up the bottle and pouring herself a glass of wine. 'So, I'm intrigued. Holden, how did you come by the name Holden exactly? Were your parents J.D. Salinger fans?'

'Yes, the perils of being born to high school English teachers.'

'Oh, that's so sweet. Do you have siblings called Jane? Oliver? Matilda, by any chance?' Rachel laughed, placing a hand lightly on Holden's arm. Sylvie felt herself stiffen.

'Yes, a sister who's an Emma.'

'No. Really?'

'Of course. They were big on the classics. Holden and Emma beats being called Hansel and Gretel I guess.' He shrugged.

Rachel laughed loudly. 'And as I've just been informed about Sylvie here, are you also a writer in disguise?'

Holden put down his wine and thought for a moment. 'I don't think writers are ever in disguise really, are they? That's the whole point. They can't seem to keep the truth inside. They are actually failures in the art of disguise.'

Sylvie felt a smile play on her lips. She wanted everyone else to go away so she could talk to this man who spoke in riddles only she seemed to understand.

Rachel raised her eyebrows. 'Spoken like a true writer. Or perhaps philosopher.'

Holden shrugged. 'I'm just the guy who runs the boat.'

'And stuffs a pretty mean chook,' said Fran. 'Speaking of food, shall we graze while we're waiting for lunch?' She carried a large platter filled with cheese, cured meats, dried fruits and nuts, olives and crackers, and set it on the coffee table in front of the fire.

They arranged themselves on various couches, cradling their wine while the storm raged outside. Sylvie sat in an armchair near the window rather than right by the fire with the others. She felt like she was on the outside looking in, like a child gazing into a snow globe. She would have liked to sit with Holden and exchange more obscure literary references with him, but he'd been pulled onto the couch between Rachel and Kase.

'Glad you're not out in that?' asked Kase, passing a cracker with a huge slice of brie to Holden.

Sylvie was reminded of Rachel and her clique at high school, the way they zoned in on the attractive males like bees to a blossom, sending subtle cues that no man could hope to decode but that every other girl understood. Kase had always been this way. Perhaps that's why she and Rachel had ended up friends. They had loved boys and boys had loved them back. Rachel was a classic beauty. And there was a wild sensuality to Kase that was like a beacon. And yet it seemed she'd chosen a connection of the mind with her husband. Henry, who was reading the paper, seemed oblivious to the thrall of Holden.

'Can I ask how old you are, Holden? Or is that too rude? Sorry, I'm a bit blunt, aren't I? Sylvie, remember how you used to constantly tell me I was too blunt?' Kase said.

Sylvie shot her a knowing smile. 'I remember.'

'I'm forty-two.'

'No. Really?'

'It must be all the UV rays and wild weather doing wonders for my complexion,' he said sarcastically.

'And yet you're like one of those criminals who look ten years younger because they haven't seen the sun,' Rachel said.

'Err, thanks?' Holden shifted in his seat. He was possibly wishing he'd just dropped the box off and left right now.

'Are you married, Holden?' Henry's voice was deep and steady. Sylvie could just imagine him delivering a philosophy lecture. He had taken off his glasses and taken up his wine. Perhaps he had been listening to the conversation after all.

Holden was silent for a beat, but his face betrayed him again. Into that silence came two words: *grief* and *longing*. Sylvie would know the shape of those words anywhere. Their etch on a face.

'I'm divorced.'

Sylvie felt these words inside her, two immiscible liquids, like oil and water. *Sadness. Hope.*

'Oh, I'm sorry to hear that,' Henry said.

'Same,' said Rachel, her hand shooting up like a schoolgirl.

'Great club to be in, isn't it?' Holden quipped.

'Any other takers? Sylvie?' Rachel asked too brightly.

Sylvie grimaced and shook her head.

'We've skirted pretty close, haven't we, Gabe? But nope, not us … yet,' said Trina, laughing.

Gabe's laugh was a low grumble, which ended in what sounded like a smoker's cough.

'So, were you all friends from way back?' asked Holden, clearly trying to steer the conversation away from the pain in his life.

'Yeah, I've known Sylvie and Gabe and Rach since we were kids,' said Kase, topping up her wine.

'These three were like extra children to me,' said Fran. 'The number of times there'd be extra kids in my house for days on end …'

'What can I say? You fed us, you're still feeding us,' said Gabe, cutting himself a thick slice of pate.

'That's what Sylvie said she remembered. My cooking.'

'That's how you show your love, Mum,' said Kase. 'It's beautiful.'

'Thanks, darling. And it's been so lovely to have you here eating everything in sight, Gabe.'

They all laughed.

Fran smiled wistfully. 'Nobody had an appetite like Tristan though. Remember how many sandwiches he'd eat in one sitting? He'd make a pile of six slices of bread and eat them in two gulps.' Her gaze drifted out the window. 'We would have been celebrating him turning forty-two this year.'

Kase's face fell behind a bank of cloud. *Shadow. Pain.* Almost everyone in this room knew the heft and weight of those words, those feelings.

Sylvie wondered about the weeks and months that followed Tristan's death. How had Kase coped in those grief-fresh weeks?

The hospital, the induced coma, Sylvie's slow rehabilitation … Kase hadn't been there for any of it. She only visited Sylvie once, but Sylvie had no memory of that visit, or of any of that time. Her short-term memory had been wiped clean, the doctors said. It was her mother who'd told her about Kase visiting. When she finally left hospital and Evangeline took her home, as she slowly regained her strength, her mind, she had contacted Kase. She was met with unreturned phone calls. *Silence.* There were only so many times you could try before you realised that the silence was actually the answer to your question.

Sylvie ran her fingers over the tracheotomy scar at the bottom of her neck. The hurt had sat lodged in her throat like the scar, refusing to fade. *Abandonment.* Sylvie had another word too: *Why?*

But now here she was, counted among Kase's nearest and dearest. Perhaps it had just been grief, pure and simple, that had made Kase shut off. People acted in strange ways when they were in pain, and grief was a deep hole. Maybe this was a fresh start, another chance, an understanding that the past was the past. Surely that was why Kase had invited her here. *I missed you, too.*

There were so many emotions the English language could not adequately express. Why, for example, wasn't there a word for the way friendships could go into hibernation for years and seemingly awaken as if no time had passed?

But time *had* passed. She looked at Kase now, leaning into Rachel, sipping her wine, a smile playing on her lips. Would that have been her if Tristan had never died? Tristan would be here with his wife and kids instead of Gabe. A tiny part of her wondered, *could that have been me?*

Kase caught her eye and smiled. Sylvie returned it, shyly. It felt like a dance, a push and pull. Strangely similar to a love story. But deeper in a way, wider and longer, though no less fraught. She'd once thought the bonds of friendship were made of a stuff more resilient than romantic love, but not anymore. Sylvie felt the loose threads of their connection wind around her now, the sweet embrace of rekindling their kinship, but the questions like tendrils sticking to her skin. While the others were here, they were in safe territory. They could skim the surface, remember back to before that night through the warm prism of nostalgia, to when they had been teenagers twinned. To before the gulf that echoed in the spaces between words, like a hole waiting to be filled.

'Lunch is ready,' said Fran, placing the steaming food on the long timber table that ran along the bank of windows fogged with breath and rain.

Sylvie hung back, waiting for the others to assume their places along the table, the way a family naturally seem to do. She was still an outlier. She registered the relief when she sat down, and it wasn't next to Kase.

CHAPTER 4

commune *(v.)* – to converse, talk together, interchange thoughts or feelings.

They walked under the moisture-laden leaves of overhanging trees. The sky was so low, Sylvie was sure if she stood on tiptoe she could touch it. Their bellies were full of good food and she could feel the wine moving in her veins, softening everything out, illuminating her from the inside, like sunlight against a blackened sky. Waves bit into the cliffs, the sea unable to forget the raging storm that had just hit the coast. But it felt like a fading bad dream now in this clean afternoon. They walked along the beach, the wet sand hard under their feet. Sylvie found herself again next to Fran.

'Sorry, I'm so slow, I've got issues with my knees. But it's so good to get outside after all that food,' Fran said. She nudged Sylvie. 'You don't have to walk with me. I'm so slow in my old age. Catch up with the others.'

Kase and Rachel were up ahead, arms linked, with Holden, Gabe and Henry in front and Trina behind at the water's edge with the kids.

'That's okay, I don't move that quickly myself. I feel a little like the odd one out anyway. Though everyone is making me feel very welcome,' Sylvie said.

Fran nodded. 'To be honest, it feels like you've slotted right back in. It's as though twenty years just passed in the blink of an eye.'

'I know what you mean,' Sylvie said. *But I haven't, not really,* she thought. *I'm no longer the person you once knew, but no one is willing to acknowledge it.*

'So, Sylvie, do you have anyone special in your life? You said you're not divorced. No kids. Are you married?'

She always found this question tiresome, as though this along with your job was the measure of your success in life. But Sylvie couldn't be upset with Fran. She knew she only ever came from a place of kindness and genuine concern. They had slipped back into the same comfortable bond they'd always shared.

She shrugged. 'No. I'm a bit of a loner, I guess. I live a very small life. I work a lot and read a lot. This is the biggest social thing I've done in the past ten years.'

A shadow passed over Fran's face, fleeting like the fast clouds above. 'And you're happy in your job? I mean, is it intellectually stimulating enough for you? I don't mean to be rude about that, but for a girl who topped all her subjects at school …'

Sylvie laughed to cover the intense awkwardness she felt. 'You sound like my mother.'

Fran raised an eyebrow. 'Well, that's something she and I agree on.'

'Yes, you two didn't always see eye to eye.'

'I just thought the fact that she never knew where you were was problematic. And that you never ate proper meals and you were so skinny. I always wanted to know where Kase and Tristan were, and that they were sitting down to an evening meal with the family.'

Sylvie felt the familiar longing she had always had around the Fowlers. 'My mother wasn't really into "family".'

Fran pursed her lips. 'I suppose that's why we took you under our wing. I did worry about you after the accident, but by then your mother was actually around for once and helping. Then we all sort of drifted apart, didn't we … and there was the move to Hobart. It was a very hard time for me after Tristan died. I apologise if you felt abandoned by our family.'

Sylvie swallowed back the lump in her throat. *Yes, that's exactly what I felt. Finally, someone has acknowledged it.* She wanted to reach out to touch Fran, but she couldn't bring herself to. 'No, it's okay. I get that you were all grieving. And I had a lot on my plate, too. I had to do so much physio and therapy just to get my brain back to functioning.'

Fran slowed. 'I was so sad to learn you never went to university like Kase, but I guess …'

Sylvie shrugged awkwardly. 'I never trusted my brain after going through all that.'

She remembered the feeling of overwhelm and humiliation at training her brain to read again, to follow simple instructions, complete basic tasks. She couldn't face not being the brilliant student for whom words and ideas flowed easily, naturally. And she didn't want concessions or anyone's pity. She would rather not have to face the difference in herself, even if that meant doing jobs others thought were beneath her.

'And I do like my job. It suits me,' she added.

Fran patted her shoulder. 'Well, we can all see how far you've come. And that's good you're happy.'

Sylvie could think of all the words for happiness. *Joy, pleasure, felicity, cheer.* But the feeling had always felt like quicksilver through her fingers.

They walked in silence for a while, until they reached Kase and Rachel, who were inspecting a shark egg on the sand.

Fran picked up a stick as an aid. 'I think I'll wander back to the kids. That's enough walking for me.'

'Mum's getting old,' Kase said as they watched her follow footsteps in the sand back down the beach. 'We're all getting old. Where did our lives go?'

She linked her arm through Sylvie's and pulled her close. Sylvie's heart began to race. She dug her nails into the soft part of her hand to stop it going to the pocket of her dress. The words were flooding her. She needed to write them down, get them out of her body, but she couldn't. *Memories. Nostalgia. Aching.* All those times they'd walked like this, at the mall, at school, the way they'd held their heads high and flicked their hair. Giggled into each other's shoulders. Joined at the hip, everyone said. Kase and Sylvie. Sylvie and Kase. It felt achingly familiar, and yet fragile, like a reflection in moving water.

This tension between them, she could feel its crackle, like the storm clouds on the horizon. Perhaps it was simply the gulf that had opened up between them over twenty-three years and everything that hadn't been said. *What happened to make you walk away from our friendship? And why did you replace me with Rachel?*

Kase hugged her close. 'Can you believe you're here? It's so weird. It feels like no time has passed at all. And yet we're middle-aged adults now. Well, I am. You're not far behind.'

Sylvie didn't resist the physical contact, but it took effort. She wasn't accustomed to being so close to others. 'I know, it's weird,' she said, trying to sound normal.

'I'm still a bit shocked you actually came. I didn't expect you to reply, you know. I was just … I guess a big milestone like this makes you look back on your life in a slightly different way. The important people in your life. You kind of see everything with a bit of perspective, like you can suddenly see the forest and not just the trees. And we were such good friends at such a formative time in our lives, you know?'

'I remember the two of you,' said Rachel, taking Kase's other arm in a gesture that smacked of possessiveness. 'Bonnie and Clyde. The outfits. Thigh-high socks and fishermen's caps.'

'All pure op shop,' said Kase. 'God, how we must have smelled? I didn't even bother washing those clothes.'

Op shop clothes were all I could afford, Sylvie thought. *They were a choice for you, but a necessity for me.*

'Maybe that's why we never had any other friends, the smell,' said Sylvie, allowing herself to laugh. She stole a look at Rachel. *You were not our friend. Why did Kase replace me?*

'What little teenage characters we all were,' said Rachel, a nostalgic smile on her lips, as though the three of them had been in collusion. The hairs on the back of Sylvie's neck stood up. 'And we were always drinking Diet Coke and chewing Extra.'

'Oh, the gum. Do you remember? How did our stomachs cope with all that artificially induced gas?' asked Kase.

'We wanted to be skinny I suppose,' said Sylvie.

'Now we all want to be smooth. Wrinkle-free. Collagen powder and Botox has replaced Extra and Diet Coke,' said Kase.

'Oh, and lemon water,' said Rachel. 'What's with women over forty drinking sparkling water with a squeeze of lemon in it?'

'I do that,' said Kase.

'Does lemon tea count?' Sylvie asked sheepishly.

'See, it's endemic in middle-aged women,' said Rachel. 'I do it and I don't even fricking know why.'

They all laughed, the tension scattering for a moment, breaking apart like the rain clouds above them.

'I'm very seriously flirting with the idea of Botox. I told myself to wait until I was forty,' said Kase, smoothing her fingers over her eyebrows.

'Oh don't,' said Sylvie.

'Do it,' said Rachel. 'I'm frozen from the armpits up.'

'Yeah, she is,' said Kase. 'And I've got to say you do look good. Not too fake.'

Sylvie had to stop herself from rolling her eyes.

'I'll text you the name of my guy. When you've made your career from your looks, being on stage, and photographed constantly, you need a good guy.'

'Sylvie wouldn't dream of it,' said Kase. 'Am I right?'

'I'm afraid it's just good old lemon water for me.' Kase and Rachel laughed and Sylvie felt the glow of their inclusion. 'I don't have anything against it, I just couldn't afford it, even if I wanted to.'

'So, what's the deal with your work? Do you really do no writing at all anymore?' Kase asked. 'How can that be? The Sylvie I knew was always writing. I thought at the very least you'd be a freelance journalist.'

Sylvie felt her insides shift and crunch, like the fragile shells under their feet. Kase kept coming back to this, as though she could somehow break her open and the Sylvie she once knew would pop out. *I never got to go to uni, my brain was recovering from the accident for years. I couldn't hold onto things that had happened five minutes ago let alone retain academic information. Cleaning houses was all I could do, okay? And you'd know all this if you'd been there for me*, she thought.

Instead she said, 'People change. Life never turns out the way you think it will when you're seventeen.'

Kase kicked at a stick. 'I guess. We wanted to be famous actresses, remember? We must have been about fourteen. We made a pact sitting by the pool one night that we'd be like Nicole Kidman and move to Hollywood. We were so sure it would come true.'

'I remember,' said Sylvie. She'd never forgotten those long-term memories. If anything, they had become stronger. The past, before the accident was something that felt solid.

'And now Rachel is living our dream as a stage actress,' said Kase.

Sylvie knew she was meant to react to this, to worship Rachel. Rachel's face shone with expectation, but she couldn't give Rachel anything because she could see how desperately she wanted, needed it, and all Sylvie could think about was her mother's same need for adoration. She looked at her feet.

'It didn't help that neither of us could act, I guess. We enrolled in that drama school with the dodgy chain-smoking guy who ran it who kept telling you your legs were too perfect to be on a kid. And what were we, like, sixteen?' said Kase.

'That didn't even seem weird in the nineties.' Sylvie grimaced.

'And you got that TV commercial. What was it for? Rice? I was so jealous,' said Kase.

'I'd completely forgotten about that. It was bread. That doesn't even seem like me,' said Sylvie.

'And we were popular at school for about a week after that and then the novelty wore off and we were just considered weird again.' Kase shrugged.

Sylvie laughed. She wanted to say, *I remember how Rachel Williams commented on how she liked my shoes, and we were so starstruck because she was the most popular girl in school. But then she said something bitchy to you, and it was all over. And now you have her here and I don't understand why.*

'Were we?' Sylvie asked instead.

'Yeah, don't you remember?' Kase nudged her.

'I really don't remember much,' said Sylvie.

'Kase, you must feel like all that eccentricity early in your life makes total sense now. You were a brilliant artist waiting to emerge, like some worm turning into a butterfly,' said Rachel.

Sylvie felt this dig, low in her gut. She was still the eccentric worm in Rachel's eyes.

'Ah no, I still just feel like a worm,' said Kase.

Their eyes met and a silent amusement moved between them.

Rachel looked puzzled. 'Really? So, all the accolades and awards … the money, it doesn't make you feel accepted by society now? Superior somehow?'

Kase laughed. 'God no. It all just feels like a massive fluke that will unravel at any moment.'

'I always liked your low self-esteem,' said Sylvie, feeling a sudden rush of affection for Kase.

'You can talk. Sylvie, the smartest girl in school with this mermaid hair and sweetest personality and she could never see her worth,' said Kase.

Sylvie shrugged, hated the feeling of their eyes on her.

'And you don't seem to have changed all that much. You're still living a life that doesn't match your brilliance,' said Kase.

Sylvie stiffened. Here she was thinking Kase didn't judge her the way everyone else did. That their soul connection was still somehow, after all these years, intact.

'Sorry, I didn't mean –'

'It's okay.' Sylvie shook her head and fixed a tight smile on her face, swallowing back her hurt. *You have no idea what I've been through.* She reached for her notebook. If she didn't write the words down now, get them out, she was going to scream. She took the book out of her pocket. 'I'm still a weird misfit. I have to write down things periodically in a notebook, so I don't forget where I'm up to, so to speak. It's a leftover from the accident.'

She broke away from the awful silence of the other women and wrote: *Disgust, humiliation, shame.*

Sylvie breathed out and put away her notebook again. Mercifully Kase and Rachel had continued along the beach. They were probably discussing what a weird worm she was.

* * *

Sylvie saw Holden up ahead. He'd taken a long stick and was drawing something in the wet sand near the water's edge.

'You're a bit of a sand poet, I see,' Sylvie said, trying to make out the words he had written in a sloping script.

There was a storm on the day you were born.

He looked at her quizzically, a small smile twitching his lips. 'What did you say?'

Sylvie shrugged. 'I said, you're a sand poet.'

'My daughter used to call me that.'

'What, a sand poet?'

'Yes.'

'You have a daughter?'

'I used to call her Pippi Longstocking. But her name was Pip.'

Past tense. Gone.

'Oh, I'm so sorry.'

'Every time I walk on the beach, I write her a message. It's what we used to do. Sometimes if she was feeling bad about something it was the only way for her to voice her emotions. In the sand. It's our tradition.'

'Oh Holden, I'm so sorry.' Sylvie wanted to ask more but intuited that he had already revealed more than he intended. *Hidden. Pain. Raw.*

'It's okay.' He shook his head and smoothed the sand with his hand, the words gone. 'Sorry, I normally wouldn't have shared that, it's just that you called me a sand poet, and that was quite … uncanny.'

He brushed the sand from his hands and stood. The vulnerability was gone and all she could sense was its ripple. 'So, would you like to see where Tail and Claw keep their nest?'

'I'd love to,' she said, walking with him down the beach.

She wondered what he thought of her limp. It became more pronounced when she was anxious and around other people, and when the weather was cold, a stiffness in her bones. She knew Kase and Rachel would have noticed it. Strangely, she didn't feel as self-conscious with Holden. She wasn't sure why at first, but after what he'd just revealed, she knew. Sometimes you recognised a vulnerability inside another person, and you knew it was the same silent thing you carried, and so they would not judge you for it, for they too felt its weight.

The wind had picked up, rattling the leaves of the twisted blue gums that clawed their way to the ocean at the far end of the beach. The cliff rose sharply, dark rocks surging with whitewash. It smelled wild, like salt mixed with soil and eucalyptus. The meeting of sea and land. Sylvie hugged herself, wishing she'd worn something warmer than her porous sponge of a jumper.

'There's a track that follows the shoulder of the island,' Holden said, stepping off the beach and into the bush. 'The nest is this way.'

The bush was dense and wet and the path muddy, but Sylvie sensed that this was Holden revealing himself to her. Not through spoken words, but through nature, through the senses. Through carvings in sand. Through the taste of wine, through the seeking out of small treasures.

They reached the headland that Sylvie had seen from the boat.

He craned his neck and pointed. 'Can you see the nest in the arm of that gum?'

'Yes. Are there chicks?'

'Listen.'

Above the surge of the water on the rocks below she heard a high note, tiny squeaks. 'I can hear them.'

'There are two chicks. Mum and Dad are likely out getting food. They're white-bellied sea eagles. They're monogamous. It's quite romantic – they form permanent pairs and stay together until one of them dies. Their calls at night are said to foretell danger.'

'Oh no,' Sylvie said, crouching down. A ball of fluffy brown feathers lay in the muddy ground beside her. 'It looks like this little one didn't make it.'

Holden was beside her, scooping the tiny bird up in his hands. He smoothed the feathers away to see the small shut eye, the stiff beak and curled claws. Sylvie's heart ached as she watched his face fall into shadow. His throat worked to swallow back emotion.

You know this loss, she thought.

The feelings of others were not something intellectual that Sylvie could regard at a distance, she felt them in her own body, she wore others' scars as though they were her own. Feelings were catching things. They were alive and physical. *Felt. Held. Broken. Mended.* Holden's bruises were blooming below her skin as though they too were her own. She looked at her pale arm, expecting to see purple shadows there.

After a while she spoke. 'Shall we bury it on the beach?'

He looked up and their eyes met, and she saw pain carved into him, like years of water against rock. She had witnessed this pain so many times, but it never failed to strike her deep.

He was silent for a while, staring at the dead chick. 'Maybe we should return it to the sea.'

They made their way down the headland until they reached the rain-slicked rocks at the edge of the sea. The cloud ceiling had lifted and the sun warmed their skin with its bright fingers. Holden had placed the chick on a large leaf, which he held out in front of him, like an offering.

The sea foam frothed about their feet, freezing Sylvie's toes inside her wet shoes. 'If we put it on the rocks the tide will reclaim it,' she said, her voice snatched by the salt air.

He placed the bird's body carefully on the rocks. They stood back and waited, scanning the sky for the two eagles who were monogamous until death. It seemed the world felt their turmoil, the water bubbling, the sky leaden with leftover cloud, clotting at its corners. They waited in the loud silence.

A wave crashed over the chick and took it. Holden looked up towards the white sky and Sylvie saw tears shining on his skin.

SPRING 1996

The op shop had that same comforting smell of old people and potpourri. Kase felt her skin ripple in anticipation of the treasures they might find. Sylvie, as usual, went straight for the second-hand book section. Kase found the red floral dress she'd been looking at and held it up for Sylvie.

'You're going to look stunning in this. I'm about to be majorly jealous of you.'

Sylvie looked from the book in her hands to the dress. 'How much is it? I HAVE to buy this book.' She held up a battered copy of *The Catcher in the Rye*.

Kase made a dismissive gesture. 'Oh, I have that at home, you can have mine. The dress is fifteen dollars. But it's a good label.'

Sylvie shook her head. She showed Kase the tiny writing on the inside. 'This is an early edition. And it's four dollars.'

'Is it worth anything?'

'I'm not sure but it's worth a lot to me. Look at the inscription. "To Breen, from Harriet. All my love." Imagine.

Who were Breen and Harriet? Don't you just want to know?' Sylvie pressed the book against her chest.

'I want to know if this dress fits you.' Kase pulled Sylvie towards the changeroom, which was a shower curtain draped over a corner with a mirror balanced on a chair.

Sylvie reluctantly put the book down, unzipped her uniform and pulled the red dress over her head. They were used to sharing changerooms together, but Kase knew Sylvie was self-conscious. Kase felt happy in her own body – she had good boobs and a flat stomach. Her legs weren't as long as she would have liked, but she had a dancer's body, just without the being a dancer part. She could do the splits and was massively, inexplicably flexible. It was a source of secret pride and her go-to party trick. She didn't see the big deal about swanning around semi-nude. It was a body. Everyone had one. It annoyed her that Sylvie was so coy when she was so much more gorgeous with her long limbs and effortlessly slim, catwalk-model body. Of course, the dress looked fricking amazing, like it was made for her.

'I can't afford it.' Sylvie shook her head and began to peel off the dress.

'What, because you have to have Breen and Harriet's book?' Kase rolled her eyes. Sylvie and her ratty second-hand books. 'I'll buy it for you. Come on, don't be a buzzkill, we have to look hot for the party. And I'm totally straightening your hair and doing your makeup.'

Sylvie made a face. 'You can't always buy things for me. You know I can't pay you back.'

Kase stretched a skin-tight black velvet dress over her head and scrunched up her nose. 'Too slutty?'

'No, it'll be hot with your Docs.'

'And dark red lippy,' Kase said. 'Don't worry about the money. You know it doesn't matter for me.'

Sylvie did the thing with her shoulders that meant she was uncomfortable. Kase nudged her. 'Don't worry about it. It's only fifteen bucks.'

'And the doughnuts and the movies from the other night and all the other stuff you buy me.'

'Look, it's Dad's money. He's never around to enjoy it, so we may as well. It's cool beans. Promise.' Kase gave her a quick squeeze.

'Which city is he in at the moment?' asked Sylvie, peering into the mirror. 'Is this foundation too dark for me, by the way?'

'It's okay, but you can sort of see it near your jawline … Next time get the lighter shade,' she said. 'And I can't keep up with Dad. He's doing a new route to Europe. He said he'd have some time off from flying soon.'

Sylvie wandered out into the store and began looking through the accessories. 'Oh, this bag would go with your dress.' She passed Kase a red velvet purse with an antique clasp.

'Oh my God, it's perfect.' Kase opened it. 'Hey, come here.' She pulled out a piece of paper. It was rolled tightly. 'You're going to die. It's someone's phone number. Elliot.'

Sylvie's eyes grew wide.

'We have to ring it. Tonight. Vodka for courage.'

Sylvie elbowed her. 'Oh alert. Rachel Williams and her gang have just entered the store.'

'Argh. How dare they. This is our turf. They should be shopping at Portmans.'

'They're coming over.'

Rachel had dyed black hair and green eyes that she enhanced with lashings of kohl. She was incredibly pretty with her naturally light hair, but the dye job made her look gothic, mysterious and cool, the ultimate aim of every girl their age. It better matched her sharp tongue, which coupled with her beauty, had earned her the wary worship of the entire year.

'Snuffling around in the old people's stuff again, you two?' Rachel arched a brow.

'Yep, want some mothballs?' Kase held Rachel's gaze.

She looked past Kase to Sylvie, who had her legs and arms twisted as though she was standing in front of a snake that was ready to strike.

'Hey, I hear your mum's pretty cool. Reckon she'd be able to get us some wine and/or weed for the big end-of-year party?' Rachel asked.

Kase watched the blush creep up Sylvie's neck and into her hairline. She twisted the fabric of the dress in her hand. Kase felt an overwhelming need to protect her, but she held back.

'Um, yeah, she's a mum you know, so essentially lame, but … yeah, I guess she's okay with us drinking. She says she'd rather us do it around her and have philosophical discussions over red wine instead of drinking metho in a park.'

Kase felt a little rush of pride at the fact that Sylvie had such a cool mum, and she knew exactly how to downplay her to Rachel for maximum effect.

'We'll be drinking on the beach. Things might get philosophical.'

Rachel's three friends, the second, third and fourth prettiest girls in Year 12 after Rachel, laughed. They all had varying shades of blonde hair and the air of dolls that Rachel had collected.

Rachel met Kase's eye. 'We've been invited to the party too. You're not the only one with a hot older brother.'

Sylvie and Kase exchanged a look they both knew meant *not that hot*. Sylvie wiggled her eyebrows in a way that she knew full well would set Kase off and a bubble of laughter fell out. Kase clapped a hand over her mouth.

Rachel's eyes narrowed. Kase braced herself. Sometimes Kase felt as though Tristan's friendship with Gabe was all that was stopping Rachel from destroying her and Sylvie at school. They were both top of the grade, something that immediately marked them as deeply lame. Having a hot older brother was their only protection. And Tristan was protective. Kase knew deep down that despite their constant ribbing and sibling banter, he'd do almost anything for her, unlike the dynamic between Rachel and Gabe, where Rachel appeared to be the older, more protective one.

Rachel smirked. 'Oh you two, you're so *goddamn* quirky.'

Kase shot Sylvie a look that said *Oh, no, she didn't just say that*. Sylvie widened her eyes ever so slightly in a *Yep, she just did*. God, Rachel was a manipulative bitch. She'd milk them for what she wanted until they were of no use to her and then the *quirky* would just become *weird* again.

'Well, let me know about the philosophical wine, Sylvie Dane,' she said with a smile that hardly even had time to find her lips. 'I'm about to die of noxious old-person gases.'

And she and her dolls turned and walked out of the shop.

CHAPTER 5

burn *(v.)* – to be on fire, to give light,
to feel strong passion.

The bonfire roared, scattering the night's inky skin with flecks of burning orange. Sylvie huddled closer. The wood smoke infused her hair, lacing her woollen jumper, and when she breathed it in it almost felt purifying. The cold air clawed at her back, but her cheeks were aflame. She was woozy with the heat and the wine. They had made a circle on the beach, camping chairs elevating them off the cold sand. The flames hissed and the wood popped, mingling with the rush and pull of the dark waves. Holden was cooking a breakfast-dinner on the beach, with bacon spitting over the flames and damper wound around sticks. She shoved her stick deeper into the glowing embers and it caught. Holden was beside her pulling it from the flames and blowing the blackened dough.

'Easy there. Don't stick it right in. Unless you want charcoal for dinner.' His hand was warm on her cold back.

She laughed. They hadn't spoken much since they'd farewelled the chick at the lip of the ocean. The sky had started spitting icy drops even while the sun shone down, and they'd raced back through the bush to find the others meandering home down the beach. But there was something between them now, something unspoken but lingering, like the clouds that had clung onto the edges of the evening, illuminated by sheet lightning. Sylvie longed to have him alone. To ask him about beach poetry, and why he carved out his sorrow into soft sand. She had wanted to brush away the tears on his face as he said goodbye to that bird.

She'd always been drawn to the broken, the wounded. She collected lost souls, injured bird-men. They flocked to her as though she were crumbs scattered to the wind. She allowed herself to take flight for a little while, for them to peck around her perimeters. Most of the time she took them under her wing for a little while and then found she couldn't give them what they wanted.

She thought back to the last man, Phillip. It had been more than a year ago. He was a reader too and they'd met through an online book group Sylvie had been part of for a while after her mother had urged her to be more social.

'You've passed the window for childbearing, which I wouldn't necessarily recommend anyhow,' Evangeline had said over the phone from her Istanbul apartment, the call to prayer a swell of music in the background.

'Thanks, Mum.'

'I'm just being honest with you, Sylvie. I've always been honest with you, haven't I? I'm not sure you're cut out for it. I certainly wasn't.'

'Hmmm,' said Sylvie.

'But don't you think you should find a lover?'

'Not everyone needs a stream of lovers.'

'Really? Why not? It's not like you need to settle down with them all. And it's not like you don't have the time. Have you done anything lately? Been out? Seen anyone?'

Sylvie had told her she and her landlord's wife, Josie, had been for a drink. It had just been a cup of tea in Sylvie's courtyard behind their shop, and Josie was around sixty, but Evangeline didn't need to know that. Besides, she loved Josie's company, talking about the books they'd read lately, making herbal tea and pottering in the garden.

From the start, Phillip felt like her mother's idea. He was older than her by ten years, with a tall lanky body, kind eyes, and speech that hinted he'd been a stutterer as a child. This had endeared him to her immediately, and he'd read all the classics she admired. He was also an aspiring writer.

'You're too beautiful to be single at your age,' he'd gushed on their first date at a coffee shop inside a bookstore.

They'd both had books on the table in front of them, small comforts that they smoothed with their fingers like a pet's coat. She'd blushed a deep shade of red that probably matched her lipstick. She knew it was his way of complimenting her, but it still felt uncomfortable, wrong.

If I was ugly, would it be perfectly normal then? she'd wanted to ask him. But she wasn't confrontational. And in her opinion, she wasn't beautiful anyway. She was acceptable-looking, as long as her curls were tamed.

Instead, she said, 'Maybe there's a reason I'm single at my age.'

He had laughed, but she'd felt the familiar thread of doom move through her. She had listened to the sad story of his divorce and a detailed rundown of the novel he was writing, *The Iliad* meets *The Magician*. They had finished their coffees and moved on to wine, and the talk had progressed to their similarly frustrating mothers.

Is this what relationships are meant to be like? she wondered. *They talk and I listen?* When you hadn't had a long-term relationship by your late thirties, you simply didn't know. *How does this work? How does this last? How does this not get exhausting?*

There had been one man who had asked her questions. So many questions. About her past, about her future dreams, about what she ate for breakfast. How she exercised. He'd called it his 'technique'. She'd felt like they were in a job interview. That had been exhausting in a different way. He'd had an intensity in his eyes that had made her nervous. And when she called it off after a few dates, around the time he was insisting they take things back to his place, he began spamming her with needy messages and she'd wished she hadn't answered all those questions.

Phillip had lasted longer, and she'd actually liked him. He was a little self-obsessed, but his intelligence and their mutual love of literature kept the conversation afloat and they were able to drift to a fairly familiar place of him cooking her dinner at his home several times.

She couldn't find the words to say why she was open emotionally to some of these men at the start but then shut down as soon as things became physical. Why the connection she felt with another person, even attraction on occasion, couldn't be translated into the physical plane. She had found words, of course, ugly, shameful words – *cold, frigid* – but they didn't explain it, not properly. They didn't explain the emptiness she felt, as though they were taking everything from her and giving nothing. There was no way to put that into words without breaking things. And so, it was easier to be alone.

But being here now – gathered around the fire, Holden's warmth as he crouched close to her, the familiar ring of Kase's laughter in the air – she almost couldn't imagine that she'd been alone for most of her life. Because her seventeen-year-old self had never been alone, and she could have been that half-girl, half-woman again right now, her best friend laughing, drunk, and Sylvie catching eyes with the boy she liked.

Holden pulled a camping chair beside hers. They ate their damper in silence for a while, licking the butter and bacon fat from their fingers and washing it down with red wine.

'Kase is a classic,' said Holden, wiping his hands on a paper napkin and nodding across the fire, where she was gesticulating wildly.

'Yeah, she is. She hasn't changed in twenty-three years. I thought it might be weird seeing her again after all this time, but it's the opposite, which is also a little … weird.' *And it feels like I'm torn between loving her and resenting her.*

'I thought you were friends since you were kids?'

Sylvie paused. She'd just shared this with Holden so naturally, as though he already knew. *I'm tipsy,* she thought.

'Oh, yeah. We were, but then we sort of drifted apart over the years.'

'Yeah, it happens, people get busy. I don't see many of my schoolmates anymore. One owns a pub, so I see him the most.'

Sylvie laughed. 'Did you grow up here?'

'In Hobart. It was a nice place to be a kid.'

Silence opened up between them and into it came the words,

Pippi Longstocking. Sylvie wanted to ask him what had happened to his daughter, but he spoke first.

'So, this is a long-lost reunion of sorts then, between you and Kase?' He filled up her wineglass.

'I guess you could call it that.'

'How many years since you hung out exactly?'

Sylvie pressed her lips together. 'A long time.'

'Did you have a falling out, or –'

'No, we just … I don't know, stopped calling each other. I guess life got in the way.' Her hand dipped into her pocket, but she didn't take out her notebook. *White lie. Fib. Safer.*

'Yeah, I had that with a good mate. And you wonder if it was just the time to move on with your lives, a natural drifting apart, or whether you did something they could never talk about with you, offended them somehow …'

Sylvie's throat ached. 'I was pretty sick, and she'd just lost her brother so … it was too hard, I guess.'

'Oh, that's not good. You're okay now?' Shadow lines of worry danced on his face in the firelight. *Beautiful. Kind.*

'I'm fine. It was just head trauma.'

'Just head trauma? That sounds pretty damn serious, Sylvie Plath.'

Her face warmed and she pressed her cool hands to her cheeks. She was telling her life story to this man so readily, but it felt like they had already shared so much. 'Oh, well, yes, I guess it was. I hit my head pretty hard and it took me many, many months to get back to normal. I lost my sense of smell and my short-term memory. I still have issues sometimes.'

'I have issues all the time,' Holden said, his eyes flicking to hers, his mouth crinkling into a smile.

Sylvie laughed. She heard Sylvia's voice in her head. *Be brave*. 'Holden, were you okay today? I mean, with the bird? After what we talked about with your –'

'Oh yeah.' He shook his head and ran a hand through his hair, laughed awkwardly. 'Sorry, that was all a bit … I get emotional about those birds. I'm quite attached to old Claw and Tail.'

White lie. Fib. Safer.

Your daughter. Sylvie left it. He wasn't ready to talk. Of course he wasn't. They'd only just met. It just didn't feel like that. She'd never felt such an immediate connection with a man and she wasn't sure what to do with this energy running between them, just below the surface.

He stood and wiped his hands down his jeans. 'Well, I'm going to get some more blankets from the house. That wind is picking up.'

She watched him walk off towards the house. *You scared him away*.

Kase sat down on Holden's chair, pulling her cardigan close. 'You and Holden seem to be getting on quite well.' She raised an eyebrow.

'Oh, no, it's nothing like that.'

'Are you sure?'

'Gosh. I've given up on relationships. I think you get to the age where it's just easier to be alone.'

Kase nodded. 'I know what you mean. Men need a lot of tending to. You'd think they'd be stubborn weeds, but they're actually tender flower buds that need constant mulching and watering. It's bloody exhausting.'

Sylvie laughed. 'Nice metaphor. Though Henry seems more weed, less pansy.'

Kase laughed. 'He's somewhere in between. Maybe a climbing rose.'

'Oh, well that's okay then, though he's not who I'd –' Sylvie stopped herself.

'What? Not who you'd have pictured me marrying?' Kase nudged her. 'It's okay. He's not who I'd pictured me marrying either. But it works.'

'That's great.' Sylvie's voice held a note of false brightness.

'Mainly because we have an open marriage.'

Sylvie was struck dumb for a moment. 'You do? Really?'

'Oh God, the Sylvie I used to know wouldn't have been shocked by that.'

She reddened. 'I'm not shocked.' She hated how defensive she sounded.

'You can't hide it. I still know you.'

Sylvie squirmed and heat seared through her chest. *No, you don't. You haven't known me all my adult life. You have no claim over me.* But she said nothing, picking up a stick and prodding the fire. Sparks erupted into the cold air. She wanted to get up and walk away down the beach towards the dark waves, but she forced herself to stay.

'Anyway, it's surprising what you can get used to,' said Kase, staring into the flames. 'It didn't start off that way. The first ten years we were devoted to each other. Both on the same page. Neither of us wanted kids and my career was taking off. *The Then and the Now* had just won the award, and … I found out about him and a student. I know, what a cliché. A philosophy lecturer and his 25-year-old charge, all starry-eyed and in awe of the big brain that is my husband. He said he was having an existential crisis. That he envied my success. And the student had pursued him. God.' Kase threw a stick into the fire and shook her head.

Sylvie pursed her lips in sympathy. 'What a way to passively bring a successful woman down.' Kase had always been such a mass of contradictions. Bold, almost brittle on the outside, but soft on the inside. Sylvie could feel the deep pulse of her pain. 'Hence the climbing rose. He has thorns.'

Kase smiled and took Sylvie's arm and hugged it to her. She rested her head on her shoulder. 'I've missed you. Not having to explain everything. Having my mind read.'

Then why did you abandon me? Why did you replace me? But the words wouldn't come. This was about Kase's second big life heartbreak. She didn't need Sylvie to pile on more drama.

'And so, I decided I'd just have an affair too. You know me. I love men. John, a friend, was the first. Terrible in bed, but it was fresh. It was something. It felt like Henry and I were on even footing then. And I told him, and he's so logical – everything is a puzzle to be worked out. He said he was fine with it as long as we were upfront. Honest. He kept seeing the student for another year.'

Why didn't you leave him? Sylvie wanted to ask, but she could see the resignation on Kase's face. She understood that Kase's energy was no longer tuned to men. Sylvie knew what that felt like.

As though reading her mind, Kase said, 'You know, there's something freeing that happens to a woman when she reaches a certain age and finds her worth beyond the male gaze.'

I have spent my life avoiding the male gaze, Sylvie thought. 'And what about you and Henry now?' she asked.

Kase shrugged. 'I don't have the energy at the moment.

I haven't for years. I have my next book due soon and I don't think Henry has any active cases. We're almost a normal, middle-aged boring couple.'

Sylvie laughed. 'Is that what you call them, active cases?'

'Yeah, romantic, huh?' Kase gripped her arm. 'But you. You *were* a romantic. How have you ended up single?'

Sylvie's skin prickled, like salt drying on skin. 'I've had lovers.' God, she sounded like her mother. 'But nothing has stuck. Not long term, anyway.'

Kase opened her mouth to speak, but just then there was a whistle from behind. Holden was walking down the beach carrying a paper lantern lit bright against the cold night.

'It's a birthday-wish lantern,' he said. 'You make a wish and send it into the sky.'

Kase took the fragile globe of light into her hands. 'Oh my goodness, it's beautiful. What should I wish for?' she asked Sylvie, her eyes dancing. She might have been fourteen again and blowing out the candles on her cake.

Sylvie shook her head. 'I don't know. You've got just about everything.'

Kase smiled and Sylvie felt the words press into her sternum like a hand. *Sadness. Regret. Hope.* She thought about everything Kase had told her. Maybe it would be lonelier to live with someone and feel alone than to simply be alone, like Sylvie was.

'I don't have everything,' Kase said. She hooked her little finger through Sylvie's, just like she used to do. 'I wish for you to be in my next forty years.'

Warmth flooded Sylvie, from the tips of her fingers to her toes. She gazed at the trail of light as it rose like a moon, until it burned clear into the atmosphere, Kase holding her hand.

SPRING 1996

It was their place, that's what they called it. It smelled like the insides of old books, and the outside world shut out. It felt like a word-cocoon and they lingered for hours, cushioned and stirred and inspired. There were armchairs spilling stuffing, lamp-lit desks nestled into dark corners, and wooden stools to reach the top shelves. The daybed caught the afternoon sun and sometimes had someone reading or sleeping on it, but they had to compete with Victor Hugo, the Blue Russian cat who ruled over his domain like a languid despot.

Zola ran the shop and knew them both by name. She didn't mind that it was a Tuesday morning and they wore their school uniforms and should have been in maths class. Someone named after a French novelist would never care about such things, Kase decided. Zola seemed ancient, but they respected her literary tastes above all others, except perhaps Evangeline.

'Be not inhospitable to strangers lest they be angels in disguise,' Kase said in greeting as she and Sylvie entered to the sweet chime of the door.

Zola had fashioned her second-hand bookstore off the famous Shakespeare and Company on the Rue de la Bûcherie in Paris, and its motto was inscribed at the entrance. Neither Kase nor Sylvie had been to Paris, but this was a portal into another life, one deeper and more profound than their northern beaches upbringing allowed.

There were always people in the shop, usually ones with a slightly itinerate, bohemian air. One boy-man – not quite man and yet no longer boy – was asleep on the chaise lounge, glasses pushed high on his head, a book over his stomach, feet crossed at the ankles. A girl in her twenties wearing a green felt beret, who Kase imagined she'd one day befriend at uni, was pecking at the old typewriter in the corner under an industrial lamp. She ripped the piece of paper out and inspected her work before placing it in a neat pile beside her. Kase longed to see what was written on those pages.

'*Salut, mes chéries*,' said Zola, tipping her red hat. 'Tell me if you need anything.'

'Thank you, Zola,' they chimed. They parted, like lone ships in a calm sea, Sylvie for the classics and Kase for Zola's newest acquisitions. The cover struck Kase first. It was a deep aquamarine with gold lettering, and moons and stars orbiting two bodies entwined as though they were rose stems. It was a hardcover but nearly small enough to fit into your palm. Kase ran her fingers over the embossed title: *Soul Friends*.

She sank into a faded green armchair and began to read. It talked of twinned souls, the notion of deep connection between two people that transcended a label.

Sylvie squished in beside her on the armchair, a book of Celtic poetry in her hands.

'Look at this book, it's gorgeous,' said Kase.

Sylvie smoothed the cover just as Kase had. 'Is that what we are? Soul friends?'

'It's about how a soul connection, a twinning, morphs in each lifetime. The idea that the soul finds its home in one life as a friendship, in the next as a lover, and yet the next life as a mother.'

'Ha. Not likely,' said Sylvie.

'No, your mother is definitely not your soul connection in this life. But for some it's their lover, or it might be a sibling, or a parent or a friend. It takes a different form in each lifetime.'

'So, we only get one,' said Sylvie.

'Yeah. One for each lifetime.'

'So, you and me, that's it for us, right?'

Kase laughed. 'We can stop searching for our soul mate in a man.'

'What a relief.' Sylvie put her arm around Kase's neck and their heads touched. 'I do feel like I've known you in about a hundred other lives before this one.'

'Do you believe in reincarnation? That the next life it might be my soul, but in the form of your lover? Your mother?' asked Kase.

'I would love you to be my mother. I bet you wouldn't let me drink vodka at fourteen.'

Kase took a piece of Sylvie's hair and began threading it through her fingers, plaiting it. 'No, I'd ground you and make you toasted cheese sandwiches after school and packed school lunches, and pick you up from parties when you're crying.'

'Aww. You'd just be Fran.'

'Yeah, I would.'

'I want to believe that there are more lives for us. But maybe that's why we have books. Don't you ever find it sad that you're confined to your own story? That your life is bounded by your mind inside your own head?'

'Deeply sad.' Then Kase brightened. 'I believe in reincarnation though. Surely there's more than just this incredibly lame life we're living, which is basically, you know, school. What do you think I was in a past life?'

Sylvie inclined her head thoughtfully. 'Hmm. I think you were a Hindu prince.'

Kase grabbed her hands. 'And you were my princess, but you were engaged to marry another man and our fate was never realised.'

'How tragic. Star-crossed lovers.' Sylvie pressed her hand to her heart. Victor Hugo sauntered over to them, weaving in and out of their legs. 'Oh, even kitty cat is impressed.'

They laughed and bent down to pat him.

'But over many lifetimes we've finally reunited as best friends who spend their days in musty bookshops talking about weird shit. Soon we'll be mad cat ladies,' said Kase, pulling Victor Hugo onto her lap.

'Can we never stop talking about weird shit?' asked Sylvie. 'Other people talk about such boring, normal things. The other girls at school, don't they get bored with the sound of their own voices? Aren't they interested in exploring the edge of things, the unknown and unknowable, the darker places?'

'Nope. They're all, "What moisturiser do you use, yada yada."' Kase rolled her eyes and the cat nestled into her lap. She stroked Victor Hugo thoughtfully. 'Syl, you know how we're different from the others … do you think it means we'll be something in this life? I don't know, sometimes I feel like because we're always over analysing everything and we're on the outside looking in, there's stuff we've got to say, I mean, to make life matter somehow. I feel like we have to make it matter if it is the only one we get.'

'Maybe we'll write books,' said Sylvie, resting her chin in her hands wistfully. 'Make portals for people to escape into other lives. Take them to the edges, the dark, interesting places, the unknown and the unknowable, because they don't know how to get there themselves.'

'There are already too many books in the world. Look at them all. How could we ever add to that?'

Sylvie shook her head. 'How can my soul mate say this? There are never, ever, too many books or stories in the world and one day Kase Fowler, you will add another one.'

'That's your prediction, is it?'

'Yes. Absolutely. We're buying this book from Zola, aren't we? So, she won't mind if I write in the front.' Sylvie took a pen out of her schoolbag.

I hereby predict that in 20 years' time, Kase Fowler will be a famous author and Sylvie Dane will be married to Tristan Fowler with a kid, addicted to vodka and writing depressing but searing, brilliant poetry.

'That sounds like Sylvia Plath,' said Kase.

'Ha. It actually sounds like my mother.' Sylvie rolled her eyes.

'And we'll be friends forever, the Hindu prince and his princess.'

Sylvie rested her head on Kase's shoulder. 'We'll just keep returning to each other in each new lifetime, haunting each other until the end of time. We don't even have a choice.'

CHAPTER 6

found *(v.)* - to set up or establish on a firm basis or for enduring existence. To base or ground.

Sylvie sat up in bed, her gaze drawn to the wall of glass overlooking the bay. There was a dull thump in her skull, but even that couldn't detract from the beauty in front of her, or from the lingering glow in her chest from last night. Her feet touched the cold wood and she winced. She had heard the soft song of the sea all night, dreaming she was adrift on a boat. Gentle rocking. But she knew it had just been her wine-addled mind.

She stood and placed her hands against the cold glass, her breath a fog. The sun was watercolour pale as it leaked through the clouds that gathered at the horizon like smoke plumes. From her window she could see the oyster flats gleaming black, slick with salt, frothy with whitewash, as though the ocean had brushed its teeth. She could almost taste their plump, creamy flesh with fresh lemon. Holden had promised to take them all oyster-shucking today. Or had she dreamed that? She wondered if dream and memory were as slippery for others as they were for her. Since the loss of her memory the two had felt more intertwined. She mistrusted memories as though they might be merely dreams, and dreams as though they may have actually happened.

She did remember last night, though it was hazy, glazed by the firelight and wine. They had all drunk too much. Snippets surged back to her like the creamy waves outside. Henry talking about theory of mind. Rachel telling them about one of the famous actors she'd worked with whose name had now slipped from Sylvie's mind. Gabe making everyone laugh about the pitfalls of parenthood. Kase forcing whisky on everyone even though they'd already had too much wine. The satisfying heat of it in her stomach. Holden calling her Sylvie Plath, their eyes snaring.

She looked around the room. The timber floor was overlaid with a handwoven rug, there were lamps with knotted rope bases, and pillows in slate grey and cream, the colours of the ocean. There was a small ceramic jug with a mug for fresh water. It was a beautiful room, but it was cold, with a note of salt spray in the air, as though the elements refused to obey the timber walls. She got back into bed and curled under the soft covers. She could stay here for days, looking up from a book to measure the passage of time in the tides.

Her mind wandered. Last night had been something. *Alive*. Yes. She had felt alive. *Kindled. Lit. Blazing*. She had forgotten the way being around other people could feel. Not their ghosts, or their abandoned possessions, but actual alive people. The sharing of food. The sharing of stories. The gathering around a fire. *Elemental*. And no one had required anything of her. She had been allowed to just listen. To absorb. She'd forgotten how much she was capable of absorbing.

How long had it been since she was in a group? She had no family group. Her father had never been known to her. Her mother and she were two, but that wasn't a group. Sometimes she went to the funerals of the people whose houses she cleaned. She saw the way humans amassed. How there were blood ties, love ties. How they seemed to crave this connection. But it never felt like something accessible to her. She was on the periphery. A reader of a story written by someone else. Except for the Fowler family. They felt more like family than her own ever had and they'd drawn her in again as though those twenty-three years of estrangement had never happened.

She slipped out of bed again and found some socks, pulled them onto her icy feet. There was a thick white bathrobe in the bathroom and she wrapped herself in it. She listened for noise below, sounds of the house waking up, but heard nothing. Everyone was probably sleeping in. She ran her fingers along the dusty spines of the books in a small bookshelf next to an antique writing desk. Fran had always been a voracious reader. Kase's talent for words seemed to come out of nowhere, unlike Sylvie's so obviously passed down from her mother. But Fran loved books. A memory flashed, bright and clear from those early years – Fran sitting in the sun in her reading chair that overlooked the white arm of Palm Beach.

She slipped a few books out, smoothing their worn covers, their browning pages, wondering about the others who had read them, the tea that might have been drunk over them. How their stories may have shaped their readers' lives. There were a few she hadn't read. One caught her eye. *The Bell Jar*, by Sylvia Plath. Her chest warmed as she thought of Holden.

She would have to tell him what she'd found in her room – Sylvia Plath's only novel. She pulled it out and examined the cover. A woman's silhouette under a bell jar. *That could be me*, thought Sylvie, a shiver running through her. She'd studiously avoided this book during her teen years, knowing how much her mother loved Plath's poetry. Knowing she expected her daughter to read this rite of passage classic authored by her namesake. It had been a childish kind of rebellion that she never did. She knew of it, of course, and that Plath had written under the pseudonym Victoria Lucas, so that her mother wouldn't realise she'd written it while still at school. Sylvie understood. The way we hid ourselves, the things we did to obscure and protect ourselves, even from those we knew and loved.

She opened to the edition page. 1967 Heinemann. It was in good condition, considering its age. Her fingers found the first page. *It was a queer, sultry summer, the summer they electrocuted the Rosenbergs, and I didn't know what I was doing in New York.*

She got the same tingle she always got when she read the first sentence of a new book and it snared her. Something about the cadence, the rhythm of the words. Something about falling under the spell of the writer. It seemed silly and stubborn now that she hadn't read this in her youth. She'd devoured all the other rite of passage books – *On the Road* by Kerouac, *Lolita* … *The Catcher in the Rye* … all of Austen. She realised how much she wanted to see Holden today. She flicked through the pages and lifted the book to her nose. Tea leaves and dust. There was an inscription on the first page:

To Franny, may our fates be always entwined. Love, Eve

Sylvie ran her fingers over the words, so familiar and yet so foreign. Her heart was loud in the cold room. Her mother's handwriting. She'd recognise its distinctive script anywhere. Her mother was always scrawling notes. *I won't be home until later. Food in fridge. Have a good day at school. E x*

Sylvie stared at the words. *Franny and Eve. 1967.* Her mother would have been fifteen. Of course her mother and Fran knew each other, but Sylvie had believed it was only through her friendship with Kase. Did they share a past? Their mothers were so different, chalk and cheese. Nurturing, warm, wealthy Fran and free-spirited, permissive, destitute Evangeline. They'd never exchanged more than polite platitudes at each other's doorsteps as they dropped one or the other of their daughters off. Sylvie did remember wondering why their mothers couldn't have a friendship, like she observed in some of the other girls' parents. She'd always assumed it was because Evangeline looked down on the other mothers and probably thought Fran a boring, stuck-up, stay-at-home mum, and that Kase's family had looked down on Evangeline for living in a granny flat behind someone's house with a kid on a scholarship to the poshest school in the area.

Sylvie bit her lip and sat down on the bed with the book. Maybe it wasn't her Evangeline, or Kase's Fran. She couldn't imagine them being called Eve and Franny, either. Eve and Franny sounded like different people. Not their mothers. And what did 'may our fates be always entwined' mean?

She slipped her legs back under the doona and snuggled down into the nest of pillows, the pull of the words strong as she read the second sentence, and then the third. The rain spat at the window as she disappeared into the world of the protagonist, Esther Greenwood.

SUMMER 1967

Franny gazed out to the place where the lake almost, but not quite, met the sea. It was separated by a thin wedge of land, an isthmus that held fast despite its fragility. A tall row of pine trees always drew her eye. From the kitchen sink you could see all the way up the peninsula, or that's what her mother kept telling people through puffs of cigarette smoke when they rang on the phone and she was describing their new house. It felt as though it was perched on the plateau, like a bird waiting to take flight. Franny hated being here, in Sydney, leaving all her friends behind in Hobart, but she did love this house with its view, and its overgrown gardens tumbling down the hill in a dense green jungle.

Her eyes were drawn to the granny flat hidden at the end of the garden under the folds of the giant maidenhair ferns. Franny had hoped to make it her own, being nearly fifteen, but her parents had refused, saying they planned to get a tenant in as soon as they were all settled.

It had been a hard few months settling in. It was lonely being the new one. The girls at school were so different from her friends back in Tasmania. There was a sophistication that Franny just couldn't seem to keep up with. Her hair felt too long – the other girls had chic short hair – and she didn't wear makeup to school because it was against the rules. She had asked them what books they were reading, and they'd gawked at her like she was an alien. All they could talk about was a show called *Homicide*, which she'd made a note in her journal to start watching immediately.

'Franny, could you put that book down and set the table?'

She looked up to see her mother dressed in a silk evening gown with rollers in her hair and a glass tumbler in her hand.

'Oh, you're not even reading. Daydreaming out the window, as per usual.'

'Who's coming for dinner?' Franny expected it was one of the important businessmen from Daddy's new work.

'The new tenants. They're moving in tomorrow. There's a girl your age. I'm sure you'll be friendly. Come on, get dressed into something nice and put out the good cutlery. I've made beef bourguignon.'

Franny rolled her eyes. Parents thought being the same age as someone was enough to make them a friend. How quickly adults forgot what it was like to be young. She wondered why her mother was making such a fuss when these people were living in their back garden. She went to her room. It still didn't feel like hers, even with her Beatles posters staring down at her lovingly. But the view from her bed did make her happy. The clouds were turning pink and orange, as though crisped by the sun. She changed out of her school uniform into a skirt and top and gave her hair a brush. How would she look with shorter hair like the others? She could hear her parents in the kitchen, and she snuck into her mother's room and stole her eyeliner and rouge. She had seen the girls at school practising lining their eyes in their little compact mirrors at lunch. She made a complete mess of her face and wiped the makeup off with a wet washer.

The doorbell rang and she went to answer it. The man was dazzlingly handsome, with blond hair and tanned skin and those eyes that look at you like they know a secret. Franny had no idea how Daddy was going to feel about that. She could tell exactly how her mother felt about it, as she bustled up behind her and ushered him inside the house. The girl followed behind. She was tall and had the same quality of startling beauty. Her hair was long and dark, with a sweeping fringe that made her look awfully sophisticated. She wore white boots, paisley stockings, a miniskirt and a white shirt under a black vest. Franny wished she hadn't wiped her makeup off.

'Hi, I'm Eve,' the girl said, stopping in front of her. A small smile flitted across her face. 'Can we be friends? I hate all mine.'

Franny laughed. 'I'm not too keen on mine either.'

'It's settled then. Show me your room.'

Franny led the way down the hall into her room. The sun was nearly set, but the last glimmer of light had turned the water into a still, silver mirror.

Eve walked to the window and pressed her hands up against the glass. 'It makes me want to cry, it's so beautiful.'

Franny looked and there were actual tears in Eve's eyes, and she knew at that moment that they would be friends.

CHAPTER 7

open *(v.)* – to disclose or reveal one's knowledge, thoughts, feelings, etc.

Sylvie sat up, her mouth dry and her face flushed. How long had she been reading? She looked outside to see the sun had risen, though it was still a pale imitation of itself behind a curtain of cloud. She found her phone. Almost 11 am. Instinctively she reached for her notebook on the side table. *Shocked. Embarrassed. Outsider.* She dressed in a long floral frock and cardigan, and fingerless gloves. She slipped the notebook and pencil into her dress pocket. It was the first thing she looked for in a dress; it had to have a pocket. She looked longingly back at the book and bed. She wasn't in her little flat anymore, where whole days could slip by sunk into the pages of a story. She'd forget to eat, forget to drink. She'd become the character. Esther was like a friend.

She could smell toast. Her stomach growled. She pulled her curls back from her face. She thought of Holden and applied some blush and mascara in the little mirror above the bathroom basin. Before she left the room, she picked up the book once more. Should she show this to Kase? It felt like she'd been snooping, but she'd just been doing what she'd always done with books … finding the story within the story. Was there a story here? Or was her overactive imagination finding meaning, finding ghosts where there were none? She hesitated in front of the bookshelf before slipping the book back among the others.

Esther's world trailed her like a mist, ghost words, as she descended the stairs, passed Gabe's kids playing video games in the lounge and entered a kitchen full of people.

'Oh, you've decided to join us,' said Kase warmly, breaking off a piece of crispy bacon and putting it into her mouth. They were arranged around the kitchen table before another of Fran's beautiful spreads: bacon, eggs, sourdough, muesli, a fruit platter, orange juice, tea and coffee were set out.

Part of her was still in New York, but she smiled. 'Sorry. I slept in, it was so dark.' She knew it was more normal a response than *I've been swallowed up in a book for hours and couldn't get out.*

'Sit, eat, before Gabe gets all the bacon,' said Fran.

Gabe protested and took two more pieces. Fran's cheeks were flushed from being over the stove and she swiped him with a tea towel. This surely wasn't the Franny who had read into the dark corners of Esther's soul.

'Thanks. This looks beautiful, as ever, Fran.' Sylvie helped herself to grainy sourdough toast and topped it with avocado and crunchy bacon. The tea was strong and bitter, like the book. She wondered if other people took a while to leave their book worlds behind.

'Holden's taking us oyster-shucking,' said Kase.

'Holden can shuck my oysters any time,' said Rachel, flicking her hair.

Sylvie felt a thread of discomfort and Kase's and Sylvie's eyes met. Kase knew she liked Holden. You couldn't be friends with someone in those formative years without intuitively knowing such things.

'I didn't think he'd be glamorous enough for you, Rach. Rachel likes to date playwrights and directors.'

Yes, only people who are useful to her. Sylvie shot Kase a glance. *Thank you.*

Kase's eyes flashed with mischief.

'I do like the rugged type too, you know. I'm not a one-trick pony,' Rachel said, clearly affronted, or pretending to be. Sylvie found it hard to tell the difference.

Kase looked at Sylvie and rolled her eyes. A giggle escaped Sylvie's mouth but she clamped it shut. Rachel clocked their connection and tried but failed with her frozen brows to frown. It made Sylvie laugh more. Kase was laughing too, but silently, with her hand concealing her mouth. Everyone was staring at them.

'These two,' said Fran, shaking her head with a smile. 'Anything can set them off.'

Kase pressed a hand to her chest. 'No, I'm just … we get a bit hysterical when we're tired,' she said, finding her breath.

Sylvie felt again the embrace of Kase's inclusion. *It's true. We did. We still do.*

Fran clapped her hands. 'Okay, okay, I know everyone's tired after last night, but we're collecting oysters for tonight's piece de resistance – the official birthday party dinner,' she said.

Kase regained her composure and wrapped her arms around Fran's neck. 'Mum, you're too good to me.'

'Does everyone eat lobster? I thought we'd do a big seafood platter and a paella on the beach – it's forecast to be a fine night. With plenty of champagne.'

'Sounds terrible,' said Gabe.

'I'll help with the cooking,' said Trina.

'Me too,' said Sylvie.

Fran rose from the table, clearing away some empty plates. 'Now, I've got some gumboots we can wear out onto the oyster flats.'

'No, no you sit down and finish your coffee,' said Sylvie, taking the plates from Fran's hands. 'We'll clean up.'

Sylvie and Trina cleared breakfast, loaded the dishwasher and washed up. Sylvie warmed to Trina for the simple fact that she insisted on helping. All their conversation so far had been over the scraping and washing of plates, and usually centred around the domestic and child-rearing, something Sylvie knew little about, but which understandably consumed Trina. Sylvie could see that Trina was a practical type. A good mother. She was always wanting to know where the kids were, encouraging Gabe to spend time with them, and making sure they had snacks. A few times she referred to Sylvie's cleaning job, and she now understood that Trina felt this bound the two of them. That perhaps Trina considered herself in a kind of domestic servitude at this point in her life.

Rachel, on the other hand, was exactly like Evangeline, who would never offer any domestic assistance and expected to be treated like a queen. But now after having spent some time with her, Sylvie could see how she and Kase were friends. Rachel had a dry wit and was often darkly funny. Her and Kase's relationship was one forged by their shared wryness.

* * *

The clouds had parted by the time they squelched out over the sand, through the rock pools and onto the black, oyster-strewn rocks. The sun was warm, and Sylvie tied her dress into a knot above her knees, pulled up her leggings and took off her cardigan. Holden was there with buckets, dressed in an old army-green shirt rolled up to reveal tanned forearms. He looked at her and it felt as though she'd just swallowed the sun. She thought about *The Bell Jar* and how she would tell him that she'd found it in her room.

'Find the belly of the oyster and slip the knife in to cut the muscle right here.' Holden demonstrated how to prise open an oyster and place it into a bucket. He crouched beside her, his eyes crinkled with warmth.

'You're a natural, Sylvie Plath.'

'You look like you could be a rebellious young character in a 1950s novel today,' she said, slipping the knife below the flesh.

He smiled. 'That's funny, because I was thinking the exact same thing about you. And how impractical it was to wear a beautiful dress with gumboots and yet somehow, you make it work.'

Sylvie blushed, smiled, met his eyes briefly. She felt strangely emboldened. Perhaps Esther Greenwood's panache still hadn't worn off. She handed him the oyster.

'Perfect. I have a rule that you must eat the first one.' He reached into his pocket and took out a lemon, sliced it cleanly on the rock and squeezed its juice into the shell.

She could feel him watching her as she tipped her head back, sucking in the tart lemon and creamy, salty flesh.

'Well, that was …' He raised his eyebrows suggestively.

Her face glowed with an intense self-consciousness she knew he could see. *Sensual. Weirdly erotic. Delicious.*

They laughed softly. She wanted to kiss him. She was shocked by the sheer, simple force of her desire.

'Holden, can you help? I can't shuck it.' Rachel's voice. Sylvie cringed.

Their eyes met and he told her silently that he didn't want to go, but he stood and walked over to the others.

When they'd filled their buckets, they took off their gumboots and walked barefoot along the beach, the kids weaving in and out of the waves. Sylvie watched Gabe with his children, swinging his little girl around until she squealed, and racing his son along the shoreline. Gabe still carried his droll indifference, his sense of natural confidence, in the square set of his shoulders. As though he was privy to knowledge no one else had access to. Just as Trina and Sylvie had naturally adopted a solely domestic connection, he and Sylvie had naturally assumed their roles as being outliers in the group. It was funny how dynamics didn't change, even after half a lifetime.

She watched Fran stroll along the sand with Kase, arms linked, chatting companionably. She wondered again about *The Bell Jar*. About Franny and Eve. Maybe she'd ask Kase, though she was sure she'd be just as disbelieving at the prospect of their mothers having once been friends. Sylvie watched for an opening when Holden was alone again, but he was busy with the others.

The kids were getting hungry, so they turned and walked back down the beach and then up to the house. There was an outdoor shower and they washed the sand from their sea-numb feet. Holden took the oysters to the laundry to prepare them for the party. Sylvie hoped he'd stay for lunch.

She went upstairs to change. She was so cold she ran a shallow bath. She slipped the book from the shelf and closed her eyes as she sank beneath the warm water. She remembered the smell of him, close, mixed with the ocean, the colour of his eyes. The way he'd bitten his lip when she ate the oyster. She'd never felt something so intense. Not since Tristan. But she had been young then. The heady feeling that only teenagers have. This was different. This felt real. *Close. Reciprocated*. Holden was like a puzzle that needed to be solved, like a story that needed to be told. She needed to know how it was going to end.

She opened *The Bell Jar*. She only allowed herself a chapter. She found she didn't long to disappear into a book the whole weekend, even one this good. She wanted to be around the others, have lunch. It was a rare feeling, this hunger. She'd eaten more food in the past twenty-four hours than she had in days, but she was still hungry for more. She dressed in the same clothes and went downstairs. She helped Fran make grilled cheese sandwiches and chop up a salad. Kase and the others were on the deck in the sunshine, drinking beer.

As she ferried the Gruyère sandwiches from the buttery pan out to the table, she thought about casually raising the book she'd found in her room with Fran. But the notion of their mothers being friends, of the long ago lies that would imply, seemed so ridiculous in the face of preparing lunch, that she didn't. They sat and ate with greasy fingers, the warm sun on their backs. Conversation flowed easily and Kase suggested everyone take naps before preparing for the party.

Having spent the morning in bed, Sylvie found herself drawn instead to the beach, where the air was soft with salt, and Holden was sinking torches into the sand. She felt a curl of anticipation in her belly as she approached. The sun was sliding in the sky, casting long afternoon shadows down the beach. It would be a still evening and a spell of calm had finally been cast over the water.

'Are you on party prep as well as being the chef, Holden Caulfield? Looks like you might need some help.'

He looked up and smiled. 'Hi there, Sylvie Plath. Yes, that would be tremendous. I thought I'd make a start before setting up the paella burner. Maybe you could help set the table.'

She placed cutlery and wine down the centre of the trestle table and then found herself collecting shells and arranging them next to lanterns she found in a box. The house was quiet when she stole into the lounge to collect throw rugs, which she arranged on the backs of seats.

'Wow. Looks eminently better than what I could have done,' said Holden, brushing sand from his hands.

'Thanks.'

'What did you say you do again for a job? Interior design?'

She laughed. 'If you call cleaning out the furniture of people who have passed away interior designing.'

He nodded and smiled, but sadly, she thought.

'Gosh. That's quite a job, Sylvie Plath. A tad more emotionally demanding than being a cleaner.'

She made a non-committal noise. 'It seems to suit me.'

'And let me guess, you wear your beautiful flowing dresses to do that job as well as to shuck oysters?'

She put down a lantern and looked at him. Was reminded of Kase's comment about her dresses and her job. How Kase had known she'd still be wearing vintage dresses while cleaning.

'Actually, yes.' She didn't feel the need to explain, and he didn't demand it.

He smiled again. He had the kind of smile that hid something. She felt the nonsensical urge to try to make him laugh, to crack open that close-lipped grin.

'You seem to have a particular sartorial bent too. You always wear hats. I seem to recall your literary namesake being partial to hats.'

Holden tipped his beanie. 'A red hunting hat, I believe it was.'

'I remember.'

'I have one. Naturally. It's got ear flaps, too. Perfect for the Tasmanian cold.'

'Do you now?'

'I do. Listen, I've got to pick up a few more things for tonight from the cabin. Do you want to walk to the headland with me and see my Holden Caulfield hat?'

'Oh, you live here, on the actual island? I did wonder how you would have gone driving your taxi to the mainland last night.'

Holden smiled. 'It's just a cabin. Nothing like Fran's place. But the view makes up for what it lacks in charm.'

She shivered, a tiny ripple on the surface of a still pond, at the prospect of glimpsing into his world.

CHAPTER 8

hide *(v.)* – to conceal from knowledge; keep secret.

Holden and Sylvie walked down the beach, the sinking sun in their eyes, the sand soft beneath their bare feet. A hush had fallen over the shoreline, as though the water were sleeping, as though it were listening.

'Are you okay to walk for a little while? It's a bit further than we went before,' Holden said gently.

She felt her face colour. She knew by the timbre of his voice that he was referring to her limp. She was so vulnerable in this moment. *Raw, exposed* but also *seen*. She felt no judgement from him. Only care. She blinked back the tears building behind her eyes. 'I'm fine. It's only when I get really tired that I notice it, that it makes me slower.'

He didn't try to dismiss or cover up her direct reference to her body's weakness to hide his own embarrassment. He wasn't embarrassed, like so many others were. The authenticity, *the trust* that was then allowed to settle between them felt as open and beautiful as the sky above them.

It was as though the final barrier of politeness had dissolved and Sylvie felt like a child, suddenly. She wanted to grab his hand, to know everything about him. His favourite colour. His favourite food. Where he had found his Holden hat. There were so many words crowding her mind that she didn't know where to start.

Instead she said, 'You'll never guess what I found today up at the house. *The Bell Jar*, by Sylvia Plath. It was in the bookcase in my room.'

'Don't tell me *Catcher in the Rye* was there too. Now that would be fate.'

The surface of the water rippled with a soft breeze and she shivered with the implication of his words. She felt herself blush. 'I don't know. I'll have to take a closer look.'

'I think you'd better do that,' he said, smiling out of the corner of his mouth, looking at his feet, and she knew they weren't talking about books any longer.

They walked in a thickening silence that had nothing to do with the evening growing blue around them and everything to do with the words that hung between them, unspoken. The sand was growing cold under her feet, the sun was losing its heat, but all Sylvie could feel was warmth.

She slipped on her sandshoes as they left the beach. The bush was scuttling with dusk activity, birds calling from the trees and small animals moving in the undergrowth. They walked until they came to the headland where the eagles nested. From here the curve of the beach below looked like the stroke of a pen, luminous under the sun's dying rays.

They walked until they came to another place where the cliff fell into the water.

The cabin was small, with timber walls on a stone base and a rusted tin roof. There was a balcony with two rattan chairs that had been bitten and beaten by the weather coming in across the bay.

'It's not much, but it's home,' he said.

Sylvie thought of her own home. The tiny flat behind the cafe, the smell of coffee pervading her furniture, her clothes, the slant of the afternoon sun as it fell in the courtyard. Her succulent plants basking in their little pots. Her reading spot under the window – the old armchair she'd reupholstered. The tea table next to it with her current stack of books and her teapot. It wasn't much either, but at least it felt like her little cocoon.

He opened the unlocked door and flicked on a light switch. It was already dark on this side of the island. She could smell the damp and knew it was always colder here, like the dark side of the moon. As she moved into the cabin, the damp smell was overlaid by burned wood, with a hint of the dinners he had eaten. There was a small kitchen in the far corner with dishes neatly stacked and drying. The living room was demarcated by a couch positioned in front of a potbelly stove. There was a door, which must have led to a bedroom. She found herself reading the room as though it were one of her jobs and stopped herself. The living had houses that felt different from the dead. Though this house was readable mainly through what it lacked. Lack of personal details. No pictures on the walls. No photographs. No books. It was like a cabin that might be rented out for a holiday house. But there was also something more that made a home. Something intangible. It was a feeling that was missing. This was not Holden's cocoon. What had made him come and live here at the end of the earth? Was it losing his child? She wasn't sure why she expected to see photographs of Pippi. She knew that people grieved in vastly different ways.

She thought of her own home. She didn't have much either, but she had a few pictures of her and Evangeline, cushions she'd covered with pretty fabric and vintage teacups that she sipped from while she read. And the heaving bookshelves, of course, which told her whole story, in the way that books map one's internal journey through the world. She had tried to part with some of them, but it felt like giving away pieces of her soul.

'Are you cold? Shall I make us tea?'

'That would be nice.'

He put teabags into mugs and lit a gas stove with a box of matches.

'I can see why you need a Holden hat living here. It must get freezing in winter.'

He rubbed his hands and blew into them as the kettle steamed into the chill air. 'Yeah, it gets pretty cold in the bush. It took me a while to acclimatise, but if life has taught me anything, it's taught me that humans can get used to almost anything.' He poured water into the mugs and then disappeared into the other room.

She thought again of his daughter. Of the chick.

'Here it is.'

Sylvie took the soft red and black hat with shearling in her hands. It was like a small animal. 'Put it on,' she said.

He slipped it over his head and she could see the boy he used to be. He grinned self-consciously and went to take it off.

'No leave it. It suits you, Holden Caulfield.'

His lips parted and she saw his real smile, his teeth. 'If you say so, Sylvie Plath. Did Sylvia wear hats?'

Sylvie chuckled. 'I don't believe she was a hat wearer of any particular distinction.'

'More the shame,' he said, laughing.

They took their tea to the window overlooking the cliffs and the sea below. The whitewash surged and drew. *The ocean's lungs*, she thought.

'Don't you think Plath should have been a hat wearer?' asked Holden. 'I mean, if a writer can't wear hats, who can? She appeared, like Caulfield, to embrace, to wallow in her eccentricity.'

Sylvie sipped her tea. It was hot and sweet. 'Hmm, I'm not so sure. I think she, like Caulfield, was the original loner. But they were both torn between being different and being accepted. They wanted to embrace their uniqueness, take strength from it. But they also wanted to fit into the world on some level. This is also Esther Greenwood's struggle in *The Bell Jar*.'

'And where do you fit on this spectrum of fitting in, Sylvie?'

It was the first time he'd just used her own name. She felt her cheeks colour, avoided his eyes, sought the movement of the water out the window. 'I clean out dead people's houses and live alone and read books. Where would you say I sat?'

'But then you're friends with people like Kase and Rachel. A famous writer and a famous – or at least she acts like she's famous – actress.'

Sylvie smiled. 'Hmm, am I?'

'They seem to like you.'

'You can like anyone for a weekend,' she said, raising an eyebrow.

'Even if they're wearing a silly hat?'

She laughed. 'Especially if they're wearing a silly hat.'

Their eyes met and the air no longer felt chill. It felt like that low sun over the beach at dusk, shining right into her. *Dazzling. Squinting. Incandescent.*

'I think I've always been partial to people who are different. Loners, people who wear silly hats –'

'Hey, who said I was a loner?' He shot her a cheeky look.

'Oh, I don't know, the cabin at the end of the earth?'

'So, I'm partial to a bit of space. And nature.'

'A bit of space. Hmm …'

'You don't sound convinced.'

She glanced at him sideways. 'There's only one thing I don't fully understand. I know a literature lover when I see one … but no books? Even at the end of the earth? You must get so much time to read and yet …' She gestured around the small, bookless room.

His lips twitched into a grimace before he hid it with a thin smile. 'No. Too hard to bring all the way out here. Speaking of all the way, we should get moving.'

The air was chill again, that syrupy sun set behind a cloud suddenly. *What was it about the books? What did I say wrong?*

'Oh, of course,' she said, trying to keep the hurt out of her voice.

'The others will be coming down to the beach soon for drinks. I have to start cooking.'

He had shut up to her like an oyster on the beach. Like a closed book. His vulnerability hidden. She bristled at his sudden coolness. Wished she could find a way back to the soft place they'd just inhabited, the authentic place they'd found together on the beach. He took the mugs and put them in the sink. She wanted to say something, anything, but she had lost her words.

He disappeared into the room off the lounge and emerged wearing a jacket and no hat. He pulled his hood up. *Hidden, secluded, secretive.* She wanted to say, *What, no Holden hat?* But it felt like the bond between them was gone, cut like a rope and she was floating adrift again. She had recognised him too well, too fast. She'd scared him. She had been naive to think that this person she'd known so fleetingly was somehow connected to her through books.

He picked up a box from the kitchen table and wordlessly closed the door of the cabin after her. They began down the path. Darkness bled into the cold air. The shadows grew long, leaking doubt into her gut. They parted on the beach. She felt the hope that had been buoying her like an invisible life raft abandon her. As she walked up to the house, she wondered what on earth she was doing here.

CHAPTER 9

memory *(n.)* - a mental impression retained; a recollection.

She wasn't in the mood for a party any longer. The feeling of wanting to escape into a book had returned. To curl up in bed and shut out the uncertainty. To shut out the world. She wondered how people lived full-time in reality. How they remained tethered to the ground, instead of freeing their minds to float into other worlds.

The house was quiet and dark, except for a lamp in the living room. Maybe everyone was getting ready. She climbed the stairs to her room, opened the door and started. Kase was standing at the foot of the bed.

'Oh, hi,' said Kase, clearly startled too. 'I thought you were napping like the rest of us and wondered if you'd fallen asleep reading in the bath, you know, like you used to.'

Sylvie shifted uncomfortably.

'And then I saw that you're over halfway through this.' Kase held out *The Bell Jar*. 'Now I know why you were so late to breakfast.'

Sylvie gave an awkward laugh. She felt exposed. *Wrenched. Torn.* She wanted to show her the inscription in the front of the book, but she sensed Kase had been snooping. Or maybe she was just getting the disappointment of Holden mixed in with Kase. That happened to her a lot. An emotion was so strong that she couldn't decipher its origin any longer; it just spread like a fine mist over everything.

She decided to give Kase the benefit of the doubt.

'I found it in the bookshelf, and look.' She took the book from Kase's hands and opened it to her mother's handwriting. 'What do you think when you see this?'

Kase took the book back. 'Eve and Franny.' She looked up and their eyes met. Kase's expression was puzzled. 'You think it's our Fran and Evangeline?' She pursed her lips in doubt.

'It's just that this is my mother's handwriting.' Sylvie traced the script with her finger. It felt like they were sharing secrets again. *Known. Sacred.* A memory floated into her mind of the old bookshop they used to frequent to find literary treasures.

'Really?'

Sylvie nodded and they shared another quizzical look. 'It's pretty distinctive.'

'But they hardly know each other, aside from all those years of dropping us off and picking us up. But they only exchanged polite hellos,' said Kase, scratching her head.

'I know. And the date in this book is 1967.'

'This is weird.'

'Maybe they knew each other when they were kids. That would have made Mum about fifteen. I was tempted to show the book to Fran.'

Kase's brows drew together. 'No, she's having a hard time of it. It's always extra hard on milestones. I don't think she needs any more dredging up of the past. If that's what this is.'

Sylvie nodded. 'Oh, of course. Do you think it's possible though? That this could be them? That they knew each other? My mother does adore Sylvia Plath.'

'Hmmm. I think her dad, my grandfather, used to call her Franny. It rings a bell. I know where we can look.'

Kase took her hand. It felt as strange and strangely familiar as the handwriting in the front of the book. She led her down the hall until they reached a set of small stairs.

'These go up to a little office. But under the stairs here is a lot of our old stuff. Photo albums, newspaper clippings. Mum's mother died when she was young. There's the newspaper clippings from that. I remember going through them when I was younger. I remember thinking it was somehow wildly romantic that my grandmother had committed suicide. God, I was so young and naive.'

'She did? That's so sad. Poor Fran, no wonder you don't want to bring up her youth.'

Kase opened a small door that led under the stairs. She pulled a chain and a tiny light clicked on overhead. It smelled like dust and old memories. It was only just big enough for them both to crawl in. Cardboard boxes were piled along the walls and there were stacks of old books that almost reached the ceiling. There was a faded blue beanbag with a resolutely deflated air in the middle.

'I come here sometimes. I like going through all the old photo albums of me and Tristan growing up.'

Sylvie felt a shiver from her shoulders through to her fingertips. She imagined Kase here, sitting in this blue beanbag awash with grief and felt a wave of sorrow for her friend, who she had judged so harshly for abandoning her. She might own a whole island, but she was still alone and broken, licking her wounds in this small space where she felt safe and held.

Kase picked up a brown photo album and carefully unstuck its pages. 'Isn't it funny? The kids of today won't be able to do this. All the photos are on phones or computers. But there's something so romantic about looking through an old photo album. It's a glimpse into a world that's now lost. Half my memories of childhood are from these albums. It's sad really, the thought of not having that anymore.' She looked up at Sylvie. 'Does it make you sad that you never had kids?'

Sylvie smiled. 'Evangeline told me I shouldn't. That I'm not cut out for it. She might be right. But yes, sometimes I'm devastated I haven't had kids, other times I'm relieved. Maybe if I met someone, things would become clearer.'

Kase nodded. 'I'm sad. I feel like it's now or never. But Henry doesn't want them, and I don't want to bring a child into our marriage when it's so …'

Grief. Disappointment. Regret.

Sylvie reached out and touched Kase's arm. 'You have your books. They're like babies, I imagine.'

'Maybe.' Kase passed Sylvie the album. 'This is the photo I kept looking at after Tristan died. We were at my grandfather's place in Collaroy. He had this beautiful home with a big garden overlooking the lake and it was Christmas Eve, and I remember Tristan and I swimming all night in the pool and taking turns to run into the house to get Christmas cake … and just this sense of … I don't know. Anticipation. Hope. If you asked me to pinpoint the most pure happiness

I've ever felt in my life, it was this night. I must have been around ten or eleven.'

Emotion swelled in Sylvie's throat and she swallowed it back with difficulty. She smoothed the photo, veiled by the yellowing patina of age. Tristan was tall and brown and smiling, and Kase was all teeth and spiky fringe. Both teetering on the cusp of what was to come. Adolescence. The end of innocence.

Laughter bubbled out of Sylvie, surprising them both. 'Oh my goodness, what is going on with your hair? Do you remember how cool we used to think we were?' she asked, nostalgia and mirth mixing inside her at the memory.

'What do you mean? My hair was my best feature,' Kase said. 'Especially when I gelled the fringe up. And you had to leave one bit straight and the rest kind of bouffed back in a wave.'

'And remember we used to try with mine, but it turns out curly hair should never have a fringe. I was so jealous of yours.'

'I was jealous of your Doc Martens,' said Kase. 'You had the boots that went past your ankle, but Fran would never let me wear them because she said it made me look too much like a sassy soldier. She meant *slutty* soldier. So I just had the normal shoes. So uncool.'

Sylvie shook her head. 'But you did have the boots. We went into the city to buy them. It was a big thing, remember? We'd been planning it for weeks. And at the bus stop that man came up to us and told us to smile, that it would make us prettier and life wasn't that bad. And without missing a beat you said something like … "Dude, we're not the middle-aged man talking to schoolgirls at a bus stop."'

Kase gasped at the memory, grabbing Sylvie's hand and squeezing her eyes shut. 'Oh my God, I did. And his face. I remember.'

'And then you did that weird dance.'

'And it completely freaked him out.' Kase laughed.

'And then he couldn't get away from us quickly enough.'

Sylvie was laughing too. She looked at Kase, who stood awkwardly in the tiny space and replicated the dance, forcing Sylvie's stomach to ache as she pressed her hand into it and tried to breathe.

'Oh my God.' Kase was gasping too, tears squeezing out of the corners of her eyes. Each time they looked at each other a new wave of hilarity washed over them. They were fifteen again and sitting at a bus stop with enough money for the fare, food court Chinese, and a pair of brand-name shoes. They were Kase and Sylvie against the world again. Indifferent to the disapproving stares of strangers as they tried and failed to tame the hysterical laughter that bubbled through their chests.

Kase rested her head on Sylvie's leg. She looked up. 'Sylvie, your memory is actually perfect.'

Sylvie flinched. She couldn't help it. 'Long term is fine. Everything before the accident.'

There it was again, the line in the sand. She wiped the moisture away from under her eyes. She looked at the photo again and pressed her fingers to her lips. She had not seen Tristan's face in twenty-three years. His memory had warped over time into something else. *Mythic. Unreal.*

'You loved him, didn't you?' said Kase, propping herself onto her elbow.

Sylvie's breath caught and it felt as though all the air in the small space had been sucked out. She swallowed. *Truth. Pain.*

'Did I?' The words stuck to the roof of her mouth. *Insincere.*

'Sylvie, do you really not remember what happened that night? Still?' Kase's eyes were searching, her hand on Sylvie's arm.

Sylvie's face felt numb, as though all the blood had drained from her head. She shook it. Her breath was shallow, and she drew her arms around her. 'No. The doctors said I have retrograde amnesia. I lost memories of the events before the accident, and the accident itself.'

'Where do you remember up until?'

'I … ah.' The rush of blood in her head was so loud it took up all the space and all the sound. She searched for the words. 'The beach.' She shook her head. 'I remember us at the party on the beach before we went up to the lighthouse.'

'And then …?'

Sylvie willed the words to come out of her mouth. They flitted through her mind. *Nothing. I remember nothing. And I still don't understand what happened.* She opened her mouth. A single word came out. 'Nothing.'

'Hello? Kase? You back here? We're opening the champagne, but we have no birthday girl.' Rachel's voice drifted down the hall.

'You don't remember him falling?'

Sylvie shook her head, feeling sick. The air was too hot, too close, too dusty. She coughed. She'd never been so glad of Rachel's presence.

Kase opened the door a crack. 'We're in here, Rach. Under the stairs.'

She ran her fingers along another album, this one an older style, mustard-coloured. The pages were tacky and the images were black and white. 'Here.' Kase peeled back the plastic and slipped the photo out. 'When I saw Franny and Eve written in the book, this is what I thought of. Is this Evangeline? Is this your mother?'

Sylvie took the photo and her hand went to her mouth. They were sitting on the bonnet of an old white Valiant, faces open in laughter. It was like looking at a photo of herself and Kase but in black and white.

SUMMER 1967

Eve was like a flash of light come into Franny's life. Like the lightning storms they'd watch unfurl over the lake while doing their homework on Eve's bed. Like the bright images playing across the screen at the cinema as they watched the Sunday movie. They had only known each other two weeks but it already felt like forever. After school, Franny would dump her bag at the house and make her way down through the wet, teeming jungle garden to the granny flat. The summer air was thick with the scent of frangipani and she'd stripped down to shorts and bare feet. Her legs were tanned from the baby oil she coated them in on the weekends when she and Eve sat by the pool drinking lemonade and eating crackers.

Once, her handsome next-door neighbour, Teddy, popped his head over the fence and introduced himself to Eve, but he was in the middle of exams and to be honest, Franny felt relieved. She wanted Eve and their new, golden afternoons all to herself. She wanted Teddy and their connection to stay separate.

Franny had been sweet on this boy ever since she saw him loading his surfboard onto his old car out the front of his house the day they moved in. With his surf-browned skin, sandy hair and green eyes, she was soon to discover that he was prime real estate at school, just like their adjacent cliffside homes.

Teddy surfed every morning, and she eagerly took up his invitation for her to tag along. She even had a go on his longboard, both of them laughing when she couldn't manage to do anything other than get dumped. But she went along every time he asked, sometimes swimming, other times just sitting on the sand, watching his board cut through the glassy waves and the sun slide up into the sky. Perhaps it felt so easy between them because they were at the same school, but she knew it was finding the fairy penguin that had bonded them. She hadn't even known what it was when she first spotted the dark shape near the rocks at the far end of the beach. One of its tiny wings was torn and it was trying and failing to walk thanks to some fishing line caught around its legs. She waved at Teddy madly from the beach until he saw her and came in.

'Oh, cute little guy, you've been caught in a fishing net,' said Teddy, shaking the water from his hair and kneeling down in the sand.

'He's injured. Look at his wing,' said Franny, crouching beside him.

Teddy reached out gently, slowly. 'You'll scare him,' said Franny, but it was as though the animal was somehow sensing that they were trying to help it and it didn't resist when Teddy removed the line that was tangled in the poor little thing's legs.

'We can't just leave him here. He'll be attacked by other animals, he's weak.'

'Yeah, he will be,' said Teddy. 'He still can't walk. There must be something wrong with his leg too. Wait here, I'm just going to grab something from the car.'

Teddy returned with a towel in a cardboard box and, as he lifted the little penguin into the box and soothed it with his voice and covered it with the towel, she knew in some startling and yet simple way that she could fall in love with this man. They tended to the penguin in shifts for the next two days, hiding it in the corner of Franny's garage and feeding it dog food and sardines from a tin. It was their secret. Their joint mission. When the penguin seemed stronger and could walk a few steps across the garage floor, they returned to the same rocks where they had found it.

'I'm not ready to let Ringo go,' said Franny as they placed his box carefully on the sand. They laughed as they watched him waddle around, his wounded wing no longer dead by his side, his leg mended. 'See, he doesn't want to leave us either.' She looked at Teddy and she could tell he didn't want to say goodbye.

Teddy brushed his eyes with the back of his hand. Franny touched his arm lightly and he grabbed her hand and squeezed it. 'Come on, we've got to be strong. Ringo can't live in a garage for the rest of his life, can he? He's got to go find the rest of The Beatles.'

They laughed, and Teddy's hand was rough and warm, and she didn't want to ever let it go as they watched their little charge shoot off into the waves. And every so often, when they were hanging out making snacks at Franny's place, swimming in the pool, Teddy would say, 'I wonder if Ringo has found Paul, John and George yet?' And they'd both start laughing and humming Beatles tunes. It felt like they had something special between them.

But now she also had something special with Eve. On weeknights, Eve's dad worked late – he was a tradesman, and his work took him all over Sydney, so they had the flat to themselves. It smelled of damp, that wet humidity that Franny imagined was the garden breathing. They burned incense on the porch and watched the lake turn into a silver mirror through the trees. Franny had dreamed of making the little space her own, but now it was made so by Eve. Her tiny room – almost a closet really – was hung with posters of Jim Morrison, filled with flowers picked from the garden and the stacks of books Eve carted from place to place.

They sat on the bed eating Sao crackers from the pack. The Doors were playing on a record player propped up in the corner by books.

'I'm destined to fall in love with a boy who looks like Jim Morrison,' said Eve, flopping onto the bed and sighing, languidly plaiting her hair. 'Don't you ever want to know what your husband is going to look like? Maybe we could catch the bus into the city and see that fortune-teller that I told you about. Wouldn't that be fun?'

Franny thought of Teddy's sun-browned face. Instead, she said, 'Gosh, maybe. Although I don't know if I want to know any of that.'

'You could ask her if your parents are going to get divorced.'

Franny made a face. 'Did you hear them fighting again last night?'

'It's impossible not to. I can't hear your dad so much, but your mum screaming is …' Eve scrunched up her nose. 'You should just come down here when that happens again, and we'll drink Dad's beer.'

'Maybe I will. Last night I locked myself in the bathroom and lay back in the bath so my ears were underwater for as long as I could, so I didn't have to listen to them. And then they freaked when Mum noticed the door was locked and she started banging on the bathroom door. At least it stopped them fighting. It must make you glad your parents aren't together. Do you remember them fighting? I mean, before your mum left?'

Eve shrugged. 'No, not really. I don't imagine they even would have. Fought. They were never married and I was an accident, so Mum just took off when she realised being a mother wasn't fun. My dad is more the loyal type. And he never talks about her badly, even though she just left him with a kid and no money. I mean, she's obviously a piece of work.'

'Your dad is a sweetheart. I think my mum has a crush on him.'

Eve rolled her eyes. 'Every mum has a crush on Dad. Why do you think we have to move around so much?' She laughed.

'Really? Is that why?'

'I don't know, I think he likes to think he's some kind of Casanova. I mean, I guess he's pretty good-looking. And I do see the way the mums look at him. But there haven't been any actual scandals that I've known about. He likes this woman called Carole, and they're very on and off. She's like a queen and expects to be wined and dined and my poor dad doesn't have the money, but he adores her, I can tell. Every so often he takes her out for a fancy dinner. It's probably why we're living in other people's granny flats. One day I want men to take me out for fancy dinners.'

'But only men who look like Jim Morrison,' said Franny, helping herself to another Sao.

'Exactly.'

They laughed and then Eve snorted and that set Franny off, her stomach aching. Somehow their laughter built until they couldn't even remember what they had been laughing about in the first place.

They were hungry and there was nothing in the tiny fridge at the flat, so they went up to the main house and found peaches in the bowl and took them out to the pool to eat with the juice sliding down their arms, watching the sun set over the ocean and the lake.

'This is the perfect view for us,' said Eve. 'You're like the still lake and I'm like the choppy ocean, and there's just a thin wedge between us but we're made of the same substance.'

Franny smiled. Sometimes she couldn't believe the things that came out of Eve's mouth. She seemed so much older than fifteen, but maybe that's what happened when you grew up without a mother and had to find your own way in the world.

It was the first time in a long time that Franny felt happy, in a simple kind of way, with the sweet fruit in her mouth and the sun on her face, the cool water around her ankles. But she knew it was really because she didn't feel alone anymore.

CHAPTER 10

broken *(adj.)* - having undergone breaking.

Rachel insisted they get ready together. Sylvie had forgotten these female rituals existed. She and Kase had done such things in their youth, but she hadn't ever been anyone's bridesmaid, or been married, so the fanfare felt like a long-forgotten religious ceremony.

Rachel brought styling tongs and nail polish into Kase's room and insisted on smoothing Kase's hair while she drank champagne in a bathrobe. She wanted to do the same to Sylvie, but Sylvie said no, she wanted to keep her hair natural. The look of disapproval on Rachel's face made her squirm, and something inside her whispered that she used to enjoy these things. She thought of Esther from *The Bell Jar*. Esther would not have partaken in such a ritual. She too would have felt stifled by it. Somehow this comforted Sylvie. Book characters always comforted Sylvie. If only everyone was as transparent and honest as a person on the page. Truths were harder to come by, honesty was harder to find, in real people.

She agreed to let Rachel paint her nails a shade of blue that matched the ocean. The slow, careful way Rachel applied the brush felt like a baptism of sorts.

'Kase, you'll have to come to Sydney for my next opening night. We'll do lunch overlooking the harbour, followed by a day spa. I have the most fabulous new facialist.'

'Sounds good,' said Kase, threading gold earrings through her lobes in the mirror.

Sylvie knew this invitation was a clear demarcation, a reminder that Kase belonged to Rachel. She'd seen the flick of jealousy cross Rachel's face on finding the two of them closeted under the stairs. Did Kase feel it? This tension?

There was also another demarcation, and that was wealth. Kase and Rachel had always been rich. Sylvie knew their friendship was long distance, but that they flew between Sydney and Hobart frequently to attend literary and arts events together. Kase had never missed a play's opening night and Rachel had never missed a book launch.

Sylvie wondered what it was like to move in that privileged, moneyed world so easily. She supposed at school she'd at least had the cultural credibility of winning the scholarship. Now she was just a cleaner. She couldn't afford lunch on the harbour and a day spa. It wouldn't have even occurred to Rachel to invite Sylvie, she fell so far out of that sphere. People like her meant nothing to people like Rachel. And yet, somewhere in the recesses of her mind she remembered a time when she'd had the upper hand over Rachel. When she had been stronger, smarter, more powerful. The wound inside Sylvie solidified to something more defiant.

'Sylvie, you should join us next time,' said Kase. 'You'd love some of the plays Rach stars in, she's so brilliant.'

A shadow passed over Rachel's face and her mouth scrunched at the corner.

'Oh, I wouldn't want to intrude,' said Sylvie, smudging a perfectly painted nail.

'You know, it's funny how we weren't all better friends at school,' Rachel said, smoothing her hair in front of the mirror. It fell like a perfect sheet against her symmetrical features. 'The two of you were just so exclusive. I mean, when I found you both sitting under the stairs like that before, it just took me right back.'

We weren't better friends at school, because you looked down on us, Sylvie thought. *And now I'm back and you're scared. Threat. Hazard. Risk.*

'Well, we're not fifteen anymore. We can have more than one friend,' said Kase. 'Your hair looks perfect. How does it always look so damn perfect?' She reached out and touched Rachel's hair.

Rachel softened at the compliment.

'And you're forgetting, Rach, you always had your crew. Remember the three blondes? You surrounded yourself with people who did your bidding. Sylvie and I were exclusive because we were both loners. We didn't fit in anywhere but with each other. Isn't that right?' Kase looked to Sylvie.

Sylvie nodded. 'I still don't fit in anywhere.'

Rachel crossed her arms. 'Oh, poor you. You think you have a monopoly on that? That it somehow makes you special? Here's the truth: most people don't feel like they fit in. Most people feel like they're pretending. Do you think I believe I deserve to have all the success I've had? I still feel like an impostor. Like someone's going to tap me on the shoulder and send me off the stage. Back to drama school, where they said I had the looks but not the talent. And I may have had the three blondes, but I spent all of school lonely and misunderstood. At least you two had each other.'

The room fell silent. Sylvie fought the urge to leave. She felt like Rachel had just performed the closing act of a play, and was awaiting her audience's applause.

'I didn't realise you felt like that, Rach. On the outside you seemed so … confident,' said Kase. She took a step towards Sylvie. 'Though I'm pretty sure your idea of not fitting in is a bit different from ours.'

Sylvie felt the rush of warmth from Kase as though a summer wind had blown blossoms between them, branch to branch. She wanted to reach out and take her little finger, but she just stood there with her tacky half-wet nails.

Rachel's eyes were cold and her full mouth was pulled into a thin line. 'You know what you're always mistaking, Kase? Brokenness for brilliance.'

Sylvie thought immediately of Henry. Of how palpable his brokenness had been when they'd first met. How she had intuited it in him because she had the same thing in her. She knew Rachel was right, but it made Sylvie love Kase fiercely suddenly. For her ability to see hope and beauty in frailty.

Rachel turned and left the room.

Silence. Sylvie could hear Kase breathing, the ocean breathing on the other side of the glass.

'I still don't think Rachel likes me,' Sylvie deadpanned.

A smile slipped onto Kase's lips and she began to laugh. It infected Sylvie, and she felt laughter issue from her like a silky ribbon. When their eyes met their laughter built, until tears squeezed out of Kase's eyes and they were breathless. They didn't have to say anything. Sometimes you just knew and there didn't need to be words. They linked arms and went downstairs. Kase picked up a bottle of opened champagne and took a swig. Sylvie did the same as they made their way down to the beach. They didn't have to say it. They were friends again.

SPRING 1996

The bus to the city was filled with old people in suits. Kase turned to Sylvie, who was sitting by the window, the wind blowing her hair back from her face, raised to the morning sun. She looked so free, so beautiful. Kase wished she had a camera to capture this moment. They were on school holidays and days of freedom stretched out before them like a sun-flooded beach.

She grabbed Sylvie's arm. 'Please, Syl, tell me, *promise me* we're not going to be lame office types riding a bus to work every day with no soul in a few years?'

Sylvie laughed. 'They're not all soulless. Turn around.'

Kase turned and saw a woman with tightly curled red hair listening to her Walkman and making passionate hand movements to the music with her eyes closed. The people on the back seat were giving her a wide berth. 'Okaaaay.'

Sylvie shrugged. 'I'd *waaay* rather be her. She doesn't care what anyone thinks. She's free, it's only everyone else who's cringing.'

'I wonder what she's listening to?'

'Alanis Morissette,' said Sylvie.

'*Jagged Little Pill*,' said Kase at the same time, and they laughed.

Sylvie opened the window wider and they sang the lyrics to 'Ironic', their favourite song off the album, the breeze on their faces, smiles on their lips. Kase could sense the eyes of the other passengers on them and she sang louder. It felt like they were invincible. It felt like they would never be bus-business robots.

'Should we go to Pitt Street Mall before getting your boots at Oxford Street? I want those sticky honey prawns and prawn crackers from the food court,' said Sylvie.

'Oh my God, I'm so hungry, don't. Is it bad that I chucked Evangeline's pancakes in the bin?'

'Oh my God, I can't believe she made them out of buckwheat. They were like rocks.'

'Well, at least she made us breakfast,' said Kase.

'That's only because I gave her a guilt trip about how Fran makes us pancakes with maple syrup when I stay at yours and I think she actually felt bad. So, we got to eat rocks.'

'At least she's trying.'

Sylvie shrugged. 'I guess.'

They had stayed up all weekend watching music videos on *Rage* and eating ice cream from the tub spiked with Baileys from Evangeline's liquor cabinet. Kase guessed that they'd had about three hours sleep total, but she didn't feel tired.

They crossed the Harbour Bridge and Kase felt the familiar gut rush of excitement in reaching the city. It felt so full of possibilities here among the tall buildings and shadowy streets – so much cooler than the lame suburbs. They got off the bus, arms linked, necks craning up to the sky.

They passed a homeless woman sleeping on a bench, the smell of urine and stale sweat making Kase almost gag. Sylvie shot her a sad look before taking two coins out of her purse. She was such a softie; by the end of the day Sylvie would have given half of what little money she had to the city's outcasts. Kase made her put away her coins and dropped her own money into the bowl beneath the handwritten sign.

A man wearing a cracked leather jacket and a sleazy look approached them. *Here we go*, thought Kase.

'Cheer up, girls, why so glum? Give us a smile. You're beautiful, young, what more could you possibly want?'

'Ah … how about not being cracked onto by strange fifty-year-old men,' said Sylvie, arching a brow. 'That would really make us smile.' Then she pasted a fake grin onto her lips and Kase laughed and clapped her hand over her mouth.

The man frowned and muttered something, and Sylvie cocked her head. 'Why so glum? Oh yeah, that's right, because we're young and beautiful and you're old and creepy.' She did a little dance on the spot, which ended in a deep bow, grabbed Kase by the hand, and they began to skip, shooting the man beaming smiles over their shoulders. He shook his head and they let out a whoop of laughter and ran.

CHAPTER 11

party *(n.)* - a group gathered together for some purpose, as for amusement or entertainment.

The night was soft and full, and a low salt mist hovered over the sand. It almost felt like the summer it was meant to be. There was no wind and the moon had risen over the headland, spilling a trail of light over the sea. The air smelled of fire, salt and fish cooking. Candles and lanterns winked like fireflies along the sand. Kase took her seat at the head of the table and they ate paella, lobster and fresh oysters, washed down with champagne. It felt like days ago that Sylvie had shucked the oyster on the rocks, had walked to Holden's cabin. Had seen his underbelly and felt him shut to her, like a sea creature protecting its soft insides. He was busy, helping Fran to serve food and top up drinks. Every so often she thought she saw him gazing out at the ocean. Every so often she found his eyes resting on her. But she did not meet them.

Henry clinked his glass with a fork and they fell silent. He raised his glass. 'I guess this is the time to say something about the woman of the hour. I know she wanted this to be informal, but I'd like to say a few words to mark the occasion, if I may. Thank you all for coming to the end of the earth. But what an end of the earth it is. Kase has always loved this place and it's so special to be able to celebrate here. Thank you, Fran, for being the perfect host. And for the magnificent food.'

Fran gave a small smile, a nod.

'Kase is a force to be reckoned with, as we all well know. And I don't know that I've managed to tame that force, nor would I dare to, mind you. Especially not when she's on a writing deadline.'

There was a ripple of knowing laughter around the table.

'She is a brilliant mind, having produced an extraordinary body of work, which I couldn't be prouder of. It has been a pleasure to be married to you, Kase Fowler.'

Sylvie studied Kase's face. She had tears in her eyes. *Kase didn't want you to tame her, she just wanted you to love her.*

Rachel stood with a dramatic flourish, a glass of wine held aloft.

'Kase, as your closest friend I just wanted to say something too. Your friendship has meant so much to me. And, I know, to Gabe. We're so proud of everything you've achieved. So many amazing books published, several amazing houses purchased, not to mention your own island.'

Everyone laughed.

'The actor, the author and the newspaper editor. Who would have thought we'd come this far? To my beautiful Kase.'

Sylvie's flesh rippled with repulsion. *Possessive. Self-centred. Narcissistic.* Rachel always had to make it about herself. And where were all the other words for Kase? *Funny, tender, warm, vulnerable, quirky, kind.* All they were celebrating were her achievements. Not who she was. It was as though both of them had seen the pretty cover, but hadn't opened the pages of Kase.

I know her better than both of you.

Sylvie's hand hovered at her glass. Her legs twitched. She wished she had the strength to stand up and speak. What would she say? Could she really pretend to know Kase better than her husband and her best friend? Perhaps that's what adulthood, what growing up, was. Leaving behind the people who saw your raw formation, and surrounding yourself with people who were more aligned with the ideal you. Just because Sylvie hadn't managed such a thing, didn't mean that others weren't able to. Life was speeches at parties now, and career achievements and marriage; it was more than an internal monologue of doubts. Perhaps Sylvie had just read too many books. Had been in too many heads. Just because she wasn't able to do any of it, didn't mean Kase couldn't.

She took a long drink of her wine. Rachel's cruel words came back to her. *You're mistaking brokenness for brilliance.*

Rachel made a big show of giving Kase her present. It was obviously a painting, considering its shape and size. Kase peeled back the wrapping to reveal a portrait of herself. Sylvie knew the photograph the painting had been inspired by. Kase had made the prestigious cover of the arts section of a major newspaper for her last, most lauded novel. She stood in front of a bookcase, looking distinguished. Unsmiling. Wearing a blood red blouse. It was a beautiful painting, by a famous artist friend of Rachel's. They heard all about how his paintings were in the Art Gallery of New South Wales and how he'd wanted to enter the painting into a big competition, and still might.

Sylvie's fingers found her present in the pocket of her dress. It felt small and inconsequential. A locket she'd happened upon in an antique store that she'd imagined Kase wearing close to her throat, as she'd always worn her necklaces. Now she was filled with doubt. It was such an immature present. A present meant for a teenage Kase. Sylvie's cheeks burned at the thought of even giving it to her.

While everyone was admiring the painting Sylvie snuck away, excusing herself and heading up to the house. She had nowhere to put her overwhelming emotions, except into words. The wine was heightening everything, making things unravel. She headed for the bathroom near the kitchen. Her paleness met her in the mirror, eyes lidded with too much wine. She looked like an impostor, with her bare face and wild hair, untamed by Rachel. She took out her notebook and began to write.

She heard others come into the house. The crash of cutlery in the sink. She couldn't bear the thought of going back out there. She felt like a stowaway on a ship that was already at sea. She opened the door a crack, intending to sneak upstairs to the safe haven of her room. Her book. Kase and Gabe were by the sink. Instinctively she slunk back behind the door. They were speaking in hushed tones. Sylvie's pulse thickened along her wrists. She watched them through the crack, too drunk to stop herself from spying.

The pair of them were standing too close. *Illicit.* Were they having an affair? She thought of Kase's open marriage. Of Trina and the kids, and Gabe's constant jabs at parenting. Of all those days when they were young – swimming, watching movies, studying together. Kase had never mentioned any feelings for Gabe.

'I've been trying to talk to you properly since we got here. You've been avoiding me,' he said, raking a hand through his hair.

'I've been kind of distracted, if you hadn't noticed. I'm turning forty, apparently. Thanks for the painting though. You guys must have pulled a few pretty spectacular strings.'

Gabe wiped a hand down his face and shook his head. 'Why, Kase? Why the hell did you invite her?'

'She's my best friend, for God's sake.' Kase moved away from him, aggressively scraping plates with a knife.

The sound put Sylvie's teeth on edge. She dared not move a muscle. Dared not breathe. Had Gabe and Rachel had a falling out? Why didn't he want her here? Why was he talking about his sister that way?

'I thought we'd agreed,' said Gabe.

Kase stopped stacking plates and shook her head, pushed herself back from the sink. 'It was twenty-three years ago, Gabe. We were kids. She doesn't even remember.'

Sylvie felt herself slipping and she grabbed at the doorframe to steady herself. The room spun. She felt sick. Were they talking about her?

'What if she does? Remember?'

'She doesn't, okay? I asked her.'

'And how the hell did you do that? You seem very confident about a person you haven't seen for twenty-three years.'

'I still know her. None of us have changed that much. We all like to think we have, but we haven't.'

Gabe grunted, turned away and rubbed the back of his neck. 'You say that, but she's changed. She's clearly not the person she once was. Not as sharp. And we all have things at stake now. People at stake now. Everyone except her.'

Silence. Sylvie wondered if they could hear her breathing on the other side of the door. She wondered if they could hear her body shaking.

The conversation under the stairs. Kase asking her what she remembered about the night Tristan died. Was that what this was about? There was a loud blood beat in her ears, filling up all the room in her head. She couldn't think. The bathroom walls were closing in. Sylvie slid down until she was sitting on the cool tiles.

She was just starting to feel close to Kase again. Now she didn't know what to feel. Kase was hiding something from her, but she'd also called Sylvie her best friend. Not Rachel, fabulous Rachel, giver of art, queen of the stage, but Sylvie. Plain, ordinary, broken Sylvie. The feeling of that was soft and hopeful under the bruising of those other words.

Footsteps sounded and Gabe opened the door to the veranda and walked out, the slam of it breaking the quiet. Kase stilled her aggressive cleaning, like a ship's sails losing wind. Her shoulders curled inwards. Sylvie couldn't see her face, but as she pushed her hair behind her ears, she saw that Kase was shaking.

SPRING 1996

The afternoon sun poured onto the deck and the surf was a low roar on the rocks below. The light shifted through the leaves above, casting patterns over her books. Kase squinted into the brightness and stretched her arms to the sky. Her shoulders ached from hunching over textbooks and her brain buzzed from too much caffeine. They were on the final stretch before their HSC exams. The table was strewn with highlighters, empty Diet Coke cans and biscuit packets. She could feel the beady eyes of the black birds in the gum trees above, biding their time.

'I can't read another sentence. It's too hot. Let's go for a swim,' she said.

Neither Sylvie nor Tristan moved. Sylvie was sprawled out, devouring *Wuthering Heights*. Tristan's face was scrunched in concentration over a thick textbook.

'Come on, nerds. And by the way, Syl, why are you reading that book *again* when you should be studying maths?'

Sylvie shrugged. 'I've finished revising.' She glanced at Tristan, twisting a strand of hair around her finger.

'Is that ...?' Kase rolled her eyes and picked up some maths papers next to Sylvie. 'Has Sylvie been helping you with maths again, Trist? You're *meant* to be a year ahead of us. Sylvie why are you doing his TAFE exams for him?'

Tristan made a flicking motion with his fingers, indicating his displeasure.

'He was doing that thing he does – clicking his tongue when he's trying to work something out. It was annoying, so I just showed him some tricks to make it easier.'

'Uh huh.' Kase crunched through the last of the crackers and washed them down with a sip of Diet Coke.

Tristan pushed the textbook away from him and onto the floor where it landed with a thump. 'I'm done.' He pressed his face into his palms. 'How the hell is she so smart? I still don't get this stuff.'

'Oh, you're talking about me?' replied Sylvie in mock surprise, eyes widening, hand on her chest.

'Bloody hell, Syl, you're so lucky. You barely have to study for your HSC.' Tristan rubbed his hands down his face.

The familiar spike of frustration rippled through Kase. Tristan put Sylvie on a pedestal in many ways, and yet he couldn't see what was right in front of him. It was painful to have to witness day in, day out. Boys could be so dumb. 'You should know by now that Sylvie studies for fun.'

Sylvie shrugged innocently, her eyes never leaving her book.

Tristan checked his watch. 'Oh my God, how is it lunchtime already? Shit. I have so much more study to get done today.' He stood and stretched.

'Come on, we need a break. You know what Mum always says,' said Kase.

'Brain food,' Tristan said, rolling his eyes. He followed Kase into the cool relief of the kitchen and flung open the fridge, standing there staring, like he always did.

He's going to drink the OJ straight from the bottle now, Kase thought. 'Yep.'

'What?'

Kase sighed. 'Can you not? We don't all want to be drinking your spit.'

'Fine.'

She stood with her hands on her hips as he sculled the entire carton. 'Sylvie and I might have actually wanted some of that.'

He took a bottle of apple juice out of the fridge, found two glasses, dropped ice cubes in them and poured the juice. He handed one to Kase with a flourish. 'Your spit-free juice, madame.'

She laughed and punched him as he put a tea towel over his arm like a waiter and took a juice outside to Sylvie, still reading on the deck.

When he returned a moment later, Kase watched him remove half the contents of the fridge and arrange it on the counter. 'Are you ever moving out? I can't believe you're still here when you don't have to be.'

He shrugged. 'I can't seem to leave you, my darling sister. Plus, I need Sylvie's study tips.'

She poked her tongue out at him. 'What you need is Mum and Dad to pay for your food.'

Truth be told, she didn't actually want him to move out. The balance would feel off. Their family felt like a four, not a three. And she did secretly like having him around, the dag that he was.

'So, do you want the Tristan study special or not?' he asked.

'You mean a ham and cheese sandwich?'

'With pickles. The pickles are the key.'

Kase rolled her eyes. 'Fine. Sylvie, do you want one of Tristan's weird pickle sandwiches?' she called. She ducked her head out to the deck to see Sylvie shake her head.

Kase and Tristan ate the sandwiches perched on the kitchen stools in the easy silence that came from a lifetime of sharing meals together.

Kase put the plates in the sink, went onto the deck and grabbed one of the now-dry towels from their morning swim. She threw it at Sylvie. 'Come on, Cathy. Put Heathcliff down. We're going for a swim.'

Their skin was still salty from this morning, swimmers sandy under their clothes. It was burning on the beach, and they danced on hot toes to the waterline. Gabe was just coming in with his surfboard. He'd taken a gap year and was spending it surfing, drinking beer, going to parties and distracting Tristan. He threw his board down on the sand and he and Tristan crashed through the waves, pouncing on each other like puppies.

Kase eased into the shallows, the coolness cutting through her hot core. It felt like dissolving from the outside in. She closed her eyes. The sea was calm. The horizon was a haze of salt spray beyond the gentle swell. She let the water rock her gently, turned onto her back and floated. Sometimes the soft lull of the sea was the only time she felt whole. All the other parts of her drifted away. The pressure to do well at school. The need to be beautiful. The need to be thin. The need to be as smart as her brilliant best friend. The yearning for something she couldn't articulate. The fear that no boy would love her. The way the world felt too big and too much and it made her want to burst into it and shrink and hide from it, all at the same time.

She felt Sylvie's skin brush hers. She was on her back too, her hair floating out from her head like a seaweed queen. Their little fingers interlaced. She would always have Sylvie.

'I'm scared,' Kase whispered, to the sky, to the sea. The salt on her lips tasted like tears.

Sylvie's face was a pale moon shielding the sun above her. 'Are you okay?'

Kase closed her eyes. 'I don't know. It all seems too big. Too hard.'

'What? Exams?'

'Life.'

'Mmmm. I know. But we just have to get through the next little while and then we're free. Free! No more school, ever. We can start living life our way.'

'But what if it doesn't turn out like we hope? What if all our grand plans just, I don't know … what if we're just destined for boring, ordinary lives, like the bus robots? Don't you get scared?'

Sylvie smiled. 'It'll never be boring and ordinary as long as we have each other. Whatever our souls are made of, yours and mine are the same.'

Kase laughed. 'You've been reading too much *Wuthering Heights*.'

'Is there such a thing though? I don't think *Wuthering Heights* can be quantified. It's in the same category as chocolate.'

'Is there a love like that out there for us, do you think? I mean, a big love. A dramatic love. A chocolate love. A love fit for fiction.'

Sylvie's eyes went as glassy as the glinting green sea.

'You thinking about Tristan?' Kase asked.

Sylvie smiled, sadly, and disappeared underwater. When she came up for breath Kase touched her cool flesh. She wanted to tell her friend that she was destined for bigger things than her brother, but then Tristan and Gabe were there, thrashing through the stillness, the tender ripples of their conversation gone.

She watched Tristan pick Sylvie up and throw her into the whitewash, shrieking. Did he know deep down how much she loved him? Was he simply blind to her? The smart friend of his little sister.

Gabe came up behind Kase and she splashed him ferociously to stop him touching her. Sometimes she felt his eyes sliding over her body. The feeling was not unpleasant, but there was something that made her hold him at arm's length. Some instinct that she couldn't voice but that she knew to listen to. Like the rip pull under the waves, like the sting of salt on the skin. Like the time she was getting out of the shower and had felt *watched*, and she'd put her eye to the keyhole and gasped. An iris, a pupil, dilated. Blinked shut. Gone. She'd wrapped the towel tight and swung open the door. But the hall was empty. Surely it hadn't been her own brother spying. It could only have been Gabe.

He caught her arm now and she broke away and grabbed Sylvie's hand, and swam, breathless, for the shore. The two of them ran all the way back to the house, taking the stairs up the cliff two at a time, the boys in pursuit.

CHAPTER 12

dare *(v.)* – to have the necessary courage or boldness for something.

Kase wiped under her eyes with a tea towel and took a deep breath, steadying herself at the sink. Then she went out into the night. Sylvie crept from the bathroom. She felt painfully sober, assaulted by the bright kitchen light. She wanted to scuttle upstairs to her bedroom and crawl under the covers, create a shell, like a crab. Shut out the light and those harsh words spoken under them. Go back under *The Bell Jar*. But she knew Kase would come and find her. Kase always found her. Even after twenty-three years she had found her. And how would Sylvie explain her antisocial behaviour on her friend's birthday? How would she find the words?

Why were you talking to Gabe about me and that night that Tristan died? Why are you scared?

But she couldn't say any of it, because it all led back to those same words that sat between them like a tender bruise. *How could you have abandoned me?*

She walked out onto the dark deck overlooking the beach.

It was black at one end, bright with firelight at the other. The burning wood toasted the air. Voices carried softly across the sand. She felt like that stretch of beach, the warm brightness of their inclusion cocooning her at one end, the darkness of everything left unsaid creeping cold into her bones at the other. She felt numb. Immobile, unable to take a step further.

'Do you think Kase liked her present?' Sylvie jumped at the voice behind her. His cigarette smoke drifted over to her before the shadows gave him up.

'Oh, I didn't see you there, Gabe.' Her laughter sounded thin, nervous.

He remained in the shadow of the house, but his voice was as clear and deep as the night air.

'Sorry, it's just that Trina doesn't like me smoking, so I have to hide. But it comes with the job. Newspaper editors always smoke. I've tried to quit many, many times but there are just some things that can't be quit.'

She drew her arms around her. Gabe had a way of talking that didn't seem to need a response, but she tried to think of something to say. 'It must be nice having a break from running a newspaper.' *Fake. Surface.* But she realised she wanted to seem normal to him and hated herself for how his perceived power affected her just like it affected everyone else.

'The reception here is pretty shit, but I can't say I miss having to make the big decisions for a few days. It never stops. The news never stops. Human hankering for drama never stops. Though we pretend we don't like reading bad news.'

'No, I don't suppose it does … stop, or that we stop … pretending,' Sylvie said, chastising herself for her eternal awkwardness.

Gabe dropped his cigarette and extinguished it with his foot. His hands went to his pockets. He stepped into the light. 'So, you're back in the Fowler fold. It's sure been a while.' His face held a question, as though she were his interview subject.

Sylvie felt the hair on the back of her neck prickle as he walked towards her, but it wasn't fear, it was something else. It felt like he was the only one honestly addressing what everyone else was thinking.

'We were always the hangers-on, weren't we?' he kicked at the ground, his mouth creasing into an unexpected smile. 'Tristan and Kase. And we just revered them, didn't we? Oh, to be let into their orbit, even for a summer. All those afternoons we spent at the beach.'

Transparent. Vulnerable.

Sylvie shifted to face him more fully. 'Yes, we were like little moons going around their warm sun.'

'Hmm. You were always good with words, Sylvie. Maybe you should be on my staff.'

It wasn't the job offer or its easy arrogance that made her breath catch. It was the first time he'd used her name for as long as she could remember. And he'd spoken it with more warmth than she thought him capable. More humility, in acknowledging the way in which they were the same, both still here, both still hanging on, perhaps still feeling like interlopers.

He took a cigarette pack out of his pocket and held it out to her. 'Remember all those times the four of us bummed cigarettes and smoked under the deck?' *Peace offering.* 'For old time's sake.'

She hesitated a moment. She didn't smoke, but she took one and let him light the tip, aware that she was no longer feeling on edge. She drew the smoke into her lungs. It burned like hot asphalt under bare feet, like sunburned skin, like memories seared into the mind.

Trina's voice carried on the wind. 'Gabe? I can smell your goddamn cigarette smoke. Come down. We're playing a party game and it needs Dad jokes.'

'Busted,' he said.

Sylvie laughed, and suddenly they were schoolkids hiding under the wooden slats, rays of light angling above, with Fran calling them all for dinner. Part of her was annoyed at herself for letting him disperse the tension so easily, especially after what she'd just witnessed in the kitchen. *I'm so needy for the past*, she thought.

He took both their cigarettes and extinguished them.

'Coming.' He walked away from her, down the slope towards the beach.

'Where's Sylvie? We can't start without her.' Kase's voice reached her on the wind.

She dug her hands into the pockets of her dress and followed. A light breeze eased over the sand now, tickling the flames of the fire, which had burned low. It was funny how predictably humans arranged themselves around a fire. Equidistant from the burning core, but close enough to feel the warmth. Holden had brought his red hunting hat after all. Kase was drinking from a bottle of whisky and Fran was sipping thoughtfully from a glass of red wine while staring into the fire.

Kase jumped up from her log and snuck her arm through Sylvie's, drawing her close. 'I thought we'd lost you for the night to the bath and *The Bell Jar*.'

Sylvie's chest contracted, the familiar ache. Like a magnet at once repelled and attracted. 'You nearly did. I'm not very social these days.'

Kase fixed her with a look. 'You were never very social, any of the days.'

Sylvie laughed despite herself. *Known. Seen.* 'Touché. Yes, I guess …'

'I still know you, Sylvie Dane.'

Kase handed her the bottle of whisky and she took a sip. The liquid burned pleasantly through her. Maybe it was Dutch courage, but she squeezed Kase's arm and took a deep breath. She needed to know what had just gone on in that kitchen, but first, she needed to stop pretending that no time had passed, that nothing had changed and that Kase hadn't ignored her for twenty-three years.

'Kase, you know me. Still, after all these years. It's amazing actually, as though no time has passed, but Kase, I –'

Rachel was suddenly upon them, squealing as she tackled Kase playfully from behind. She tugged the bottle from Sylvie's hands. 'Come on, bitches. Let's play.'

Sylvie resisted, but Rachel dragged them to the log next to the fire and sat them down as though they were wayward children. She clapped her hands. *God, this woman just needs a constant audience,* Sylvie thought.

'Okay. This is a party, people. We need games. As unofficial MC we're playing Two Truths and A Lie. We play it in rehearsal all the time to loosen up and it's hilarious.'

Her unbridled enthusiasm endeared Rachel to Sylvie for a split second, as though she'd glimpsed beneath the veneer to a vulnerable girl. The feeling discombobulated her.

'So, you've got to say three things about yourself and everyone has to guess which is the lie,' Rachel instructed. 'Everyone who guesses wrong has to take a sip of their drink. And naturally, the birthday girl has to start. Of course, it's going to be easy because we all know her so well.'

Sylvie felt Kase nestle into her arm, a gesture she knew meant Kase was reluctant.

'Oh God.' Kase ran her hands down her face. 'In front of my mum, really?'

'Mothers know a lot more than you give us credit for,' said Fran, raising her wineglass.

'Okay, give me a moment. Um. This is going to be lame. I … um … sometimes use a fake name at restaurants? I've been arrested? And I'm a terrible swimmer?' Kase cringed.

I know, will they? Sylvie thought.

Henry made a gesture as though he was swimming, and then drowning.

Rachel rolled her eyes and looked at Kase as though she were a child who hadn't understood the instructions. 'God. That's *waaaay* too easy, hon. As if you've ever been arrested. And we all know you can only do breaststroke and really badly, and that you don't like people to make a fuss of you at restaurants.'

'Sorry.' Kase hung her head and Sylvie gave her arm a reassuring squeeze. She hadn't known for sure about the restaurants, but she'd intuited that Kase wouldn't use her power to demand things from others.

Rachel pressed a hand to her chest. 'Okay, I'll start. It has to be a little bit risqué. There needs to be some *spice*.' Rachel cleared her throat as though she was about to go on stage. 'I had a dog called Drummy as a child and he was decapitated in a freak accident. I have an album on my phone with outfits I've already styled on myself for events. And … my first kiss was in front of my whole Year 6 class.'

Oh God, thought Sylvie.

'They all just sound so dramatically Rachel,' said Kase, reading Sylvie's mind.

They went around the circle, each struggling to pick Rachel's untruth.

'Sylvie? What do you think?' asked Rachel, when it came back around to her.

Sylvie took another swig of the whisky to hide the grimace that wanted to form on her face. 'Well, the dog sounds so far-fetched that it must be true. The outfit album sounds the most normal for your line of work, so it's probably the lie hiding in plain sight.'

Rachel slowly clapped her hands, shaking her head. 'Sylvie's the only one who got it. God, imagine, all my closest friends and family here, and the person I know least picked it.'

Person you like least, you mean. Sylvie felt the familiar knot of resentment tighten in her gut.

Rachel made a dismissive gesture. 'I would *never* be that organised. My other actress friends do it for events and get stylists to help, but I like dressing myself and spontaneity too much. Everyone else, drink up!'

'Poor Drummy the dog,' said Holden, sipping on his beer, and they all laughed. 'How did he get decapitated?' His mouth scrunched in sympathy.

You are a nice person, Sylvie thought.

'Gabe, do you want to tell the story?' Rachel asked with a flourish.

'How come I haven't heard about Drummy's tragic demise? I didn't know he was decapitated,' said Trina, elbowing her husband.

Gabe scratched the back of his neck. 'My darling sister is clearly intoxicated, so she's dug up the source of the family's greatest shame.' He glared at Rachel, but his mouth was twisted in dark amusement. 'Let's just say Dad was in a rush one day and Drummy didn't get out of the way of the tyres in time and well, Rach and I both saw what was left of his head. It came clean away from his body.'

'Poor Drummy. It's etched into my mind forever,' said Rachel, pouting.

'God,' said Trina.

'Can we play something a bit more joyful, please? This is a birthday party, a celebration of *life*, not death,' said Fran, making a face.

Kase shot Fran a disapproving glance.

We never stop feeling slightly embarrassed by our mums, thought Sylvie. But she felt sorry for Fran. She'd done so much to make this celebration wonderful for Kase.

'Okay, Fran. You've obviously got no skeletons in your closet. Give us some happy stuff,' said Rachel.

Fran's hands twisted in her lap. 'Well, I never said I had *no* skeletons ...'

Sylvie and Kase shared a look. *Collusion. Secret.*

'I just don't want to hear about a beloved pet's head being squished,' said Fran. Kase put a reassuring hand on her mother's arm. Fran's eyes were glazed with wine and she was clearly tipsy.

'Okay, I've got something to cheer you up,' Holden interjected. 'I once had a deaf cat that survived being run over three times.'

'Oh, good Lord,' said Fran.

'You wanted a happy story, Fran.' Holden smiled and rubbed his jaw.

'Okay. At least he lived.'

'And number two: I travelled to the other side of the world to see the Northern Lights and slept through my alarm. And three: this hat once belonged to a terrific friend of mine, who was the son of a famous author.'

A smile crept onto Sylvie's face. *Secret. Message.* The circle made their guesses, which were mostly that the cat was the lie to cheer up Fran, because how could a disabled cat *really* cheat death that many times? And then it was Sylvie's turn. The alcohol had made her bold. She met Holden's eye. 'While I won't call you a complete phony, you're the most terrific liar I've ever seen in my life.'

Holden took off his hat and bowed. 'Sylvie has indeed picked the lie.'

Sylvie felt herself flood with warmth.

'Err, did I miss something?' asked Rachel, taking a swig of the whisky.

'The hat was the lie,' said Kase. 'They're chanelling *Catcher in the Rye* to each other. As you do. Holden Caulfield always said everything was "terrific" and people were "phony".'

'What makes you so damn good at picking lies, Sylvie?' asked Rachel, her hand on her hip.

Sylvie felt her face grow hot under Rachel's gaze.

'Sylvie reads so much fiction that she lives in some liminal place between the blurred dream world of the author and reality,' said Kase. 'So, as a result, reality, truth, feels starker for her. Like a constant feeling of coming out of the cinema into a world of taxis and hamburgers and people on the footpath.' She nudged Sylvie. 'Am I right?'

Sylvie knew exactly what that felt like but instead she said, 'Err, that's very philosophical. Maybe. I guess so. You're the writer, you must have it too then.'

Kase bit her lip in thought. 'No, I use my fictional worlds to tell lies, to hide the truth, so that I can't tell what's real and what's not anymore.'

Her face fell into shadow and Sylvie wanted to ask her what that meant exactly, but Gabe spoke.

'Hey, journalists are pretty good at this stuff, too,' he said. 'I live squarely in harsh reality and so I know first-hand that truth is indeed stranger than fiction.'

'Then why aren't you better at this game?' asked Rachel. 'Okay, it's Henry's turn.'

Henry, who'd been silently observing from behind his glasses, legs and arms crossed in front of him, raised his eyebrows as if only just waking up. 'Oh, God. Really? Okay. Uh, I hate the French accent. I've read all of Kase's books twice, and I've never eaten McDonald's in my life.'

'Oh God, really? Are you that much of a snob?' Rachel asked, and Sylvie found herself laughing despite herself.

Kase scrunched up her face. 'You know, I'm actually not sure which is the lie.'

'You don't know if your own husband likes or dislikes the sexiest accent on the planet, how many times he's read your books or whether he's ever eaten Macca's?' Rachel cocked her head in disbelief.

They have an open marriage, thought Sylvie. *Why are you surprised?*

'Well, I've never seen him eat McDonald's in all the time we've been married. And I have no idea if he's read my books more than once. Though I'd highly doubt it. You haven't, have you? Hmmm.' She tapped a finger against her chin.

'Come on, Sylvie, give it to us. What's the answer?' asked Rachel, her voice resigned.

Her blood felt like it was rushing in her veins, from the alcohol, the heat and the tension and attention these intimate questions were creating. 'Oh, I'm not some kind of psychic ...' But they were all waiting for her, so she went on. 'Um, okay. I think he does hate the French accent, has read Kase's books twice.' *Out of guilt*, she thought. 'But he secretly loves McDonald's.' *Because he behaves like a boy and not a man.* 'So that's the lie?'

'Are you sure you're not psychic?' asked Henry, raising his glass to Sylvie and looking over the top of his glasses in mirth. She met his gaze.

Kase shook her head at her husband. 'McDonald's Really? Do you, like, squirrel it into the philosophy building at lunch?'

Henry shrugged. 'Sometimes. I like the pickles.'

Kase threw her hands up. 'And you think after ten years that you know everything about someone and it turns out you know nothing.'

'Unless you're Sylvie,' Holden clarified.

Sylvie felt his words surround her like a hug.

'Oh, yeah, well.'

Sylvie shook her head. 'I swear I honestly don't know how I'm doing this. I promise I'm the least psychic person on the planet.' She laughed and pressed her cool hands to her cheeks, flushed by Holden's attention.

Fran drained her glass. 'Me next.' Her words were slippery on her tongue.

'I once visited a psychic who told me something that came true and it's haunted me ever since.'

Everyone let out a joint 'Oooooh' sound. Sylvie and Kase exchanged a look.

'Um … I once ate two packets of Sao crackers in one sitting and threw up in the pool, and I had a fairy penguin as a pet for ten days.'

'Ohh, they're good ones. They're all weird. Truth is stranger than fiction. Gabe? This is your domain,' said Rachel.

Gabe screwed up his face in deep concentration. 'Oh, the pressure.' He rubbed his temples. 'This is worse than covering a breaking news story. Okay, the fairy penguin is the lie. I know what I just said about the truth being stranger than fiction, but that assaults my common sense. Those little guys are impossible to get a glimpse of, let alone catch as a pet.'

'I think you're overthinking it, bro. What does the almighty seer say?' asked Rachel, turning to Sylvie dramatically.

Sylvie rubbed her temples. 'Argh. The pressure.' She screwed up her mouth. 'I'm saying the psychic is the lie.'

Fran clapped delightedly. 'You're both wrong. The Saos was the lie. I ate a lot of Saos in my time, but I never threw them up.'

'Sylvie, you have been dethroned,' said Kase. 'Drink.'

Sylvie took a large swig of the whisky. She felt it spark in her veins.

'How the hell did you get a fairy penguin as a pet?' asked Gabe.

'We found it injured on the beach and nursed it back to health. It was the sixties, before you did things like call WIRES. We fed it dog food.'

'Wow,' said Gabe, shaking his head.

'So … the psychic? What did they predict that's haunted you ever since?' asked Trina.

Fran's face darkened. 'Oh.' She shook her head. 'Maybe that was a bit of an exaggeration. I'm getting confused. I think I've had a little too much wine.'

'Oh, Fran, you can't do that to us,' said Rachel.

'Oh, I …' Fran pressed a hand to her chest, her voice wavering. 'I don't like to talk about it … Sylvie just reminded me, talking of psychics …'

Kase put her arm around her mum. 'I think it might be time for some tea up at the house.'

'Come on!' said Rachel. 'Your psychic is the most interesting part of this whole night, aside from Henry's secret McDonald's fetish.'

He snorted.

Leave Fran alone, thought Sylvie. Kase shot Rachel a warning glance and helped her mother to her feet. Fran seemed frail, older, suddenly. Sylvie stood and took Fran's other arm, but everything wavered at the edge, like a mirage. The liquor had worked its way into her without her realising just how much.

'Oh, don't go yet! Okay, okay, at least stay for one more. Sylvie, what about your three?' Rachel pressed, like a bossy child who has been left out.

Sylvie was tired suddenly, so tired. The alcohol swam inside her, muddying her mind. The exhaustion of so much socialising without a break had finally caught up. She couldn't pretend to be normal any longer and she knew Rachel would just harass her until she capitulated. She realised it didn't matter what she said. None of these people really knew anything about her life as it was now. Not a thing. They only knew the past. That comfortable, safe cushioning of nostalgia between them. But it was a lie. The words tumbled out of her like underwater bubbles. Slow and rising to the surface.

'I have twenty-seven cacti in my courtyard. French linen sheets are my sole extravagance … aside from books. Many, many books. I am extraordinarily drunk. And I am *so* confused about why I was even invited to this party after all these years.'

She only realised what she'd said when she saw the look of hurt cross Kase's face and heard the silence of no one picking a lie.

SUMMER 1967

A peal of laughter startled Franny from her stupor. Her school uniform stuck to the backs of her legs and a tremor of sweat hovered above her lip. Ray's milk bar bustled with schoolkids, all waiting for one of his frothy cold delights to appease the afternoon heat.

Franny felt trepidation pull through her. The laughter had come from a group of girls at the far end of the milk bar. The Untouchables. They all lived and died for The Beatles and it was rumoured Audrey Wakefield, the beauty of the year, had gone backstage when the band toured here.

Even though she and Eve went to different schools – Franny to the expensive private school where the Untouchables reigned, Eve to the local high school down the road – Eve had already become a subject of gossip among these girls. Franny wondered how they knew her.

Eve slid into the booth, eyes flashing. 'Sorry, I was reading, and I totally lost track of time and missed my stop. It's a new novel, *Picnic at Hanging Rock*. Have you heard of it? It's so good. I can't wait for you to read it so we can discuss.'

Ray approached with a stainless steel milkshake cup. 'Hello, Miss Eve. My regards to your father, as always. Milkshake's on the house.'

'Thank you, Ray. I'll tell Dad you said hi. And thanks for the shake.'

'Your favourite.'

Eve slid the milkshake to Franny and watched her suck the thick, cold milk through the paper straw.

'I told you it was the best milkshake on the planet.'

'Oh, it's out of sight,' said Franny, the cold sweetness numbing her mouth pleasantly.

'So, you know Ray personally, do you?' Franny turned to find the languid voice attached to Audrey Wakefield, hairband perfect in her cropped hair, hip out, eyebrow arched.

'Oh, hi Audrey,' said Franny, licking the mix of sweet froth and salty sweat from her top lip.

'I didn't realise you two were so friendly.'

Eve threw her arm around Franny. 'Hi, Audrey Wakefield. Me and Franny are like sisters, actually.'

'As far as I'd heard, you've just moved into Franny's old granny flat at the bottom of her garden. Get thrown out of another backyard, did you?'

Franny felt Eve stiffen. How did she know about that? Franny lowered her eyes and took another sip of the milkshake. Eve was beautiful, motherless, with a charismatic father who let her run wild. All things that should have made her the envy of these girls. Maybe they did envy her, and so saw her as a threat. Franny wished she had the strength to stand up to Audrey, to claim Eve, but she felt herself shrink under Audrey's cool gaze.

Audrey's face transformed suddenly, softening, her mouth growing full, like a smiling feline. 'Teddy. Hello there. We don't see you around these parts much,' she cooed.

'I've come to see Franny, actually.' Teddy's tone was cool, but it warmed Franny's heart and she felt herself blush. He slid into the other side of the booth as though it was the most natural thing in the world, stretching his brown arms on the table and leaning back into the sticky leather. Teddy was the kind of person who always looked like he belonged, no matter where he was.

Franny knew Teddy liked Audrey about as much as a pin in the eye. It was pure coincidence that he was here, but he wasn't going to let Audrey know that. She exchanged a knowing smile with him, and Franny felt lit up by it.

Audrey took a silver flask from her pocket. 'Want a dash in your milkshake?' she asked, clearly trying to impress Teddy.

Eve grabbed the bottle from Audrey's hand and took a swig. Her face betrayed nothing of the burn that Franny knew would be scorching the back of her throat.

'We prefer things straight up,' said Eve, locking eyes with Audrey.

Teddy stifled a laugh.

Audrey snatched the flask from Eve and fixed her with a stare. 'I gotta split. You know where we are, Teddy, if you want to have some real fun.' She turned and flouted off to join the Untouchables who were craning their necks to see what had just transpired.

Teddy stuck his hand out across the table for Eve to shake. 'I've been so jolly busy with my finals, we haven't really met properly, but I see you and Franny have been hanging loose, which makes me know I'll like you. I already admire you because we have a common enemy.'

'Oh, that girl. She's insufferable,' said Eve.

Franny again felt the warmth of Teddy's words and glances. She cleared her throat, suddenly feeling the need to introduce them properly. 'Teddy, this is Eve. Eve, this is Teddy, my … our neighbour.'

'I've heard music coming from the granny flat,' he said. 'I see you've discovered Jim Morrison too.'

Eve pressed her hands to her chest. 'Oh my God. "Light My Fire" or "The End"? If you *had* to choose.'

Teddy rubbed his chin, lowered his voice. He began to sing 'The End'. Franny felt herself blush at how magnetic and brooding he looked with those words issuing from his mouth. It was a different Teddy from the one she usually saw – darker, more daring.

Eve grabbed his hand, her voice matching his in drama as they sang the words looking fiercely into each other's eyes.

Teddy's face grew serious as he reached the spoken word part of the song, the bit about the son wanting to kill the father, that frankly, Franny found a bit creepy. She jumped as he suddenly let out a high-pitched scream just as Jim Morrison did on the record. Every eye in the place flicked towards them.

Eve was transfixed. Teddy's eyes blazed. They laughed, their bodies moving towards each other, and it felt like they had entered a different realm from Franny. Words flew between them, flitting like translucent wings as they traded lyrics. Jumping into their conversation felt like trying to get the timing right jumping over the tracks between oncoming trains. Franny felt her heart contract. Her connection with Teddy was through The Beatles, through Ringo – she was unsettled by this darker version of him that Eve and her Door's obsession had unleashed.

'So, what's the deal with you and Audrey anyway? How does she know you and that you're living in the granny flat?' Franny eventually asked, managing to break the spell between them.

Eve shrugged. 'Girls like that always hate me. We were at the same school for about a term at one point. That's all it took for her to have an unwavering interest in my life, apparently.'

'Why only a term?'

'We moved again. I've lost track of how many schools I've been in.'

'You and your family move around a lot?' asked Teddy, scratching behind his ear in a way Franny found adorable.

'It's just me and Dad, and yeah, we're itinerants. I used to hate all the chopping and changing, but now I'm used to it. Though if he tries to separate me and Franny too soon, I'll kick up a stink all right.'

Franny felt the train slow down, Eve's words surround her like a caress. 'No. You're not allowed to leave. We just found each other. Can you believe it's only been a few weeks? It feels like I've known you forever.'

'How do you know we haven't known each other forever?' asked Eve, inclining her head towards Franny like a cat wanting to be stroked.

Franny patted her head. 'You're my soul kitty cat.'

'Meow.'

They both laughed.

'I'd love to get out of my boring life, move around a bit,' said Teddy.

'As long as there's a beach nearby,' said Franny.

'Well, yeah.'

'And tell me,' said Eve leaning back into the red leather of the booth. 'What do you read, Teddy?' Eve's fingers skimmed over the cover of *Picnic at Hanging Rock*.

He shook his head and Franny found her shoulders dropping in relief.

'Not a reader. Not if the surf's up,' he said.

His Valiant sedan grumbled at dawn every morning outside her window and she wondered when the next time would be that he'd ask her along.

Their conversation went back to The Doors, but Franny knew with a rush of relief that she wasn't going to lose Teddy to Eve, or Eve to Teddy, any time soon.

CHAPTER 13

harbour *(n.)* – any place of shelter or refuge.
(v.) – to conceal; give a place to hide.

'Ah, I'm pretty sure that was four truths … and no lie,' said Holden, who was suddenly by Sylvie's side. The fire burned low, only the embers glowing. 'Which was, technically, cheating.'

When Sylvie didn't take her eyes off the fire he reached out and touched her arm. 'Are you okay, Sylvie Plath?'

She moved over on the log so he could sit down. She felt like she was dissolving in the heat of the fire, into the alcohol in her blood. She just wanted to lie down and close her eyes. 'I don't have twenty-seven cacti, I only have twenty-five. I'm not *that* much of a freak. And I really like your hat.' She patted his head as though it was a small animal and he laughed.

'Okaaay. So, there *was* a lie. And I think we've established that you're very fond of my hat.'

'Have we though?' she asked. Their eyes met and, as much as she tried to, she couldn't draw hers away. She felt the twang when their connection finally snapped.

'Well, you sure know how to wrap up a party fast,' he said.

Kase had recoiled as though Sylvie had slapped her with her words, and Sylvie had waited for a biting retort, but Kase turned inward, her shoulders rounding as she put her arm protectively around Fran, who was looking exhausted. Kase turned her back on Sylvie, guiding Fran up the beach towards the house. Sylvie felt guilt and sadness ache through her, making it hard to swallow. And then Rachel was at Kase's side, seizing on the fissure that had just opened up.

'Ah, I should go and check on the kids,' Trina had laughed awkwardly. 'We all got a bit carried away with the whisky, didn't we?'

Sylvie was grateful for her diverting the group's focus away. Henry and Gabe had both agreed, and drained their drinks, and they'd all made their way up the sand to the house, which glowed against the bank of dark bush.

The beach was deserted now, save for a flock of gulls roosting on the sand, white ghosts that took off and hovered before settling again.

'Do you want me to help you back to the house? I'm not sure I'd trust your balance at this point,' Holden said. 'I've just got a bit of cleaning up to do here, but I'll leave the bulk of it for the morning.'

'No,' she said. 'I'll just sleep on the beach.'

His eyebrows lifted. 'Will you now?'

'I don't belong here.'

Holden grimaced. 'So you told everyone.'

'Well, what am I supposed to think? Radio silence for twenty years and then it's all back on. We're all buddy-buddy besties divulging all our secrets?' Sylvie felt her jaw clench.

'But didn't you say you and Kase just picked up from where you left off? That you had that kind of friendship? You seem close to Fran, too.'

'Where we left off was a night just like this. A summer party where her brother fell over a cliff and then she visited me in hospital once when I was unconscious. Even though she knew I loved him too.' She felt tears wet her skin and she rubbed them away with the heel of her hand. 'And then nothing. I reached out for months.'

'Oh,' said Holden. He got up and poured Sylvie a glass of water. 'Here, drink this.'

She drank, feeling the cool water move through her, clearing her mind a little. She looked past the fire to the dark waves, glowing like white horses galloping to shore.

'Do you think I ruined the birthday party?'

Holden smiled. 'Kase doesn't strike me as someone to have a fabulous night ruined by one little truth.'

'But it isn't a little truth. And she's actually very sensitive.'

His eyes held a question.

'What?' she asked.

'Why don't you just go and talk to her? Ask her what happened. She knows now that she hurt you.'

'No, no, I can't. I can't go back up there. Can you take me back to the mainland?'

'What, now? You can't just leave. And you're in no state.'

Sylvie stood on unsteady legs and brushed sand from her lap. 'I stayed for the party. It's done. I'll just sneak up to the house and get my stuff at dawn and … go …'

Holden shook his head, but his voice was soft. 'Not a good idea, Sylvie Plath. You have to sort things out with Kase, or you'll just be wondering for the next twenty years. Another abandonment. Another question left unanswered.' His face darkened. 'Believe me. You don't want that.'

She looked into his eyes and the pain she found there told her that he was talking about Pippi. He took her hand. It was warm and rough. She let him pull her back down to sitting. It felt like the most natural thing in the world to rest her head on his shoulder.

'I'm not going back up there tonight.'

He took his hat off and pulled it over her head with such tenderness that tears welled again. 'You're going to need this to keep warm.'

She swallowed back the salty tears in her throat. 'Thank you.'

'I'll stay on the beach with you. We've got blankets and leftover cake.'

'Oh, cake,' she said, and he laughed.

They cut thick slices of the chocolate layer cake that had been fashioned into the shape of a book with gold-edged pages and a blue cover. Holden boiled water for tea over the low fire. They licked the sticky icing from their fingers and washed it down with black tea that scalded their mouths.

Sylvie spread a blanket on the sand and lay down, pulling another blanket over her. The sand moulded to her body and Holden's hat was warm and she felt the welcome tug of sleep.

Holden sat down next to her with his arm resting on a bent knee. 'Not a bad plan, Sylvie Plath. Not bad at all. Look at those stars.'

They both looked up into a sky awash with starlight. The silence that fell between them was filled by the soft rush of waves, the quiet calls of the nesting gulls.

'Thanks for staying,' she said. 'Now that I'm sobering up, I feel terrible about spoiling the party.'

'You couldn't help it. *In vino veritas.* The truth is in the wine.'

'Holden, what would you have said if you were just telling three truths in that game?' Sylvie asked.

He lay down beside her and she offered him some blanket. She could feel his body heat.

His voice was as soft and fine as the sand. 'I've only been in love once. I don't read books anymore because it's too painful. I miss my old life.'

Sylvie let his words sink into her. *Stripped. Bare. Vulnerable.* She knew not to speak, not yet.

'Do you ever feel like you're living on the periphery of your own life, Sylvie Plath? Like you know what it was meant to look like, but you can't get there?'

She turned her face to look at him. She could feel his breath, he was so close. 'Yes,' she said simply.

'Back at the cabin it really threw me when you asked about why I had no books. No one's ever asked me that. I don't think I'd even realised, not consciously.'

She nodded in recognition. She knew that things were tied together under the surface in ways that were hard for the conscious mind to fathom.

He took a deep breath and rubbed at his jaw. He kept looking up at the stars. His face in profile was strong, beautiful. 'I stopped reading after Pippi died.'

'Oh,' She couldn't help the word, which sprang from her mouth like a sigh.

'I know, it's strange. But … it's hard to explain. Books, words, were my life. Our life. I taught English at her high school.

Books were a portal between our two worlds. Even as she grew up, as she hit being a teenager, we could still communicate with stories. Ever since she was a little girl I read to her every night, and even though I didn't sit on her bed and read her *The Hobbit* anymore, I'd buy her books and leave them on the end of her bed, especially if she was having a rough time. And she'd leave books on my bed, too. And because of that, even if we were busy, or feeling resentful about something with each other, it always felt like we understood each other on a deeper level, you know? Like the books protected something between us. Protected her. Books had always been there for me – to teach me, reassure me, keep me feeling safe in life. But they didn't … I couldn't …' He covered his face with his hands.

'Oh, Holden.' She put her hand lightly on his arm. She could feel his turmoil, like a cold current beneath his warm surface.

He kept staring at the sky as though speaking to the stars. 'I couldn't protect her. She was fifteen. Words in books couldn't protect her, and somehow I'd thought they could. So naive. I thought they could buffer her against life, but I was so stupid.'

She kept her hand on his arm and stayed very still, as though calming a wounded animal. *Quiet. Careful.* She knew if she contradicted him about his perceived folly he would cower or bolt.

'Holden, I'm so sorry.' As she spoke, tears spilled down her cheeks and he turned his head and saw them.

He gave her a sad, watery smile.

'Can I ask you what happened? How Pippi died?'

He sniffed and wiped under his eyes. It took him a long time to answer. 'She got into a car with her friends and never got out again.'

Sylvie heard herself make a noise, as though all the air had been pushed out of her lungs.

'And after that, stories didn't seem … enough. It all seemed flimsy. Unreal. Indulgent.'

'I can understand that,' she said. *It would be terrifying to live a life without stories*, she thought.

'I had to leave it all behind. It was too painful to stay in that life after she was gone. I worked with teenagers … and books.'

It hadn't been easy to see the scars on Holden. But they were cut into him and barely healed over. If you ran your fingers over them they would be mountains. Now she understood the moment with the chick on the headland.

'I've wanted to just keep moving. Doing things with my hands until I'm exhausted and fall into bed. That's why I took this job. There's always so much to do.'

A haunting cry floated in the wind and Holden raised himself onto his elbows. He pointed towards the headland. The eagles that mate for life soared low over the horizon before swooping back up into the dark trees.

'Aren't their cries at night meant to foretell danger?' She shivered under the thin blanket.

He didn't respond as they listened to the eagle's mournful song, and it sounded like the grief of parents who have lost a child.

'I don't think I've ever heard anything so beautiful as what you and Pippi shared with your books. I'm sorry that she's gone … and that they carry such pain for you now. I know I hide in my books. They're my crutch. My real life feels … like I'm always waiting for the quest to start, you know? The grand adventure that propels the hero into the story. But it never happens. I feel like there's some big life out there. But I can't grasp it. There's a line in *The Bell Jar*. Esther sees her life branching out before her, like a green fig tree: "From the tip of every branch, like a fat purple fig, a wonderful future beckoned and winked."

'One of the figs represents marriage and children, another fig represents her being a famous poet and another a brilliant professor. But Esther can't decide. She's immobilised. And so, she sees the figs wrinkle and blacken and drop to the ground and she starves.'

She looked at Holden and his eyes were dark and shining like the water.

'Maybe it's just because I've read too many books.' She laughed sadly. 'We don't all get the grand adventure. The bigger meaning. I mean, why do I even expect it? Poor Pippi. I'm so sorry, Holden.' Tears spilled down her face. 'Life is hard and painful at worst. Ordinary at best. It breaks my heart to say that.'

Holden very gently used his thumb to brush the tear from her cheek. 'Sylvie Plath, you're like someone I dreamed up.'

She smiled. 'You did. Sylvie Plath doesn't exist.'

'I feel like she does.'

'I am transparent though. Like a ghost moving through life.'

'I see you,' he said, finding her hand under the blanket, threading his fingers through hers. He moved closer, so they were both lying on their backs, like two stars fallen from the sky.

A feeling, as luminous as the infinite swirls above, brightened her chest. *Dazzling. Inconceivable.*

They stayed like that for a long time, still and quiet, listening to the eagles that couple for life call to each other, and to the wash of the shore breathing, until they fell asleep.

SPRING 1996

The bush dazzled them – cicadas shrill in the trees, sun bright under a high blue sky. An earthy scent rose from the track and mingled with the salt spray coming off the sea. She and Sylvie were behind the boys on the overgrown track. No one spoke. It was too hot for words. But it was better than sitting in maths class with Mr Rider, the airless room smelling like broiled human flesh. Kase had finally convinced Sylvie to wag school. She envied Sylvie's absolute freedom. She'd simply told Evangeline that she was feeling tired and was going to read in bed today, and her bohemian mother had scrawled a note saying her daughter was having a rest day, and left her in the house.

Kase had concocted an elaborate list of sicknesses that could not be tested with a thermometer. She'd gone with a simple gastro bug and had, she thought, made a pretty convincing show of doubling over in pain. She knew Fran would be too busy getting out of the house herself to insist she go to school. It was one of her mother's two work days at the local library.

Sylvie and Kase had made detailed plans. They would catch a bus into the city and walk through Hyde Park, buy rosary beads at St Mary's Cathedral and solemnly light candles and pretend they were in Europe. They would walk up to Glebe and drink strong coffee at Badde Manors and try to pick the Arts students and the boys they might next year fall in love with. They would try to buy cigarettes and if they succeeded, smoke them nonchalantly on street corners.

But as soon as Tristan's eyes met Kase's over her uneaten breakfast, he'd shaken his head, miming his disbelief at her farce behind their mother's back. And Gabe was the one with the access to liquor and cigarettes, and so somehow now they were all going to the boys' favoured swimming spot – a place that was always deserted because the only way to get there was via an overgrown bush track. And of course, Sylvie had immediately wanted to go because of Tristan. Kase had rolled her eyes and briefly mourned the day they had planned together in the city, but the truth was, she wanted Sylvie to be happy, and being around her brother did that.

They reached the place where the trees met the sea, kneeling down with their knotted branches as though to sip from an azure pond. It was a tiny cove scooped out of the coast like an afterthought. The boys ran onto the powdery sand, their torsos already naked, already baked brown by the spring sun. They dived in and emerged glistening like wild sea creatures. She and Sylvie followed, relieved when their feet met the lip of the sea. The water was like a long, cool sigh.

They watched the ferries make their way past the heads, heaving their bulk over the swell like old men with bad hips. Gulls called to each other on the wind. There were no breaking waves, just the gentle push and pull of the undercurrents, colder below than on the surface.

'Shark!' yelled Gabe, and Kase felt a surge of adrenalin throttle through her. Tristan sent a pelt of water at his friend's head, laughing.

Kase gasped with relief. 'Dickhead,' she shouted. 'Don't do that. There could be.'

She looked over at Sylvie, waist deep in the water. Her skin had taken on a blue tinge, as though the blood had stopped pumping through her body.

'There is one,' Sylvie said, still frozen, her voice barely audible above the loud throng of nature. And then it was as though she suddenly kicked into life. 'Out! Get out!' she cried.

Tristan and Gabe were rushing through the water towards the shore. Kase felt their bodies collide with her, collect her, looping their arms under her armpits. They stood on the beach and shielded their eyes against the glare. She saw it then, sluicing through the water like a knife. A perfect triangle. A harbinger of doom. It looked like a scene out of *Jaws*. None of them said anything. Their bodies were rigid with the visceral knowledge of how close they had come to real danger. They watched the triangle until it slipped beneath the water.

Gabe waded into the shallows up to his shins. 'What do you reckon? A great white? My pick's a bull shark. Come on. Who dares go back in?'

Tristan hugged Kase from behind, toppling her to the sand. 'You okay, sis? Freaked out enough?'

Kase pushed him away, brushed the sand from her knees and stood. 'Don't be a dag.'

'What's the dare?' asked Sylvie. She had regained her colour and stood with her hands on her hips.

'Whoever swims out the farthest without stopping wins.'

Kase shot both her friends a look of disbelief. As if anyone was going back in that goddamn water.

'Wins what?' Sylvie asked.

'Dude, you totally crazy,' said Tristan, shaking his head slowly.

'Our U2 tickets,' said Gabe. 'Sold out show.'

'Don't you dare.' Tristan punched him in the arm.

'Dude, she's not going to do it.'

'You sure about that?' Sylvie dug her toe into the sand and met Gabe's eye.

'Syl, he's just being an idiot. Ignore him,' said Kase.

'If I win, what will you give *me*?' asked Gabe, his chest puffed out.

'My mum's weed plant.'

'Done,' said Gabe, walking into the water, shoulders squared.

Kase caught Sylvie's arm. 'He's just baiting you. It's all bravado, you know Gabe. Don't do it. It could still be out there.'

'We're going to that concert.' Sylvie's arm slipped from her grasp like a fish, and then she and Gabe were neck and neck in the water, arms cutting a path through the place where the aquamarine turned dark blue.

Kase felt her stomach drop. 'Tristan, stop them,' she cried but her brother only shook his head, his arms braced around his body.

She scanned the water for the stealth shape. It was true, Sylvie had always had more mettle than her. She was so soft and wafty, until she wasn't. There was something galvanising just below her serene surface, like a cold current drawing around an ankle, like the place where the coastal shelf fell away to deep water. Kase supposed the pain in Sylvie gave her this courage. It wasn't apparent to everyone, but it was apparent to Kase. She didn't really know how to articulate it, but it was to do with a sense of security, of love. Sylvie didn't have the emotional safety net that Kase knew she and Tristan had, would always have. She was more vulnerable, but it made her tougher, harder, as though she somehow had less to lose. Because maybe, truth be told, she did.

They were far out now, almost in the slip stream made by passing vessels. Kase yelled their names but her voice was lost on the hot salty breeze. The wind had picked up, frothing and churning the water further out.

'Oh, they've reached a buoy, thank God,' said Tristan, hands on top of his head, squatting on the sand. 'Bloody hell, they're far out though. They'd better be more scared of the boats than the shark at this point.'

Kase squinted into the burning sun. Their two forms were clinging to a white buoy. Were they in distress? Would they come back? Who had won? Surely they wouldn't keep going. They'd get pulled into the wake of one of the ferries.

They were both coming back. Relief rushed through her and she dropped to her knees. The water in the shallows felt as warm as a bath. But their bodies seemed too small against the swell. They were tiring. It was still such a long way in.

'Tristan, go out, will you? Help them. They're getting tired.'

'I can't. They'll just grab onto me. That's the first rule of lifesaving.'

'God, why didn't we bring boogie boards or something.' Kase's gut clenched with regret.

One of them had stopped. It was Gabe. Had he seen the shark? Felt it? Kase shivered at the thought of a dark shape beneath their legs. His head was bobbing on the surface, as pale as the whitewash. And then he was gone. It was impossible to tell if he'd gone under or was just hidden by the peak and trough of the swell. She scanned the water. 'Where is he? Can you see him?'

'Shit,' said Tristan, wading into the water, ready to swim out, but Kase could tell he was scared too.

And then Sylvie was swimming back to where Gabe had been. And somehow the two of them were both there again, treading water next to each other.

'What are they doing?' asked Kase.

'I don't know,' said Tristan.

'Go out to them, help them,' yelled Kase, her heart drumming in her chest. But Tristan remained in the shallows, his body rigid.

Kase rushed at the water, suddenly up to her waist. She was about to dive in when she saw Sylvie wave. It wasn't a wave of distress, but to say they were okay. And then they were swimming again towards the shore.

'What the hell?' Kase cried when they were within earshot. She dragged them both out of the water. 'You idiots!'

'What the hell happened out there?' asked Tristan.

But neither Gabe nor Sylvie spoke. They couldn't speak. They collapsed onto the sand, Gabe spread-eagled like a stingray in the shallows and Sylvie bent over, looking like she might be sick. They stayed like that for a long time, with Kase rubbing Sylvie's back.

There was no talk of who had won or lost U2 tickets or weed plants. They picked their way back through the track, the dried salt prickling their backs. The bush had grown silent with the thick lethargy of afternoon.

Gabe drove them back to Palm Beach with the radio loud, and even though Fran might come home and find them not at school, they didn't care. They had endured bigger things than a mother's rage. They made themselves toasted sandwiches and drank Midori and lemonade with ice out of plastic tumblers while watching *Jaws*. Somehow by laughing at the absurdity of an enormous shark they were able to process and dismiss what they'd actually experienced. No one mentioned the dare, or what had happened out there in the swell, but Kase felt Gabe's silent humiliation shimmy along her skin, refracting like the light through the trees outside. Sylvie didn't make eye contact with him and she was subdued, they all were, until the giant shark bit a body in half and they laughed hysterically like that couldn't have possibly happened to them.

CHAPTER 14

hope *(v.)* – to trust in the truth of a matter.

Sylvie opened her eyes. Dawn colluded with the smooth horizon so that she imagined she could almost see beyond where the world ended. The sky had hushed the sea – daybreak's spell. The night came back to her, gossamer thin, like a thread, a web she had to follow and unstick in her mind. *The eagles. Holding hands. The stars.* Ever since the accident her memory was not something she could trust. It was as hazy as old photographs. As slippery as thoughts. Maybe that's why she trusted written words. They were solid. You could commit them consciously to memory and always find them again.

The sadness of the night came back to her, too. Holden's deep loss. Kase's hurt face. The whisky. The thump of her hangover had begun at the base of her skull. And Holden was gone. Now she felt the coldness of dawn in her bones. How alone she was on this beach.

Had it all been a dream? A story she'd read once?

She sat up and saw his words, etched into the sand with a stick.

Good morning, Sylvie Plath. Today we will eat figs.

She laughed, a full sound. Her heart was beating fast. She reached out to trace his sand message, written in cursive. No, not with a stick, *a feather.* White, tapered. It lay next to the full stop. It was not a gull's feather. *No, this is an eagle's feather.*

She ran her fingers over its soft plume and drew her knees to her chest. The light of the new sun felt like a tender kiss. She wished Holden was here so she could say to him, *Do you ever find yourself in a single moment and it feels like it might be the most perfect of your life? And you wish you could still time forever and live in the perfect promise of it?*

She stood and looked down the beach towards the headland and Holden's cabin. She looked up at the house. Its windows winked like bright eyes in the morning light. Her instinct drew her towards the cabin, but she remembered Holden's words from last night. *Another abandonment.* She would have to face Kase today. She shivered and drew the blanket close. Holden had packed up the detritus from the party. Only the table remained, like a skeleton picked clean of flesh.

She took the feather and wrote her reply: *That sounds terrific, Holden Caulfield.*

She wanted to wait for his return, but she knew why he'd left. What she must do. She could feel his care and intention for her – it felt as soft as the sand beneath her fingers. She folded the blanket that had held them for the night and placed it on the table. She left the beach and walked up the dune, the grass and shrubs strung with morning dew. She held her breath as she opened the front door. Silence. The house was like a sleeping dog, twitching, on the edge of wakefulness as the light crept through it. She poured herself a glass of water and drank thirstily, then tiptoed up the stairs. Her room was cold, and she closed the door quietly behind her. She was about to strip and crawl into bed when she saw her. Kase was huddled under a blanket at the window seat overlooking the beach, *The Bell Jar* next to her face. A feeling as tender as the morning light moved in Sylvie. Had she been watching over her on the beach? Waiting for her to return?

She dared not move. She felt suspended, as though she were a butterfly pinned, her wings stretched from her body. *Inert.* Her breath sounded too loud. She backed towards the door, but the floorboards creaked in protest and Kase stirred, her eyes slits against the light.

'Syl?' Her voice was thick with sleep.

Syl. How long has it been since you called me that? 'Sorry, I … I didn't mean to wake you.'

'No, sorry, I must have fallen asleep.' Kase wiped the side of her face, the skin crinkled. Blinked.

'I slept on the beach. I mean, I fell asleep on the sand … I was so drunk.'

Kase sat up with difficulty, rubbed her eyes. 'We all were. Oh my God.' She pressed a palm to her forehead.

Sylvie went to the jug of water on the side table and filled a cup. 'Here. This will help.'

Kase drank the water and closed her eyes. Took a deep breath. 'I finished the book.'

'You did?'

'Yep. Possibly the first time I've ever beat you to it.'

Sylvie smiled. 'How do you know I haven't finished it?'

'You still fold your pages. A travesty.'

Sylvie rolled her eyes but smiled. 'What did you think?'

Kase ran her hand over the cover. 'I know how Esther feels … inside the bell jar.' She flicked to a page that she'd marked. '"To the person in the bell jar, blank and stopped as a dead baby, the world itself is a bad dream."'

Why would your near perfect life feel like a bad dream, Sylvie thought. But instead she said, 'I haven't got to that bit yet.'

Kase crossed her legs and tucked them under her. She pushed her hair behind her ears. 'Sylvie, what you said last night. Did you really mean that? That you don't know why I invited you here?'

Sylvie's hand impulsively found her notebook in the pocket of her dress. She needed to get the panic rising inside her out. Instead, she grabbed *The Bell Jar* from beside Kase, a shield of sorts, smoothed the worn cover. Pressed it to her chest. She couldn't look Kase in the eyes. 'It's just … I don't … You're kind of a big deal. I'm just …'

Kase reached out and grabbed her arm. 'Don't you feel it? Our connection? It's like no time has passed. We can still read each other … like an open book.'

Sylvie felt conflicting emotions move through her. 'But Kase, the book was closed, wasn't it? When Tristan died. And I feel like … I feel like I've missed the main part of the story. I'm just here for the ending, but …' She looked out at the sun sliding behind low clouds.

'I know you loved him too, Sylvie.'

Sylvie shook her head. 'It's not about him anymore. I feel bad to say that but … Kase, you never called me after the accident.' Her voice wavered and tears gathered behind her eyes. She swallowed them back. 'I must have reached out to you what? Twenty times at least. More. I know your brother had just died, but my friend had just died too. And I was recovering from a brain injury. It was so hard. I needed you.'

Kase looked into her lap. She bit her thumbnail and looked out at the sea. A single tear slipped down her face, but she brushed it away quickly. 'I'm so sorry. I didn't know what to say.'

Sylvie's chest ached. 'You didn't know what to say? I didn't need you to say anything, I just needed you there. You guys were like my family. You *were* my family.'

'I …' Kase shifted uncomfortably.

'And you didn't say *anything* ever again to me for more than twenty years. And then you invite me here and it's like nothing happened. What am I supposed to think?'

The silence felt too thick, too charged. Blue black like thunderstorm air.

Kase swallowed, her hands twisting in her lap. 'Sylvie, I'm so sorry. I'm sorry, I … I still don't know what to say.'

Sylvie shook her head. 'What? Why? I don't understand.'

Kase bit at her lip. 'I've realised these past years, I just … I missed you too much. But maybe it was selfish of me to invite you here.'

'Selfish? Why?'

Kase's eyes filled with tears. She closed them and they spilled down her face. She took a deep ragged breath.

'I don't understand.' Sylvie felt pressure building behind her eyes.

'Do you really want to know?' Kase asked. 'Because Sylvie, hitting your head like you did, it was a small mercy that you didn't remember. That you don't remember. Can't we just leave things where they lay and still be friends? Can't we let the past rest?'

Panic stretched through Sylvie's chest and her words came out breathless. 'What are you talking about, Kase?'

She shook her head. 'We were all so drunk. We were acting stupid. God, we were young. So young. It was all just a horrible accident. No one meant for it to happen.'

'I know. I know all this. It was awful that Tristan fell. And I know you were in shock and grieving, but so was I. Why did you shut me out? Why couldn't you talk to me? Why couldn't we help each other through that time? I lost everything all at once. Him and you.'

Kase went very still. She looked out the window. The wind had picked up. The water had become choppy, as agitated as Sylvie felt.

'Are you trying to tell me something else happened that night?'

Kase shook her head, a sad smile on her lips. 'You could always read my mind. I never wanted to have this conversation. I never …' She looked into her eyes and the depth of the sadness Sylvie saw there felt like an arrow piercing her sternum.

'Sylvie, you told Tristan your true feelings for him that night, and … he didn't take you seriously. He laughed at you, and you were … humiliated, and just devastated. Understandably. And drunk. We all were. You were upset, angry. You launched at him. You pushed him, and he … he stumbled backwards and … he fell. It wasn't your fault. It was just a terrible, terrible accident.'

Sylvie felt her body go cold, as though all the blood had stopped flowing through it. She felt herself shaking her head and a deep pain tore through her chest. *No*, she thought. *No, no, no, no.*

Kase reached out and took her hand, pressed it between hers. It was much warmer. Cloying. Sylvie snatched her hand away. 'What? I don't –'

'You don't remember. I know. We were all so thankful in a way that you didn't, and that the doctors said you had memory loss, and that you might never fully recover your memory of the night.' Kase paused and looked into her lap. 'I saw him go over and it has haunted me my whole life. I will never unsee that moment as long as I live. I was in shock. And then … I pushed you. I'm so sorry. I didn't know what I was doing, just like you didn't know what you were doing. We were all acting on instinct. Bad instinct. Teenage drunken instinct. And you hit your head. And the blood. It was everywhere. And Tristan was gone. And Sylvie … it all just happened so fast.'

Sylvie's words stuck in her throat like fish bones. 'No. I couldn't have. I'd remember. I wouldn't have … I would never …'

Kase reached for her again. 'I'm sorry. I'm so sorry for telling you. I'm sorry for not telling you. I just … I didn't know how to talk to you. I didn't know how to process everything that had happened. In the space of a few minutes our whole world was destroyed. I thought I was protecting us all. You, Fran. That it was better for you to forget. And I'd already lost Tristan. I couldn't lose you too. But I realise now that I did lose you, and I …' Tears filled her eyes again. 'I wanted at least one of you back. And that's why you're here. I've missed you my whole life.' She wiped her tears away and her eyes met Sylvie's.

Sylvie stepped away from Kase and stumbled, falling to the floor, her bad leg failing her. An image of that dead chick came to her. Its legs bent back the wrong way.

Kase rose to help her, but Sylvie shielded herself with her arm. 'Don't.' She scrambled to her feet and turned, making for the door.

'Sylvie, wait. Don't go. I'm sorry for hurting you. This is what I was afraid of … Don't –'

But Sylvie was already out the door. Everything was a blur. She stumbled down the stairs, aware that she was probably waking everyone in the house. She didn't care. Let them wake. She felt like she'd been woken from the deepest slumber, mid-dream. Reality was too bright. Caustic. It burned her skin. She had to get away. She needed to find Holden to take her to the mainland. It had been a mistake coming here. It felt like the past had been torn open, its neat stitches ripped and its guts spilling, too warm, too sticky. Like some long-wounded animal that was still rotting. She couldn't breathe – the stench was too much.

The wind had picked up, and whipped her hair about her face. The soft morning she'd woken to felt like a lifetime ago. She headed onto the sand. Cold droplets stung her face. It was raining. Or maybe she was crying. She couldn't tell. She found herself walking towards the headland, towards Holden's cabin. She didn't know where else to go. Her body felt as heavy as the lone broken log on the beach. Her foot had begun to drag, and she cursed it. Cursed herself.

Just as she was about to leave the sand for the bush, she turned to see the house. Was Kase still at the window in her room? Still watching her? Self-loathing rolled through her. That was why Kase and Gabe had been acting so strange in the kitchen. It was herself, not Kase, who she should be angry with right now. It was her own mind that had deceived her all these years. Kase's words followed her like a horrible song she couldn't get out of her head.

You were upset, angry. You launched at him. You pushed him, and he … he stumbled backwards and … he fell.

Oh God. She had killed Tristan. The only boy she'd ever loved. It was like her brain had shut down, her memory slammed shut, like a door. Maybe she'd chosen to forget. Kase was only trying to protect her from herself. *He rejected you. You launched at him. You pushed him.*

Nausea washed over her, and she keeled over, trying to force air into her lungs. She began to run, but her bad leg felt like a dead thing, a dead weight. She could not get away from her own broken body or her mind, her swirling thoughts, the sickness in her gut. She stopped again and caught her breath, doubled over, gasping. And she realised she was still holding *The Bell Jar* in her hand.

SUMMER 1967

'June and Jack seem to be getting rather friendly.' Eve was lying on her side, her hair sweeping over her shoulder like warm honey. She twirled a lock lazily around her painted fingernails.

Franny sat up so quickly that the Sao packet on her stomach scattered biscuits over the deck. A strange mixture of excitement and dread flitted through her. 'What, my mum? And your dad? What have you seen?'

Eve arched a brow, her fingers skimming the glittering surface of the pool. 'June was in the front garden watering when I came home from school yesterday and Dad was there. They were just talking, but I went round the side of the house and spied on them. Those azaleas sure got a soaking.'

'Could you hear what they were talking about?' Franny couldn't imagine what Jack, a tradesman, and her mother, a housewife, would have to talk about at any length. Although she also couldn't imagine her mother and father having a conversation that didn't involve either her, or the same old problematic domestic issues.

'It was hard to hear because of the hose, but my dad likes plants, he does a bit of landscape gardening on his building jobs, so I think they were talking about the garden. Boring, really.'

'But did they seem –'

'Flirtatious?'

'What do you think? Did you see your mother's face that first night we came to dinner at your house? She looked like the moon she was beaming so much.'

Franny laughed. 'She certainly spent a long time doing her hair.' She took a sip from her bottle of Coke and passed it to Eve. Franny lay down on the deck, feeling the pleasant burn into her bare back. The chlorine from the pool mixed with the smell of frangipani growing over the fence and she closed her eyes. 'What if your dad and my mum got married. It'd be the best. My parents would stop fighting and you could move up to the big house and we'd be sisters.'

'What about your dad?' asked Eve, propped onto an elbow.

'God. He'd be happier with almost anyone else. They annoy each other so much.'

Eve pressed the sweating glass of the Coke bottle against her forehead, rolled it at the back over her neck. 'Let's ask the fortune-teller.'

Franny squinted at Eve. 'You're serious.'

'I found out more. She works out of a Chinese restaurant in Kings Cross. This girl at my school went to her and she said she predicted she'd fall for a boy called Bobby and sure enough, she's now going steady with Bobby Randall.'

Franny felt a pull in her belly. She couldn't tell if it was excitement or anxiety. 'Really? I don't know ...'

'Her name's something like Madame Butterfly. You go and eat in this restaurant and then she comes to your table and does your reading while you're finishing your honey prawns. The thing is, it's only late at night that she does these readings, so we'd have to sneak out. Well, we'd have to sneak out anyway, because I'm pretty sure your parents wouldn't want us going to Kings Cross at any time of the day.'

Franny scrunched up her face. 'Hmmm, my mum's the lightest sleeper. But it would be kind of cool to go to Kings Cross at night.' She searched Eve's face. She did want to do something adventurous, something risqué, but mainly she wanted Eve to be impressed.

'You could stay at the granny flat and we could sneak up the side when everyone's asleep and catch a bus or hitchhike into the city.'

'What about your dad?' Franny asked.

'He wouldn't even care. And he sleeps like the dead.'

'Yeah, my dad snores like a train. Nothing wakes him. But Mum would hear us – we'd have to go right under her window and the gate creaks. She's like a fox, always on alert.'

Eve cocked her head. 'I think I have a solution for that. We make her a cup of tea, mix in a bit of mother's helper.'

'What's that?'

'Valium, silly. All the mums take it. Your mum will have some in the medicine cabinet for sure. It's what Sally McFarlane puts in her mum's tea the nights she sneaks out too.'

'She does?' Franny sat up and shielded her eyes against the light. The tight feeling in her gut was there again.

'It's just a sleeping pill. All the mums take them. It's totally safe.'

'Well, as long as it's totally safe.' Franny slid back onto the deck. It felt hotter now than before and she gasped.

'The trick is not to make it too weird that we're making her tea out of the blue.' Eve poured baby oil into her palm and smoothed it over her legs. 'So, we can start tonight. Let's watch *Bellbird* up at the house and just casually ask if she wants a cup of tea. We could even try to bake something – mums love that stuff. And then on the weekend it won't be that weird.'

Franny considered this. Her mum would love having a cup of tea and some cake made for her. It made her feel bad that she'd never thought to do such a thing before having an ulterior motive.

Teddy's face appeared suddenly over the fence. 'Hi,' he said.

Eve waved him over. 'Oh, come and have a swim.'

He disappeared and a few minutes later came down the side of the house dressed only in his togs and carrying a portable record player. Franny was intensely aware of his body, the golden hairs on his arms catching in the afternoon sun. And of her own bare arms and legs. He placed the record player down. 'I thought I'd bring the party to the pool.'

He took a packet of cigarettes from his pocket and offered one to Eve who placed it carefully between her lips.

'Franny, are you smoking?' he asked, and she felt herself grow hot with embarrassment. Eve looked so sophisticated lying on the deck like that, like a brunette Brigitte Bardot. And Teddy knew full well that Franny didn't smoke.

'Yes,' she said, taking the cigarette and cursing her asthma.

'My dad taught me to smoke,' said Eve. 'He said if a gentleman offers you a cigarette, a real lady should accept with grace. And that it's a sign of elegance and confidence.'

Franny felt the flush reach her cheeks.

The first notes of 'Break On Through (To the Other Side)' floated on the air as Teddy lit their cigarettes. Franny drew the smoke into her mouth but not her lungs, but she coughed all the same. She tried to look relaxed.

Teddy tipped his head back and blew smoke into the air. 'What plans were you two concocting anyway?'

Eve pursed her lips. 'Our grand escape plans,' she said, glancing at him sidelong.

He flicked her a smile. 'That sounds fun. Can boys come?'

Franny's eyes met Eve's and she knew it was their little secret and that Teddy wasn't included.

'No, no boys,' said Franny, unable to conceal her smile.

Teddy lay back, cigarette dangling from his mouth, his head resting on Franny's belly. She felt like her thighs were on fire. She could smell him – smoke mixed with the hair oil he used and that scent that was just him. She couldn't help the feeling of pride that Teddy had chosen her, not Eve, to relax his beautiful body into. She scanned Eve's face but found nothing but her eyes squinted against the smoke drifting from her mouth. Of course Eve breathed the tobacco all the way into her lungs.

They lay that way for a while, feeling the sun's sting slowly subside, Jim Morrison's mournful songs moving over them, through them, like warm water. Franny felt melted under the weight of Teddy's body. She was cocooned in this moment, in this smooth feeling that must surely have been happiness.

CHAPTER 15

drench *(v.)* – to wet thoroughly; steep, soak.

Sylvie reached the cabin as the rain turned into a downpour. Her hair was stuck to her face and her teeth were chattering but she didn't care. She felt raw, stripped away by Kase's words, by the rain, like the tender flesh of an oyster prised open. Her tears mingled with the rain so she didn't know where her turmoil ended and the storm's began. The sky cracked with lightning and she cowered. What was she doing here? Was he even here? She knocked meekly, then realising he probably couldn't hear above the pelt of the rain on the tin roof, she knocked louder.

Holden opened the door, rubbing his eyes against the light. His hair was messy and he had a shadow of stubble grazing his jaw. She wanted to reach out and touch it, but she simply stood there, on his doorstep, blinking water from her lashes.

'Let's get you inside,' he said and reached for her, his hands encircling the cold, bare flesh of her arms, pulling her inside into the warmth. He took the book from her hand, its cover beaded with moisture, its pages as swollen as the soft skin around her eyes, and dried it carefully using his T-shirt. It moved something in her, watching the careful way he treated this book.

She was about to speak when he touched her face, the place just above her brow with his thumb. It was so tender, like fingers of sunlight reaching into a winter's day. She closed her eyes, leaned her cheek into his palm. The cup of his hands encircled her face and she felt the warmth of his breath on her lips before his kiss. Her eyes rolled back, closed with the sweet relief of it. Like water finally flowing after a lifetime of being dammed.

He brushed her hair from the nape of her neck. His fingertips left warm trails along her wet skin. It felt like melting. She fell into him with more abandon than she could control. All the doubt and regret, the fear and the anger left her and it felt like she was on fire. All those half-hearted embraces, the thinness of those other kisses over the years, they were nothing. Empty and strange. Not like this.

His hands were in her hair, the taste of him flooding her as their kiss lingered on, like a morning dream, like a song. She felt half-conscious with it. But then another image – indistinct, half-formed – came to her. *Tristan.* A flash. Intense. Burning. His hand cupping the back of her head. His hot lips on hers. The looseness of her body, of his.

She pulled back from Holden abruptly. 'I'm sorry. I –'

Tristan. He kissed me.

Holden shook his head. 'No, no. I'm the one who's sorry. I just … You're wet. Here, let's get you dry.' He pulled a blanket off the couch and wrapped it around her shoulders.

It was only when she was covered that she realised she was shivering. She sank into the lounge and Holden fed the potbelly stove with wood. It seemed impossible that they'd been kissing only moments ago.

'Do you want coffee? Or tea. You're a tea drinker, aren't you? Are you as hungover as me?' Holden spoke over his shoulder.

Sylvie only nodded. She was overwhelmed with emotion, with cold. Images appeared in her mind, as hazy as the smoke rising from the damp wood. *Tristan. That night. Kase said he rejected me, so why did he kiss me?*

When the fire was roaring, Holden moved to the kitchen and spooned coffee into an Italian coffee pot, which he placed on the stove. The sound of him opening the cupboards, running the tap, was comforting. She smelled eggs cooking, and then the rich scent of coffee.

'For someone so good with words, you're awfully quiet,' Holden said as he set a plate of eggs and a cup of strong black tea in front of her. 'Sorry, I know you were expecting figs today.'

She smiled, a small laugh issuing from her lips.

He sat down next to her. 'I hope it's okay that I … that we … I didn't read it wrong, did I?'

Sylvie looked up from her mug. His uncertain eyes moved her, and she wished she could reach for him once more.

'No, no, you read it right,' she pushed a strand of wet hair behind her ear, suddenly self-conscious. 'Thank you. For breakfast and for … what you wrote in the sand, about the figs. For really listening. I just … I can't go back there, to the house. I did what you said. I talked to Kase. But what she told me …' She shook her head and looked into her lap.

'What? You asked her why she never called you all those years ago? What did she say?'

Sylvie pulled the blanket tighter around herself. 'She told me things about that night at the lighthouse when Tristan died. Things I didn't know. Memories I don't have. I …' She wasn't ready to divulge everything to Holden yet. It felt too wrong to say out loud. Too dangerous. Too awful. *I pushed him. I killed him.*

Worry creased Holden's face – a reflection of what her own face must have held. 'So, it didn't go well, I take it. It's okay, you can stay here.'

She wanted nothing more than to be here with Holden in this warm, safe little cabin on the edge of the world, cocooned by the rain. But her instinct told her she must go. Who else knew what she'd done to Tristan? Did they all know? Rachel and Gabe? Not Fran surely. Guilt and shame sluiced through her. And yet there was the tiny glimpse of memory she'd just had, of Tristan kissing her, like a faraway sound, barely audible. It whispered something else to her. Something she was straining to hear, but couldn't yet make out.

'I need to get off the island. Can you take me?' she asked.

She saw hurt cross Holden's face and she hated herself for causing it. She focused on her meal. The bread was crusty and the eggs creamy and salty and comforting, but she struggled to enjoy the food.

'What about all your stuff back at the house?' he asked.

She shook her head. 'It doesn't matter. I can't go back there.' She knew she was being irrational – she would need her wallet and her phone – but she couldn't face Kase ever again.

'What about if I get your bags for you?'

'I don't want to put you in that position.'

He squeezed her arm. 'It's okay.'

She softened. 'I'm sorry, I'm just … Maybe you could just grab my wallet and phone. My handbag. The rest doesn't matter.'

'Okay.' His voice was quiet, despondent, she thought, and she hated herself for abandoning him. *Them.* If that's what this was. Or could be. It felt like the opening chapter of a book you knew you could fall into, that might change your life. But she'd snapped the cover closed before the end of the first page. The story, the words, were gone.

They finished their breakfast in a silence as thick as the salt mist rising from the bay below.

'At least it's stopped raining,' she said, trying to sound normal. 'Thank you for breakfast. Thank you … for everything. I'm sorry. I could stay here forever … with just you. I just don't know what else to do but leave.'

'Don't,' he said. 'Don't leave. Please.' He implored her with his eyes.

'It feels like their island. And I can't be on it anymore, not after what Kase told me.'

Holden shook his head. 'Do you remember anything she told you about that night?'

Sylvie bit her lip, tempted to let everything spill out. She gave her head a tiny shake.

'How about I get your stuff from up at the house and I'll take you off the island. But please promise me you won't go back to Sydney, not yet. I was going to take you somewhere today, to pick figs from the trees. To Bruny.' His eyes met hers, earnest, pleading. 'I have a place there.'

She saw on his face what it had taken for him to mention this. It must have been his home with Pippi. Sorrow and empathy twisted inside her. 'You do?'

'An old cottage on farmland near the water, surrounded by fruit trees. My ex-wife Charlie's family still owns it, but she doesn't mind me staying there sometimes. It's empty at the moment.' He paused, looking down. 'It was our family home.'

Sylvie reached out and put her hand on Holden's arm. His skin was warmer than hers. He took her hand in between both of his. 'You're still cold.'

'That's funny, I feel warmer now.' She felt the flick of pages, the easing open of the spine. She smelled the pages, the ink, the hope. And she knew their story wasn't over, not yet. She nodded. 'I'd like to taste those figs.'

He smiled.

She picked up *The Bell Jar*, opened its soggy pages. 'Do you have a pen?'

Holden got up and retrieved a biro from the kitchen.

Sylvie opened to the title page of the book. Under the inscription that may or may not have been her mother's handwriting, she wrote two words: *I'm sorry.*

She handed the book to Holden. 'I need you to return this to Kase.'

SUMMER 1967

Franny pulled her doona over her head, but it didn't stop the sounds. She used to pretend they were birds squawking at each other – the shrill high strain of her mother overlaid with the low call of her father, like some deep swampish bird. But tonight she couldn't pretend anymore, and she couldn't block them out. There was a loud crack and then a thud. Probably something being thrown against a wall. Hopefully not her mother. Franny screwed her eyes shut and hugged her knees to her chest. She knew her mother wasn't blameless. She had a temper and would rail and rant, but she also knew in some deep elemental way that her father had crossed a line. That he had hit her before, and he would hit her again. Franny listened. Silence. She opened her door a crack. Their bedroom and the study doors were shut. They had retreated to their safe places. A crunch under her slippered feet. A vase lay in pieces – her mother must have thrown it before barricading herself in her room.

Franny made for the door to the deck, following a thin trail of moonlight. The garden was filled with the shadows of tree ferns, fanning like dark feathers, and the insistent click of night insects. She followed the path through the garden, the air cool on her flimsy night dress. A light was on in the granny flat and she followed the soft trail of music and the smell of incense.

The kitchenette was empty and smelled of the noodles Eve was fond of cooking for herself most nights. She heard laughter from the bedroom and a shiver of apprehension ran through her. Was that Teddy's voice? She knew the answer in her gut even before she pushed the door open.

Teddy was there, sprawled on Eve's bed, hands behind his head, legs crossed, as though he was sunbathing. She was about to flee, a gash of pain opening in her chest, when Eve was in front of her.

'Franny.' There was a moment, fleeting, when Franny saw that Eve was startled, but she smoothly reached out and drew Franny into her. 'Oh no, is it your parents again?'

Tears erupted from Franny's eyes even as she fought them back. She didn't want to be vulnerable when Eve's betrayal was causing her more pain, more hurt. She wanted to push Eve away, to say, *How dare you and Teddy hang out without me?* But the words wouldn't come. And then Eve was rubbing her back, pulling her inside the bedroom. Teddy saw her tears, and guilt and horror passed over his face. His eyes looked everywhere but into hers. She wanted to slap him.

She thought of the times before Eve had come along when they had swum in the pool, biked to the beach together, played card games in his room on hot, sticky afternoons, listening to The Beatles. But now the tune had changed. The Doors and cigarettes had replaced card games and swims. Their connection had felt so known, so solid. Like friends. Like the siblings neither of them had. Like the simplicity of the dawn they had witnessed together as he surfed and she swam.

'Franny's parents are at it again,' said Eve by way of explanation, drawing Franny down onto the futon so that she sat between them. The tension in the room felt like a string that could be twanged, like a discordant note from a guitar.

Teddy turned the music down. 'They fighting again? My parents hear them too, you know.' He rubbed the back of his head.

Franny sniffed. 'Yeah. It was just worse this time.'

Eve fixed her with a serious look. 'I saw June and Jack sitting on the pool deck together after lunch yesterday. Dad was smoking and he was sharing his cigarette with your mum. They seemed to be talking pretty … intimately. Let's just say it was a progression from the watering-the-garden chat.'

'Really?'

'And then your mum fixed them drinks, all fancy like. Cocktails. I don't know where your dad was.'

'He was visiting Grandma yesterday,' said Franny.

'Maybe he's jealous. Maybe he came home and saw them. Maybe that's what sparked this latest fight.'

Franny put her head in her hands. The smoke was making her breathing shallow. She needed her asthma medication but she knew she wouldn't bother taking it. 'Maybe.'

'Have your parents got something going on?' asked Teddy. 'I mean, for real?'

Eve shrugged and put a cigarette to her lips. Teddy went to light it for her, but Eve grabbed the lighter from him and lit it herself. 'Teddy you have to leave.' She hugged Franny tightly.

'I think this is the night. Franny and I are going to Kings Cross to see the fortune-teller.'

Teddy shifted onto an elbow. 'I'll drive you.'

'No, it's *our* adventure.' She linked her arm through Franny's and Franny felt the tears dry on her face. *Their secret. Their plan.* She was back with Eve, just the two of them. Her heart lifted.

Teddy shrugged and drained his bottle of beer. 'You two are little rebels. Suit yourselves,' he said as he stretched and stood.

They watched him lope out the door, but then he turned. 'Franny, want to do an early morning beach swim? It's been a while.'

Eve squeezed Franny's hand. 'I think we'll be back pretty late. We may only get home at dawn.'

But Franny couldn't hide her smile. 'Maybe one morning before school?' She turned to Eve. 'You could come, or …'

Eve waved a dismissive hand. 'God no. I'm not a morning person. Or an exercise person.'

Franny's eyes met Teddy's before he gave them a wave and left.

Eve grabbed her elbows. 'Let's get dressed up. I'll do your makeup.'

'What about Mum? She might hear us. I don't want her to worry … She's already so upset.'

Eve stood and held out her hands to Franny. 'We're going to take her a nice cup of tea before bed, just like we did the other night. It'll make her feel better, too.'

Franny felt a twinge of anxiety, but she let Eve pull her up. Eve went into the tiny bathroom and returned with a bottle of pills. She took one out and crushed it into a powder with the back of a spoon on the kitchen bench.

'Maybe we should have a little bit too, it just relaxes you. Takes the edge off.'

Eve took a small glass bottle of Coca-Cola from the fridge and carefully put some powder in it. She took a sip and held the bottle out to Franny. Doubt wormed inside her, but she took the bottle and drank. Soon they'd know if their parents would be together. Part of her felt sad for her dad, but all she wanted was to have the fighting stop, and for her mother to not be brittle and frightened. Soon June would be relaxed and happy and everything would be all right.

She followed Eve up the path to the house. Her mother was in the kitchen, standing at the sink eating from a tub of ice cream. Franny could tell she'd been crying. The familiar smell of liquor lingered around her, as though she was sweating it out of her pores. Yes, it had been a bad one. It felt natural to make her sit down and tell her they'd make her a cup of tea. Eve was so charming as she put the mug in front of her that June reached out and smoothed her hair and told her that she and her dad were the best things that had ever happened to their family.

CHAPTER 16

book *(n.)* – a written or printed work of some length.

Sylvie left the island the same way she had come – under dark storm clouds, the pale yellow grass and deep green trees shrouded in thick mist. Eagles circled in the sky above. The sea baptised her once more, and she felt chastised. She never should have come here, she knew that now. The sea had known. And yet ... She looked across at the man who had promised her figs.

They passed the Bruny ferry that would have taken her back to the mainland. She let herself be carried past the safe return to the steady narrative of her life and over the heaving waves of the channel.

Holden steered them along the wild coastal stretch of Bruny Island. Cliffs filled with tall pines fell steeply to deserted beaches. Rocks jutted from the sea like sharp black teeth and then the landscape flattened. She saw the low buildings of a small town, and smooth water washed into luminous stretches of sand. In the distance the island's lighthouse was a tiny white spot against the bruised sky. A shiver ran through her. Whispers rose into her mind, images flashed: Tristan's face, beautiful, eyes closed, lips warm. Another image came, fragile, transparent, like mist. Kase and Sylvie linking arms, looking up to the Palm Beach lighthouse, the smell of summer. Smoke from a fire.

'Will you take me to the lighthouse?' she asked into the wind.

'I'll show you everything,' he said.

She didn't know what she would find here, but she knew it was a place where ghosts resided, and not just Holden's ghosts. She knew now that her story was not yet told. She'd thought she knew the ending, but this place had plotted out a different one. It was dark, but luminous too.

It was a full moon that night … I am remembering. Her doctors had told her she may one day recover her memory of that night, but that the memories would return like pieces of a jigsaw puzzle, in random order. The only piece she had was Tristan's kiss, but it felt like the corner piece, the piece from which all the others would fit. She hadn't tried to remember over the years, not really, if she was honest with herself. She'd needed to bury the person she'd once been as much as she'd needed to bury the pain and loss of that time.

They docked at a jetty, a lone marker in a sea of white trunks. Tasmanian blue gums, blackwoods and huge pines grew from the water's edge. The water was calmer here, and green, as though the leaves had seeped into the sea and stained it. The rain had eased and a tentative sun washed a weak warmth over the land.

'It's so untouched. I expected there to be more people,' she said into the silence, as Holden cut the motor and they drifted into shore.

'It's just us and the trees. The farmhouse isn't far. We can walk from here,' he said.

And then he was tying the rope to the jetty and helping her out. He'd brought her bag as he'd said he would. He had given Kase *The Bell Jar* with Sylvie's message inside, and then he'd left. Sylvie didn't ask about what his working arrangement was with Fran and whether he could just disappear.

Sylvie followed him up a narrow track through the bush, birdcalls and the soft wash of the bay filling up the silence. It smelled like eucalypt and lemon. It smelled new, fresh, as though the bush had just got here instead of being ancient and timeless. They didn't talk – the walk stole their breath. Eventually they came to a dam and above it, a small farmhouse. Its roof was corrugated iron painted the same green as the trees, and its walls were a yellow fibro that had suffered the assault of salt air. There were stacks of logs at the entrance and a rusted old pushbike on the porch. The place skirted a fine line between romantic and derelict.

Holden skuttled some cobwebs away from the entrance with a stick and found a key under the doormat. The house smelled of the many fires that had been lit to cushion the cold beyond its thin walls. There were gumboots, jackets and hats hanging at the entrance, which led into an exposed brick kitchen with an old-fashioned stove. Beyond that, Sylvie glimpsed a lounge room. *A library.* The walls were lined with books.

Holden noticed her wonder and smiled.

'May I?' she asked.

He gestured towards the lounge room. 'I told you you'd like it here.'

It was like walking into a second-hand bookshop. Three sides of the room held overflowing bookshelves, as though the cottage walls were really paper thin. There were old paperbacks and heavy tomes. Reference books and picture books. There was a lifetime of reading material. The furniture was worn and the paint peeling, but all she could see were the books, all she could smell was knowledge, and stories.

'You asked why my cabin didn't have any books. This is the answer,' he said, taking down a beautiful hardcover book. It was a copy of *Pippi Longstocking*. He opened it like he was opening his heart. 'You've reminded me about the beauty of stories.'

She turned towards him. 'I have?'

'Yeah.'

She touched the book and then his arm. 'Thank you for showing me this,' she said.

'I didn't know I needed to show anyone until you came along.' He threaded his fingers through hers and they stayed there a while, feeling the warmth of each other's bodies.

'What other books did Pippi like?' Sylvie asked.

He went to the other side of the room. There were dozens of young adult fiction books.

'Her tastes tended towards the dark. She started with *The Hunger Games* at age ten, and she loved *Wuthering Heights* and anything dystopian, like Margaret Atwood. These are her books.' He ran his hand along their spines with a tenderness that Sylvie felt sigh along her skin. 'And I've kept all her baby books.' He pointed. 'I guess I'm not very good at letting books go.'

'You should see my flat. I feel some deep obligation to rescue and home books. It's almost maternal. I'm a book womb.'

Holden laughed. He took a heavy dictionary down from a shelf and they sat on the faded fabric lounge. 'A bibliophile … a restorer. That doesn't seem quite the right word.'

'A gatherer. We are book gatherers,' she said.

He closed the dictionary. 'I don't need a dictionary when I have a Sylvie.'

She smiled and the taut, invisible line that ran between them tightened. He took her hand and pulled her off the couch and outside. 'There's more to see.'

She followed him into the gentle sunshine. The view from the veranda was across the still water of the dam and out past the forest to the bay beyond. He led the way higher up the slope, through fruit trees, pointing out a small olive grove, some citrus and nut trees. He passed her lemons to hold to her nose and almonds to crack open. And then they came to a row of fledgling figs, not like the ancient ones she knew, with their knotted roots growing along the Sydney Harbour foreshore.

He reached up and picked a piece of fruit. He was smiling as he handed it to her. It was purple, ripe, and she breathed in its sweet scent. Sylvia Plath's words whispered inside her, like the breeze in the wide green leaves above.

From the tip of every branch, like a fat purple fig, a wonderful future beckoned and winked.

She expected him to tell her to eat it, to say he'd fulfilled his promise in the sand, but instead he took a bite and then kissed her. He tasted like summer and sunshine and hope, and she could feel the coil of tension in her belly unfurling.

He passed the fig to her to finish. 'I've never shown anyone this place since Pippi died.'

'Thank you for bringing me.' She pressed a hand to his cheek. 'How often do you come here?'

'Every few weeks. I do some maintenance, make sure the fruit trees have enough water.'

'Is it hard to come back? Does it make you miss her more?'

He kicked at the soil and shook his head. 'It did at first but then you realise that this is all you have left. The place where the memories are. And then you want to preserve it. It's scary for a while, and then it becomes precious.'

'I understand,' she said. 'When I clean out people's houses after they die it's because many of their loved ones don't want to do it. They don't want to face it, because the places we live hold on to our memories. I believe that. I've felt it.'

'And it doesn't frighten you?'

Sylvie thought for a moment. 'No. I find it beautiful, sacred. I guess I never had a family home that felt like a place I belonged, so when you come across that history, that longevity, it's amazing.'

'Is that because your mum always moved about?'

Sylvie nodded. 'For many years, Kase and her family home at Palm Beach was the only solid thing in my life. My mother … she went from lover to lover, from place to place. We lived as she lived as a girl, in the back of people's houses, in their granny flats. I mean, she was also a struggling writer when I was growing up. There was never any money. Even now that she's found success and has money, she still moves, but now it's country to country instead of suburb to suburb; she can't stop and put down roots.'

'So, you spend your life going into the places where other people have put down roots and cleaning them out and saving their precious things. Their books.'

She smiled. 'Yes. I hadn't really thought of it like that.'

'And that's why it was so hurtful when the place where you felt those roots was gone suddenly. When Kase and Fran abandoned you.'

The truth in his words felt like a cold slap and the dread pooled in her gut again. *Because I killed their brother, their son. God.* The sweet fruit that had fallen on the ground around them suddenly smelled of rot. A wave of nausea washed over her. Could she really stay here with Holden, taste the sweetness he offered her?

He touched her arm. 'Are you okay?'

'I just feel a bit lightheaded,' she said.

'We should have some lunch. Come on, there's a market not far from here. I'll drive us in the old truck. We'll get sourdough and some cheese and oysters, and fruit and vegies. The produce here is very good.'

She grabbed his arm. 'Are you sure, Holden? I don't really know what I'm …'

She couldn't say *I don't know what I'm doing here*, because of the figs, because of what they'd shared, because of the pull they both felt. It would be disingenuous. But at the same time, could she really run away from her life? Could she just hide from what Kase had told her? Had she really done that to Tristan? She thought of the Bruny lighthouse hovering like a ghost from the boat. About how places held memories. She had not been to a lighthouse in twenty-three years.

He looked into her eyes. 'You're standing under the fig tree, Sylvie Plath. I know what fig I want you to choose. I think I've made that abundantly clear.'

She allowed a smile to creep onto her face. 'It was a delicious fig.'

He put his arm around her and kissed the top of her hair and she felt that soar of hope again.

'And you haven't even tasted my best cooking. Let's take it one day at a time, shall we? Tonight we'll eat on the veranda under the stars and then tomorrow we can return to the fig tree.'

She smiled up at him and let her body rest against his. She didn't know what this might mean, spending the night with this man who saw her so clearly, but he was telling her he wouldn't rush her. That the figs were her own to pick and eat as she pleased.

They walked higher, hand in hand, to the top of the hill and the sun was warm now, the leaves of the fruit trees obscenely green. The farmhouse and the dam were picture-book idyllic, and beyond that, the bay sparkled. There was no hint of the storm that had blown them here. Everything was golden.

Holden pointed through the trees. 'You can just see the tip of the lighthouse from here. We can pick up fresh oysters and cheese and visit tomorrow, if you like, take a picnic.'

She felt cold move through her bones, but the white streak of the lighthouse in the distance would not release her. She nodded and followed him down through the orchard, the taste of figs on her lips.

SUMMER 1967

Flashing lights and the boom of music greeted them as they stepped out of the taxi. The night was humid, and the air reeked of cheap fragrance mixed with cigarette smoke and rubbish. It was exotic and dangerous. A woman wearing what appeared to be a silk dressing gown with scant underneath, sauntered past, her kitten heels clacking on the pavement. She flashed Eve and Franny a gold-toothed smile.

'Oh my goodness, her teeth,' Franny whispered, aware that her first fifteen seconds in Kings Cross had revealed more about the world than the fifteen years that had preceded them. She gripped Eve's arm. Nerves and excitement jangled together inside her, as large and uncomfortable as the earrings hanging from her lobes. She hiked her dress down, all of a sudden acutely aware of just how short it was. She couldn't believe they'd snuck out in the middle of the night and caught a taxi to the most dangerous place in Sydney.

There was shouting, and two men fell out through a doorway shaped like a pair of enormous red lips. A scuffle ensued and they stumbled from the footpath onto the road. People dragged the men off the street and cars honked their horns. Franny felt Eve's fingers dig into her arm. She was glad she wasn't the only one who was scared.

'So, where's this Chinese restaurant?' Franny asked, trying not to let her voice betray her nerves. She wanted to get off this strip with its loud, dark brazenness.

Eve took a piece of paper out of her bag. It had directions scrawled on it. 'Ruby Street, which is off the main drag near the fountain. Let's find the fountain. I think it's this way.'

They walked past clubs flashing with lit-up cartoon body parts, and men with dark eyes that followed them. There were people everywhere – women with elegant hairdos and fabulous dresses, men in suits wearing sunglasses at night, buskers sitting on the pavement banging tin drums and homeless people lining up at a soup kitchen. A cafe spilled out onto the pavement, still open at midnight and filled with patrons smoking and sipping wine, couples in glamorous outfits, as though they'd just returned from a show.

Franny felt very young and very old all at once. But her whole body was zinging with a feeling she'd never had before. It was as though the world had suddenly opened its wide arms and Franny had fallen into the embrace. She suddenly saw that life was so much bigger than the four walls of her bedroom filled with Beatles posters, bigger than the petty dramas of her schoolfriends, and the smash of vases hitting walls.

They slowed in front of the cafe, arm in arm. She could tell Eve was seduced too. There was a man with a painted face playing a violin on the street and its romantic, mournful song added to the allure of the scene. Eve pulled her towards a little round table on the street. They sat, and Eve took out her cigarettes and handed Franny one. She crossed her legs and lit it and she thought at that moment that she had never and would never again feel so utterly and entirely sophisticated.

A waiter dressed formally in a bow tie approached them and Franny was about to ask to see a menu or order a milkshake when Eve used a voice that sounded much more grown-up than her own, to order them two glasses of red wine. Franny waited for the man to refuse, but he simply scribbled in his notepad and left.

She squeezed Eve's hand under the table. 'Can you believe this place? I feel like I'm in Paris.'

'Oh, I feel so at home here. This is a place for dreamers and bohemians and artists,' said Eve, her voice now breathy and more like her own. 'Look at that man writing in his journal, drinking espresso in the middle of the night. Doesn't he just look like a writer?'

Franny's eyes followed Eve's gaze to a man with a mop of unruly curls, dressed in an ill-fitting suit. The fingers of one hand toyed with the stub of a cigarette, while the other hand scribbled in a leather-bound book. Yes, definitely a writer.

A woman with an extremely low-cut top served their wine and they clinked glasses and took tentative sips.

'I can't believe we really did this,' said Franny. 'And no one's acting like we're out of place … thanks to your makeup skills. We obviously look eighteen.'

'We just look like uni students having supper after the theatre on a Sunday night. Oh, can you imagine the life we'll have in a few years? How exciting it'll be? We'll get a flat here and we'll both be writers during the day and work at cafes like this at night and meet all kinds of interesting people to put in our stories and take as lovers.'

'Look, a second-hand bookstore across the road. Oh, I'm going to work there. Oh my gosh, it's still open. Let's go in after our wine,' said Franny.

'What about our fortune-teller? We have to see if June and Jack are destined to be together and if our Kings Cross university dream will come true.'

They finished their wine and the complimentary bowl of nuts, and left money on the table, feeling very cosmopolitan in the process. The main drag was a little quieter now and they wondered if the Chinese restaurant would even be open at this hour, but they turned the corner and saw it, lit up like a paper lantern and buzzing with bodies bent over bowls of noodles.

The aroma of fried meats and garlic suffused the air and Franny realised she was hungry and a bit drunk. They were seated at a table under a painting of a golden fish and Eve asked the waiter about the fortune-teller who visited tables late at night. The young man looked barely older than them and told them she didn't work this late on Sunday nights, but then possibly seeing the disappointment on their faces, said she was actually his mum and she'd get out of bed for twenty dollars.

They pooled their cash and nodded their agreement. They had to forgo the noodles they were craving and instead ate the prawn crackers on their table and waited for Madame Butterfly. Franny had been picturing a striking Asian woman wrapped in an ornate blue robe, with flowers in her hair and destinies flowing from her mouth. The woman who arrived was wearing a housecoat and slippers, with rollers in her hair. She and Eve exchanged a look. Maybe the waiter had tricked them to take their money.

'Madame Butterfly?' asked Eve.

'How old are you two?' asked the woman in a deeply accented voice that did match Franny's expectations. She pulled a chair over to seat herself beside them and fanned a pack of mysterious looking cards onto the table with an expertise that told them she was indeed a fortune-teller.

'The same age as your son,' said Eve, and Madame Butterfly narrowed her eyes.

'Well, you are brave girls, I give you that. Do your mothers know where you are?' she asked, eyebrows raised, chin high.

'Our mothers are bohemians,' said Eve. 'They let us run free.'

The woman humphed. 'And what about your friend? She hasn't said very much. Your mother is also a bohemian, I take it?' She raised an eyebrow.

Franny reddened at the sarcasm in the woman's voice. She called out something in what was probably Cantonese and her son appeared, bearing steaming bowls of soup with noodles. 'On the house, because you both are too skinny,' she said, with a wave of her hand. 'Now, let's have a look at the divine tarot.'

The cards were beautiful, colourful, with gold-trimmed edges and symbols that Franny didn't understand. They gave her a funny feeling – the same feeling she had when she smelled incense burning or singing in a language other than English. She slurped some of the soup. It tasted spicy and as exotic as the cards laid out before her.

'And I'll also need something of yours to hold. A piece of jewellery, for example.'

Eve pulled a ring from her finger and chose three cards as directed by Madame Butterfly.

'Well, you are the more dominant one in the friendship, that is clear without divination,' the woman said, glancing over a pair of glasses she had slipped on from around her neck. She looked at the cards, her mouth pursed in thought, and then closed her eyes while she pressed Eve's ring between her palms.

Eve and Franny shared a look of wonder. 'What are you sensing?' asked Eve, leaning in, captivated.

'That you need to talk less and listen more, and eat your soup,' the woman said, opening one eye. 'There is much restless energy. I am sensing a nomad, a seeker. You seek a figure in your life who is missing. You miss someone. That is what these cards are telling me. And so, you reach and seek but you have not yet found what you're looking for.'

Eve's eyes flashed as she squeezed Franny's hand beneath the table. Maybe this woman did know what she was talking about, her look said. Franny didn't believe in fortune-tellers, not really, but this experience was totally unlike what she'd been expecting.

'You will travel the world, that is certain. You will create great things from nothing. But what you need to learn is closer to home. It is something your friend already knows.' She narrowed her eyes.

Franny and Eve shared a confused look.

'What is it?' asked Eve.

'It is not for me to answer. That is your lesson. And life will teach it to you.'

Eve's mouth scrunched in frustration. 'Can I ask a question?'

The woman nodded as she ran her hands over the cards.

'So, what we really want to know, why we came, is to find out if our parents might end up together. We want to be sisters, you see. Can you see anything about that?'

'The cards do not work that way. Let me take a look at this one.' She indicated for Franny to choose three cards. Franny shot Eve a disappointed look before handing over a charm bracelet from around her wrist.

The woman closed her eyes for a while. When her gaze met Franny's there was sadness in it. Franny's stomach lurched.

'You have chosen a card that looks beautiful on the surface.' The woman smoothed the card as though it were a cat. She had long painted nails – they were the kind of hands that also fitted Franny's impression of a fortune-teller. 'I am wrestling with whether to tell you this, but I can see that you are brave girls, who seek more from life than most, and at such a tender age.' She smiled, meeting their eyes. 'That will stand you in good stead in this life.'

She reached out and took Franny's hand and the gentleness with which she did so gave Franny butterflies. 'This is, in actual fact, a difficult card. When people choose the Death card they panic, but there are other cards that herald darkness. And perhaps I should not say this to you, but I feel protective, as a mother myself.' She nodded over to her son, who was quietly folding cutlery into napkins on the other side of the room. 'Your fates are intertwined in a way that I rarely see. This can herald something very beautiful, very good, or something very bad, depending on how you act. And this is why I've chosen to tell you. So that you may be warned to always act in a way that is kind and gracious.'

Franny's eyes met Eve's, which were wide and more uncertain than she'd ever seen them.

'What does that mean exactly?' asked Eve. 'Does that mean our parents do end up together? Is that why we're entwined?'

The woman reached over and took Eve's hand, patted it and then placed it into Franny's. 'It is rare that life bestows upon us such a connection and so early in life. You two are lucky ones. To come here together, inspired by a common purpose.' She nodded. 'You are special girls. Your friendship is special. Often we seek life partners in the opposite sex all our lives, God knows I have. Divorced twice.' She rolled her eyes. 'But sometimes it is friendship that is our true life calling, our true soul connection. You two have that soul connection. I see it plain as the nose on my face. These are eternal and rare and mystical and as such they burn the brightest. Most of our relationships, even very loving ones, are revealed to be only temporary. Soul connections are forever. It doesn't matter what happens in your lives … you may not see one another for a very long time, you may be separated by the whims of fate, but you will always meet each other on a very deep level. What you have will never fade. Remember that, girls. What you seek here, you have already found.'

Franny squeezed Eve's hand and Eve squeezed back.

'But what is it that Franny already knows, and I don't?' asked Eve as the woman stood and pocketed the cash on the table.

'That is something the pair of you will need to figure out. Now finish your soup and go home to your mothers.' They watched her go, stopping briefly to kiss her son on the head and then parting a beaded curtain at the back of the restaurant and disappearing.

'What on earth?' said Eve, pressing her hand over her mouth. 'What just happened?'

'I got the Death card – no, the worse than Death card,' said Franny, scrunching her mouth up.

'We don't even know what that means. Maybe she was a crazy old lady. She didn't actually tell us much.'

'She seemed to be saying in a roundabout way that June and Jack are going to be together. Why else would we be linked?' Franny shot Eve a worried look.

Eve hugged her. 'Come on, don't worry. At least you've already learned the lesson that I supposedly have to travel the world to understand ...' She rolled her eyes. 'Let's go to that second-hand bookshop you liked the look of.'

Eve approached the waiter on their way out. 'Is your mum actually the real deal?' she asked.

The boy shrugged. 'The Kings Cross mafia come to her, so ...'

The girls shared a wary look. They left the restaurant and walked in silence, arm in arm, back down the main drag, past the staring men to the bookshop. It looked like a soft bubble in the brash loudness of the rest of the street. The door dinged as they walked in. It was tiny, lamplit and empty, save for a man at an old desk piled with books. He didn't move or look up from what he was reading, and Franny thought he looked like a garden gnome. She found the smell of the old books comforting. It felt like a safe port in the sea of chaos outside. She ran her fingers along the dusty spines, trying to still the unease worming in her stomach from what Madame Butterfly had said. She pulled a few books out and inspected them, breathed in their tea-leaf pages, thumbed the dust off their stained covers. Eve sat at a little writing desk in the corner, lit by an ornate lamp, as though it was the most natural thing in the world to do. Franny wondered if people were allowed to just come in and sit at this desk and write. *How wonderful*, she thought. *Maybe we will live near here and come and write at night when we can't sleep.*

'What are you writing?' Franny asked.

Eve flashed her a mysterious smile. 'It's a surprise.' She had a book in her hand. She went over to the man, who looked up with surprise, as though just realising he had customers. She handed him the book and some loose change from her pocket. Eve pressed it into Franny's hands. It was *The Bell Jar* by Sylvia Plath.

'Open it,' said Eve as they stood at the shop's entrance, on the threshold between two worlds.

Franny opened the book and read the inscription:

To Franny, may our fates be always entwined. Love, Eve

CHAPTER 17

adventure *(n.)* - an undertaking of uncertain outcome.

They drove along the coast. Sylvie unwound the window to smell the sea. The landscape was raw, scrubbed. There was an untamed energy here that felt different from the private island. It was bigger – the forests, the views, the cliffs. The other island had been Kase's. This was Holden's island. He pointed out the trees – Tasmanian blue gum, myrtle, blackwood, acacia, native cherry and sassafras.

They stopped the old truck at a drive-through oyster bar and bought cold white wine, a dozen oysters and soft sourdough. They found a beach that curled into a headland and sat on the truck's hood, sipping wine straight from the bottle and letting oysters slip down their throats. Sylvie felt tipsy and full. She strolled the deserted beach, picking up glistening strands of seaweed. Holden crushed leaves between his fingers for her to smell. Her senses were alive with sea and air and forest. She wondered how she had spent so little of her life up until this moment in nature. They walked and talked until the beach ran out. She felt like they were the only people on the island. She felt like they had known each other for as long as the water had known the land.

Back in the truck they rounded a corner and green farmland stretched out towards the sea. They drove on until they reached a place where black swans dipped their long necks into shallow aqua water. They parked the truck and climbed the stairs there until they were on the top of the headland. Sylvie's breath caught as she gazed out at The Neck, an isthmus that divided the beach from the bay, two arcs of sand. The exact same topography as the place where the ocean spooned away from the bay near the lighthouse at Palm Beach. She felt the hairs on her arms rise. She was at the other end of the world, the other end of her life, but there was a strange echo that was getting louder.

They returned to the truck and continued on, and Holden pointed out places that were personal to him. The road to the swimming hole where Pippi had learned to swim, the paddock where he taught her to drive, the tiny primary school she attended until age eleven. It felt like the most precious and vulnerable place inside him unlocking for her, his pages caught in the breeze through the open window. They rounded a corner with a small white cross, over which flowers had been twisted. She waited but he said nothing. This child of his was just coming alive to Sylvie. She didn't ask if that might have been the place Pippi had died.

They reached a small village that was really just a pub, corner shop, fruit market, and petrol station that doubled as a bait and fish and chip shop. They picked up more bread, butter, brie, red wine, pasta and some fruit, vegetables and milk. It felt strangely natural to be engaged in such domestic pursuits with Holden, despite the fact that she had never in her life shopped for food with a man. It somehow seemed absurd that she'd reached middle age without undertaking such a mundane task.

The awful shimmer of what Kase had told her about Tristan floated at her periphery. Was that why there had never been any man of consequence in her life? Did she understand on some unconscious level, beyond her fractured memories, that she'd killed the only man she had ever loved? Is that how little she knew herself? She shivered and stared out the window at the pristine wilderness flashing by.

* * *

Later, back at the farmhouse, Holden insisted she sit at the timber table that took up most of the kitchen and drink wine while he made a pasta sauce on the old stove. The aroma of garlic, onion and wild herbs picked from the garden infused the air, steeping through her, warming her.

'When did you know you loved to cook?' Sylvie asked, sipping the fruity pinot noir.

'When I had Pippi. First it was vegetable purees, and then finger food, and then I started experimenting with spag bol.'

'So "fine cuisine" then.'

He laughed. 'Exactly. I cooked because I had to. Charlie, my ex, was away a lot for work. She's a singer and has gigs all over the country. And as a schoolteacher with predictable, child-friendly hours and holidays, it fell to me to be Pippi's main carer.'

'Pippi was lucky to have a dad like you. I never grew up with that father presence in my life.'

'Where was he?' Holden threw pasta into boiling water.

'Oh, it was nothing sad or anything, my mum just never really knew. Or he was inconsequential. Simply a sperm donor by accident, I guess.'

'Did you ever want to track him down?'

'God no. I have enough reluctant parents in my life with Evangeline.'

Holden shot her a sympathetic look.

Sylvie traced the marks in the timber, imagining all the meals he'd shared here with Pippi. 'Did your wife, Charlie … was she around much?'

Holden didn't look up from the sauce bubbling in an old frypan. 'She'd make sure she came home as often as she could, and she was earning decent money for the family. I can't fault her on that. But sometimes she and the band travelled for three weeks in a month. So it was just Pippi and me a lot of the time. And maybe at the age where a father and daughter would grow apart, we seemed to grow closer. That was probably partly because when she went to high school in Hobart, we'd travel forty minutes both ways together. That's also why we read so many books. She'd read them to me while I drove.'

'That is so special.' Sylvie fought a lump in her throat and busied herself with topping up their wineglasses. 'Do you and Charlie keep in touch? Apart from stuff about the house?'

'Charlie … isn't the easiest person to be around. She's in Surry Hills in Sydney with a new partner now. Still gigging. Still travelling. We didn't keep in touch for a long time. There was blame, I guess. I don't know how parents lose a child without there being blame. But I know she'll never sell this place. She'll keep it for me. And Pippi.'

Sylvie felt tears prick her eyes. 'Thank you for bringing me here.'

Holden came and put his arms around her shoulders and kissed the top of her head. 'I don't think I'll ever leave this part of the world. I'd feel like … I don't know, I'd feel like I was abandoning Pippi.'

'Oh Holden.' Sylvie felt the tears that had been threatening fall and she stood and put her arms around him. 'I think that's the most beautiful thing I've ever heard. How did I find you here at the end of the earth?'

He smiled a sad smile. 'Do two broken pieces make up a whole?'

As if to answer him, she kissed him and then pressed her cheek to his chest. She could hear the breath whisper in his lungs, smell his aroma, as delicious as the food he was cooking for her.

'You know why I'm hiding from the world. Why are you, Sylvie Plath? Why do you disappear into books? Why were you so alone in this world?'

She broke from his embrace on the pretence of picking up her wineglass. How to tell him that all the broken roads of her life led back to that night at the lighthouse? That her fractured memory had led her not to trust herself. That her distrust of men was instinctual. That her mother had never made her feel like Holden had made Pippi feel. That, at seventeen, the betrayal she'd felt from Kase, from Fran, had made her realise she was truly alone in the world, which had made her spin her cocoon of solitude tighter. And now she was only just finding out about what she was capable of doing to those who came close.

She must have paused for a long time because Holden spoke again.

'I'm sorry. You've been so good, listening to me pour out my life story, my grief. I forgot that sometimes these things take time. I just feel like we've known each other for years, not days.'

Her voice was quiet. 'I do too. Sometimes I just can't find the right words.'

'That's okay. All I really need you to do now is find forks,' he said, smiling and draining the pot of pasta.

They sat outside under a sky that went up forever and ate their meal, letting the velvety silence of the night embrace them. The moonlight smoothed the waters of the bay silver beyond the dark line of trees. Holden's voice was soft, tentative, as he leaned back and took up his wine.

'Tell me something that no one else knows about you. Anything.'

Her mind filled with an awful whisper. *I killed someone.* 'I've never had a real boyfriend.'

She pressed her hand to her mouth, cursing the wine. But at least she hadn't said that other thing. That thing hovering on the edge of her consciousness like a spiderweb – invisible but sticky, waiting for her to walk into it.

'Nothing long term, I mean,' she said, quietly mortified. She thought of Phillip, the closest thing she'd ever had to a relationship, questioning how she wasn't married by her late thirties, as though it was an abomination. Is that what Holden thought too? That there was something wrong with her?

'Well, Charlie and I were high-school sweethearts, so I've really only had one girlfriend. And it didn't exactly work out …'

It was Sylvie's turn to frown. 'So, there was no one after the divorce?'

'No. Just you.'

Such simple words but they felt like the sweetest ones she'd ever heard. They infused into every molecule of her body.

He reached across the table and squeezed her hand. 'Thank you for trusting me, for coming here with me. I'm guessing it must be … a little strange.'

She shook her head. 'No, it's not strange at all. I know we talked about being on the periphery of your own life and knowing what it's meant to look like, but not being able to get there … I feel like this is the getting there bit. Do you ever have that feeling when something's playing out in your life, that even though you didn't expect it, it kind of feels *written*. Like some part of you knew it was going to happen, and happen just like this?'

He smiled. 'That a man in a funny red hat would sweep you away to a deserted farmhouse lined with books that reminded him of his daughter?'

She laughed. 'Yes, yes, that's exactly how I knew it was going to play out.'

'Oh well, that makes one of us.' His smile was so big his face opened, like a new day, and she noticed a dimple appear in his cheek.

She squeezed his hand. 'I did. I mean I didn't know up until now, but now that I'm here it feels inevitable. I remember when I used to write stories, the same thing would happen. I'd just get this tiny glimpse, this sliver, like a peek into a world I knew would be revealed to me … but I had to be patient. I had to write into it and have faith that things would play out as they were meant to. And when it was written I'd look at it and think, yes, that's what it was always meant to be.'

'I didn't take you as someone who believes in fate,' he said taking a sip of his wine but not letting go of her hand.

'I don't really know if I do. Not really. But I do believe there's magic in the world.'

'That's what I love about you. You don't shy away from the darkness, yet you still see the magic too. I think I'd forgotten about that bit.'

'That's because you'd forgotten about books.'

His eyes glistened and he swallowed. She felt a lump form in her own throat.

He kissed the back of her hand. 'Will you read something to me?'

She already knew the book she would take from the shelves. It was her super power, she explained to him while she washed up and he dried – matching people to books. Holden said that one day she was destined to open a bookshop, because that was a gift not to be wasted. She laughed and wondered why she hadn't done that already. Just like she wondered how it had taken her half her life to meet this man.

He took her hand and led her to the main bedroom, which overlooked the dark forest and the silver water of the bay. The window was open, and the air was laced with pine and salt. Sylvie felt a curl of desire, but also uncertainty, hope and fear mixing like the sea and forest scents. It had been so long since she'd been with a man. She wasn't ready. Even though it was Holden.

Perhaps sensing her hesitation, he pulled her onto the bed but rested his head in her lap. She ran her fingers through his dark hair, the intimacy of the gesture spreading warmth through her. She opened the novel, *The Time Traveller's Wife*, one of her favourite books and the story of a little girl and a father who defy the laws of time to find each other again.

* * *

They had fallen asleep with the book lodged between them, like a child. She didn't know how long they'd been reading, or even how the words had drifted into silence, and then sleep. They had moved from one realm into another seamlessly. The early morning light fell like a veil through the bare window. The soft birdcalls, the whisper of water in the distance, enveloped her. She felt cocooned here in this new light. Holden's chest rose and fell, his eyelids translucent. This small vulnerability moved her. If she'd been a painter, she would have liked to capture him this way. One lean, muscular arm stretched behind his head, the other resting on the white sheet.

She wanted to reach out to feel his breath on her skin. She'd never slept overnight in a man's bed. In some ways this moment of waking seemed more intimate than sex. The most human time – a soft return from the dream state. The tiny hairs on his tanned arms caught the light and she couldn't help but run her fingers along them. He roused and a sleepy smile slid onto his mouth. He reached for her, eyes still closed, and drew her into his warmth. The smell of him was intoxicating. They lay like that while the morning opened her eyes, her mouth, the sun growing warm and the bird song loud.

Sylvie showered and dressed, combing her wet hair, remembering how Holden had run his fingers through it when he read her a chapter. This intimacy unfurled inside her, a ribbon of promise. Her face looked full in the mirror, the whites of her eyes bright. For perhaps the first time in her life, she felt beautiful.

They ate fruit and toast and then finished their tea on the veranda overlooking the bay. Their talk was as easy as the sun's slow ascent through the blue sky, and the glide of the water birds on the mirror surface of the dam. The tension of the past few days felt far away – Kase's island a dark shadow crouching on the horizon.

They packed a picnic of bread, cheese and fruit, and the remainder of the bottle of wine, and drove the unsealed road towards Cape Bruny. The road skimmed the coast, the bush flush against cliffs, trees testing the salty wash with their toes. They rounded a bend and the lighthouse slid into view in the distance, bright against the dark horizon. A beacon of safety, of hope. And yet Sylvie shivered. *Ominous.* She wanted to warn Holden that she was headed towards the place in her mind that had been lost, like a ship in the night. But the tide felt like it had snagged her, and she let herself be carried, an anchor of dread dragging at her.

As though sensing her mood, Holden took her hand and squeezed it, one hand on the steering wheel, his eyes crinkled against the sunlight streaming through the open window. He told her about the shipwrecks that had taken place here in 1835, prompting the building of the lighthouse by convict labour in 1836. It had been continuously manned by a keeper for 158 years.

Sylvie thought of Tristan, whose life had ended at a lighthouse at the other end of the world. The other end of her life. *You pushed him.* She knew she had to let herself meet the sharp rocks of memory, where the lights had gone out forever and she'd become lost at sea.

CHAPTER 18

headland *(n.)* – a promontory extending into a large body of water.

Sylvie had expected wild wind and salt stinging her eyes, but the sun caressed her skin, the breeze a soft breath on her neck. Gulls called as they wheeled above, joining the sound of waves crashing on rocks far below. The lighthouse was blinding white against a blue, cloud-swept sky. They walked the path towards it in single file, taking in the scoop of beach on one side of the headland, and the bottle green water of a bay lined with steep rocky cliffs on the other. She felt as exposed as the structure in front of her, her own smallness against the loud indifference of the elements. She wondered how humans ever thought they could tame nature, stop the breaking of their hulls on rocks.

When they reached the top they found a smattering of tourists and the lighthouse locked for maintenance. But Sylvie didn't need to go inside. She didn't need to be any higher up than she already was. She gazed out to the horizon and felt tears prick her eyes. She didn't know what she thought she'd find here – some clue? Some entry into the darkened portal of her mind?

Holden was beside her. He took her hand.

'Come on,' he said. 'I know a spot only the locals can get to.'

She followed him through the low scrub down a track so narrow that only someone who knew it was there would find it. She was glad to be leaving the lonely lighthouse behind. The track was steep, and the branches scratched her skin under her thin dress. They were heading down towards the bay where the deep green water met black rocks and a pebbled beach. The descent took her breath, but she scrambled to keep up. They came to a place where the cliff had fallen away and Sylvie's heart slipped like the loose rocks under her feet, but Holden steadied her. They walked perilously close to the edge, wild seagrasses twisting in the wind. And then suddenly the wind was gone. The cove was tiny and sheltered by a sheer wall of rock. The water lapped softly at the shore. They stepped onto the smooth stones that ran out into the sea. Sylvie picked one up. It was warmed by the sun.

'Do you like it?' Holden took a picnic rug from his backpack and made a place for them to sit on some sand hidden beneath a low-hanging tree. The water sparkled through the branches.

He passed her a cup of tea from a thermos. It was sweet and milky and she realised she was thirsty.

'Thank you. How do you know about this place?'

'I can't even remember, you know. I feel like I've always known it. Locals just call it The Cove. It's part of the local lore, actively kept secret from tourists.'

'It's the place people come to make out, isn't it?' She laughed. 'You've brought me to the local kissing spot.'

He smiled. 'I might have.'

Their eyes met and his face was suddenly serious and naked with desire. Before she could react, he reached for her, easing her down onto the sand. Her blood rushed in her ears. His kiss tasted like salty air and sweet tea as he ran his fingers down her body, brushing her breasts under her clothing, sending pleasure gliding through her. She ached for him in a way she hadn't known before. For the taste, the smell, the feel of his body. It was like the moment before diving into a cool pool. The sweet anticipation of relief, release. She kissed his neck, finding his lips again. It felt like her body waking up and her mind closing down.

'Are you okay with this?' he asked, pulling his top over his head. His body was browned by the sun, honed by the physical nature of his work. She nodded and unbuttoned her dress, letting it fall to her waist. She was conscious of her paleness, as pale as the fine sand beneath them. She was almost in camouflage. His fingers were cool as they traced the line of her jaw, her neck, and down her stomach. When he touched her between the legs she heard her own moan above the sound of the sea.

His breath was in her ear. 'I want to make love to you. Is that what you want?'

Her throat constricted with longing. 'Yes,' she said. And then he was above her, naked. His lean body was knotted with muscles, like branches. She felt his hardness between her hands, and wanted it in her softest places. His eyes held a question and she answered it with her hips and then they were soldered together, mouth to mouth. It felt as though every moment of being within Holden's orbit had been leading to this moment. It wasn't pleasure and it wasn't pain, it was both together and it startled her. He was tender, his breath a soft breeze against her cheek, and he was rough, a deep ocean current pulling her into him. They moved to its slow, undulating pulse. Holden cried out and she could feel the rush of the sea foaming inside her, flooding her.

She heard voices then. Distant, laughing in the bush beyond and a cold feeling overtook her. Holden rolled away and she felt hollowed out. Empty. She curled up, tight as a seashell. An image rushed at her like a wave. She was in the dark. *Voices. The full moon. Tristan. Gabe.* And Holden was pulling his pants up over his hips and her naked body was trembling, lying broken on the rocks, the lighthouse a terrifying streak in the corner of her eye.

SUMMER 1967

The street was wet and a soft rain had begun to fall. First light tugged gently at the edges of the early morning gloom. Franny and Eve had ridden an empty bus home and walked in tired silence, arms linked, down the familiar suburban street. It felt strangely comforting after what they'd seen. The frumpy, sleeping houses, so innocent, so domestic, reminded Franny of being a child. Of being safe. She suddenly wanted to be inside, in her own bed.

She saw the lights reflected in the dark asphalt before she saw their source. Blue and red flashes that seemed out of place in the quiet, tree-lined street. Eve's hand tightened around her arm. She saw her own uncertainty reflected in Eve's eyes. There was an ambulance parked in the street. It was absurdly silent, the emergency no longer pressing. A slow dread moved through Franny. She was suddenly very cold.

They stopped in front of Franny's house and stood as though in a dream. A medic standing by the ambulance approached them. 'You girls shouldn't be out here, go home,' he said. 'Nothing to see here.'

Franny felt herself float outside her body. 'But this is my house,' she said.

The man straightened and Franny saw alarm cross his features before it was quickly replaced by a sorrow that made her stomach drop. 'You live here?' he asked.

They both nodded and she could see him taking in the makeup running down their faces, their too grown-up clothes.

'We've been out, in the city,' said Eve, a sudden earnestness in her voice.

'What's your surname?' he asked, wary.

'Taylor,' said Franny. 'Is everything okay? What's happened? Is there an emergency?'

The man put his hand on her shoulder. 'Is your mother June Taylor?'

Franny felt the world tilt, as though the thing that had so seamlessly held everything together had come undone, and she found herself falling. The man's face was suddenly close to hers. She could feel his breath on her wet cheek.

'Your dad's inside. I'm going to get him, okay? You stay here. Is this your sister?' He indicated to Eve. 'She's going to wait here with you, while I get Dad.'

Franny watched the man run inside. She looked up at Eve, and couldn't tell whether her cheeks were wet from tears or the rain. Blue-black rivers ran down her face and her lips were a bright streak across her face. She looked like a tragedy. A clown.

Jack came running out of the house and wrapped Eve in his arms. All Franny could think was, *Where's my dad*? Her father walked out of the house, but his body was different from Jack's. It was as though he'd aged twenty years in one night. She could see the old man he would become.

Franny wanted him to take her in his arms the way Jack was hugging Eve. She wanted him to whisper that everything would be okay as he patted her head, as Jack was doing for his daughter. But her father stood above her, his face dark, his eyes hollow and said, 'Your mother has died.'

Franny heard laughter come out of her mouth and she wondered why on earth she was laughing if her mother had died. She grasped for her father, but his body was cold and unresponsive, like a corpse. She cried out then, because all she wanted was to be held. To be safe in her own bed, not soaking wet on the street with strange people and places filling her mind, away from this unfolding nightmare. Someone wrapped a blanket around her shoulders and led her to sit on the front steps. The same front steps her mother had walked up a million times doing things she thought would go on forever – carrying groceries into the house, watering the plants. Now they seemed absurd in their normalcy.

Franny was given a mug of something and she drank, but she couldn't feel the warmth even though she could see the steam. Eve took her hand and tried to hug her, but she couldn't feel anything, anyone.

A policewoman sat down with them. She kept saying everything would be okay, but her eyes were saying something different. Franny couldn't bear to see the sympathy there. Their fathers were talking in low voices to the medics just inside the front door. Snippets of their conversation floated by, the words like barbs embedding into her. *Found her unresponsive. Unsuccessful CPR. In the bedroom. No note. We'll investigate further. Alcohol and drugs. A toxicology report.*

A police radio blared from a nearby car and the policewoman got up. Franny and Eve were left alone. Suddenly Franny felt that they were very young, and very silly. 'They never even asked us where we went, why we were coming home at dawn,' she said.

Eve hugged her. 'I guess it doesn't matter.'

'But it does,' said Franny. 'Because we killed her. We put drugs in her tea and it killed her. That's what the ambulance officer just said. Alcohol and drugs mixed.'

Eve pulled back. Her voice was low, whispered but urgent. 'We don't know that. We don't know that at all. They said there was no note, so they think it's a suicide. And I know this is hard but June, she wasn't happy. She was in a bad marriage.'

Franny felt anger fizz up her spine. 'You said the Valium wouldn't hurt her.' Her eyes filled with tears. 'I trusted you.'

'It didn't. It wasn't … it wouldn't have been enough. I promise.' She looked around. 'Please, Franny, keep your voice down.'

Franny's shoulders bunched around her neck and she looked Eve straight in the eye. 'Why? Because you don't want the police to know you drugged my mum?'

'It wasn't just me. We both agreed. It was part of *our* plan.'

'Your plan. I never wanted to do it. Not really. I was worried. I just did it to get you away from Teddy.'

She saw the impact of her words on Eve, who swallowed hard. 'Maybe she overdosed on other pills. Maybe it was a coincidence. Or maybe she already had Valium in her system.'

Franny laughed and this time it was as dark and hollow as the look in her father's eyes. 'No, Eve. Maybe the fortune-teller was right. This is what freaked her out. I saw her face when I drew that card. Well, this,' she indicated to the scene around them, 'is the card.'

At that moment, an ambulance officer moved them gently away from the front door. A gurney with a white sheet over a body was wheeled out. All Franny could think was, *that's Mum under there*. She wanted to tear the sheet off, clamber up on that bed and curl her body into her mother's. Feel her fingers smooth the damp hair from her forehead, smell the soft floral scent of her. This was all a bad dream. It was absurd that a woman with a love of gardening and afternoon cocktails and silk scarves, a woman who fought, and smashed vases against walls and railed against her husband's oppression could have made this choice. It was impossible that she could have left Franny alone in the world.

Eve reached for her, but Franny slapped her arm away. Her words were choked. 'You stay away from me. Now I know why you move from house to house. You're a bad omen. No one wants you.'

Eve's face collapsed and Franny felt remorse twinge in her. But she thought of the fortune-teller's words, and of the real reason she'd let Eve put Valium in her mother's tea and drag her into Kings Cross in the middle of the night.

Franny locked eyes with Eve and it was the first time she'd seen total vulnerability there. She felt a fire burn up through her. 'And you stay away from Teddy. He's mine. He was mine first. He was never yours. If you come near us again, I swear I'll tell the police everything. I'll tell them that you killed my mum.'

CHAPTER 19

ghostly *(adj.)* – ethereal, spectral, strange.

'Sylvie, are you okay? Talk to me, please.' Holden hovered above her, stroking her hair, his face worried. 'Did I hurt you?' He passed her his shirt to cover herself.

She managed to shake her head and uncurl herself from the ball she'd rolled into, and reach for him. He pulled her into an embrace and sighed in relief, pressing his forehead to hers. His fingers found the dampness on her cheeks.

'You're crying.' He wiped the tears from her face with his thumbs.

'I'm sorry. No, you were beautiful … It was beautiful.'

Part of her wanted to say that making love always just made her cry, but could she really skirt the surface with him after all they'd shared? This was real. The first real thing she'd ever had. She couldn't start with lies. She knew she needed to tell him the truth.

'I told you about the night I hit my head and forgot everything. At the lighthouse? The night Tristan died?'

He nodded, understanding washing over his face. He looked

towards the clifftop where the lighthouse stood stark against the sky. 'This lighthouse … did it trigger something?'

'I remembered … something.' The cold dread of the memory slid through her and she hugged her arms, which were pricked with goosebumps.

'While making love?' Confusion darkened his features.

Sylvie pulled her dress up over her chest and drew her knees up. How could she tell him that she'd never been able to take that final step with Phillip or her other failed relationships? That Holden was the first man she'd ever felt safe with? He'd think she was a freak.

'Yes. I know it's … weird.' She shook her head and fresh tears ran down her face. 'It was like a nightmare. Not the sex. That was amazing, Holden, I mean it. It was like nothing I've ever experienced. But the memory … when you rolled off me …'

'Oh Sylvie, I'm so sorry.' Holden pulled her into a hug and she clung to him, the beat of his heart loud through his thin shirt.

'No, it's not your fault. It felt like an unlocking of something. When we were coming here, I knew I'd feel something, I knew I'd remember something. When I stood on the clifftop next to the lighthouse, I expected to feel it then.'

'You should have told me.'

'I'm telling you now.'

He kissed her hair. 'Do you want to tell me about it? This memory?'

She bit her lip until she tasted blood. Was she really going to tell him this? She already felt so raw, so exposed. Making love had stripped everything from her. She'd been cracked open.

She took a shaky breath. 'When I came to you at the cabin, I was upset after confronting Kase, because she told me something.' She swallowed back the lump in her throat, but it was lodged there, choking her words. 'She said … she said … I'd pushed Tristan off the rocks that night.' She felt her cheeks flare hot with shame. 'She said that he didn't accidentally slip like I had thought. I pushed him. That's why she didn't answer my calls. That's why there was no more contact between us.'

She watched Holden's face blanch, as white as the trunks of the trees circling the beach.

He shook his head and grabbed her hand. 'That can't be true, Sylvie. I don't think you're capable of doing that.'

'But what if I am?' She was crying now, salt from her tears running into her mouth. 'Why would Kase tell me that otherwise? She was trying to protect me all those years ago. Why would she lie?'

'You would never do that. I know you. *I know you.* I feel like I've always known you, and you'd never hurt anyone on purpose. You're the most gentle, empathetic soul I've ever met.'

She squeezed his hand, but shook her head. 'She said I was angry because I told Tristan I loved him that night, but he laughed at me, rejected me. And I was mortified.'

'You wouldn't have pushed him for that.'

'Maybe I did. I was seventeen and drunk.'

'Was that the awful memory? You pushing him?' His face was still pale.

She pressed her palms to her eyes. 'No. There's something else, Holden, something scarier.' She gulped back the tears. 'I can't see it properly, but I can feel it … the dread.' She shook her head.

'Maybe it's your memory playing tricks. You had a brain injury, Sylvie. What happened that night is so long ago, it doesn't really matter anymore. The past is the past. Who cares what Kase says? Who knows what her motivation is, or if she's even telling the truth? You're here now, with me, and that's all that matters. Stay here. I promise, I'll look after you.'

His face was so full of reassurance, of hope, of love, that it felt like it broke something in her and mended it at the same time. He wrapped his arms around her, and she sobbed into his chest.

But how? she wanted to whisper … *How can I make love to you without remembering what happened that night?*

* * *

They drove the coast road home without words, with the windows down. Sylvie let the salt air rinse her hair, the hot sun burn away the darkness. She closed her eyes against its bright reassurance. Maybe she could do what Holden said, forget the past, forget Kase and the Fowler family. She could take extended leave from work and stay here with Holden for a while, reading books to each other, the forest and the sea on their sheets. He would be gentle with her when they made love again. He would look after her. They'd never return to Cape Bruny Lighthouse. Maybe her mind would never return to that night. Maybe the puzzle pieces would stay scattered and unsolved. Maybe he was right. How could she even trust her own memories?

Holden reached out and took her hand. 'Sylvie, are you okay?'

He had stopped calling her Sylvie Plath. They had their own story now.

She nodded and smiled, squeezed his hand.

'We won't go back there,' he said, his eyes flicking to the rear-vision mirror where the lighthouse still lanced the horizon.

'No.' Sylvie shook her head.

'But I meant what I said. Will you stay for a while? I'll take some leave from the island, from the taxi. I haven't had time off in a year.'

'I haven't had time off in ten years.'

He smiled, and an understanding passed between them, that she was accepting his offer.

They pulled onto the track that wound up to the farmhouse. A flock of white swans took off from the dam and Holden stopped the truck to watch them soar into the sky.

'How's that for a welcome home?'

Home. She leaned over and kissed him deeply, her heart lifting as easily as those white-winged birds.

A bunch of wildflowers sat on the front steps, freshly picked, their stems still glistening with moisture. She shot him a look. 'Another welcome home gift?' she asked.

He shook his head and rubbed his jaw. 'They're not from me.'

She opened the envelope with her name on it, her pulse quickening when she saw the handwriting.

Dear Sylvie,

I'm so sorry for how everything happened the other morning. I'm so sorry to hurt you again. We thought you might be here with Holden. We're worried about you. I know we abandoned you last time, I don't want to do that again. I asked Mum about the note in the front of The Bell Jar – Franny and Eve. She said it WAS her and Evangeline, but that it's complicated?? She won't talk to me about it. She wants to talk to us both. She said it's important. I know you probably hate me after what I told you about Tristan, but Mum doesn't know about any of that, I promise.

Please come back. It's just me and Mum here today, everyone else has gone into Hobart. We'll be here waiting for you.

Kase xx

SUMMER 1968

Franny was coming out of the startling cold of the surf when she saw her, silhouetted against the late afternoon sky. It had been so long, but her form was familiar, yet strange too, like glimpsing your own reflection in a shop window. Her instinct was to call out. *'Eve!'* But something stronger overlaid it, and Franny turned back to see Teddy, Audrey and Bob coming out of the water behind her. They didn't see Eve, or notice that Franny had stopped, still as a shell on the shoreline. The others flopped onto beach towels, Bob passing around beers, which they sipped, closing their eyes against the hot sun.

Eve was thinner than Franny remembered, but it had been a year. Maybe she'd forgotten. Maybe Eve had always looked like bones moving beneath skin. She was wearing a wide-brimmed hat and a black bathing costume. She was alone. Part of Franny, the largest part, wanted to run to her, but her heart was beating too fast in her chest and sweat slicked her skin despite the sea breeze.

The others called to her and she felt her limbs moving towards them even while her eyes remained snared on Eve.

Franny felt Teddy's warm arms draw her to him. His neck smelled like coconut oil and salt, so comforting, as familiar as this, their stretch of beach. She knew Eve was watching her, she could feel the heat of her gaze prickling her skin. Another part of Franny, a small, sharp, cold part felt a rush of satisfaction as she leaned into Teddy's bare chest. She knew what this would look like to Eve. What it would *feel* like. The four of them stretched languidly on the sand, their easy banter. Their togetherness.

Eve was suddenly standing in front of them, her skinny arms gripping her towel, eyes hidden beneath her hat.

'Hi Franny,' Eve said, her voice small, almost lost on the breeze.

Franny sat up. Teddy's hand was still on her thigh.

'Oh my God. Eve Dane. Is that you?' Audrey's voice was loud, abrasive, like cold sand on soft skin. 'But you're so skinny. I hardly even recognised you.'

Franny saw Eve's shoulders straighten, still that defiance remained, even now. And seeing it, Franny felt her tenderness towards Eve harden. Snippets of that night came back to her like shattered glass. The shards lodged in her chest, making it hard to breathe. Eve's indifference, her brashness, the way she'd reacted to Franny's mother being wheeled out on that gurney – as though she'd played no role, instead of apologising for slipping drugs into the last cup of tea her mother would ever drink.

'Hi Eve, want a beer?' asked Teddy, and Franny felt him disengage from her. He rested his arms casually on his knees, smiled his lopsided smile.

Eve suddenly looked coy and took off her hat, smoothed her hair over her shoulders. 'Sure.'

An awful, familiar roll of fear moved through Franny. It was like pressing a bruise. Franny had told Eve never to come near them again, but to Teddy she'd only said Eve's dad had forbidden her from ever seeing her friend again after it was discovered they'd gone to Kings Cross that night. He didn't know that Eve was dead to her. Eve and her father moved away, into another small place at the back of someone's house a few suburbs away. Franny heard snippets of gossip from friends at her school who knew people at Eve's.

The smell of incense faded from the carpet and Franny claimed the flat as her own. Her father immersed himself in work and largely ignored her. She took to making dinners for them both. It was what her mother had always done, even when they'd been fighting; she always had a meal on the table. It felt, sadly, like her legacy. And it felt like the only way for her and her father to connect – baked beans on toast, sausages with mash, tuna mornay. Her father always drank whisky from a cut-glass tumbler. They exchanged polite conversation – never mentioning her mother, never mentioning June. It was as though her mother had been wiped from the face of the earth and Franny knew that if she pressed her father, an imperfect memory of her might emerge, one she didn't want to face, one she didn't want as a legacy. After dinner, her father would turn on the news and she'd retreat to the granny flat. He never protested, and she was left to nurse the mother-shaped hole in her body alone. But at least there was no more smashing glass and shouting. Now there was only the sound of the sea and shades of silence.

Franny went back to listening to The Beatles and turned off The Doors whenever she heard the sensual, languid beat that took her back to that summer of 1967. She told Teddy she didn't like that music anymore because it reminded her of her mother, and he stopped listening to it too. He had been there to smooth the tears from her face, to still her when her body shook so violently that she thought she was dying. He took her to the beach to gaze out onto the ocean on the pretence of watching him surf. Franny's grief had washed in and out like the white foam. She was grieving for her mother, but she knew deep down, she was also grieving what she had lost with Eve. The anger she felt shifted, like sand underfoot. Some days as hot and burning as the sun beating on her skull on the beach. She was angry with Eve, angry with her mother, angry at herself. Some days the pain drowned her. On others her head was ever so slightly above the water, until one day, only recently, she found that she'd spent a whole afternoon without its whirlpool sucking her down.

And as the flowers died in her mother's garden, another blooming opened her cold, closed heart. *Teddy.* Their first kiss, underwater, buzzing from beer while swimming in the pool. Their first time on the lumpy mattress in the granny flat after a party. Having Teddy secured Franny's place at school. Audrey began to be nice to her – her boyfriend Bob surfed with Teddy. The two of them spent hours on the sand watching their boyfriends slice the water with their longboards. They didn't talk about books or writing or going to university and living in Kings Cross. They talked about hair styles and makeup and who was going steady with who. But they were friends. Uncomplicated and girly, but more, they were a foursome, spending every weekend at the beach with their boyfriends. In some ways her life had worked out more perfectly than she'd ever imagined, like a TV commercial – the teenage suburban dream.

But on nights when the moon fell in long shapes along her walls at the bottom of the garden, the words of the fortune-teller returned to her. *Sometimes it is friendship that is our true life calling, our true soul connection. Remember that, girls. What you seek here, you have already found.*

Franny was brought back to the present by Audrey's loud voice. 'Oh, I don't think there's time for more beers.' She nudged Bob. 'We're going to the pictures with the others, and we've got to get cleaned up.'

Eve hovered, uncertain, having been about to reach for the beer Teddy was holding out. Part of Franny wanted to link arms with Eve and walk away from the lot of them, along the beach. She longed to hear about the books Eve had read, the dreams she had dreamed. Was she still going to be a writer? Had she returned to Kings Cross to sip wine with the bohemians? Where was she living now? The other part of her stayed still as Eve recoiled and Audrey made a show of packing up the Esky, standing and shaking sand from her towel.

'Oh, what are you seeing at the pictures?' Eve asked, stepping back from the sandstorm Audrey was creating with her towel, her voice a little too hopeful. Franny swallowed back the pity she felt.

Audrey stuck out her hip. 'Oh, there's no way you'd like it, Eve Dane. It wouldn't be anywhere near arty enough for your tastes, just something fun our boys will like.'

Our boys. There was the line in the sand, as though Audrey had taken a stick and drawn it around their group, with Eve on the outer.

Eve's face fell and she pulled her hat back on. Lightning sheeted across the horizon and Franny felt one cold droplet on her shoulder.

'Looks like there's gonna be a storm anyway,' said Teddy, obviously trying to soften the blow Audrey had just dealt Eve. 'Maybe some other time, hey? We're always ...' He shrugged and lifted his chin to indicate the waves. 'Here.'

Eve smiled awkwardly and her eyes met Franny's for a moment. Franny felt the pull of their connection – bright, immediate, like the sulphur flare of a match – just the same as the first time they'd met on the doorstep of her house, when her mother had been alive. A vulnerability and sadness came over Eve's face before she turned and walked off down the beach, until she was a small black smudge in the salt haze. Thunder grumbled above them as they left the beach and piled into Teddy's Valiant. Franny felt it at her core – relief mixed with a deep emptiness that felt like regret.

CHAPTER 20

truth *(n.)* – that which is true;
the true or actual facts of a case.

Fran looked at this woman walking up the beach towards the house and felt, what? *A pang.* Yes, that's what it was. Deep and sharp and knowing. *Sylvie.* This beautiful, quiet girl, who had tormented her in many ways. But she was an innocent. She didn't know. And the truth was, Fran loved her, still, somehow, after everything that had happened, she loved her. Not like she loved Kase, because her daughter was of her own body, grown from her own flesh. But Sylvie had been wounded by life, by circumstance, and by her mother, in a way that joined them all, just below the surface. Like the hazy moment between sleep and wake. Like serendipity. Like fate. And then Sylvie was standing on her doorstep, her wind-wild hair about her face, her expression serious and shadowed. Fran knew this day was probably always going to come. She just didn't think it would be today.

Fran drew her into a hug – she couldn't help it. She'd always wanted to protect the frailty in Sylvie, so obvious, so like her own. 'Kase will be so glad you came back. We were worried.'

Sylvie's eyes were large and the pale green of clean, shallow water. They spoke volumes more than her words. They always had. Fran knew she was upset and wondered what had happened between the girls to make Sylvie flee with Holden, and without saying goodbye. So out of character. Fran liked Holden and she could see their connection even before they had – two lone birds drifting on the same slipstream. Holden had lost his whole life, Sylvie had always been lost.

Kase wouldn't be drawn on what had made Sylvie leave, but Fran felt she knew something more. Daughters could never hide things from their mothers for very long. Mothers on the other hand, could hide things for whole lifetimes, it turned out.

She rubbed Sylvie's arm and opened the door wide. 'Come on in, I'll put the kettle on.'

Sylvie followed her wordlessly into the kitchen, and Fran called up the stairs to Kase, who had been ensconced in her study all morning.

Fran set out teacups and a pot and spooned tea leaves into it. 'So, how are you liking Bruny? It's very wild and beautiful, isn't it? And Holden's place is just the perfect old cottage.'

Sylvie nodded and sat down on the bar stool opposite. She had the air of a pale horse with its long legs folded underneath, yet ready to bolt at the first sign of danger. 'Yes, it's beautiful. So windswept and deserted.' Her voice was soft, unsure.

Fran poured boiling water into the pot. 'Sylvie, are you okay? Holden's lovely … like part of the family. But we were just surprised when you and he left so suddenly … Well, it just seemed a little out of character. But he's looking after you, I take it? Everything's okay?'

Sylvie's arms clamped around her body. 'I'm sorry. It was really rude of me to leave without saying … You'd been such a lovely hostess.'

'Did you and Kase have some kind of argument?' Fran grimaced. 'You know what she's like, she won't talk to me about it. Told everyone the party was over last night and that she needed a day of writing and they should all go to Hobart for the day without her. Even Henry.' Fran rolled her eyes. 'The moods of artists.'

Kase stepped into the kitchen. 'I did need to write. I do. I have a deadline.'

Fran arched a brow. 'You say that every time, hon, and then they wait patiently until the book is done. You didn't have to be so pushy.'

The air thickened with tension and Fran lifted the teapot. 'Do you want tea? I've just made a pot. There's some leftover cake in the fridge.'

'You don't always have to feed us, Mum. We're not fifteen.' She slid onto the stool next to Sylvie.

'I'd love some cake, thanks,' said Sylvie, smiling sweetly.

Kase glared at her. The air snapped and crackled.

'Well, it doesn't matter if your child is fifteen or forty, mothers have a deep instinctual need to feed their children.'

'Not mine,' Sylvie said lightly, getting up and taking the cake box out of the fridge.

Fran shot Sylvie a knowing smile.

'Speaking of Evangeline …' Kase opened the lid of the box, stuck her finger into the icing and licked it. 'So, what's the story, Mum? With you and her? Why are we only just finding out you used to be friends? Were you friends? And why were there never any friendly cups of tea or chats on the doorstep? Can you cut me a slice, Sylvie? I haven't eaten properly all day.'

Fran felt butterflies release in her stomach and she wrung the tea towel in her hands. 'I'll have cake, too. Let's take it out onto the front deck, shall we?' She needed the still line of the horizon to steady her. She always had. She thought back to the view out the window from her bedroom at Collaroy. Of the view from her Palm Beach home. How many times she'd looked out onto water to anchor her when her life felt like it was choppy.

'Keeping us in suspense. God, it must be a good story,' said Kase, putting a huge slice of cake onto a plate.

They went through the house and sat on the weather-beaten cane chairs facing the ocean. The afternoon breeze was soft in the wind chimes. Kase sprawled languorously on the day bed, eating cake with her fingers. Honestly, sometimes she reminded Fran so much of Evangeline, and Sylvie, sitting, nursing her teacup and saucer chastely on her lap, was just like herself. *There is an alchemy at play*, she thought. *Light and dark, yin and yang, mother and daughter. Best friends.* She could feel the weight of Kase's and Sylvie's expectation. *I must just start at the beginning*, she thought, taking a deep breath.

She looked at Sylvie. 'Your mother and I used to be dear friends. Not the kind of friends who come and go, the ones on the periphery, but the friend who … I don't know, who gets you right away, I suppose. Like the two of you.' She looked to Kase, who had a piece of cake halfway to her mouth.

'How have you not told us this before?' her daughter asked. 'Sylvie, you didn't know any of this, did you?'

She shook her head.

'No one knew. Well, your father knew.'

'What does that mean?' Kase asked.

Fran turned towards Sylvie, whose face was as still as the water beyond the waves. 'I'm sorry I have to be the one to tell you this, when it's probably your mother's place to do so … and maybe she never would have, but the truth isn't owned by one person. It's all of ours, it's the narrative of all our lives, not just Evangeline's.'

'You're scaring me a bit, Mum,' said Kase, now propped up on one elbow.

'Oh Kase, always my dramatic one. I guess you were destined to be a writer. Like her. You know what I was just thinking? How much you're like Eve, and how much Sylvie is like me.'

'You used to call her Eve,' said Sylvie. 'I've never heard her called that before, aside from in the inscription in the front of that book. It softens her.'

Fran chuckled. 'She was softer when she was younger. I fear I may have played a part in her hardening.'

Kase was sitting upright now. 'And you call me dramatic. Oh my God, I think we're going to need something stronger than tea. Bloody hell.' Kase got up and went inside.

'Sylvie, I just want you to know how much your mother meant to me. She was my best friend, my "Kase". She may not have been around for very long in my life, but it felt like a lifetime, maybe because it was in those important, formative teenage years. And because it felt like what we had, well, it burned bright. And when the two of you became friends, we couldn't believe it. But then, we sort of could. Sometimes it seems there's a strange serendipity at work in life. Something we can't always see, but we can sort of feel. And I daresay that's the little bit of magic, really, isn't it? The thing that we cling onto, hope for.'

'How did you meet?' Sylvie asked, chewing her bottom lip.

'She came to live in the granny flat at the bottom of my garden with her dad.'

'So, she's always lived in the background of other people's lives. On the periphery. She's told me so little about her upbringing.'

Kase returned with a decanter of whisky, which she proceeded to pour into their empty teacups.

'Yes, I guess she grew up a bit of a drifter and she's stayed that way, hasn't she? I still remember her standing in my bedroom that first night we met. I had a view out over the lake and ocean from my window and she … I don't know, she said she knew we were going to be friends, and … we were. Just like that. Just like you and Kase in Year 7 on day one. Some things are so simple they feel like they were always going to happen.'

'Until they aren't, and you both have children who become best friends and never tell the children you even KNEW each other.' Kase threw back a slug of whisky and crossed her arms.

'What happened?' Sylvie's gaze held so much emotion it made Fran's eyes prick with tears. She drew in a shuddering breath.

'My mother died.'

'My grandmother? June? Didn't she have a drinking problem? I always kind of got the feeling she committed suicide, but you've always been very vague about it,' said Kase. 'I've always known you didn't want to talk about it and when I interrogated Dad, he always said it was a terrible accident.'

Fran looked out onto the water, tried to draw courage from the vastness of the sea. 'I didn't. Want to talk about it. There was too much shame. My own shame. God. Give me some more whisky.'

Kase topped up her cup and she drank down the burning liquid.

'Eve was there the night my mother died. We'd snuck into Kings Cross. We wanted to be bohemians. And we saw a fortune-teller.' Saying it out loud made the skin along Fran's arms tingle.

'I had no idea about any of this,' said Kase.

'Children always think that their parents' lives started when they were born.' Fran smiled and Kase rolled her eyes. 'This fortune-teller said Eve and I were bound and always would be. And now, looking at the two of you here …' Her eyes filled with tears. 'I know what she meant.'

'I don't,' said Kase, shaking her head.

'Eve and I had a pact. She … we … put Valium in my mother's tea that night. Not anything sinister, just stupid, stupid … we were stupid girls. We just needed her to stay asleep so we could sneak out to Kings Cross – she was a very light sleeper, you see. And how could we have known that my mother drank like a fish? And alcohol and Valium are a dire combination. But more than that, the toxicology report also found other drugs in her system. It wasn't the Valium that killed her, she likely did take her own life, but, you see, I blamed Eve for my mother's death. The Valium had been her idea. It was easier to blame someone, anyone but my own mother. I banished Eve from my life. From our lives.'

The sound of the waves and the cry of gulls filled up the silence as both girls stared at her.

Fran's voice wobbled. 'But really, if I'm honest, I always knew it was because of Teddy and Eve. Sometimes it's alchemy.

They had that. And I forbade it. Like I said, I banished Eve from my life. And from his. But it was inevitable that they would meet up again. Theirs was the big love story. Teddy and I didn't have that. We were friends, really. Pals. But he was mine first, and I couldn't have Eve, so neither could Teddy.' Fran realised she was crying, but she didn't wipe the tears away. She drank the rest of her whisky. The truth felt like it was unfurling from her body like a long, smooth stretch of sand. 'I guess it was selfish in a way. He tried to reach out to Eve, but I kept her at a distance. But they found a way to be together years later, while Ted and I were married. Teddy didn't want to hurt me. He loved me in his way, and he adored you kids, but his heart was with Eve. It always had been.'

Sylvie was shaking her head, her face drained of colour. 'I can't believe … surely Mum would have told me. Something that big. Even for her that would be –'

'Maybe neither of us would have ever said anything … but when you found that book with our names in it, well, I didn't want to lie by omission any longer.'

Sylvie's eyes were large and fiercely apologetic. 'I can't believe my mother did that to you. With Ted. I'm so sorry. I had absolutely no idea. I'm mortified … all those years I spent in your house.'

Fran placed her hand on top of Sylvie's and looked into her eyes. 'It doesn't change how I feel about you, Sylvie. You've always been part of this family.'

'God, Mum! Sylvie and I, we're not … Dad isn't Sylvie's …' Kase was breathless suddenly.

'What? Oh, no. No, no, you're not half-sisters, if that's what you mean.' Fran shook her head. 'They weren't together then, in the early years of our marriage. I know, believe me, I checked.'

'Oh Mum, but how on earth did you take Sylvie into our house knowing that her mother had had an affair with Dad?' Kase's face was flushed.

Fran took a deep breath and let it out slowly. 'I didn't know at first. And then when he confessed, I cried. I railed. But he said it was over with Eve. It had all happened when you kids were small and he and I were struggling, exhausted, disconnected, as parents of young children often are, and even after I knew, I didn't want to break up our family. And what could I do? You two reminded me of who we'd once been – Eve and Franny. Franny and Eve. Your bond was so strong. And Sylvie needed us. The fortune-teller told us, the two of you are bound in ways you don't yet understand. You will always be bound. I thought the she meant Eve and I would always be friends. But it seems she meant that our daughters would be friends.'

Kase moved towards Sylvie, but Sylvie got up, her teacup falling from her lap and shattering.

'I'm sorry, I just need to process …' Her hand fluttered at her throat.

'Sylvie, I love you like a daughter. I think you've always felt that. My home has always been your home and it's the same here in this house. This is between Ted and Eve, it's not your fault. You're family. My family. Kase's family. I felt that as soon as you arrived, even after all these years.'

Sylvie's face was drawn in pain as their eyes met. Fran remembered that same look. *Betrayal. Longing.* Eve had given her the same look many years ago, before she turned her back and walked away down the beach forever.

PALM BEACH, SUMMER 1996

The moon shone a silver path over the water below and the lights of the houses winked at the shoreline. The dark path snaked before them, up towards the lighthouse. Kase was glad of the others behind, drifts of their drunken laughter reaching them, softening her unease at the sounds of unknown things moving in the undergrowth. The track was steeper than she'd remembered, and leaves and branches brushed their bare legs as they climbed higher. Sylvie was humming a song from the radio Kase had heard a million times, but couldn't quite place. She loosened the scarf Sylvie had wound around her neck. She was hot now, and a sickening dizziness overcame her. She'd drunk too much. Kase pulled Sylvie down onto a step and their bodies collapsed into each other.

Sylvie put her head on Kase's shoulder. 'I'm too drunk to be doing this,' she said. 'I just want to go to sleep.'

'Same. Hey, I saw you and Trist looking at each other earlier, by the fire. What's going on there? Did you say something?'

'What? As if. Not in a million years.' Sylvie nestled into her.

'Well, maybe he's finally realised how infatuated you are with him … and how beautiful you look in that dress that I, I repeat, *I* chose for you.'

'*Shhhhh.*' Even in the dim light Kase could see Sylvie's face flushing.

Tristan and Gabe had reached them, both drinking from cans of beer. Gabe squished between the girls, putting his arms around their shoulders. His breath was sour and his words slurred.

'Come on, we've got to get to the top. The others are way behind. Goddamn fucking lightweights. But we're here to protect you girls. You never know what kind of psychos are hanging around in the bush.'

'Yeah, you,' Kase said, and Gabe punched her arm, hard. She grunted and rubbed the spot, then took his beer and drank some. 'This isn't beer. This is the hard stuff,' she said, the bourbon sickly sharp and sweet in her mouth.

Gabe took the can back, emptied it in one gulp, then crushed it and threw it into the bush. He slung an arm around Kase's shoulders, leaning heavily into her to stay upright.

Tristan pulled Sylvie to her feet as Kase extracted herself from Gabe's sweaty embrace. Maybe Sylvie's dreams were coming true, though she spotted the same can in Tristan's hands. They were very drunk, more drunk than she'd ever seen them. Kase was sure she'd seen her brother's eyes lingering on Sylvie tonight. She did look beautiful in the dress from the op shop and her hair straightened and long, like a silver ribbon down her back. Kase decided to let them have some time together.

She punched Gabe back doubly hard and said: 'Race you to the top.'

They took off, Gabe in the lead as his strong legs powered up the path, Kase stumbling a little as her eyes adjusted to the growing dark. She looked back to see Sylvie and Tristan walking together, their heads bent towards each other in conversation. Her silly brother, so blind to what was right in front of him. Maybe he was finally waking up.

The lighthouse loomed on the clifftop above and Kase's arms and legs pumped as she ran the narrow, dark bush track, her lungs burning. Gabe was long gone, and she could no longer see Sylvie and Tristan. She was totally alone. But instead of feeling frightened, she felt a ripple of something else. The moon was growing larger, hovering over the earth like a promise. She felt free. Strong. Their exams were done. Her future felt as vast and open as the shining sea below. Maybe it was the alcohol, but she felt a shiver down her spine as she stepped onto a rock jutting over the ocean. It was so high. She stood at the very edge. She felt invincible at that moment. Like anything was possible. Like she could jump and soar and land on that silver water and walk all the way to the place where the low moon met the globe. She sat down on the edge of the rock, letting her legs dangle over the side. Soon she'd be living with Sylvie in their much dreamed about flat in Newtown, going to uni together, talking philosophy over endless coffees in cute cafes. Drinking red wine and smoking while they studied English literature late into the night. When they had to eat they'd live off Lean Cuisines and toasties. They'd meet cute boys who liked to read and write as much as they did. And preferably would write deep, tortured poetry.

She heard a rustling and soft voices as Tristan and Sylvie came along the path. They were walking close together. Closer than normal. Did Tristan have his arm around her shoulders? Kase crouched silently on her rock, watching them pass. She felt torn. She wanted Sylvie to be happy, but if she was honest, she didn't really want Tristan and Sylvie to be together. They were not a good match. Sylvie was too smart for her gorgeous but simple brother. And Kase knew he wanted kids and a family soon, a steady job, not ideas and travel and books and knowledge, as she and Sylvie wanted. In a few years, Tristan would probably be living in a house with a boat docked nearby, have a pretty wife and a baby; Sylvie and Kase would be in the south of Spain, studying in Granada and visiting Morocco on the weekends. But she could see Tristan's appeal for Sylvie, apart from his looks. He was steady, reliable, solid – something missing in her upbringing. Sylvie would want something real. Something true. Someone like Tristan. Kase wasn't ready to lose her and Sylvie's intense connection to a boy, even if it was her brother.

She rejoined the path and continued up towards the lighthouse, straining to see further ahead in the dense bush. It was darker now, even with the moon casting silver across the shoulders of the headland. She came to a fork in the track. Which way did the others go? There was a sign, but it had been vandalised and was illegible. Maybe she shouldn't have gone off by herself. The alcohol was making her reckless. The boys knew this track better than her – they'd spent years climbing up and down these scrubby trails after school. She took what appeared to be the wider, more well-trodden path. She walked for a while, but an unease grew inside her. This didn't seem right. This track was taking her down into the dark depths of the bush, not up towards the lighthouse and the moon. She swallowed down her panic and redoubled back, the muscles in her legs aching and her breath quick and loud in her ears. She reached the fork in the path again and took the other way. This track skirted close to the side of the cliff. She didn't feel lost if she could see the ocean. She stopped to catch her breath, and caught sight of the lighthouse, solitary and stark in the moonlight. She wondered how many shipwrecks, how many broken boats and ghosts still lingered here. A scuttle in the bushes nearby made her jump and she quickened her pace again. She felt a wash of relief as she heard voices up ahead.

There they were, silhouetted against the moon, on a rock that jutted over the ocean just like the one she'd been sitting on. Three shapes. But something was wrong. She slowed her steps. There was a strangled sound, like someone choking, or in pain. And a grunting. Awful. Primal. *No. No. No. No. No.* Gabe's face was contorted as his body thrust violently. And Tristan. So still by comparison. Kase heard her own shout before she knew she'd screamed. Tristan reacted first, standing up before stumbling and falling down again, then retching over the side of the cliff. Gabe laughed – awful, slow, terrifying, and pulled up his shorts.

Tristan's words were slurred. 'I swear … we were just mucking around. She said she had a crush on me, she kissed me, and then … It was just meant to be a bit of fun.'

Kase's voice was strangled. 'Tristan, what have you done?' Nausea rolled through her and she fought the urge to vomit. She dropped to Sylvie's side. She was lying on her stomach, her body flat against the rock, like a broken doll. Her cheek was raw where it had scraped against the stone.

Tears blurred her vision as she gathered Sylvie to her. She covered her body with their scarf, smoothing her hair. It was curly now, as though they'd never stood with the hairdryer to straighten it, her eyes bruised with mascara as though they hadn't leaned against the bathroom sink to carefully apply it. A fierce and protective rage welled up inside Kase. Sylvie opened her eyes and looked at her, but her gaze was glassy, empty, as though the Sylvie she knew wasn't there anymore.

'No, no, no, no, what have they done to you?'

CHAPTER 21

mother *(v.)* - to be the mother of; give origin or rise to. To care for or protect as a mother does.

The wind whipped the headland and Sylvie felt its cold fingers tug at her clothing and hair. This was the spot where they had found the broken baby bird. It was the highest point on the island and the place Holden had told her she could get the best reception. Her pulse was pounding at her temples as hard as the water against the rocks below. She stared over the cliff into the surging sea and felt vertigo. Everything felt unsteady, precarious. Her mother had betrayed her, letting her be in the care of someone who should have, by all accounts, hated her. Sylvie dialled her mother's number. She didn't care what time it was in Istanbul. She wanted to wake her in the dead of night, find her when she was sleep-addled and unsuspecting and couldn't lie anymore.

Evangeline picked up on the third ring. Her voice was thick with sleep. 'Sylvie, is everything okay?'

The worry in her mother's voice made Sylvie's throat ache. It took her a moment, in which time the hiss of the international line filled up the silence. 'Fran told me. About you and Ted.

Teddy. Teddy and Eve. Why? Why didn't you tell me? How could you let me spend all my teens in that house?'

She heard her mother's sharp intake of breath. Sylvie could just imagine her with her sleep mask pushed up, sitting on the side of the bed in the elegant silk pyjamas she'd always worn. She heard the snap of a lighter.

'So, she told you.' Her voice betrayed no emotion.

'Do you even care?'

'Of course I care. I just –'

'You just what? You've just lived your life as a lie and you don't even sound sorry?'

'I don't know what to say, Sylvie. It was a very, very long time ago. There were things that happened between myself and Fran and Teddy that –'

'That you hid from me. You just kept drifting through life, doing what you pleased. Leaving the wife of your lover to essentially raise your daughter.'

'Sylvie, there were things that went on back then that you don't know about.'

'Oh, I know everything. Fran is the only honest one among you. She told me about the Valium and how she blamed you for her mother's death. How could you do that to her, and then steal her husband?'

'Sylvie, it was more complicated than that.'

'How? How could it have been more complicated? It sounds pretty simple from where I'm standing.'

'Where are you calling from? Did you go to Kase's party? Is that why all this has been dug up?'

Sylvie said nothing. She let the silence ring out between them.

Her mother sighed. 'I guess I was just trying to protect you.'

'From what? The truth? Well, you failed. On all counts.'

'Sylvie, I know it sounds inexcusable but Teddy and I were in love. I was in love with him the moment we met, but that night, the night … Did she tell you about Kings Cross and the fortune-teller? The night June died? That night changed everything. It was a terrible mistake. I never meant for June to die. Of course I didn't. And it was the tiniest amount of Valium. It couldn't have killed her. But I shouldn't have done it. But I was fifteen. I was reckless. Motherless. June and my father, Jack, had a connection … It broke my father when she died. That's three generations our families have been connected. Through what? I don't know. Fate? Destiny? Tragedy? I lost the two people who meant the world to me that night. Franny and Teddy. You don't know how hard that was for me.'

Sylvie swallowed. She did know that feeling. She felt it burn her sternum. 'I do, Mum. I do. I had it after the night Tristan died. I lost him and I lost Kase.'

Her mother went quiet, and Sylvie could hear the sigh of her lips releasing smoke. 'I'm sorry, darling. That I kept this from you, that you had to find out this way. But life is messy, and I didn't want you caught up in it. I've always tried to shield you from heartbreak, though it might not have seemed that way to you. It was always funny, well not funny, but strange and beautiful in a way, the way you and Kase found each other. Out of all the girls in that school you chose her. The only school you got a full scholarship for. We applied for three.' She gave a breathy laugh. 'And I think Fran and I always wanted to allow you that. To protect what you had. The two of you were our peace offering to each other, in a way. That somehow, after all the pain, the two of you got to have what we were never able to have.'

'But how? How was Fran able to do it? She treated me with such …' Sylvie's voice broke. 'Love.'

'Oh, Sylvie. Fran is a remarkable woman. The very best. That's why I loved her so, why I was drawn to her so strongly from the beginning. It was like best friendship at first sight. But she's not blameless in all this. She knew. She knew what she was doing when she cut Teddy and me off from each other forever. We all have stories we tell ourselves to be able to sleep at night.'

'And what stories do you tell yourself, Eve?' Sylvie asked coolly.

Her mother's voice was more vulnerable than she'd ever heard it. 'I suppose I hoped you and Kase were our salvation. But then, when Tristan died, everything fell apart again. It all feels sometimes like a spiral, a tunnel we can never get out of. Maybe this is the thing to bring you back together after all these years. We've come full circle.'

'You say it so matter-of-factly, as though you played no role in this, as though what you did doesn't matter, you just blame the universe.' Evangeline didn't reply and Sylvie felt annoyance buzz along the tops of her shoulders. 'So, are you going to tell me what happened with Ted?'

Sylvie thought of the man who had featured in the background of those teenage years at Palm Beach. Away for days as a pilot, coming in and out of their lives, sometimes sitting, straight-backed and dark-eyed with exhaustion at the end of the table, as though he was still on autopilot. She could sometimes see the man he used to be. The foppish blond hair turning grey at the temples, the easy tan of his skin. Sometimes a smile on his lips when he and Tristan spoke about surfing. There was no part of that man who felt like he belonged to her mother. He'd shown her nothing but simple politeness.

'It clearly didn't work out, despite your "love at first sight" mythology,' Sylvie said. 'He stayed with Fran. He ignored me. Until obviously it was all just too painful for them both, and he left.'

'Don't be so cynical.' Her mother's hard edge was back. 'You have no idea –'

'That's because I was never told. I was like another accessory to fill up your whimsical life. I was just the bookish daughter to pull out when you wanted to impress your academic friends. And then when I wasn't quite so smart, after the accident, I became invisible to you.'

'Is that what you really think?' Evangeline's voice was high.

'I don't know what to think anymore. Who to trust. All I can feel is shame.'

'What do *you* have to feel ashamed about?'

Sylvie couldn't say it, even to her own mother. She could never say it to anyone. Another secret. Another layer to the curse. *I loved him and then I killed him.*

PALM BEACH, SUMMER 1996

Everything was slow. Too slow, as though the world had slipped off its axis. Kase felt the skin slough off her knees as she slid right to the edge of the cliff.

'Tristan,' she screamed. 'Tristan!' She shrieked his name into the unforgiving bush, into the ocean below, scanning for a glimpse of him. An awful silence met her – he was gone. She looked up. Sylvie was hovering there, suspended in the dark air, like a ghost. Her face was blank, impassive, a shocking white. Their eyes met and everything felt like it was shifting, teetering. 'Do something!' Kase screamed, grabbing her shoulders, shaking her. Sylvie stumbled backwards and then she was falling. There was an awful crack. Her head hitting rock.

Kase dropped to her knees. 'Oh, no, no, no. I'm sorry.' Sylvie was still. Too still. Kase couldn't breathe. She felt painfully sober, her head pounding. 'Help us. Somebody help us,' she cried. She felt wetness in Sylvie's hair. Blood. Oh God. Gabe was kneeling beside them. She'd never noticed how huge he was and she froze. 'Get away from us,' she yelled, pulling Sylvie's prone body to her own. 'Don't you dare touch her.'

Voices suddenly, and then Rachel was there, crouching beside her. Kase grabbed hold of her and sobbed with relief. Rachel yelled for the others, who were just coming up the track, to run back to the beach and get help. She was leaning over Sylvie's body. Her eyes met Kase's as she saw the blood in Sylvie's hair.

'She's okay. She's breathing,' Rachel said, her cheek to Sylvie's mouth.

'Oh, thank God.'

Rachel pressed Kase's hands between her own. 'I was just behind you. I saw. Oh my God. Tristan.'

Kase's voice was tiny. 'He went over. It's too far. He's gone. Is he dead? Tell me he's not dead. Did you see? What they were doing to her?'

Rachel placed her hand gently on Kase's shoulder and shook her head. 'They weren't doing anything.' She swallowed with difficulty. Her voice wavered ever so slightly. 'Gabe …' They both looked over at Rachel's brother who was struggling with the buckle of his belt. 'He's just really, really drunk. We all are.'

'But …'

Rachel fixed her with her cool gaze. 'I know what you're thinking. That we have to tell … But …' She shook her head again and her voice was confident now. 'It was an accident. Tristan slipped. That's all that happened. He was very drunk. We've all had too much to drink. No one did anything bad. I know you wouldn't want to lose Sylvie *and* Tristan. Just like I don't want to lose Gabe.'

Rachel got up and went to her brother, pulled him over. 'Do you hear me? Gabe.' She shook him until he looked up. 'We won't tell anyone what Sylvie did to Tristan when she wakes up, will we? We'll tell her he just slipped. We were so drunk. We don't want anyone to get into trouble.'

Kase grabbed Rachel's arms. 'But she'll remember what Gabe and Tristan did to her.'

'Kase, you're so drunk. You're imagining things, isn't she Gabe? Tell her. We're all friends. No one meant to hurt anyone. It was all a bit of drunken fun.'

Gabe was quiet. A slow dread crept through Kase. No. No, this wasn't right … but her mind was muddled. Her brother, how could he be gone, and Sylvie lying there lifeless? What was happening?

Rachel was smoothing her hair. 'I'll look after you,' she said. 'I'll do all the talking. I'm practically sober. All you have to say is that it was all an accident and how drunk we all were. You want to protect Sylvie, don't you? She didn't know what she was doing when she pushed Tristan, just like Gabe didn't know what he was doing. Okay? Okay? Kase, are you listening to me? Do you understand what I'm saying?'

Kase wiped her face. It was wet with tears. She didn't understand, but she nodded. Her eyes met Gabe's. They were darkened, shrouded with drink and he couldn't even focus on her. *Maybe none of us knew what we were doing*, she thought. *Maybe it was all just a terrible, terrible accident.*

CHAPTER 22

ravine *(n.)* - a channel, depth, gap, hollow.

Sylvie was walking down the beach towards her. Kase could tell from her gait – so changed since the accident, but still so Sylvie – that she hadn't seen her yet. It was funny you could know someone so well that their body betrayed them, even from a distance. It was no wonder Sylvie had never left Kase's consciousness. They were bound by the loves and betrayals of the generation before them. Even after all these years, Sylvie felt like a recurring dream, like a promise yet to be fulfilled. There were nights when Kase had felt so alone that she'd wanted to pick up the phone and call her. Once she even had. But it was an old number, disconnected. She'd been very drunk after her latest book launch – she should have been elated, the book was already shortlisted for a major award, and a bestseller before it was published, but instead she felt empty. It hadn't helped that Henry had invited his lover. Kase had invited hers too, but the revenge tasted as sour as the gin cocktails being served.

Afterwards, she'd sent her lover home and walked to the bottle shop around the corner, intending to buy herself some expensive whisky and get totally drunk. Instead she'd bought Midori, as iridescent as the grass the summer they'd first tried it. She supposed she'd wanted to taste what life had been like back then, before she had known loneliness. When she'd been hopeful and naive and thought having her writing dreams come true meant she'd be happy. She hadn't realised that what she'd felt on those long summer afternoons on the deck at Palm Beach with Tristan and Gabe and Sylvie, legs slick with sweat, hair stiff with salt, had been happiness. She'd been waiting for something else, something bigger, something more. It had taken half a lifetime to realise happiness was deceptively simple. She'd poured herself a glass straight. It was sickly sweet and nothing like she remembered. She'd drunk it down like radioactive mouthwash, gagging until she began to cry. She had woken the following morning to find it had spilled and the green had seeped into the pages of her freshly printed book.

Sylvie had seen her now. Her arms drew tight about her body. For a moment Kase thought she might launch herself into the sea. She slowed. Her limp was more pronounced on the sand, forcing her to work harder. Guilt sluiced through Kase. She'd known Sylvie had struggled with her memory after the accident, but the fact that it lingered still in her body, the slip of her hand into her pocket, the notebook she always kept there in case she forgot, pained Kase.

She heard voices on the wind and turned towards them. The others were disembarking from a taxi boat at the jetty. Gabe and Trina and the kids, Rachel and Henry. She quickened her pace away from them, towards Sylvie. It felt like Kase's life had narrowed into this thin tunnel of water and sand. *Past and present. Truth and lies.* She reached Sylvie and they both stood for a moment, awkwardly, before Kase pulled Sylvie into an embrace. She could feel Sylvie's reticence. Cold water rushed at their ankles and Kase drew back and shook her head. She could hear her own breath, loud and uneven above the soft sigh of the water.

'Did you have any idea?' she asked.

Sylvie shook her head, her arms still soldered to her body. 'No. Did you?'

'No. I remember us lamenting that our mothers weren't friendly. And here we thought it was because they were so different.'

'I've just spoken to Evangeline.'

'What did you say? What did she say?'

'She has no guilt about Fran taking me in. Fran somehow owed her for denying her and Teddy their big love for so many years, apparently.'

Kase dug her toe into the sand. 'Your mother has an uncanny knack for turning herself into the victim.'

'Yes.'

'So, it was your mother and my father. The grand love story. And poor Mum, caught in the middle, trying to do what was best for everyone, as per usual,' said Kase.

'Which turned out no good for anyone,' said Sylvie. 'Because none of us got to be with the people we loved, in the end.'

Kase's heart swelled and fizzed, like the cool foam around her feet. 'Sylvie, you're like my sister. Our families are bound in ways we could never have imagined. I love you. I've always loved you. You're part of our family. Fran said it. You're home now. I'm so, so sorry that I abandoned you when you needed me most. I was young. I was scared. I was in so much pain.'

Sylvie's face shifted, the edges of her mouth tugging down with emotion. 'But it was more than that, wasn't it? I can't stop thinking about it all. Seeing you all again … None of it makes any sense to me. And I need to know, Kase. I need to know … What really happened that night? You said I pushed Tristan. It's killing me to think I did that to him. But there's something else, isn't there? I can feel it. It's like a puzzle.' She shook her head, pressed her fingers to her temples. 'But I don't have all the pieces. They're scrambled. He kissed me. Tristan kissed me on that headland. I remember the feeling. He didn't reject me, like you said, so why on earth did I push him? There's something else. I can feel it just beneath my skin. Please, Kase, if we really are family, it's time to be honest with each other. I need to know. Please. I'm begging you.'

Kase took a step backwards. It was instinct. Self-preservation. *Fear.* The others were making their way up towards the house. She didn't want to have to face this. Have to face what she'd hidden from Sylvie. There was an almost crushing relief as Rachel appeared beside them, slightly breathless.

'Hey, what's happening? You're back, Sylvie. You and Holden getting it on, I hear. You move fast. You were always a bit of a dark horse. Got to watch the quiet ones. Go you.' She punched her arm, and Sylvie flinched. Kase felt like punching Rachel.

Kase could feel Sylvie's eyes on her, waiting. Kase answered for her. 'They make a good couple, don't you think?'

Rachel raised an eyebrow ever so slightly. Their conversation the night after Sylvie arrived returned to her. They'd been sitting outside on the veranda after everyone else had gone to bed.

'What the hell, Kase? How could you spring this on us?' Rachel had asked

'It's my fortieth. She's my childhood friend, my oldest friend. I honestly didn't know whether she'd come.'

'Well, she broke out of her reclusive life and she's here and who knows what her motivation is. She's got a limp, and she's not as sparky as I remember. I mean, she was a genius, right? That's got to be from the accident. She's got to be bitter under all that serene sweetness.'

'Rachel, the last time I saw her she was in a coma and then when she woke up she couldn't remember what someone had said two minutes ago, let alone what happened that night. The doctors said she'd lost all memory of it. You see how she still writes in her notebook to help her remember things.'

'Let's hope it stays that way. And if it doesn't,' Rachel had fixed her with a pointed look, 'you know what to say.'

Kase had felt dread move through her and she'd shivered. She'd finished the wine in her glass in one long drink, waiting for it to numb her.

Rachel had nestled into her. 'You know you're the best thing that ever happened to me? If it wasn't for that awful night, we'd never have become so close. All those nights I held you while you wept. Do you remember? All the late-night trips to the servo for cigarettes and chocolate?'

'I was a mess,' Kase had said, unable to soften the hard edge to her voice. She'd wanted to push Rachel off the seat and run upstairs to Sylvie. Instead she'd poured more wine and drank it, waiting for the uncomfortable feelings to fade away.

Now they were standing on the beach, the light too bright, Sylvie's face too vulnerable, her eyes too serious, searing in their paleness.

Kase turned towards the house. 'Come on, let's go up. It's getting cold.'

Rachel linked an arm through Kase's. 'I'm starving. It's all this brisk sea air.'

Sylvie didn't move. 'You were there, Rachel, weren't you?'

Rachel turned, her perfect posture stiffer than usual, her voice bored. 'Where?'

'The night Tristan died. At the lighthouse. You were the one who talked to the police and paramedics. That's what I was told anyhow.'

'We were all there. Frankly, you're lucky you don't remember.'

Her voice was dismissive, cold. Kase wanted to reach out to Sylvie, but her arm was under Rachel's in a kind of vice.

'Am I? Really? It doesn't feel much like luck,' said Sylvie. The wind whipped her hair against her cheeks and she wrestled it away. Her face was wet with tears and Kase felt moisture prick her own eyes.

Rachel must have realised too. 'Oh hon.' She let go of Kase and embraced Sylvie. 'We all miss Tristan. Our lives were never the same, were they? Such a tragic thing to happen. A horrible accident. We were all just babies.'

Sylvie disentangled herself, stepped backwards. 'Is that what you tell yourselves? That we were just young? Stupid? Drunk?'

'Well, we were young, stupid and drunk. That's exactly what we were,' said Rachel, her voice heavy with condescension.

Kase had a flashback of young Sylvie, before the accident, how she would have silenced Rachel with one cutting word. How she would have done the same. The familiar fist of guilt and self-disgust closed around her heart.

Sylvie's voice was cold. 'Well, we're old and sober now, so don't you think you finally owe me the truth? It's a day of truths, wouldn't you say, Kase?'

It almost felt like the old Sylvie was back. Kase felt all the blood drain from her face. The brave Sylvie who had walked back into the water despite the lurking shark in the harbour that day. The brilliant Sylvie who aced exams without studying. Kase felt dizzy. She swallowed back the taste of the self-hatred broiling her insides. Her eyes met Rachel's momentarily and she saw fear in the other woman's face. Sylvie must have seen it too, but mostly Kase knew Sylvie was reading her reaction, her shallow breath, her darting eyes, looking anywhere but into Sylvie's.

'Kase, I saw you talking to Gabe in the kitchen the night of your party. Something happened. You're scared of him. I saw it. He did something … to you? To me? It's coming back. Being here with you all. Holden took me to the lighthouse at Bruny. It reminded me of Barrenjoey Lighthouse at Palm Beach. And I've started to remember.' Sylvie swallowed hard. 'What happened that night was terrifying. I know that much.'

'God, you haven't lost your drama for storytelling, that's for sure,' said Rachel. 'We were all so envious of you with your bohemian mother and your brilliant mind and shiny future.'

Kase felt anger ignite deep in her gut. God, Rachel was so adept at this, gaslighting everyone around her until they were shells of themselves, smaller, weaker, more unsure.

Pain passed over Sylvie's face then and something else Kase couldn't read. She ached for everything Sylvie had lost.

'Maybe it was terrifying because you killed the boy you loved,' said Rachel. 'Kase told me you know now what you did to Tristan.'

Sylvie brushed away tears. 'I was hurt. I lashed out. Tristan let him … he let Gabe do that to me. Gabe … he did something to me … Is that what happened?' She sunk to her knees. 'Please.' Her face was in her hands, her body shaking. The brave Sylvie was gone now and this shell of the person she'd once been was back.

Guilt screwed her chest tight and Kase couldn't breathe. *I was protecting you.* But hadn't she covered up the truth? She'd caused her friend this trauma that had haunted her, destroyed her, hobbled her. Why hadn't she stood up to Rachel and Gabe? Over the years she'd put it down to shock. *I was in shock. My brother had just died. I couldn't lose Sylvie too.*

Kase stepped forward to hold Sylvie, to comfort her, but Rachel gripped her arm. That line in the sand between them, clear and deep as a ravine. It had been there all along. As deep and dark as the place Tristan fell. For her whole life she had been looking into it.

Rachel's voice was close to Kase's ear, an urgent whisper. 'Don't do it. He will destroy you.'

Kase's eyes locked on Sylvie's. Kase nodded her head, almost imperceptibly. Hot tears ran down her cheeks. 'I'm sorry. Please, Sylvie, forgive me. I'm so sorry. But think of Fran. After everything she's been through. Please spare her this. We're family now.'

She saw Sylvie shrink, as if she could get any smaller. They'd silenced her again. Kase broke free of Rachel's grip and put her arms around her friend. Sylvie clung to her. But Rachel was pulling them apart, just as she'd done twenty-three years before, their tears mingling, their skin rasping against rock.

SUMMER 1996

The hospital corridor was cold, and the air tasted metallic, like cleaning products and medicines. Evangeline breathed in the essential oils she wore at her wrists for comfort, for grounding. She found the intensive care unit and pushed an intercom button at the door, her pulse racing.

She'd come as soon as the police called about the accident, but a sliver of guilt sliced through her. *You didn't even know where Sylvie was. It took the police hours to find you.*

A nurse spoke to her through the intercom and let her enter. Her beautiful daughter was lying small and pale on a bed in the corner, hooked up to too many machines that beeped and flashed. There were tubes going into her arms and neck, and bandages wrapped around her head. A wave of nausea washed over her. *You are a bad mother.* Evangeline took a shaky breath and stepped into the room. She startled when she saw Kase by the bed, her forehead pressed to Sylvie's hand.

Evangeline rushed to her daughter's side. 'Oh, my darling, I'm here now. I'm here. I'm so sorry. You're going to be okay, I promise. I promise.'

She pressed her cheek against Sylvie's. It was too cool, too clammy, too lifeless, and fear iced through Evangeline. She wished all this would take was a dose of Rescue Remedy and some herbal tea, her simple but effective cure for all Sylvie's illnesses over the years, but Evangeline knew it was bad. The doctor at reception had told her that Sylvie was stable now, but that she'd suffered a head injury, a swollen brain or something, and they had to put her into an induced coma so her brain could rest, could heal. It was too awful to even contemplate. She placed her hand on Sylvie's heart, willing her to open her eyes, but she remained still. Her lips were blue. Evangeline looked around the room. There were nurses everywhere, attending other patients behind curtains, and she wondered why they weren't here with Sylvie. *Do something*, she thought. *Make her better.*

'How is she?' It was a silly question, but all Evangeline found herself capable of asking.

Her eyes met Kase's and Evangeline's heart squeezed. The skin around her eyes was red and her nose was swollen. She had clearly been crying for hours.

'She won't wake up. The nurse said she's in a coma.' Kase's eyes were glazed and unfocused, as though she herself had just woken up from a bad dream.

Evangeline got down on her knees and embraced this child who was like her own, so twinned was she with Sylvie.

'Oh Kase. I'm so sorry. About Tristan.'

A deep, guttural cry came from Kase, and Evangeline held her as she shuddered and shook and still more tears poured out of her.

She smoothed the hair from her wet face. 'Where is your mother? Where's Fran?' Even after all these years, Evangeline still needed to know about Franny. Poor Franny who'd just lost her son, who'd be feeling ten times the fear and grief Evangeline was when she looked at her deathly still daughter.

Franny barely tolerated her, of course. How could she expect anything else after what happened with Teddy? She could say she regretted it, but that wouldn't be honest. Teddy was her fate. Denying herself that love would have been like holding her breath until she died. And truth be told, the first person she thought of calling when the police finally tracked her down tonight had been Teddy. And she couldn't promise herself she wouldn't call him, even though he'd asked her not to, begged her really, even though he'd chosen Franny and his family in the end. Their connection was too strong, like a perfect circle they had tried so many times over the years to sever, to change into another shape.

There had been so many times dropping Sylvie off at their house that Evangeline had wanted to climb those steps and close her eyes and go back thirty years to how things had once been between the three of them, listening to The Doors and smoking and drinking Coca-Cola in the sun by the pool. But even after everything that had happened, the care they showed for each other's daughters told Evangeline that Franny didn't hate her.

Kase shook her head. 'Mum's … at home. They've given her sedatives.'

'Oh, poor, poor Fran. How did you get here?'

Kase looked bewildered. 'Dad dropped me. I started to walk. I had to see Sylvie.'

The poor thing was in shock. 'You shouldn't be here. I'll take you home,' Evangeline said, rubbing her back. 'You need to be with your parents.'

'But Sylvie ...'

Evangeline's chest ached with equal parts love and sadness. She kissed Kase's cheek very softly. 'I know I haven't always been the best mother, and that you feel you need to protect Sylvie, but I promise, I'll stay with her. The doctors said we need to wait and hope and pray she wakes up. I'll stay.' She took Kase's hand in one hand and Sylvie's in the other. One warm, one cold.

A nurse came over to the bed. 'Are you Sylvia's family?' she asked. Evangeline hadn't heard her daughter called her proper name in so long. She and Kase looked at each other for a moment and then they both said, 'Yes.'

2004

The bookshop had glossy timber shelving and smelled like furniture polish, freshly unboxed books and red wine. The front of the store had been cleared and there were tables holding rows of wineglasses and a cheese platter. Kase walked over to the book-signing table in the corner and ran her fingers over the embossed title of her first novel. A tingle of nerves, mixed with elation ran through her. It was actually happening. She couldn't believe this was all for her.

She heard her agent's voice before she saw her. 'Well, you've certainly got friends in high places.' Elizabeth arched a brow and kissed Kase on both cheeks. She passed her a newspaper article.

The review was brief but glowing. The words floated inside her. *Lyrical, raw. A searing portrayal of grief. A new literary talent.* Kase smiled. She thought of Tristan. It was all for him. Tears welled in her eyes and a fierce joy rose inside her chest. It overlaid all the anxiety of waiting for guests to arrive.

'There are seasoned writers, successful writers who would give an arm to be reviewed in this paper, let alone such a glowing review. And here I was counselling my 25-year-old author to manage her expectations. Well, you showed me, Kase Fowler, Miss "One To Watch". I'll read this out to the guests tonight. I've got a little speech prepped.'

'Thank you, Elizabeth. I honestly didn't expect –'

'None of us did, kid, but your publisher obviously believes in you to be throwing this little shindig. You even got a cheese platter. It really is a wonderful book though. And I'm proud to be the one who discovered it.' Elizabeth ushered over a waiter and handed Kase a flute of champagne. 'Here, your guests are starting to arrive.'

Kase greeted Rachel and Fran, pressing the newspaper into her mother's hands. Fran had tears in her eyes before she'd finished reading it.

'Oh Mum.' Kase hugged her mother. The tears were never very far away, even after all these years.

'Sorry. I told myself I wouldn't cry. It's just … I'm so proud of you, darling. What an accomplishment. Writing this book. Dedicating it to Tristan. It's just very special for a mother to see one child doing something so incredible for the other, especially after he's …'

'I know. Thank you, Mum. This book is for you too, you know.'

Fran patted her hand and stood up straight, composing herself. 'Okay, we've got to pull ourselves together. Look at all these people arriving.'

Rachel brought Fran a glass of champagne. 'Oh my God, it's too much. My brilliant friend. All my acting buddies are reading it. Loving it. And Gabe is coming with the editor who wrote the review for you. I'll point him out. He's very influential in literary circles, I'm told. It's he who makes or breaks an author.'

'I still can't believe it, it sounds so weird – I'm a published author,' Kase said, taking a sip of the cool champagne. Elizabeth held her glass aloft from across the room, and Kase nodded her silent thanks. The bookshop was starting to fill up. Kase had invited some uni friends but so far it was mostly people Elizabeth had invited. They were wearing dark clothing and dark-rimmed glasses. They looked like literary people.

Sylvie floated into Kase's mind, like a ghost. All those times they'd dreamed of this. Of writing a book. Of being an author. And here she was. Without Sylvie. Something heavy and dark pulled through her. She'd thought of contacting Sylvie; she'd wanted her here, deep down. But it was a book about loss, grief. Tristan. It didn't feel right that Sylvie wasn't here, but Rachel and Gabe were coming. They would freak out. And Gabe was bringing the editor friend. Pain lanced her chest, and she pressed her palm hard against her sternum. The truth was she didn't even know how to contact Sylvie anymore.

And here was Gabe coming towards her wearing a navy suit and tie. It still took her a moment to place him. He was frozen in her mind in the same place as Tristan – young, hair scruffy with salt, suntanned. Both boys. But now Gabe was a man. A newspaper man. That reckless, aimless bravado had honed into a steely ambition after Tristan's death, and he'd somehow secured himself a three-year cadetship on the paper and now he was the youngest night editor in the publication's history.

Fran caught Gabe before he reached Kase, kissing him on both cheeks. 'Oh Gabe, I hear you arranged this wonderful review for Kase. You're a good boy, looking out for your own.'

She pressed the newspaper article into his hands, as though he hadn't read it.

Discomfort and dread moved inside Kase as Gabe's eyes met hers. She would never forget. It was a dark, deep, cold current that ran beneath them, like the shadow of the shark under the surface as they swam in the harbour. It had wound around her heart since that night when everything had changed. It was the feeling that had prompted her to write, to get it out of her body. She had made something beautiful with words from the devastation, but at this moment standing opposite Gabe, it all felt like a lie.

And then the literary editor was by her side, gazing at her over his glasses and pumping her hand. 'Nice to finally meet you, Kase. I'm Graeme. Gabe told me Tristan was his best friend and as such I was so keen and honoured to read this book.'

'Thank you, Graeme. I'm so humbled by your review.'

'You don't have to thank me. I lost my wife two years ago, so it resonated with me. Kase, you should be very proud of what you've written. It will touch a lot of people.' He shook her hand again before pushing his glasses onto his nose and wandering towards a cluster of people who quickly assimilated him into their tight little circle. He didn't seem like the intimidating book reviewer Elizabeth had described, but a man with kind eyes.

'Not bad for a 25-year-old,' said Gabe now beside her, one hand in his pocket, the other holding a beer. 'We're both prodigies in our own way. I think Rachel is a bit jealous. She'd hoped to be a famous actress by now.'

Kase shrugged, trying to keep things surface, away from the shadow depths. 'Oh, I'm sure it won't take her long. Once she gets out of drama school the world won't know what hit them. She tells me she's just scored the role of Juliet in *Romeo and Juliet*.'

'I know, poor Romeo,' said Gabe.

Kase smiled.

He scratched behind his neck. 'She's still charming the acting school's theatre director, I hear.'

'Yes. He's besotted, despite, or perhaps because of the age gap.'

'Well, no one can accuse my sister of not knowing what she wants.'

It was safe territory talking about Rachel. Kase wished she'd come over so she didn't have to face Gabe one on one like this. She'd largely avoided it over the years, but she'd grown so close to Rachel that she heard everything Gabe did by extension. And he was always there for Easter and Christmas and Tristan's birthday dinner. Fran made sure of it. But they had never talked of what happened on that headland again.

'Oh well, congratulations on the book. I'm sure you'll be the talk of the town.'

Kase blushed. 'Thanks to your connections. Thank you for that, you didn't have to do that.'

Gabe's eyes were dark, serious, when they met hers. An almost imperceptible twitch of his mouth. 'I think I did.'

Kase's heart rammed against her chest. *Penance. Atonement.* That's what this was. The silent whisper that haunted her at night, that sat alongside her brother's death like a shadow among shadows. That leaked unease through her like poison and pressed her heart into a shape too small for her body. It had happened. Gabe did remember. The darkness in his eyes told her that. Was this his way of saying sorry?

'Tristan would have wanted me to help out his sister.' Gabe held up his glass. There was moisture in his eyes. 'To Tristan.'

Kase raised her own glass. Emotion swelled in her throat, behind her eyes. 'To Tristan.' The clink of their glasses was lost in the voices of all the people filling the room.

This is all for Tristan, she thought. *Gabe is a good man now.*

CHAPTER 23

dirty *(adj.)* – soiled with dirt; foul, unclean.

Sylvie stood on the jetty and waited for Holden's boat to appear on the horizon. It was funny how your whole life you were just waiting for a person who you could trust would always come to get you. *Collect you.* Maybe that's all love was. The knowledge that they would always come. Evangeline had not been that person. Kase had not been that person. Her own father, who she'd never known, had certainly not been that person. Only Fran had. Fran, who should have been the last person to love her.

Sylvie had once called her at 2 am from a payphone, Fran sounding old, her voice steeped too deeply in sleep.

'It's Sylvie. I'm so sorry. There are no more buses and I don't have enough money for a taxi. Evangeline isn't answering the phone and it's too far to walk home.'

'No, that's okay. Where are you?'

'At the mall.'

'Where are the others?'

'They're still at the party. They're all staying overnight but I didn't want to.' She couldn't explain it. Sometimes she felt like she was looking in from the outside. The others having fun while she observed from afar.

'That's okay. I'll come and get you. Just stay near the phone. In the light.'

'Are you sure?' Guilt lodged inside her, but it was quickly rinsed away by relief. She slumped against the cool glass of the booth.

'Yes, I'm sure. I'll be there soon.'

'Thank you, Fran.'

'Stay in the light and don't talk to any strange men.'

Sylvie slept in Kase's bed that night, the doona smelling like the sweet vanilla perfume Kase wore. She wondered what it would be like to grow up with the inherent knowledge that someone would always do an hour round trip just to make sure you were safe.

* * *

The boat appeared on the horizon as a speck and took shape. Holden had come for her.

She was sure she could feel Kase and Rachel watching from the house above the jetty. Would Gabe be watching too? Had he always been watching her? She sat very still. Betrayed nothing. They had left her on her knees on the sand, but now at least, finally, she knew the truth. She'd seen it in Kase's eyes. She'd seen the hard tug as Rachel pulled Kase away. Kase had implored her with her eyes to understand, as she was dragged over the sand. Sylvie understood. Finally, she understood.

'How did it go?' Holden asked as he helped her into the boat. His hands were so warm and she wanted to press them against her cold skin. She wanted never to be alone again. The hope on his face made her love him fiercely. But how to tell someone your life had been cracked open like an eggshell and the viscous fluid was filling up your lungs and you couldn't breathe, couldn't speak?

'Come on, let's get you home and make tea,' he said simply, then put his arm around her shoulders and hugged her.

The wind was brutal and purifying. Its roar filled her up, calmed her, as they sped across the bay. Could she live here forever in this wild place at the end of the earth? Maybe she could get a job locally and leave behind her lonely Sydney life, all those empty houses. All those empty memories. Leave behind the fragile shell of her own memories. She had been longing to know for so long and now that she knew, all she wished to do was forget.

As they reached the jetty on Bruny Island, crabs scuttled in the rocks and a fish jumped, making a perfect circle in the bottle-green water. She watched its ripples spread. She was still feeling the ripples of something that had happened twenty-three years ago. They were moving over her skin. Her body had always known. Her mind may have forgotten but her body had not. She thought of all the difficult intimacy over her life. The way men's bodies repulsed her. She shirked from touch. She had always felt it a personal failing. *Shameful.* And now she knew why. *It's not my fault. But maybe it is my fault. Maybe I was too drunk, too flirtatious … and then I killed Tristan.*

Holden took her hand, kissed it then began walking down the jetty. She let him go. She couldn't move. Would he still want her if she told him? She felt dirty. Ashamed. A bad secret that everyone had known about but her. She remembered now another puzzle piece: how long they'd taken to get ready for the party that night. She'd let Kase do her hair and makeup. She'd said Sylvie looked sexy with her straight hair and eyes rimmed with kohl. She'd wanted to look sexy. For Tristan. She remembered the way his eyes slid over her body. How good that had felt. The soft shock of his kiss.

She slipped off her shoes. Reached the place where the jetty ended and the deep green began. It looked cold, clarifying, bottomless. She longed to feel the green water around her body, purifying her.

Holden turned at the other end of the jetty. 'Sylvie, what are you –'

And then the cold ache of the water engulfed her and the searing shame inside her was gone, replaced by numb shock as her skin cried out and her lungs sought air. Her feet touched the bottom. She looked up. It was bright but she knew there would always be ripples on the surface. Memories jumping like fish, falling flat and hard against the water.

2010

Candlelight reflected in expensive glassware and the women wore beautiful jewellery on their wrists and at their throats. The room smelled of perfume and the three-course dinner they were being served. Fran couldn't believe she was here, right at the front of the theatre, with them all. The actress, the newspaper editor and the author. A pelt of pride moved through her as she watched them around the table. Kase in a black gown that revealed her shoulders, twisting her wineglass, Gabe in a grey suit whispering in Trina's ear, and Rachel at that moment sweeping onto the stage.

Fran squeezed Kase's hand under the table. Rachel looked like a goddess, her hair and gown shimmering gold under the bright theatre lights. She'd always been a pretty girl, but there was a striking beauty to her now that age had conferred. The crowd applauded as she stopped in front of the microphone. She wasn't what you'd call *famous* famous, but she'd appeared in some critically acclaimed theatre productions and she was dating one of the most well-regarded directors in the Sydney scene. Or that's what Kase told Fran. The fact that they'd asked her to present at the literary awards was a testament to Rachel's growing status. Or maybe Gabe had pulled some strings.

Fran suddenly felt Kase's arms around her, her daughter's cheek damp against her own.

'Oh my God,' said Kase, looking into Fran's eyes. 'I won.'

'You did?' Fran had somehow missed it, as though everything had slowed down and speeded up at once. A rush of white noise filled her ears. And then Kase was moving towards the stage and everyone was clapping and Gabe was pulling Fran into a hug and other people she didn't know were pumping her hand, their eyes sparkling.

And Fran didn't know where to put the emotion. The enormous, shimmering pride of it. The wonder when your child accomplished something beyond what you had ever imagined possible. Eve came into her mind then. She'd never been able to think of her as Evangeline, though she'd used that name in their brief, perfunctory encounters as they'd dropped off or picked up Sylvie and Kase over the years. Eve was an author. She would read about this. Would she be wondering how it was Kase and not Sylvie here, as Fran sometimes did? Poor Sylvie. She'd never been the same after that night. They'd lost Tristan, but Sylvie had lost something too – perhaps the part of her that was strong and brilliant enough to go down the same successful path as the others. She wondered who Sylvie was now and what she was doing. She knew that Eve was abroad and writing moderately successful books. The mother in Fran ached to think that she was still living her own whimsical life, no doubt still selfish, paying little thought to the needs of Sylvie. But the mother in her was also still mourning Tristan. The loss never went away, not even after all these years.

And then Kase's words were reaching her, like a warm embrace through the haze.

'I'm sure I'm only standing up here tonight because of the very surprising and humbling success of my first book, which was dedicated to my beautiful brother, Tristan. I wish you had been here to see this. This book is for you, too. It is all for you.'

The crowd sighed collectively, and people were on their feet and her daughter was clutching her award on stage, her face soft with gratitude. Kase had mythologised Tristan. He'd passed out of the realm of the living to be immortalised in words. Such beautiful words. And Fran found she was crying, and the crowd was still clapping, but Gabe was beside her now, passing her his napkin and pouring her a glass of water, which she gulped down until she could breathe.

* * *

Evangeline put down her cup of tea and went inside to pour herself a glass of red wine. It was nearly midday, wasn't it? She didn't care that she was still swanning around in her silk pyjamas. She gazed across the rooftops of Paris. Drinking wine in your pyjamas, *c'est naturel*, she told herself. *If you can't do that in France, where can you?* She'd just seen the news of Kase's latest literary triumph on an industry website, her face glowing as she accepted the award. Franny was pictured next to her daughter, dabbing at tears. Teddy was not there. She knew only that he was somewhere in the Middle East. She always knew where he was, and he always knew where she was. Sometimes, that was enough.

Evangeline poured the leftover wine she'd shared with Gil, a friend who'd recently turned into a lover, and lit a cigarette. She returned to her tiny *balcon*, the white dome of Sacré-Coeur in the distance. She had been invited to the awards. She knew Kase and Franny would be there. She was tempted to fly back to Australia, but for what? Her latest book had not been shortlisted. Was she jealous? Yes, but not so much for herself. She was jealous for Sylvie. She couldn't help but think about her daughter, working as a cleaner, living alone in Sydney in that sad little flat. *God, all the sad flats we lived in over the years. I conditioned her to believe that's all she's worth.* Evangeline finished her cigarette and took a sip of wine.

Kase, meanwhile, was somehow walking that elusive line between critical and commercial success and this new award would only add to it. Kase was talented, yes, of course, Evangeline would not begrudge her that, but no more than Sylvie had been. She remembered reading their creative writing pieces, their essays at school, and marvelling at those bright, new words on the page. Evangeline knew she was biased, but Sylvie had always possessed a depth, a self-possession, a daring, that had elevated her writing. Kase had not had the strength of her daughter, of Sylvia, who was named after a brilliant poet, born of an unknown father, and who had all her words stolen from her in one terrible night. But she would find them one day.

One day Sylvie will write something, and it will blow you all away.

CHAPTER 24

ripple *(v.)* – to form small waves or undulations on the surface, as water.

Sylvie breached the surface with a cry. The sky was low and bright and she longed to return to the cool green darkness below, but her lungs would not allow it. Holden was in the water beside her, pulling her towards the shore. She let her body float. She wondered if this was what it would be like to fly.

And then she was on the land, the sand solid beneath her, and she was shivering but it didn't feel like it was from the cold.

He wrapped his arms around her. 'What happened, Sylvie? Talk to me.'

His lashes were heavy with water, his tanned skin white with cold. She looked out to the water and watched the ripples. She couldn't bear to look into his eyes. She couldn't bear to have him touching her as she told him.

She braced herself, pulled her legs into her chest. 'The puzzle, I've found the last pieces. They were there the whole time, but scrambled, like the doctors said. You said my memory couldn't be trusted, but I saw Kase's face when I confronted her.' She swallowed. The words felt wrong, pathetic, but she said them anyway. 'Gabe raped me. That night on the headland. And Tristan didn't stop him. I loved him and he betrayed me … and so … I pushed him.'

A fish jumped, its silver gleam catching her eye. It took everything to stay on the land when all she wanted to do was return to the water, disappear.

Holden was silent. She searched his face, expecting to see shock or revulsion, and instead she saw sadness. He was crying. It was she who comforted him, pulling his body into hers. They stayed like that for a long time.

'I'm sorry.' He clung to her. She smoothed his wet hair from his face. Kissed the moisture from his lashes, which tasted like the sea's tears.

He wiped his wet sleeve across his face. 'I'm sorry. It's me who should be comforting you. God. I'm so sorry. What they did to you.' He shook his head. 'What they hid from you.'

Sylvie took his hand. 'They were trying to protect me.' *From the monster that I am.*

Holden's face contorted. He pulled away from her. 'Is that what you think?'

'Kase was trying to protect me. I pushed Tristan. I killed her brother.'

'But what about what they did to you?'

Sylvie pressed her palms into her eye sockets and shook her head. There was a searing pain in her chest. She didn't have the room inside her to fathom all of their betrayals along with the betrayal of the only true friend she'd ever had.

'Rachel and Gabe made Kase cover it up. Rachel dragged Kase away from me when she was trying to tell me what Gabe had done. Kase was protecting me because I killed Tristan. It's not her fault.'

'What? You don't believe that.'

'Holden, you don't know what you're talking about. There are other things you don't understand. About Kase, about Fran.'

'There's nothing to understand, Sylvie. They've hidden something terrible, something that's hobbled you forever. I can see it in you. I can feel it in you. Your reticence. Your fear of intimacy. It's written all over your body.'

Sylvie got to her feet. Her clothes were stuck to her skin. Cold and clinging. He had seen her. All of her. *Exposed. Naked. Broken.* She covered her face with her hands.

Holden was up and next to her, pulling her hands away from her face, but she struggled out of his grasp.

'Sylvie, please listen to me. This is not your fault. I know you think it is, but none of it is. Kase and Fran have hidden this from you your whole life.'

A steely anger shot through her and she squeezed her hands into fists. 'You have no idea, Holden, what Kase and Fran have been through. Fran has no idea about any of it. Kase has been intimidated her whole life by Rachel and Gabe. I can see it so clearly now. I saw Gabe threaten her in the kitchen the night of her party. She was terrified of him.'

Holden shook his head. 'It's no excuse. Can't you see that? There is no excuse for hiding what they did to you. You have to do something. Gabe needs to be held accountable.'

'You don't know!' She screamed it, her own rage shocking her, blood pounding in her head. 'Fran took me into her home, even after my mother had an affair with her husband. That woman picked me up when I was drunk in the middle of the night, she fed me, gave me the love my own mother never could. And …' She closed her eyes. 'That's what opened this whole thing up. She told us. She and Evangeline were best friends. Our mothers, who we thought were just school mums to each other. So you see, it's much more complicated. It goes back further than what happened that night.'

She was shaking now. Holden stepped towards her and hugged her, and she let him. He kissed her forehead and took her hand, picked up their shoes from the jetty. Her body felt heavy as they walked up the track towards the farmhouse. They didn't talk. It took all her energy just to move. When they got into the house, Holden said he'd make tea while she took a shower. She stood for a long time under the scorching water. She stood naked in front of the mirror. For so long she hadn't recognised her own body. Slower than before. Damaged. And now she knew why. Her whole life had felt like a question and now she had the answer. But she had nowhere to put the answer. And the answer had caused a rift with Holden that she could feel yawning wider and wider, like an invisible wound.

Holden had made toast and tea and had changed out of his wet clothes. They ate looking out onto the trees and water beyond, so they didn't have to look into each other's eyes. If Sylvie wasn't so exhausted she would have asked him to take her back to the mainland, so she could return to her old safe life where there was no one to hurt her anymore.

Holden put his mug down and placed his hand over hers. 'Sylvie, I know you want to forget. I know you just want it all to go away, and you feel somehow protective of Kase and Fran. But will you let me show you something? I need to show you, because the truth is, I haven't been completely honest with you, either.'

CHAPTER 25

daughter *(n.)* - one related as if by the ties binding daughter to parent.

The sun was low in the sky as they pulled into the shoulder of the road. Sylvie recognised this place from before. The small white cross was decorated with different flowers to the last time they'd passed. These were purple and white carnations. The shrine looked lonely, stark against the twisted spines of tree trunks, the dense green foliage. Sylvie's heart contracted to think about what it really meant. Of the lives lost in this deserted stretch of road.

Holden's face was closed, his lips tight. Sylvie kept her distance from him. She felt so fragile already, like she could shatter at any moment. Something else that had been kept from her. Another secret. The only reason she'd agreed to go with him was because she sensed that somehow this had to do with Pippi. And now she knew she was right.

The air inside the cabin of the truck felt too close. Holden got out and Sylvie did too, relieved to feel the evening on her skin. He took something from under the seat. White daisies that he must have picked from the garden. He placed them on the ground next to the cross. The sight of their limp bodies made her sad.

'I always imagine that she died here,' he said. 'It's just easier that way. To have somewhere to come.'

'This isn't where her car crashed?' asked Sylvie.

He shook his head. Perhaps this was some other tragedy, some other family's small shrine. Perhaps Holden didn't know exactly where his daughter had passed out of the realm of the living. Sylvie pressed her hand against her chest to stop it aching. She understood the need to demarcate places. Emotions were tied to places, she knew that now.

He knelt at the shrine and brushed gum leaves and sticks away. He picked up one of the purple flowers. 'Purple was her favourite colour. It never changed. As soon as she could say the word purple as a child it was her colour, and it was the colour of the dress she was wearing when I found her.'

'Oh Holden, no.' Sylvie got down next to him on her knees in the gravel.

'To have something bad happen to your child is easier than to have them do something bad to themselves. But it wasn't her fault. She was on a drug, for her acne. It made her depressed, but we didn't know that at the time. She was in a bad way mentally, emotionally. I could see it, but I thought it was normal teenage hormones, I don't know. She needed her mother. I gave her books – it was the only thing I knew how to do. Charlie was off touring. She would have been able to help. But it was more than that. More than just the drug – that was just the final straw. I found her diaries, after she died.' He shook his head. 'I wish she could have talked to me, but maybe because I'm a man ...'

Sylvie put her arm around his back. He seemed small, boyish suddenly. She wanted to protect him. She felt the depth and breadth of his goodness under his grief.

His hand went to his pocket and he took out a folded page. He handed it to Sylvie. It smelled like her own childhood when she opened it – strawberry stickers. *Innocence.*

I cannot fight it anymore. I am too tired. Every day is a battle and I never had any armour. It was always me fighting with my bare hands, my raw knuckles. The bruises are blood leaking under my surface. If you pricked my skin I would bleed out. That's how he left me that night. Bleeding. That blood has never stopped. And it never will, and I cannot face its awful red trail anymore, so I choose to stem the flow. Finally. I choose. My dad named me after Pippi Longstocking, because I have red hair and live in an old house, like her. She put bullies in the trees and made burglars dance with her for gold. He used to tell me her stories every night and I know that the real reason he named me after her was that Pippi was the strongest girl in the world.

Sylvie looked at him through her tears. There were no words after reading Pippi's. They could have been her own. Sylvie folded the piece of paper very carefully and handed it back to Holden.

'That was the last thing she wrote. The boy who I believe did that to her died here. He was driving too fast around the corner. When Pippi found out, I don't think she felt relief. She didn't know where to put the emotion, or how to heal the wound. And she couldn't live with it anymore.' His shoulders slumped forward, and he wiped his hand down his face. 'And so, somewhere along the line, in my mind, this became the place she died. And I tell people who don't know that she was killed in a car crash, because that's something people can understand. And really, I feel like she died the night he did. When she knew she'd never be able to get justice, or find peace.'

Sylvie was crying but she made no sound. It felt like she was being silently strangled.

Holden looked at her. Really looked at her and then he drew her to him and held her until her body stopped shaking. 'I'm so sorry I lied to you.'

It took a long time until she could speak. 'I understand about the stories we tell ourselves. It's okay, Holden.'

He drew back from her. 'No, Sylvie, it's not okay. Nothing is okay. I don't want you to have to live with this burden anymore, this shame you carry is not yours to bear. That's why I brought you here. To show you what happens if the truth gets buried.'

'Holden, I can't. I can't face the truth. They're the only family I've ever really had.'

'But look at how they treated you.'

She got to her feet. 'You said it yourself – it's so long ago. It's in the past. Opening it up again will destroy everyone.'

His face was hard. She saw the lines grief had made between his brows. 'They deserve to be fucking destroyed.'

'Do they? They were kinder to me than my own mother. They're the ones who had the decency to tell me the truth about her, even though it must have destroyed Fran. I can't do that to her. I can't sully the name of her dead son, or of her substitute son. And, Holden, I want a family. I'm so tired of being alone.'

His eyes were full of hurt and longing mixed together. 'I can be your family. We can have our own family.' He grabbed her hands. 'But I saw how you carry this in your body. It has scarred you in ways you can't even fathom. I want to be able to make love to you without seeing fear and shame in your eyes. Why does everyone always believe the reputation of the man is more important than the safety and sanity of the woman? Sylvie, what if facing this helps you heal? I want you to be able to heal.'

She gently extracted herself from his grasp. 'I know that's what you think I need, because of what happened to Pippi. But I'm different. I've survived. I've survived my whole adult life without you, without anyone.'

'But it hasn't been enough, has it? You've been hiding. I've heard what they say about you behind your back. That it should have been you, not Kase who was the celebrated writer. That you're gifted. Brilliant with words.'

She felt her skin flush and she narrowed her eyes, shook her head. 'That was before, Holden. Everything changed because of the head trauma. You don't know what the hell you're talking about.'

'You're wrong. You can be that person again. You're brilliant. You just can't see it. But, Sylvie, you need to face the past. You can't bury the truth anymore.'

Her hands curled into fists. 'What if I want to bury it? What if I don't want to face it? What about what I want?' Her voice was high and loud, not her own. 'And how can you say that to me when you're using me to get redemption for what happened to your daughter? When you lie about what really happened to her?'

Hurt darkened his face and Sylvie turned away. She couldn't be here anymore. She got into the truck and started the engine. She looked up, expecting him to stop her, but he didn't, and she drove away without looking back, leaving him by the side of the road, with a purple flower in his hand.

CHAPTER 26

abandon *(v.)* – to leave completely and finally; forsake utterly; desert.
(n.) – a giving up to natural impulses; freedom from constraint.

The road forked up ahead and Sylvie slowed the truck to a crawl. Her vision was blurry. She was no longer trying to wipe away the tears. She shouldn't have left Holden on the side of the road. She lowered her forehead to the steering wheel. What kind of person left someone at the place that had made their daughter take her own life?

She stopped the truck and got out, running her hands through her hair. She began pacing, breathing hard. Behind her was her future. All she had to do was turn around and go back. She should go back. Holden could be her everything. She knew that. She would never get another person to be her person. But Fran was also her person. Kase, even after everything, was her person. All these years she thought Kase had abandoned her, but she'd been protecting her with her silence, hadn't she? And yet she had risked everything inviting her here – an act of defiance. And what Holden wanted, no, *needed* Sylvie to do … He just didn't understand. She wasn't capable of it. She was too weak, too broken.

Sylvie stood on the deserted road listening to the sounds of the bush. Bird cries, cicadas, the wash of the shoreline nearby. Up ahead was a sign. One way pointed to the ferry back to the mainland. She could go home. Away from all of them. If only she'd stayed listening to life muffled, muted, from the other side of her bedroom wall. Escaping into books. Living other people's stories. Remembering nothing.

The other way pointed to her past. To the lighthouse. A chill moved through her and she drew her arms close. She couldn't return there. It was strange how the past lingered in places in the present. It took so little. A smell. A certain quality of the light. A white lighthouse in the blue of early evening. She got back in the truck. She sat there for a long time as the evening softened the edges of the sky. She realised this wasn't about Kase or Holden anymore. She thought of Pippi's note. She took her own notebook out of her pocket, filled with words, fragmented memories. She knew which path she had to take.

The day was closing down as she parked the truck. The clouds were moving quickly across the bay, mist collecting in the pockets of the coast. A group of tourists filed past, laughing, talking, their cheeks pink from the wind. She wondered if she could ever be happy in that simple way. She thought about sitting at Holden's kitchen table eating the food he'd cooked her. The sea-salt taste of the oysters they ate sitting on the hood of the truck. The soft flesh of the fig he fed her. Of the roar of his boat cutting through the bay. The brush of his hand across her neck as they kissed. Yes, she could be happy. But she had to be brave. She had to face this.

The gravel crunched under her feet as she followed the path through the tangled scrub towards the lighthouse. The wind was wild, tugging at her hair and biting into her skin. It was colder, wilder than last time. The lighthouse loomed above her and below the waves heaved and crashed onto the sharp rocks. She thought of a soft body brutally meeting those rocks and nausea washed over her. She hugged her arms around herself. The headland was deserted, and the wind roared in her ears, took her breath. It was almost dark. The air was blue, just like that summer night. She turned around. She should leave. It wasn't safe being here. It wasn't safe going back. *Maybe we were all just young. We were all drunk. Leave it be. It was so long ago.*

The tourist bus drove away down the unsealed road. She was utterly alone now. The headland was hers. The wind was brutal. She let it buffet her body. She didn't cower. And as she stood there watching the waves pound against the rocks, a memory hit her. Gabe's face, white with cold and fear as they both reached the buoy in the harbour. They'd both felt it, they'd both seen it. The shadow moving below their legs, deep down where the current was cold. It had made them both stop, paralysed by fear. But she saw in that moment that she was braver than him. And he saw it too. She told him to grab the buoy, to cough up the water from his lungs. She was the one who counselled him to follow her to the shore, the muscles in their arms and legs burning while the threat stalked them below. And then his words when they felt the soft relief of sand beneath their feet. *You think you won, don't you? Well, you didn't. You'd better not tell them.*

Sylvie remembered how strong that young woman had been. How bright and simple things were, and how little Gabe's words had affected her at the time. She hadn't told Kase or Tristan that Gabe had freaked out and panicked out there in the harbour, but he knew she could. She hadn't needed to humiliate him. But he had needed to humiliate her.

She began to walk. She followed the same overgrown path etched into the low scrub that she'd taken with Holden. She came to the cliff's edge. She looked down to the dark water below, then up into the darkening sky. The lighthouse was behind her. She closed her eyes. Holden was right. This would never go away. It was an awful beacon. It was the thing everything crashed into. It was drowning her.

She took her notebook out of her pocket, its pages filled with words. So many words. They didn't mean anything. They were not connected. She had thought they were a path to follow, something to grasp hold of, but they were singular. Alone. They were her last crutch. A way of remembering, a way of forgetting.

A long howl issued from her mouth and she hurled the book into the sea below. Her body screamed again into the wind, this time louder, from somewhere deeper. She knew it was her own voice, but it felt like the whole landscape was roaring with her. She bent over with the force of the wind, her own heaving breath. Her pathetic notebook was gone.

I should have written whole, brilliant books, not nonsensical ramblings and other people's words on scraps of paper. I should have gone to university to stretch and ignite my mind instead of struggling to piece together what I'd done between breakfast and lunch. That beautiful, confident, clever girl I used to be should not have died that night on the headland. I should have been able to give, I should have been able to receive … love.

One man's toxic hatred and sickening entitlement had robbed her of her whole life. He, with his successful career, unscathed, completely unremorseful, sitting at the pinnacle of society with a family and his reputation intact. And Kase, who'd lived the life the two of them had dreamed of sharing – of being writers, living a life of the mind, inventing beautiful worlds in their heads. She might be in a loveless marriage, but Kase had had choices, she'd been able to live her potential. She knew what Gabe had done and stayed silent. Sylvie's whole body shook with anger. And Tristan, who she had thought cared for her, who she had hoped loved her, did nothing to stop his friend from raping her …

They had all betrayed her and then left her completely alone. The tears came now in wracking sobs. She cried for what she'd lost and for the cruelty of the ones who were meant to have loved her. She crouched until she was on her hands and knees on the cold, hard rock.

The memories came then, and she let them. She let them fill her head, roar through her body, as brutal as the waves on the rocks below. Tristan's arm around her neck. The hard rock beneath her back as they lay kissing under the low moon. The crash of waves against the rocks below. She remembered the way her desire felt, how the world was spinning too fast. And then she was losing her virginity to the boy she'd always loved. She was scared, but also elated. He loved her too, after all this time, he loved her. She was drunk, but it felt good. His breath was warm on her cheek, his hands brushing her hair from her face. But then something was wrong. A hand pushed her chest hard, pinning her against the rock. Gabe's voice. 'God, she loves it. Come on, mate, my turn.'

Tristan laughed weakly. 'No, come on, mate.' But Gabe pushed him off her and then she was being dragged down the rock. Her skin ripping, her dress tearing, and she was trying to turn over, because Tristan was gone and there was only Gabe. He was so strong. The horrible, hard force of him against her body. And she tried to move, she tried to scream, but she was shocked with terror, soldered to the rock. *Cold. Hard. Brutal.* And then she heard Kase's voice. She was screaming the sound that had lodged in Sylvie's throat. The scream that would not come. Gabe got off her. And Kase was there, smoothing her hair, covering her body with their scarf. She'd forgotten who owned it first. It was both of theirs. Interchangeable. It smelled like a mix of the perfume they wore, vanilla and musk.

Kase was standing now. Screaming at Gabe. 'How could you do this to her? You monster. Who are you?'

She turned to Tristan. 'And you! She loved you. How? How could you let him do this to her?' Kase was screeching, like the cockatoos in the trees on summer mornings that woke them at Palm Beach. And Sylvie wished she was there, sleepy and safe in the spare bed in Kase's room, smelling the butter from the pancakes Fran was making them for breakfast.

But Sylvie felt very wide awake now and Kase was pushing Tristan. Her fists pummelled his chest. He stumbled backwards, but Kase kept pushing him and he didn't stop her. He didn't say a word. He let her strike him again and again. But he was too close to the edge and Sylvie felt an inner vertigo, as though she was on the precipice herself and she squeezed her eyes shut, and then suddenly, shockingly, he was gone. A long wail issued from Sylvie's mouth, and she was scrambling to her feet and running towards the place Tristan had been. She reached Kase, whose face was a white mask.

'Do something!' Kase screamed and grabbed her, and they stood suspended for a moment before the whole world shifted and Sylvie stumbled backwards. Sylvie tried to balance herself but her dress was wrapped about her legs, her underwear tangled around her ankles and then she was falling, falling. She tried to put her hands out, to break her fall, but everything went black.

CHAPTER 27

boy *(n.)* – a male child or young person.

Rachel shut the bedroom door behind her and leaned against it, her hands behind her back. She let out a dramatic sigh and let her head fall back. The way she moved, as though everything was just a set piece waiting for her to perform. Other people mere secondary players to her main act.

'What the hell was that?' Rachel pushed herself into the room and began to pace.

Sometimes Kase thought Rachel truly believed she was the star of a one-woman show, perpetually in one of her plays. Kase sat at the bay window. *The Bell Jar* was on the bed where she'd left it and she closed the book. She looked out to sea to stop herself from feeling trapped in the small airless room. She wished the window opened, imagined herself jumping out, away from Rachel, away from the ghosts of the past that were gathering like an impending storm. She realised the only place she wanted to be was with Sylvie.

Rachel was beside her, pulling her into a hug. 'I know you feel bad for Sylvie but …' Rachel shook her head and pressed her hand to her chest. 'It was so long ago. What good would it do to tell her now?'

Kase extracted herself and gripped the other woman's elbows. 'We should have told her twenty-three years ago, Rachel. Why didn't we tell her then? Why didn't we support our friend, protect her after the worst possible violation?'

Rachel smoothed a strand of hair behind Kase's ear. She wiped the tears from Kase's cheeks. 'Because we were all in shock. Because it was bigger than Sylvie. Tristan died. Your brother died. We were all in complete shock.'

'But when she woke up in the hospital. I should have told her. Why didn't I tell her?' Kase put her face in her hands.

Rachel rubbed her back, as though she were a wayward pet. 'But, Kase, you're forgetting. You were a mess. Fran was a mess. And Sylvie didn't remember. You didn't tell her out of mercy. If she'd known what really happened, she would have been devastated. Devastated. It was better that she just never knew. And she was really struggling … mentally. Who knows if she would have even understood back then? It was kinder.'

Anger ached along her shoulders and Kase squared them. 'No. It wasn't kinder, it was cowardly. It was untruthful.'

Rachel straightened. 'Maybe you're right. It's true. We were all scared. We were fucking terrified actually. I was terrified.' Her voice broke and Kase saw in Rachel's eyes how afraid she'd been. 'Gabe worked so hard to show you how sorry he was. He is.'

Kase couldn't look at Rachel. She shifted her body away, her gaze drawn by the sea. All those times Gabe had leveraged her. And she'd let him. Each time a betrayal of Sylvie. She picked up *The Bell Jar* and opened to the page where their mothers had inscribed their girlhood names.

'We have to tell her now. I have to tell her. She's my best friend. I love her.'

Rachel stood. Her eyes flared and she pressed her fingers into her temples. 'What are you even talking about? Don't you even think about it. Don't you dare.'

For a moment Kase wasn't sure whether it was jealousy or defiance in her face. Maybe it was both.

'But she knows now. She's remembering. She deserves to know the whole truth.'

Rachel dropped to her knees and took Kase's hands. Her eyes were large and Kase saw that for all her selfishness and faults, Rachel did love her.

'Please, Kase, listen to me. How quickly you're forgetting everything Gabe has done for you over the years, how much he helped with your book about Tristan, the strings he pulled for you when you were just starting out.'

Kase bristled. 'Maybe he did it to bribe me.'

'Do you really think that? He's here every birthday – yours, Tristan's, Fran's.' Rachel paused as though to let her words sink in. 'Kase, he made a mistake as a boy. He was very drunk and very young, and things were different back then. Standards have changed now, and Gabe would be held to them in a way his nineteen-year-old self could never have imagined. He would be crucified. He has a wife. Kids. I think he's made amends.'

Kase shook her head and extracted herself from Rachel's grasp. 'To me maybe, but not to Sylvie.'

Rachel rose and began pacing again, wringing her hands, as Kase had watched her do when rehearsing difficult lines.

'Anyway, I'm not worried. Sylvie doesn't have the gall to take this any further, even if she has started to remember. It's her word against ours. Three people in the public eye with reputations, against one person who it's achingly apparent is very damaged. And we have money. The best lawyers. All we'd have to do is get a medical specialist to attest to the fact that she had a brain injury and that she's not fit to remember. A jury would never be convinced beyond reasonable doubt.'

Kase pressed *The Bell Jar* against her chest. *What would Esther Greenwood do?* 'And what if I tell her the truth?'

Rachel's head snapped around and her eyes narrowed. 'Are you forgetting that you'd destroy your dead brother's memory forever? Are you forgetting how it would destroy Fran?'

Kase felt a strange calm come over her. She spoke slowly. 'No, Rachel, it's you who's forgetting. You told me to stay quiet. You told me not to say anything about what Gabe did to Sylvie. Boys being boys. Isn't that what you called it?'

Rachel's mouth went hard. 'I don't know. Is that what *you'd* call it? You're the one who writes fiction with a feminist slant. I can't think your devoted readers would take too well to the knowledge of what you hid for a lifetime either. You've built your career on a lie.'

Kase felt the impact of Rachel's words like a slap. The book dropped from her hands onto the floor.

'I could tell you that Gabe would destroy you, but let's face it, Kase.' Rachel's face was hard, her symmetrical features, so striking on stage, frightening close-up. 'You'd destroy yourself.'

CHAPTER 28

home *(n.)* - a house, or other shelter that is the fixed residence of a person, a family.

The house was dark save for a single light in the kitchen. Holden was sitting at the table, an empty beer bottle in front of him. All her life she'd felt like she was looking in at life through a fragile glass pane, invisible but impenetrable. She opened the door, feeling as though she was about to step past the glass. He looked up when she entered.

'Didn't know if I'd ever see you again.'

His voice was flat, his eyes downcast. Sylvie couldn't tell if he was angry, or just sad. She remained in the doorway, one foot still in the safety of the night. The crickets sang in the dark trees.

She stepped into the light and placed the truck keys on the table. Their eyes met. 'Holden, I'm sorry I left you there. It was … inexcusable of me.'

'I don't blame you.' He looked away and shook his head. 'I shouldn't have lied to you about Pippi.'

Sylvie sat down at the table. She saw then that it was set and that Holden had prepared a meal for them. The pasta with herbs from the garden that she'd loved the first night she came. It had been the act of cooking for her, caring for her, rather than the meal itself that had warmed her. The golden threads of pasta a simple devotion. The herbs picked and cut with care. It was plated now and sitting on the bench. The simple act of his hope that she would return made tears spring to her eyes. She took the bowls and placed them on the table, touched his shoulder lightly, then sat down. Holden poured red wine into their glasses. She realised she was starving. She twisted the fettucine around her fork; it smelled like thyme and butter and salt. It still tasted warm on her tongue.

'Is it good?' he asked.

'It's beautiful,' she said, and they both knew she wasn't just talking about the taste of the food, but what the making of it meant. They ate in silence for a while and then she put down her fork.

'Holden, I understand that a story has a time to be told. That you weren't ready to tell me yet. I understand that you told yourself a fiction about how Pippi died because it was less painful. It was the only way you could live with it. We all do that. Maybe our memories play tricks so that it doesn't hurt as much.'

Her hand slipped into her pocket, but her notebook wasn't there. She put her pencil on the table. 'Holden Caulfield was right. There's a line from *Catcher in the Rye* about how people are always thinking things are all true but, sometimes, they're only partly true. We make our own stories, our own realities, from all the shades of grey in life. Books are the same. They speak partly of the truth and partly of what is imagined, hoped for.'

Holden picked up the pencil. 'Sylvie, where's your notebook?'

'I threw it away.' Sylvie could barely look at the shock on his face. 'I went back to the lighthouse.'

Holden's brows furrowed. 'Why would you do that?'

She felt all the emotions she'd experienced on that clifftop crystallise into something powerful, deep inside her. 'Because I was telling stories to myself too. I told myself I'd forgotten, but I knew. Deep down I knew, but I didn't want to face it. Just like you didn't want to face what really happened to Pippi.'

'Knew what, Sylvie?'

'What they did to me. And that it wasn't me who pushed Tristan over the edge.'

Holden shook his head, confused. 'It wasn't?'

'No, it was Kase.'

'What? You remember?'

'Yes. I remember. She was so angry at what they did to me. She was screaming at them, at Tristan, for betraying me, and she pushed him again and again, until he fell.'

Holden put down his wineglass. 'Oh my God. Are you telling me she killed her own brother?'

'Yes. Defending me.'

He paused. 'But then she made you believe that you pushed him.'

Sylvie shook her head. 'I know. She killed her own brother out of anger for what he did to me and yet she betrayed me. They all betrayed me. But hers feels the worst.' She put her face in her hands.

'Why would she do that?'

'I've been trying to untangle it all. Maybe so that I'd never say anything to anyone, if I started to remember? Maybe Rachel and Gabe are holding the fact that she killed Tristan over her. Blackmailing her?'

'And yet she invited you back into her life. That was a bit of a risk, if that's the case.'

'Yes. I saw how scared of Gabe she was. Is.'

'You need to talk to her.'

Sylvie shook her head. She felt the new strength inside her galvanise and pressed her hand to her chest. 'No. I've tried twice. I've seen the truth in her eyes, and I know her too well. She wants to tell me, but she won't. She's too scared, or too weak. Both. My whole life has been defined by other people's stories, Holden, their lies. I've finally found the truth for myself and I'm going to do something about it. I don't need Kase for that.'

He took her hand. 'What would that look like, Sylvie?'

She took a deep breath. 'I'm not entirely sure. Going to the police? I haven't thought about logistics, I'm still processing what I learned on that headland tonight.' Her eyes filled with tears. 'I didn't know if I could come back from that place.'

Holden pulled her towards him, wrapping his arms around her. 'You came back to me.'

'You found me when I was invisible. You saw me. You made me dinner.' Her voice was small.

He smiled. 'I want to look after you.' He pulled back, looking into her eyes. 'I shouldn't have pressured you like that before. I'm sorry. You know you don't have to do anything. You could stay here and I'll make you food and we'll eat and walk and read. You've brought books back into my life, Sylvie. You've allowed me to face the things I couldn't. You're helping me heal. We can be happy, I know we can.'

Sylvie kissed him. He tasted delicious. 'I've been waiting for you my whole life.'

'We can live here. I'll come to Sydney with you and help you pack up your life. We'll start fresh. I know it's sudden but it feels so right … if you want to.'

Her heart swelled with hope at the thought of this life. But what she'd just experienced on the clifftop hung like a dark curtain veiling this bright dream. 'What about what you said, about how … damaged I am?' Tears fell from her. She didn't try to stop them.

Holden wiped them away with his thumbs and kissed her. 'It doesn't matter. I love you for who you are. We'll find a way. I want to protect you, help you heal, like you've helped me. Sylvie, just so you know, if you took it further you could be trotted out in front of the media because of who Gabe is, because of who Kase is. I wasn't thinking of all that. It would be your word against theirs. That's if there's enough evidence for it to get to court, given it's a historic case. And the conviction rate for sexual assault hovers around fifty-six per cent, when it's seventy-five per cent for manslaughter.' He grimaced at her raised eyebrows. 'Sadly I know the stats. I know everything about this stuff now.'

Sylvie pressed her hand to his heart, thinking of all the hours he'd spent researching how he could have saved his daughter. 'Oh Holden.'

He kissed her fingertips. 'I'll support you whatever you decide, but please don't feel like I'm asking you to do that. It won't bring Pippi back, or somehow avenge her.'

Sylvie gripped his hand. She felt the dark veil lift. 'Maybe not. But I think it might bring me back.'

CHAPTER 29

evidence *(n.)* – that which tends to prove or disprove something.

Sylvie entered the police station alone, as she knew she must. Alone was all she had been because of what he'd done to her, and so it seemed fitting almost that she stood here with only the drone of the air conditioning and her body turning as numb from cold as it already was with fear. She dinged a bell on the counter. Still nothing. Maybe it was a sign. She walked out of the station, grateful for the soft spell of early autumn. Holden was sitting in the driver's seat of her car. He didn't see her – he was reading a novel. She watched him for a while, the way he tilted his head slightly as he read, the way he licked the tip of his index finger to turn the page. It was all she needed to find the strength to go back into the station.

Every night Holden cooked for her. In her tiny flat behind the cafe, he made her warming stews and soups. Cakes that tasted like oranges. He collected sourdough for them every morning, which they ate at the small table in the weak sunlight. She'd resigned from her job, but was seeing out a few more weeks so as not to abruptly leave her employers, who had been good to her for so many years. They drank tea wrapped in blankets in the courtyard looking up at the stars each night. She and Holden didn't talk about what she was building up the courage to do – go to the police, make a statement. They didn't talk about the past at all, instead they talked about the books they would sell in their shop. Holden had some money set aside and they spoke of opening a bookshop in Hobart, setting up a little kitchen so he could cook simple meals, and Sylvie could match people with books. The farmhouse would become their sanctuary. They would spend their days fixing it up, tending to the gardens, making it back into a home. But they would leave the library exactly as it was.

When she couldn't sleep and memories from that night on the headland haunted her, Holden read to her until the words blurred and the dreams began. Building up to this moment felt like the worst of times, but their days were bookended by hope and love.

Sylvie sat across from the police officer now and waited as he wrote in the pad in front of him. The room was so cold. She had run out of words, of trying to fit her feelings into a meaning this stranger would understand. The officer kept referring to it as a sexual assault. *Rape*, she wanted to scream. A sexual assault sounds like a wayward hand, not the scraping of skin on rock, the brutal pounding of a body. The man shuffled the papers in front of him. Even before he said the words, Sylvie knew what they would be. She could tell by his apologetic eyes.

'I'm afraid in cases such as these, particularly historic cases from so long ago, there's just not enough evidence to get it to court. You have no witnesses, as the other three present, including the accused, will, you say, deny there was a sexual assault. And given the status of those involved, it's unlikely to go beyond … best-case scenario, a plea bargain. I wish I could tell you a different story.'

Sylvie kept her voice strong, clear despite the disappointment pooling inside her, threatening to drown her. 'Is there no other way? Nothing at all?'

She had to turn away from the look he gave her. She stood, and to his credit, he did too. There was silent pity in the twitch of his lips. He simply nodded at her before she left the room, and as she made her way down the soulless hallway all she could think was that sometimes the words didn't even get to feel like anything, they didn't even get a chance to exist. They were just lost. *Hidden. Suppressed. Buried.*

It was only then that she let the tears sting her eyes.

CHAPTER 30

reckon *(v.)* - to settle accounts, as with a person.

The wind was brutal, howling along the city street, throwing up dust and the rust-coloured leaves that had been stripped from the trees. Sylvie wrapped her coat around her and slipped into the cafe. It was almost empty, as she'd known it would be. She also knew he'd come.

The plastic chair shrieked as she pulled it out and sat down. Her hands were shaking. She looked around this sad little cafe with its fake pot plants and formica tables. This was the only place left for her to settle things. She had, in her naivety, imagined a man who had committed a crime being held accountable in a court of law, rather than a tired city cafe. In all the powerlessness she felt, coming directly to him seemed the only powerful option left to her. It was hard to articulate what she wanted from him, needed from him. Perhaps there was a small, deluded part in her that hoped he had remorse for what he'd done, that if she saw his contrition, she could somehow move on with her life. Beyond that, she needed him to know that she knew. She remembered now.

She watched him approach, head down, checking his phone, strides purposeful, confident, the easy way he had in a world made for men like him. She'd made sure to make it his territory, so he'd feel in control. That's what it had always been about, after all.

Gabe spotted her and raised a leather-gloved hand. He stopped at the coffee machine as he passed it. He didn't bother to ask her what type of coffee she drank. He shared a laugh with the barista and made his way over to her table.

'Sylvie,' he said, nodding, neither shaking her hand nor attempting to kiss her cheek. She remained seated.

'Gabe.' She nodded back, tried to ignore the thrum of the blood at her temples. 'Thanks for meeting with me.' She marvelled silently at his gall in coming after everything that had happened. Was it an opportunity for him to further control the situation? Revel in his power? Or did he not even realise what he'd done to her? Was he entirely oblivious?

'Well, I did technically tell you to look me up about a job, didn't I? And …' He stripped his gloves off. 'We do go back a long way. The Fowlers are my family and I like to help out my own. And I know they view you as part of the family, too.' He shook his head. 'God, Fran is a good woman, isn't she? A good woman.'

She caught the subtext, his thinly veiled threat, leveraging Fran as his protection. *You are not worthy of her love*, Sylvie thought. She had to bite her tongue to stop the rage coursing up her spine from coming out her mouth. She was shocked by the force of it. She took a deep breath, steadied herself.

She laced her fingers under the table as the waiter came over with their coffees. He had ordered her a latte. It was hot and bitter on her tongue.

'How did you know what kind of coffee I liked?' she asked, smiling.

He returned her smile, just as she knew he would, and leaned in as though sharing a secret. 'I'm good at reading people. And I buy a lot of coffees for people. It's a skill I've honed over a lifetime of journalism. One of the first things I learned as a cadet was that if anyone ever invites you into their house for an interview and offers you a cup of coffee, always say yes. The act of saying yes to a warm drink inspires trust.'

A shiver moved through her body and she clenched her jaw to try to hide it. She kept her voice light and steady. 'I must admit I was shocked you became a journalist. I seem to remember a boy who spent most of his time surfing and hanging out with girls.'

He splayed his large hands on the table. 'What can I say? I got ambitious, eventually.'

'Do you ever think about what Tristan would have been when he grew up?'

Gabe stiffened, ever so slightly, and ran a hand through his hair. 'God, I think of him all the time. It's so strange, so indistinct, such a long time ago. Such a small part of our lives now and yet that was all he got. Tragic.'

Sylvie placed her hands on the table. They weren't shaking anymore. 'Does it really seem like a small part of your life, Gabe? I'd imagine it looms pretty large, losing your best friend at that age. And raping me.'

His cup clattered in its saucer, spilling coffee over the table. He swore and mopped it up with a serviette. For a second their eyes locked, and Sylvie saw fear there, plain and simple. The same fear she'd seen swimming in the harbour, the shadow lurking below.

Then Gabe leaned back in his chair and laughed.

'God, you're still a little piece of work. I thought you'd changed. Softened. With your pathetic limp and your brain, not quite so quickfire as before.' He leaned in, a twinkle of amusement in his eye. 'What exactly is this about? You've lured me here on the pretence of a job. As if I'd ever give it to you out of anything but charity, out of my allegiance to the Fowlers. What do you want? Money? You want to bribe me, that it? It's my word against yours. You always thought you were better than me, but not anymore. As if anyone would believe you over me. You had a fucking brain injury. And honestly, I mean really, is that how you remember that night?' He leaned in so close she could smell the coffee and cigarettes on his breath. 'Because I remember very well that you were a drunk little minx. Tristan didn't really want you, he was just pissed, so I did you a favour and gave it to you. You call that rape? I call it charity. And then you went and pushed Tristan off a cliff.'

Sylvie's face, her whole body flooded with heat. She couldn't breathe. She could barely stop herself from hitting his smirking face. She leaned in even closer. Her voice was a whisper.

'Was it really so humiliating for you that I beat you and then had to save you that day in the harbour? You had to find a way to win in the end, didn't you?'

His eyes flashed with anger, but there was vulnerability there too. He laughed derisively and stood up, the whole table moving with his bulk. 'I don't have time for this shit.'

Sylvie looked up sweetly and smiled. 'Hmm, that's funny, I've got as long as it takes.' She rose from the table, turned her back on him, walked a few steps, and then looked back. 'Oh, and Gabe. Next time you want to inspire trust … I don't drink coffee, I drink tea.'

CHAPTER 31

survive *(v.)* - to remain alive or in existence after the death of someone or after the cessation of something or the occurrence or some event; continue to live.

Evangeline poured the fragrant chai into Sylvie's cup and then took a sip.

Sylvie shook her head and smiled. 'Help yourself, why don't you, Mum?'

Evangeline put her hand over Sylvie's. It was softer, older than she remembered, but still covered in jewellery, the bracelets and rings her mother never took off. That, and the smell of sandalwood and cigarettes took Sylvie back to her childhood. It was funny how Evangeline had crossed continents and lifetimes and still smelled like her mother.

'Sorry, darling, I just wanted to taste it.' She made a face. 'Nothing will compare to Turkish tea, I'm afraid.'

Her mother had returned at another crisis point in her life, as though her internal compass was trained to the true north of drama. But Sylvie was grateful for her presence. Sylvie had phoned her in tears after meeting with Gabe. All the bravado that had propelled her to confront him had abandoned her. She'd felt the momentary satisfaction of seeing the fear flash in his eyes, but it wasn't enough. She'd been stupid to think he would feel remorse for what he'd done to her, but she hadn't expected the depth of his indifference, his cruelty.

It felt like the end of the road, and even though her mother had disappointed her so many times, Sylvie had just needed her mum. Evangeline had told her she was getting on a plane and that she had 'connections' they could utilise. Her mother always kept tabs on the power she held over people.

Sylvie looked around the tiny cafe on the other side of her known four walls. She remembered how frightening it had felt to sit here only a few months ago. Now Holden was on her left, drinking coffee and skimming a newspaper, his warm hand resting on her thigh, her mother on her right, delicately peeling layers off a croissant. Sylvie was sitting in the same place in the sunshine under the window, but she was no longer alone.

'So, what's our plan of attack?' Evangeline grabbed her hand again and Sylvie remembered that for all her faults, her mother had always been tactile, had always hugged her close.

'You can't give up. I sat with you in that hospital bed when you didn't even remember your own name. And now look at you. I know someone who we can take this to. An old journo friend. She's got a weekly op-ed column in the rival paper to Gabe's. I'll call her and see what we can do. If we can't have a trial in the courts, we'll have a trial by media. That seems fitting, doesn't it?'

Sylvie shook her head. 'Mum, they won't even be able to name him. The police don't even have a case.'

'I know, honey, but I want you to be able to tell your truth. I want you to get it out of you, even if it goes nowhere. You need to be given the dignity of being able to tell your story. Holden agrees with me, doesn't he?'

Holden squeezed Sylvie's hand and their eyes met. His smile was sad, but it held such intimacy, such knowing, such promise, that she felt she would never be trapped behind that thin pane of solitude again. He nodded very softly.

Evangeline wiped the tear from Sylvie's cheek. 'I know I haven't always been around for you, but I'm here when it matters. And I know you, Sylvia Dane. You're my daughter, and your voice needs to be heard.'

* * *

The trees in the garden were bare skeletons. The air was so cold it hurt to breathe. Sylvie felt naked as she climbed the stairs to the house. Her mind was clear but a great bruise, tender to press, bloomed inside her chest. It was the same bruise she'd carried at her core for twenty-three years, but at least she knew now the depth and breadth of it, the blunt force, the pressure that had caused it. She had Holden and her mum as a balm against it. And she had the memory of the fear in Gabe's eyes.

Evangeline knocked on the door and Holden blew his breath against her fingers.

'You're going to be fine,' he said. 'All you have to do is tell the truth. It might be complicated for everyone else – police, courts, media, but not for you. For you this is simple.'

She pressed her forehead to his, feeling all his strength and love flow into her. She sensed all the words that didn't need to be spoken hovering between them.

A woman with a greying bob, about her mother's age, opened the door with a smile. 'You must be Sylvie. Welcome. I'm Katelyn. Come in. Lovely to see you, Evangeline.'

She and her mother exchanged kisses, and Sylvie saw the warm squeeze Evangeline gave Katelyn's arm. She wondered about their connection, why this woman was doing this for her, for her mother. She wanted to ask, but it was not Evangeline's way to go into such details.

Katelyn chatted companionably about the weather, how cold it had suddenly got, as she made them tea in the kitchen. Sylvie thought of Gabe's cynical comment about how accepting a coffee inspired trust. It fed the disgust that sat deep in her gut, the disgust that she'd turned on herself for so long. They moved into a comfortable lounge room with an outlook over trees and a wood fire in a small hearth. They arranged themselves around a large coffee table with their mugs. Sylvie sat where she could see the trees. It wasn't what she had imagined telling her story would be like. There were no lawyers, no police, no people of power. It was just someone's lounge room and the smell of brewing tea leaves. But she could feel Katelyn watching her. Sylvie immediately recognised her gentle attention and care in the calm, slow way she'd prepared their tea. She trusted this woman.

'Now Sylvie, Evangeline's told me a little of what you've been through. I think what you're doing is very brave and I'd like to help give you a voice, if I possibly can. I can't promise anything – we're bound by the confines of the law and potential defamation, but I'm here to listen to you. To take account of your words, your story. So, I've got a Dictaphone here and I'm going to be taking some notes while you talk. Take your time and stop if you need a break. I want you to start at the beginning, or the end. Wherever you like.'

Sylvie took a deep breath. It felt like jumping into that icy water off the end of the jetty at Bruny again. Her heart was racing, but she was finally making ripples. 'Thanks for listening to me when it feels like no one else will. I've written something I'd like to read out, if that's okay. It starts at the end.' She looked at Holden and then unfolded her piece of paper.

'There was a girl. Her name was Pippi. And I'm here for her, not just for myself, because alone I feel like I'm too weak and this process is too hard. But Pippi was stronger than me. She was named after a girl with red hair who put bullies in the trees and made burglars dance with her for gold. And this is what she would have wanted.' Sylvie couldn't look at Holden. She knew there'd be tears in his eyes.

She took a breath, felt the softness of the ripples spread outwards from her body. 'I'm here for every girl who's been told to forget the crime committed against her and get on with her life. Because we can't. Our bodies won't let us forget. Our lives end the moment a man takes away our dignity, and silences our voice. So all we have left are our words speaking the truth. The truth isn't something any one person owns. It is its own entity and it is powerful.'

She swallowed and continued. 'I know his name will probably never be known, because somehow everything seems bent on protecting the reputation of the man rather than protecting the dignity and worth of the woman, but Gabe Williams raped me when I was seventeen.'

She stopped reading, the ache in the back of her throat too great to continue. She'd never before borne witness to those words, not properly. A single tear slipped down her cheek. She let it, and others, fall. She let herself sob. It felt like a release, after twenty-three years of holding everything in.

Holden and her mother held her until her body stopped shaking. But she was not finished.

'It has taken me a whole lifetime to find the truth and to find a way to process what he did to me. I have struggled to have relationships, because I have never been able to trust … I felt ashamed of … revolted by my body without understanding why.'

She imagined Gabe's smirking face in that cafe. She pictured him surrounded by his family, protected by his money and status, when really he was that weak, drowning boy in the harbour. 'This is the victim impact statement I wanted to be able to read out in court, but that avenue is denied to me. So, I'm here to tell the story that no one wants me to tell.'

CHAPTER 32

light *(n.)* - that which makes things visible, or affords illumination.
(adj.) - of little weight; not heavy.

The reporters were so close, Kase could smell their sweat and expectation in the room. She felt nauseous with it. They were in a sea of black camera lenses and microphones. Sylvie's story had been in the press for a week.

Newspaper editor accused of historical sexual assault.

Kase's heart had shrunk and exploded at the same time. She'd been skimming the weekend papers on the kitchen bench when Sylvie's image had appeared, her face in profile gazing out a window to the tops of trees. It felt like she'd been punched low, in the gut. Panic spread through her shoulders, rising through her neck as she read the headline and then the story.

Gabe had not been named. The article said only that the man in question had worked as a newspaper editor, and the details of the incident were deliberately vague. Sylvie had been seventeen at the time and the man, nineteen. The panic and fear were replaced by an ache deep within her as she read Sylvie's words over and over. The article filled less than half a page. It was too small a space for Sylvie to occupy. Kase was being wrenched inside, part of her terrified of everything she stood to lose, the other wracked with guilt at the selfish self-preservation that had been guiding her for so many years. She'd left the newspaper smeared with tears, hidden under a pile of books.

Though the story was small, the media was alight with commentary about how little power a woman had over her own traumatic past. There was careful speculation about who this man may have been. Several other women had come forward citing sexual misconduct with high-profile men in the press.

'Why on earth would Sylvie lie about something like this?' Fran had asked, her eyes full of tears when Kase had eventually summoned the courage to show her the article.

Gabe and Rachel had called Kase, their threats no longer masked. *Stick to the story. Don't contact her. And don't worry – there's no police investigation, no case. Gabe hasn't even been named.*

All she could say to Fran was that she didn't know, and then make excuses about needing to write. *She can't know what Tristan did to Sylvie, it would break her. It would destroy Tristan's memory forever.* And the selfish voice whispering to Kase in the dark hours when she couldn't sleep, *it would destroy me.*

She heard Gabe's voice on speakerphone when Fran confronted him. Her mother was standing in the kitchen, her eyes trained on the horizon out the window. 'What's all this about, Gabe?' Her voice cracked when she said his name.

Gabe's voice was steady, reassuring, sympathetic. 'I'm not sure if it's part of her brain injury, false memories of that time, or if she's wanting to somehow extort me for money. There's absolutely no police case against me. They can't even name me. She's obviously very confused. Maybe Holden has put her up to this. You know me, Fran, you've known me since I was a kid. I've always been like your surrogate son, for Christ's sake. I would never do that.'

But all Kase could think was, *Mum has known Sylvie since she was a girl, too*. But Sylvie wasn't Fran's daughter. She was, after all, the child of her husband's mistress. Gabe had been there for Fran for the past twenty-three years.

When there began to be calls for the man implicated in the article to name himself, as more male journalists and editors fell under suspicion, as more women came forward, Gabe asked Fran to visit him in Sydney. He told her that he needed her. Fran didn't hesitate in saying yes.

Rachel called Kase and said, 'You know you need to stand with us.'

Kase felt a stab of self-disgust as she hung up and booked their flights. She opened her phone and dialled Sylvie's number. It rang out. She texted. *I saw the article. Can we talk? Sylvie, please take my call.* She was met with silence, again and again. Kase supposed there was a sad serendipity to that.

And now they were standing on a small, raised stage in front of a lectern covered with microphones. Gabe and Rachel, Fran, and Kase, with a few other people Kase presumed were Gabe's staff. Gabe had decided to take matters into his own hands and call a press conference in the media room at his newspaper. It was, he said, the only noble thing to do, to ensure his media colleagues didn't continue to be smeared by a barrage of speculation and allegations.

He stepped up to the microphone with a confidence that was breathtaking to behold. *He still doesn't even think he did anything wrong*, thought Kase.

His voice was strong and clear, a leader's voice. 'I am standing here to protect my colleagues and to ensure their reputations are not destroyed by a baseless article that has been published this week. The woman who has brought false accusations against me was known to me twenty-three years ago. She suffered a brain injury in an accident on the night in question, and is not a fit witness to what happened. She lost her memory, a fact that medical records attest to.'

He straightened and looked out into the crowd. 'Let me be very clear – there was no sexual assault and there is absolutely no police investigation into this matter. And I will not have a trial by media in my own newspaper when the police are not even pursuing these allegations. My sister and my best friend, an eminent actress and a bestselling author, are here beside me today attesting to my character.'

He gestured towards Rachel and Kase, and Rachel grabbed Kase's hand. Her grip felt like a vice.

'They were there on the night in question when we were all teenagers. Kase Fowler, who many of you will know, dedicated her award-winning novel to her brother, my friend, Tristan Fowler, who we lost in a terrible accident that night when he tragically slipped off a cliff.' Gabe paused for a moment longer than was normal, his mouth twisting with emotion.

You're crying crocodile tears, Kase thought. *You're holding me hostage with my own brother's death. And I am not your best friend.*

Gabe's voice was softer now, emotional. 'I would never hurt a woman. I love and respect women. I have a wife, a daughter …'

Anger surged up her spine and Kase wrestled her hand from Rachel's. She was looking down, over that dark cavernous place where Tristan had fallen, and she was about to propel herself into it. Kase unfolded the newspaper article in her pocket. She looked at the picture of Sylvie, her vacant eyes staring into the distance. She was wearing a red dress, so like the one Kase had bought her from the op shop. The dress they had chosen for the party. The dress Gabe had ripped. Around her neck was a scarf like the one they had both worn, the piece of fabric Kase had covered Sylvie's shaking body with that night. Sylvie could have been seventeen again. *No*, Kase thought. *The Sylvie I used to know died with Tristan.* Sylvie's eyes weren't filled with hate or anger, they were empty. They were the same eyes, but they no longer shone.

Gabe was still standing at the microphone, the journalists' questions whizzing past their heads like bullets. 'I won't be taking any questions or making any further comments on this matter,' he said finally, putting up his hands.

He stepped away from the microphone and Kase felt her body move towards it, propelled by some unknown force. She stood for a second, hovering, unsure, at the cliff's edge. She looked out onto the faces of the media and vertigo hit her. A tiny voice inside her screamed. *You can't destroy Fran. You can't destroy Tristan's memory. She won't survive it. You can't destroy yourself.*

But Kase looked back at Fran's face behind her. It was crumpled and tired, like a piece of paper that had been balled up and then smoothed out. This had already destroyed Fran. A lifetime of lies had destroyed them all. Kase was sure Fran knew, deep down, she knew.

Kase swallowed hard. She took a shaky breath. Her whole body was quivering. It felt like stepping over the edge. 'I'd like to say something,' she said.

She turned and saw Fran next to Gabe. His eyes were filled with uncertainty, but Fran's hand was on his arm, placating him, telling him it would be okay and Kase saw the nineteen-year-old boy he used to be.

She let the words form on her tongue, the ones she'd been withholding her whole life. She spoke into the microphone. 'There was a light in my friend,' she began. 'She sparkled. She was luminous. She was clever and brave. But Sylvie's light ...' Kase's voice broke. 'It went out twenty-three years ago.'

She heard Gabe's rage before she felt it.

'This press conference is over,' he yelled behind her, his voice panicked. He was upon her now. He gripped her by the elbow and wrenched her out of the way, leaning into the microphone, his voice booming. 'We will not be taking any more questions on this matter today.'

'Let her speak.' A woman's voice in the crowd.

But Gabe was manoeuvring Kase away from the microphone with his bulk.

Two female reporters appeared beside her, putting their bodies between Gabe and herself. A third leaned into the microphone. 'Let her speak.'

Gabe surged forward but the women were there. His face was pale with shock and he stumbled backwards, into Rachel. The women moved to surround Kase. Fran joined them. Kase looked into the faces of these women and understood what they were giving her, and it lent her courage.

'My life, everything I have achieved of any worth has been based on a lie. It's been spent with the wrong people. Sylvie, you are my person. You have always been my person. I know you may never forgive me for what I've done to you, what

I hid from that night. I'm so sorry. I thought I was protecting my brother, my mother, myself, but I was condemning us all. I can't live the rest of my life without you. I'm sorry I wasn't braver for us.'

The room was loud with voices, but she looked to her mother beside her. Fran's face was streaked with tears, but she nodded, a tiny reassuring smile on her lips. Kase looked for Gabe, but he and Rachel were gone. *Of course you'd run. Coward. You've always been a coward.* Only the women remained.

'My brother Tristan's death has always been framed as a tragic accident, and recently, when Sylvie started to remember that night, we let her believe she pushed Tristan off the cliff so she'd never reveal the truth about what the boys did to her. That was always Rachel and Gabe's plan. They concocted it all that night. I was in shock. Tristan was dead and Sylvie was unconscious. And we all told the police it was just an accident. Gabe and Rachel knew I'd never say anything about the rape because …' Kase faltered. A hush had fallen over the room. She felt dizzy. 'It was me, not Sylvie, who pushed Tristan towards that cliff. They thought I'd killed my own brother and so they thought I'd never reveal the full truth, which was that Gabe Williams raped Sylvie Dane when she was seventeen years old, and my brother let him.'

A furious clicking of cameras erupted around her. She took a deep breath. 'I was so shocked, so angry at Tristan. Sylvie loved Tristan, she trusted him, and he betrayed her. I was screaming at Tristan, hitting him, pushing him, over and over. But I stopped. I stopped. I didn't push my brother over that edge. For a single moment Tristan looked at me, and in his face I saw that he knew what he'd done to Sylvie. And …' She swallowed hard, her whole body aching at the memory of the look in her brother's eyes. The look she'd never been able to forget. The utter shame and regret and sorrow on his face. 'He took a step back. Off the cliff.'

Her voice was filled with tears and they ran down her face as she spoke again. 'I thought I was protecting my brother's memory. He took his own life out of shame and regret for what he'd done, for what he'd let Gabe do to Sylvie. My brother was the toxic example of a good man doing nothing. But I thought somehow that I needed to honour him. To protect my mother, who had just lost her son. It was too hard to see my brother as a monster, so I turned him into a hero. I wrote a book dedicated to him. It should have been written for you, Sylvie. You are the hero in this story. And in staying silent, I have become the monster. I'm so sorry.'

CHAPTER 33

tarot *(n.)* - a pack of cards used in fortune-telling.

Fran slipped the letter and the tarot card into an envelope. She wrote *Evangeline* on the front, then crossed it out. She took a fresh envelope and wrote *Eve*. Fran had snuck the fortune-teller's card into her pocket the night she and Eve had visited the Chinese restaurant in Kings Cross. It had remained lodged in the spine of *The Bell Jar* for years. Fran had forgotten she'd used it as a bookmark.

She sealed the letter for delivery. She wasn't sure where Eve was staying in Sydney, but she had an idea.

* * *

Teddy's house was the same. The red-brick façade, the slanted roof with the faded blue tiles, the lace curtains. But her own childhood home, long ago sold, was unrecognisable. The new owners had erased any memory of the 1960s. The red brick had been rendered with fresh beige cement. Fran was relieved. It looked nothing like her memories of the night her mother died, the night she banished Eve on the front steps.

Fran got out of her car. It was oppressively humid for this time of year. She remembered the way the summer storms would sheet in over the plateau as though trying to shed heat. There would be a storm tonight. She could smell the electricity in the air.

She didn't even know if Eve was staying here, or if she'd want to talk to her if she was. But things had come full circle now. And there was no one else to talk to about what had happened. No one else understood the complex way they were all linked, like a spiral that only seemed to get tighter with time.

Kase had fled Sydney, pursued by journalists, and if a phone call Fran had overheard was any indication, it was finally over with Henry. Her daughter was completely alone, and she'd gone home to the island to hide and write out her pain. Kase needed her mother, and Fran would go to her soon, but she needed to do this first.

She walked up the concrete path, her heart grumbling like the distant thunder. She stood at the front door and felt fat drops of rain. Teddy had given Eve this house. Maybe it was out of respect to Fran that Eve had never chosen to live here. Eve's tastes didn't run to the suburban, but perhaps one day the home would be Sylvie's. Fran thought about pushing the envelope under the door and leaving, but then she thought about Sylvie's bravery. She straightened and knocked.

From where she stood, she could see the pool next door. It had been done up like the rest of the house, but it was essentially the same, just with better sun lounges. An image came to her of her, Eve and Teddy lying around it, the strains of

The Doors haunting the hot summer air. Nostalgia washed over her, mournful and exquisite. Memories so often felt bittersweet. Fran wondered who lived there now, what new memories, new stories were being written in its rooms.

The door swung open. Eve's mouth was a perfect 'O' of shock. Fran had no words either. They stood there for a long moment, neither sure of what to say or do. How did you find the words to speak about so many things left unsaid? All those times they had dropped the girls off and picked them up from one another's houses. It had been easier then. The anger so thinly hidden, each avoiding the other's eyes, the tension crackling along the fine hairs of their arms. It was simple avoidance. Now it was something else.

'Sorry to just turn up here,' Fran said, looking behind her, ready to leave.

Eve nodded her head, ever so slightly, to acknowledge that it was okay to enter. The decor had been updated, but it smelled like memories. The wax of Teddy's surfboard, the claret Teddy's parents used to drink. The boiled vegetables and meatloaf they used to eat. The nostalgia was so strong it was hard to breathe.

Fran held the envelope out to Eve. 'I wanted to give you this. I didn't know if you'd be here,' she said.

Eve took the letter and opened it. She held up the tarot card and her eyes met Fran's.

'I can't believe you stole the card. Did you, Franny Taylor?'

She smiled. 'It was one of my more rebellious moments. Though in hindsight, I think she let me take it.'

'Do you think she was right?' asked Eve.

Fran knew what Eve was asking. She didn't know how to answer.

'Come in, I'll make us tea.'

Eve walked into the small, timber-panelled kitchen. Fran thought of all the times she'd stood here and watched Teddy make peanut butter sandwiches. It was strange to be back here with Eve and not Teddy.

'Do you see Ted anymore?' Fran asked. She found there was no feeling attached to the sound of his name. That was the gift age bestowed. A letting go of the things that needed to be released. She looked at Eve spooning tea leaves into a pot in her striking red kimono, her hair rolled into a chignon at her neck. Some things were harder to let go.

'No. But we email sometimes. He's still flying private jets around the world. At his age! Oh well, he's keeping himself busy. He suggested I stay here while I was in Sydney. It's empty anyway.'

Fran knew then that Eve had been the one to leave Ted for the last time, and that it was finally over between them, otherwise she would not have taken up his offer of the house. She didn't know how many times they had been drawn back to each other over the years. She didn't want to know. Fran had tried to make it work with Ted for so long, for the kids, but after Tristan died, the ruse was up. Fran didn't have the energy anymore, or the room for any more pain. He'd left the house and she knew he would go to Eve.

The weight of everything unsaid filled up the silence as Eve poured boiling water into the teapot. She took a tray with the teapot and cups on it outside onto the small balcony and Fran followed. The line of the horizon was blurred, the lake and the ocean sheeted with soft rain. The granny flat was still there, decaying among the ferns at the bottom of the garden next door.

It was a relic of their youth, probably still filled with stubbed-out cigarettes and posters of The Beatles, the thin mattress on the floor.

'Is there still a hole in the fence?' Fran asked.

Eve looked up from her teacup. 'At the bottom of the garden?'

'Yes, where Teddy used to sneak in at night.'

It was the first time Fran had said it out loud, that she'd known about that hole in the fence, their night-time meetings without her.

Eve's face softened at the memory. 'I think so.'

'Gosh, weren't we just so young? Sometimes I wonder …'

'What?' asked Eve, her hand under her chin.

Fran shook her head. 'I don't know … Sometimes I just wonder what would have happened if there'd been no Teddy.'

'If it had just been you and me.'

It wasn't a question, but an answer. Fran's eyes met Eve's and she saw reflected back the same sadness and regret. She swallowed the lump in her throat. 'I'd like to see the granny flat again. Do you want to?'

Eve smiled and Fran saw a glimmer of her old cheekiness.

They picked their way down through the back garden, the rain misting their faces. The hole in the fence was still there like a portal in time, and they clambered through, sticks scratching their legs, and vines tangling their hair. Even with the pain in her knees Fran felt fifteen again. The sliding door had been left open a crack, but it took several tugs to dislodge the dirt and rust and get in. The earth had reclaimed it. Green vines crept and spread their tendrils up the walls. The carpet was black and yellow in places, blooming with mould. It had been inhabited by skinks and insects and its ceilings were laced with spiderwebs. She looked for signs that they had once been here. The place they had plotted their Kings Cross adventure the night her mother had died, the place she and Teddy had first made love. But there was nothing but the smell of rot and growth, of nature reclaiming this place.

Fran felt tears on her cheeks. 'Can you ever forgive what my children have done to your child?'

Eve took her hands. They were the same hands, bigger than her own, nails painted and fingers bejewelled. Age had only made them more beautiful. Fran was reminded of the fortune-teller's hands, shuffling the cards, so striking and strange. Franny looked into Eve's eyes and she saw the girl who had stood in her bedroom that hot summer evening and declared them friends forever. She still smelled of sandalwood and rose. She still shimmered when she moved.

'I forgave you everything the moment I met you. You were the light of my life, Franny.' Eve's eyes were full of unshed tears. 'Will you ever forgive me for what I did to June?'

Fran gripped Eve's hands. That mother-shaped loss that never closed, even after all these years. Fran's throat ached with all the years of repressed emotion. 'You didn't know Mum would die. It wasn't your fault – there were other drugs in her system. I know you didn't mean for it to happen. None of us meant for any of it to happen. But I knew. I knew Teddy loved you and I took him anyway.' The tears came now, as soft and insistent as rain on the roof. 'I wanted to punish you. I'm so sorry. I just ended up punishing myself. Maybe I ended up punishing all of us.'

Eve shook her head. 'No. You're not to blame, Franny.'

'Sometimes I think I cursed us all by stealing that tarot card. So that it all came true.'

Eve's eyes were soft. 'I'm glad that we were bound together. That our daughters found each other. Thank you for looking after Sylvie. That must have been … that was so incredibly gracious of you.'

'I always thought of them as the one good thing that has come of it all.'

Eve squeezed her hand and then pressed it against her cheek. 'Maybe they still can be.'

CHAPTER 34

angel *(n.)* - one of a class of spiritual beings ... A messenger.

The sign was still above the door: 'Be not inhospitable to strangers lest they be angels in disguise.' Rap music played in the background and a young guy sat behind the desk on his phone, but the bookshop looked and smelled exactly the same. The spines were lined up like old teeth in wobbly bookcases. Tomes were piled in dusty corners and there were still vintage records and magazines for sale. It smelled like old pages filled with lost stories.

Sylvie breathed deep. The faded green velvet armchairs were still there at the back, even after all this time. All that was missing was the soaring opera music. And Zola. She wanted to ask the boy if she still owned the shop, but maybe that wasn't even her real name. Maybe she'd died long ago. Sylvie put her box of books on the counter.

'Want to sell them?' the boy asked, picking up a copy of *Ulysses*.

'Donate,' she said. 'They're not actually mine.'

Sylvie and Holden had almost cleared her flat. They'd wrapped Sylvie's few possessions with newspaper. The faces of

Gabe and Kase came off on their fingers. The media frenzy had died down, but they were still in the news. Sylvie had watched the footage of the press conference feeling freshly vulnerable. But when she saw the fierce look in Kase's eyes as Gabe tried to wrench her away from the microphone and silence her, Sylvie remembered that other fierce love and protection Kase had shown her at the lighthouse. When Kase spoke of Sylvie's light going out, Sylvie felt the dark bruise inside her begin to ease. To have her pain seen, acknowledged, allowed a tiny sliver of light back in. Sylvie recognised the toll Kase had paid. Her atonement. She had been dropped by her publisher, her character dissected in the press. Was she a hero or a villain? Sylvie had always seen Kase for who she was: *selfish, brave, traitorous, loyal, a perpetrator, a victim.* It had never stopped Sylvie from loving her.

Sylvie knew that with Kase's confession, she could now pursue a criminal case against Gabe, but it was enough for her that his life had been irreparably damaged, made as small as Sylvie's had once been. He had lost his job and his reputation. Rachel had fled overseas after her theatre company had ended her contract. Sylvie had changed the shape of things. She'd jumped into the cold and broken the surface still breathing. She was wrapping her utensils in her perpetrator's face. She was moving to Hobart to open a bookshop with Holden, her lover, her future.

The boy disappeared behind a beaded curtain and Zola stepped into the shop. Her face was etched with half a lifetime of lines, but her eyes were the bright blue Sylvie remembered, her lips still a startling red. Sylvie smiled. She wanted to throw her arms around this woman, but she knew Zola wouldn't recognise her. Would she even remember the two schoolgirls who had visited for hours to dream? Who had typed poems on her typewriter, patted Victor Hugo the cat and spoken of one day writing their literary masterpieces?

Her gnarled fingers found the books, traced their spines lovingly. 'Thank you, dear. It's very generous of you to donate these. There are some gems in here.' She picked up a green leather-bound book with gold gilding. She turned it over and opened the cover, her face a picture of wonder. 'This is my book. Where did you get this book?' Her eyes for the first time were fully focused on Sylvie.

'I cleaned out a lady's house after she died. She lived just up the road. A beautiful house, overlooking the harbour, filled with hundreds of books. I kept the most beautiful. I couldn't bear to throw them away. Sylvia was her name.'

Zola gasped and pressed the book to her chest. There were tears in her eyes, and Sylvie knew. She'd seen the name in the front of many of Sylvia's books. *Rosemary Zola.*

This was Sylvia's Rose. Rose and Sylvia. Sylvia and Rose. Her best friend and her deepest regret. They were bound by books. Bound by words.

Zola reached out to touch Sylvie's arm. Her voice was tender and full of awe. 'You are surely my angel in disguise.'

Sylvie opened her mouth, to tell her how Sylvia had missed her, how she'd wished they'd been friends forever. To ask her what had happened to cleave them apart so long ago. To tell Zola that Sylvia had been the last person she'd thought of before she died. The last entry in her journal. To explain that Sylvie wasn't a stranger, but a girl who had come here at seventeen with her own best friend, her own soul twin, grown now. But she realised those were not the words she needed to say. There were others that needed to be said first.

She left Zola sifting through the books, a soft smile on her lips, and moved to the back of the shop. The typewriter was still there. It was the same clunky machine they had taken turns to write on, imagining that one day they would both be famous authors. There was a piece of blank paper resting in the roll as though it had been waiting there her whole life. Sylvie's fingers rested softly on the keys. The words were light, like tissue paper. She could feel them brush her skin, a sweet caress. She felt them under her skin, in her eyes, pricking to tears. She began to write.

The Beautiful Words

For Kase

AUTHOR'S NOTE

In researching this book, I read many true accounts of Australian women who have been sexually assaulted. I want to acknowledge the incredible courage of these women to come forward and speak about an event that destroyed their sense of self and their life. They need to battle not only the demons they live with but also a court system that does not support abuse victims. I also want to acknowledge women who have been sexually assaulted and have never been able to speak about it or bring their perpetrator to justice.

Women deserve to have a voice and to be heard. Women deserve to be respected and to be safe. Things need to change.

For those who may have had some difficult emotions come up while reading this story the following may be helpful: lifeline.org.au, 1800respect.org.au, beyondblue.org.au.

BOOK CLUB QUESTIONS

What are some of the key themes and symbols in the book?

The power and the fragility of deep friendship connections are explored. What was the message about friendship you felt was ultimately conveyed?

Did the text make you think about your own friendships and how they may have changed over the years?

There is an exploration of loss – of memory, friendship, of a loved one in death. What do you think was found by the end of the book?

What role did memory and its fallibility play in the book?

How did the setting reflect the unfolding action and Sylvie's emotions?

The novel explores the healing qualities of reading and writing. Can you relate?

What did you think of Holden's relationship with his daughter?

How did you feel about Kase by the end of the book?

Discuss the themes of betrayal and forgiveness as presented in the book. Do they resonate with any aspects of your own life?

Through the course of the book, which characters do you feel were most able to evolve on a personal level?

The book is about a woman finding her voice. Was there a particular moment where you felt Sylvie found hers?

What did you feel was the ultimate message of the novel?

ACKNOWLEDGEMENTS

Thank you to Anna Valdinger and Barbara McClenahan for bringing this book into the world. I'm so grateful for your insight, guidance and support. Libby Turner, Di Blacklock and Pam Dunne, you all made these words infinitely better. A huge thank you to Hazel Lam for creating the gorgeous and evocative cover and to Jordan Weaver-Keeney for helping get the message out. Thank you to the whole wonderful team at HarperCollins Australia for your support and championing. Thanks also to my agent, Jeanne Ryckmans.

Bec McSherry – one day we'll get to Tasmania together! Thank you for being a beautiful friend.

Kirstin Bokor, Karina Ware, Danielle Townsend, Ali Lowe, George Penney – I've dedicated this book to you because we're bound by our love of words and books and I'm so grateful to have you as my friends.

Charley Rico, thank you for hosting me in Hobart and taking me to sample the most incredible Tasmanian produce and for all the writing chats.

Thank you to Gemma Jones for advice on matters relating to editorial and the media.

Alexandra Joel, thank you for the moral support and our rare and precious cafe lunches.

Joanna Wolfe, thank you for your gorgeous catering – I love that we share a creative spirit.

Janneke Thurlow, thank you for the beach walks, book swaps and playdates and for having a daughter who makes mine so happy.

Thank you to Anth for the website, and to Beck, Isy and Josh for being the lovely family that you are.

To Ben, Soph, Mum and Dad, thank you for always being there for me and for believing in me.

Thanks to the Not So Solitary Scribes writers for being a lovely, supportive community during a year when such things have been so needed.

Lastly, thank you to my beautiful readers for sharing a love of language and story, and to the booksellers and librarians who help put books into hands, allowing our minds and hearts to escape and expand.

Is it more dangerous to forget ...
or to remember?

Alone and adrift after a failed marriage proposal, Phoebe flees Sydney to her family's abandoned holiday cottage. On the slow-moving river, she is confronted with the legacy of her older sister's suicide, a year before. Why did Karin leave a note written in flowers and walk into the water?

Phoebe's childhood love, Jez, has moved back to the beautiful old house, Driftwood, one jetty down. He's married now and his home has become a refuge for an unlikely little community.

As the river begins to give up its secrets, Phoebe finds herself caught up in old feelings and new mysteries.

The Lost Summers of Driftwood is a story of lost loves, rekindled passions, tragedy and betrayal set against the backdrop of an idyllic south coast town.

Beautiful, beguiling … and treacherous

Four women and their children are invited to the beautiful but remote Capertee Valley, west of the Blue Mountains. Once home to a thriving town, only an enigmatic Art Deco hotel remains – and an unsolved mystery. In 1948, Clara Black walked into the night, never to be seen again.

As the valley beguiles these four friends, and haunts them in equal measure, each has to confront secrets of her own: Nathalie, with a damaged marriage; Emmie, yearning for another child; Pen, struggling as a single parent; and Alexandra, hiding in the shadow of her famous husband.

But as the story of what happened seventy years earlier unravels, one of the women also vanishes into this bewitching place, forcing devastating truths to the surface.